DARK AEMILIA

DARK
AEMILIA
SALLY O'REILLY

Myriad Editions

Published in 2014 by

Myriad Editions
59 Lansdowne Place
Brighton BN3 1FL

www.myriadeditions.com

1 3 5 7 9 10 8 6 4 2

A CIP catalogue record for this book is available
from the British Library.

ISBN (hb): 978-1-908434-49-4
ISBN (tpb): 978-1-908434-50-0

Printed on FSC-accredited paper by
CPI Group (UK) Ltd, Croydon, CR0 4YY

MIX
Paper from
responsible sources
FSC® C013604
FSC
www.fsc.org

To Georgia, with love

Past cure I am, now reason is past care,
And frantic-mad with evermore unrest;
My thoughts and my discourse as madman's are
At random from the truth, vainly expressed;
For I have sworn thee fair, and thought thee bright
Who art as black as hell, as dark as night.

William Shakespeare
Sonnet 147

DRAMATIS PERSONAE

AEMILIA BASSANO, later LANYER, a Lady, Poet and Whore

WILLIAM SHAKESPEARE, a Poet

ALFONSO LANYER, a Recorder Player, Husband to Aemilia

HENRY CAREY, Lord Hunsdon, a Lord Chamberlain

HENRY LANYER, a Schoolboy, Son to Aemilia

JOAN DAUNT, an Apothecary and Serving Woman

ANTHONY INCHBALD, a Dwarf and Landlord

SIMON FORMAN, a Cunning-man and Lecher

TOM FLOOD, a Player

ANNE FLOOD, a Widow, Mother to Tom

MOLL CUTPURSE, a Cutpurse and Cross-dresser

ELIZABETH TUDOR, a Queen

RICHARD BURBAGE, a Player and Sharer

FATHER DUNSTAN, a Priest

PARSON JOHN, a Parson

LETTICE COOPER, a Lady-in-Waiting to the Queen

CUTHBERT TOTTLE, a Bookseller and Printer

THOMAS DEKKER, a Poet and Pamphlet-writer

MARIE VERRE, a Servant

LILITH, a Demon

ANN SHAKESPEARE, Wife to William Shakespeare

Various courtiers, players, musicians, street vendors, wives, servants, wherrymen, citizens, browsers, cozeners, plague-victims, prentice-boys, witches and wraiths

Prologue

I am a witch for the modern age. I keep my spells small, and price them high. What they ask for is the same as always. The common spells deal in love, or what love is meant to make, or else hate, and what that might accomplish. I mean the getting of lovers or babies (or the getting rid of them) or a handy hex for business or revenge. When a spell works, they keep you secret, and take the credit. When it fails, of course, the fault is yours. So a witch is wise to be cautious, quiet, and hard to find.

That was true even before they started the burnings. Across the sea in Saxony and such places, whole market squares are set alight; the thatch roars up into the night; five score witches burn at once. Most would not even know how to charm a worm out of a hole. Old, and stupid, and too visible, that was their mistake. In England too, blood is let to put a stop to magic. I saw a witch hanged in Thieving Lane. They sliced off her hands and tongue, and split her down from neck to crotch, so all her guts spilled out before her eyes. They were like werewolves, mad for gore. I can still hear the voice she made with her wound-mouth: a call to Evil and a plague on all the lot of them. (This was a true witch, five hundred years old.)

But now I want to tell you my story. About Aemilia, the girl who wanted too much. Not seamed and scragged as I am now, but quick and shimmering and short of patience. About my dear son, whom I love too well. About my two husbands, and my one true love. And Dr Forman, that most lustful of physicians. The silk dress I wore, the first time I went to ask for his predictions. Yellow and gold, with a fine stiff ruff that crumpled in a breath of rain. How my skin was set dark against it; how the people stared when I rushed by.

Act I

Passion

Scene I

Whitehall, March 1592

'The Queen!'

'The Queen comes! Lights, ho!'

It is night, and a Thames mist has crept over Whitehall, so the great sprawl of the palace is almost hid from sight.

'Bring lights!' come the voices again, and the doors of the great hall are flung open, and a hundred shining lanterns blaze into the foggy night, and serving men rush out, torches aflame, to show the way.

And here she is, great Gloriana, and a light comes off her too, as she progresses towards the wide entrance and its gaggle of waiting gentlemen, and the Master of the Revels puffing on the steps. There never was a mortal such as she. Behind her is the moving tableau of her ladies, silver and white like the nymphs of Nysa. Beyond them, the spluttering torches and the night sky. She is set among the fire-illuminated faces like a great jewel, so that as I look at her I blink to save my sight. Her face is white as bone, her lips the colour of new-spilt blood. Her eyes, dark and darting, take in all before her and give nothing back. And her hair, the copper hue of turning leaves, is dressed high in plaits and curlicues and riddled with pearls.

'Is Mr Burbage with us?' she demands, as she sets her small foot on the bottom step. 'Is he within? We've heard this is a comedy – we want his promise we shall be forced to laugh.'

I look down at the skirts of her farthingale, which is of Genoa velvet, glittering with a multitude of ant-sized gems.

The Master of the Revels makes his lowest bow. 'He is waiting, Your Majesty. He and the playwright are inside.'

'Is it witty?' she demands of him. 'We are in peevish spirits. This cloaked-up night disquiets us.'

'I laughed until I thought I had the palsy,' says the Master of the Revels. 'I trust it will divert Your Majesty.'

'Trust! Hmm. You are amusing us already. What did you say it was called?'

'It is *The Taming of the Shrew*, Your Majesty.'

'Ha!' says the Queen. Which could mean anything. I follow her whispering, simpering retinue and we go inside.

At one end of the long banqueting hall is a grand archway, built after the manner of the theatre at Venice. The archway shows a magnificent Roman street lined with gold and marble columns. Above the street is a plaster firmament. King Henry built the banqueting hall in the years of his great glory, and the ceiling, which swirls with choirs of angels, seems nearly high enough to reach to heaven itself, while the walls are hung with cloth-of-gold and tissue like the hazy outskirts of a dream. The most powerful lords and ladies in England are perched upon the stools and benches which are ranged before the stage, and above them all, upon a raised dais, stands the throne. It glitters as the pages bear their lanterns into the hall, dividing into twin processions of golden light. Even this seat itself has its own air of expectancy, as if it shares the Queen's fine discernment and knows what makes the difference between what is merely diverting, and what is worthy of royal acclaim.

The Queen processes to her throne and sits upon it with great exactness, and her ladies arrange themselves around her. When all are assembled, and after much bowing and flummery, the play begins. After a few moments, I see that this is a work of the direst cruelty. And I form the opinion that the playwright

– whoever he might be – is nothing better than a rat-souled scoundrel who thinks that belittling a woman will make him twice the man. He is not content that a woman has no more freedom than a house-dog. Nor that she does not even own the chair she sits upon, nor go to school, nor follow a profession (unless she is a widow who must work in her dead husband's place). No. He must make a mock of her, and push her down still further, till her face is squashed into the street-mud. And what grates such fellows most of all is one like me: a woman with a fiery spirit, and a quick tongue.

He makes his Katherine bold, only to call her 'Kate' and starve her of both food and her right name. '*What, did he marry me to famish me?*' she asks, and I see that it is so. A beggar is better treated than a scolding wife. If a woman is wise, she knows when to speak out and when she must be silent. Even the Queen herself plays a careful game, hiding behind paint and posture. Me? I am never quiet enough.

There is a rustling all around me as courtiers shift and make way. The consort divides like the Red Sea, and one of their number, my pretty cousin Alfonso Lanyer, drops his recorder. He catches my eye and winks at me, and I pretend not to see him. Alfonso is distinguished not by his playing but by two bad habits: womanising and losing money at dice.

The cause of the commotion is the arrival of my lover, Henry Carey, Lord Hunsdon, a man whose very tread makes all around take notice. Upright and soldierly, as this was his profession for many years. He does not suffer fools; he does not suffer anyone. Excepting only the Queen (who is his cousin) and me. He is forty years older than I am, so some may think we are like May and December in the old stories. Yet we were lovemaking this afternoon. Afterwards, he washed and clothed me with his own hands in the fine new dress I am wearing now. The farthingale is even wider than I am used to, so it seems I have a whole chamber swinging round my hips. The skirts are Bruges satin, of popinjay blue, and the sleeves are tinselled silk, stitched with narrow snakes of silver. As a final gift, he coiled my hair into a caul of sapphires. When I looked in the mirror, my reflection was so perfect that it made me afraid. I, who am not afraid of anything.

I kiss him when he sits beside me.

'God's blood, this is a rum play, by the looks of it,' he whispers. 'What's it all about? Can't he find a better jade to please him?'

I put my fingers to my lips. 'She won't obey him, sir,' I mutter into his ear. 'He is hooked in by her haughty ways, and then sets out to punish her.'

'What nonsense,' says Hunsdon, rather loudly. 'A man must choose a woman that suits his fancy, not seek to change some baggage that does not. Fellow must be a barking fool.'

'Hush, my lord,' I say. There is laughter and I cuff him lightly on the shoulder. He seizes my hand and holds it in both his own.

But then I am caught by Katherine's voice.

'Such duty as the subject owes the prince,
Even such a woman oweth to her husband,
And when she is forward, peevish, sullen, sour...'

She speaks the words of a woman beaten, or pretending to be beaten, which is much the same.

'And not obedient to his honest will,
What is she but a foul contending rebel,
And graceless traitor to a loving lord?'

'I have another gift for you,' whispers Hunsdon, pulling me closer. 'A waistcoat of quilted silver sarsanet.' For a soldier, he has a cunning eye for fashion.

'My lord! Another present?'

'I will give it to you when you come to my rooms. Tonight?'
'If you like.'
He squeezes my hand.

After the play is finished and Kate is crushed and made the most obedient of wives, there is much clapping and cheering. The Queen raises her hand. She is smiling, but her eyes are cold.

'We want to see the playwright!' she commands. 'Where is he? Let him step forward!'

He comes from behind a pillar, slightly hesitant. 'Your Majesty,' he says, with an actor's bow. He is tall, lean and watchful, with deep-set eyes. And artful in his dress, with gold earrings and fine gloves.

She regards him for a moment, her smile in place. 'A bawdy tale, more fit for a country inn than for a monarch and her great Court, would you not say?'

He bows again. He looks pale. 'I would say there is low life in it, and high-flown characters too, such as the person of Bianca.'

The Queen's smile disappears. 'A lesson, if anyone is listening, that might teach a lady to beware of being fenced in for a wife. First they trap you, then they seek to change you. And those of us with a handsome dowry must be wariest of all.'

Her ladies giggle at this, shimmering in their silver robes.

'It is a fable, Your Majesty, not taken from the life.'

This is in the nature of a contradiction. The room gasps, silently. All eyes are on the Queen's face. Her expression is blank, her vermilion mouth a flat line. 'We do not need a lesson from you in the antecedents of your little drama. There is nothing new under the sun, least of all your plot.'

Then, with a sudden smile, her mood seems to change.

'We are grateful to you for showing us what we already know. Sometimes, in our experience, this is desirable in a drama. Sometimes we want fairyland, and wild diversion spread before us, and sometimes we wish to be confirmed in our most sensible opinion. Our opinion being, in this case, that marriage favours men.'

The playwright, looking ill at ease, bows again.

'Was it not your intention? To show women the dangers of the married state? To have us run from such enslavement, in which our husband will be our lord and master in the eyes of God?'

The playwright clears his throat. 'I intended, Your Majesty, to tell a good tale of an unruly woman, who found her true vocation in the – '

The Queen interrupts him. 'Do you have such a wife?'

He blinks. 'Such a…?'

'Such a one as this. One "peevish, sullen, sour" who does not know her place.'

'Her place, Your Majesty, is in Stratford, and mine is in London.'

There is a silence for a moment, then the Queen begins to laugh, and all around her laugh too. The grinning players look sideways at the poet. The Queen flips her hands, dismissing him, and the audience breaks apart in a clamour of excited talk. It is a gay scene. The new play is a success.

Hunsdon sweeps off to consult with Her Majesty on some urgent matter, and I find myself alone in the great hall, sitting stiffly on a stool. All I can think of is this Katherine and her plight, and the cruel way that she was brought to heel.

I feel a presence, shadow-like, and turn my head. It is the playwright. He bows, even more deeply than he had done before the Queen. I stand up, my bright skirts whirl, and the stool falls over.

'I know you,' he says, which is hardly courtly.

I nod.

'Aemilia Bassano.'

I nod again.

'I've seen you... talking...'

I curtsey, mockingly. Wonders will never cease – a comely woman who can speak.

He takes a step nearer. 'So... brightly. So... full of erudition. I've heard you quoting Ovid. Like a scholar!'

I will tell him nothing. I will not say they brought me up at Court. I will not say I am a musician's orphan. I look at him, his dark-rimmed eyes. What is he after? Most men leave me alone, fearing the wrath of Hunsdon. But this one has a reckless look to him.

'Why are you so silent?' he asks.

'I'm silent when I need to be. If it were otherwise, I'd be a fool.'

'Silent with Lord Hunsdon?'

'That's no business of yours.'

'But you speak with him?'

'Of course I do! I'm not the Sphinx.'

He looks me up and down. 'The words you choose must be poetical indeed. To earn such splendour.'

'I am the Lord Chamberlain's mistress.'

'And for that great rank you sold your virtue?'

'How dare you speak like that to me?'

He waits, as if expecting me to say more, but I do not oblige him.

'Silent again?'

'I have nothing to say to you.'

'And yet, I can see you thinking.'

'Oh, surely! My thoughts are there for all to look upon, because my head is made of glass.'

'I believe that you say very little, compared to what is in your mind.'

'You have no idea how much I talk, or what I say. You don't know who I am, or what I know. But, as your play showed us, if she is to prosper, a woman sometimes needs to act the mouse.

Wasn't that your message? Better a pliant mouse than a wicked shrew?'

'Are you such a one? A secret, wicked shrew?'

I breathe deeply, wondering that my heart is beating so loudly, my face burns and yet I shiver with rage. And then the words pour out.

'I wish that you had killed poor Katherine! I'd rather you had abused her in the Roman style, and made her eat her own children baked inside a pie! Why give her fine and dazzling speeches, only to gag her and make her drab?'

He boggles at me in disbelief. 'I… *what* do you say?'

'There's not a scene in your bloody *Titus* that made my heart weep as did this dreadful tale! Shame on you, for humbling that brave soul!'

'*What*?'

'Shame on you. Your play is cruel, and beast-like, sir.'

He smiles slowly. Then he turns and strides away. When he reaches the door, he calls out over his shoulder, 'You are the most beautiful woman at Court. But I expect you know that. There's no one else comes near you.'

My head reels, my guts are water, but I gather myself, right the stool and say, 'That poisonous play is what passes for poetry, is it? If you are in the company of Men and strut in hose?'

He stops, one hand on the door handle and turns to look at me.

I know I have said too much already, but it seems I can only carry on. 'Some lame tale of witless, vile humiliation? A woman-hater's boorish jape? I could do better myself, I swear.'

He forces a sort of laugh. It is a strange noise, almost like a sob. Then he comes back and stands in front of me. He is slightly too close. His eyes are angry, but for a moment he says nothing. Then he says, 'I wish you joy of Hunsdon and your perfumed palace bed.'

'Thank you, sir. In that, I shall oblige you.'

He hesitates once more, then says, 'You're his mouse, but I would that I could make you my shrew.'

Before I can find the words to answer, he has gone.

Scene II

Hunsdon is out of sorts, complaining of cramps in his calves and pains in his belly. As I lie tossing and turning and trying to find a cool place on the bolster, I roll over to see him lying still, looking up into the darkness.

'I am growing old, Aemilia,' he says. 'I shan't live much longer.'

I curl myself around him, suddenly overwhelmed with tenderness and fear. 'Henry! What are you saying?'

'It is only the truth. You will outlive me. You will be out in the world, walking in the streets, lusted for by all who see you, and I will be dead and buried, and who knows what will happen? I was selfish to take you for my mistress.'

'No! How can it be selfish to protect and cherish me, for all these years? You are the kindest man at Court, I swear.'

'But I have ruined you.'

I swallow hard. 'My dear Henry! No one could have loved me better.'

'Another man could have married you,' says Hunsdon. 'I was greedy.' He pulls the counterpane around him and twists his old body away from me, and after a moment he begins to snore, and it is my turn to lie there, staring at the dark.

I think of the first days of our courtship, after my mother died. In the depths of my slumber, I left my chamber, close to the servants' quarters, and, dressed in nothing but my white gown, walked unknowing into the middle of a feast given in Hunsdon's honour. He led me by the hand to his own bed, returned to the celebrations, and then spent the night in his dressing room, leaving me undisturbed. Most honourable. And yet also canny, for from that day on, quite alone and sorely frightened by the constant lechery of the courtiers who wanted to have me for a night or so, I felt that here was one man I could trust.

After that, he wooed me with kind words, small gifts and imported books from the Low Countries, and the next time I found myself in his fine bed he lay with me. He was surprised to find me still a virgin and yet eager in my pleasure, and we did not sleep a wink that night. That was the first night – there have been many since. I have been his sole mistress for six years. No other man dares trespass on his territory.

Next morning, I wake late. Hunsdon has gone, but I see that he has bought me yet more gifts: a pair of new sleeves embroidered with gold angel wings, silk gloves as pale as hoar-frost, and a dainty silver knife in a leather sheath. I draw this out and look at it. Surely it is bad luck to give such a weapon to your love? I turn it this way and that, looking at the sunlight glinting on the silver blade. I touch its sharp tip with the end of my finger, and it draws a tiny drop of blood, no bigger than a ladybird. I lick the blood, wondering why God made it taste so sweet.

I go over to the window-seat and look down into the park through the small panes that make neat squares of my view. It is a clear, bright day, and the leafless branches of the oak trees are stark against the sky. When I push the window open the air is sharp, and I can smell woodsmoke and hear the hoarse cry of a stag somewhere in the forest. Yet I must not be distracted. I take up a sheet of foolscap that lies beside me and the quill that I have newly sharpened. I dip in my silver inkpot and pause, the shining nib suspended over the white sheet. I am writing a poem for Hunsdon, in the courtly style. Perhaps some fine lines might pin my passion to my lord. Besides which, words have the effect of calming me, like a long drink of ale. I love to read poetry, and yearn to write it, but what is in my head and what comes out upon the paper are never even near the same.

I have two lines so far:

My lord is like a damask rose
He smiles at me where'er he goes...

Could a lord be like a rose? In truth, Hunsdon is more like a handsome thistle. But 'rose' is easier to rhyme. For 'thistle' I have only 'gristle', which will not do. I try to think of some more martial flower. A plant with dignity and strength – and a straight back. No name comes to me. My mind is restless and distracted. Each poet, they say, must suffer for love before he finds his Muse. And I am suffering now.

A harvest mouse is climbing in the ivy growing outside. It is twisting its long tail around the stalks, and looks so dainty and moves so quick that it seems fairy-like, and as though a breath of wind might send it flying through the air. I think of my conversation with the playwright. The memory itches in my head. A secret shrew, am I? Or like this creature, a little mouse? I wonder what it would be like, to be its size and scurry into the wainscot, hidden from public sight. But if I went from here, what is there? The City streets are full of fire and noise and pestilence, and beyond them lie the brutal fields. So where is *my* place? I would rather be a female Colossus, naked to the waist, bestriding all of London with a foot on each side of the Thames. I would look down upon the sprawl of Whitehall and its chequer-board of courts and gardens, then wade across the sea to France and stroll to floating Venice and its brighter sun.

Oh, Lord. It is no use. This is not a day to stay dutifully indoors. What will become of me? I want to know. Why did Hunsdon tell me so suddenly that I was ruined? Could it be true? I have never seen myself in such a way, being given to bold thoughts about my future. Am I not admired and respected at the Court? Have I not shifted well for myself, though a bastard and an orphan, so that I am now ensconced in splendour at the heart of England? Great men push and shove and spend their whole fortunes to be part of the Queen's circle, and here I am: at its centre. Even she has told me that I am mightily well read, and sometimes speaks to me in Greek. Yet have I thrown away all hope of making my own stamp upon the world? Could this be possible?

There are ways, of course, to throw light upon such questions. If that learned Dr Dee were still at the palace I might have asked him to give me a reading, since his charts are by far the best in London, and he has always been kind to me. But he is back at Mortlake now, and not so often at the Court. The Queen believes, I think, that she has magical qualities of her own, since she was chosen by Almighty God himself. Thus her royal touch can cure diseases, and her powers of perception exceed those of any low-born man.

What to do? What to *do*? I cannot be still. All the while, I seem to see that playwright looking at me as if he were examining all my thoughts and secrets. What a vile, impertinent and damnable fellow! It is all too much. I call my servant Alice, and make her lend me her oldest cloak and most unbecoming coif, an ugly linen hood with strange ear-pieces. Tying it under my chin, I pay her a silver sixpence to keep silent, and take up a nosegay of sweet herbs. Then I creep down the back staircase of my apartments, which lead to the stable-yard, and head for the river and Whitehall Stairs.

Dr Dee is not the only famous necromancer in London. There are plenty of charlatans – like the notorious Edward Kelley – but also some whose fame recommends them. And there is one particular man I know of, a most extraordinary character. He lives at Stone

House, in the revestry of St Botolph's church on Thames Street, and his name is Simon Forman.

I make my way in haste along the narrow streets with my vizard down, picking my way around the spewed filth and avoiding the stinking kennel that gushes along beside my feet. The bright sky seems further from me now, high and pure and unreachable. I look up, and see the clouds banked into linen piles, a pattern of swallows turning first this way, then that. Between us is a veil of hidden spirits, waiting, watching, depending on mortal frailty.

Dr Forman's door is opened by an odd-looking little man, shorter than I am, with red hair, freckled skin and a yellow beard. He reminds me of a scrawny tabby-cat. Yet he is dressed to some effect, in a long purple robe with fur-trimmed sleeves, and has a confident and sprightly manner. There is no doubt that I have come to the right place.

'You are late,' he says.

'No, sir, there must be some confusion. I am not expected.'

He beckons me inside. 'I am not sure yet of your name, but you are entirely the person whose arrival I anticipated.'

'I do not see how you can "expect" a person who is unknown to you,' I say.

'Yes, yes, yes,' says Dr Forman. 'I saw that yellow dress. Though I don't believe the cap is yours, nor yet your dag-tailed cloak.'

I sit down on the chair he offers, too anxious and confused to argue further, and look around me. It is a lofty, ecclesiastic room, with a chill coming off the walls in spite of the log fire in the hearth. There are strange charts and pictures on the walls, and I notice a globe set upon a cedarwood stand, a quadrant, used to measure the altitude of the stars and a watch clock, with seconds marked around its rim.

'Now, let me see...' Dr Forman sits down beside me and looks at me intently. 'You say you know who I am?'

'You are Simon Forman. A necromancer. And you cured yourself of the plague.'

'Correct, insofar as that is of course my name; correct in that I have a physick for the pestilence, incorrect in this: "necromancer" is not my occupation. I am a physician.'

'There are as many degrees of *that* profession as there are lice upon a doxy's head.'

He smiles at me. I notice that his eyes seem paler at the centre, around his pupil. Then he rummages around in a wickerwork basket, humming to himself. Taking out a leather-bound volume and some papers, he clears his throat, picks up his quill, dips it in his ink-pot and says, 'Name?'

'I thought you knew me.'

'No, my dear, I merely said I was expecting you. Your name?'

'Aemilia Bassano.'

He looks at me over his spectacles, his ginger eyebrows raised. 'Indeed! Most interesting.' He scribbles, smiling. 'This is fortunate, a most auspicious turn...'

After a moment, he puts his quill down and clears his throat again. 'Now, what do you know about magic?'

'That it exists. That there are wise men who have spent years learning it, and wise women, who know what they are about through instinct and old tales.'

'Aha! Yes. I knew that you were clever.'

I flush in spite of myself. 'By looking at me?'

'From your reputation. And your *extra-ordinary* manner. Has the Lord created a separate degree for you? I cannot for the life of me see where you fit.'

'I don't need to "fit", sir. I will find my own place.'

'You are a scholar, so I have heard?'

'I believe I know as much as any lord, and more than all ladies, excepting only our great Queen.'

'A bold claim! There are great ladies whose knowledge of the ancients is far in excess of mine.'

'I speak of knowledge, sir, which is not the bed-equal of learning. A fool may learn, but what will he know? Teach a jackanapes his Latin and he can cant out Cicero. I speak of what comes from learning. I speak of understanding.'

'I see. And where has this "understanding" taken you?'

'To the brink of what can be borne. To a certainty that what contains me will always be too small. To a fear that I shall not be happy. To the quest for a twin soul.'

He sits back in his chair, settles himself more comfortably in his robes, and says, 'I can tell you a little of your future if you will tell me a little of your past. I see rich widows and Court ladies and all manner of womenfolk in their various degrees, but I have never seen one quite like you.'

So I tell him. I tell him that I do not think of myself as clever, or unusual, or in any manner different from any other girl whose father had been murdered before her eyes, or for whom music and poetry are a daily joy.

He strokes his beard. 'Who killed your father?'

'I don't know. Some years before his death, there was a first attempt, and the conspirators were tortured and banished. But we don't know who murdered him. No one knows.'

He nods. 'What did your mother say about this?'

'It was never spoken of.'

'Not even after he was murdered?'

'Not even then. We talked about his life, not his death. How his father made instruments for the Doge of Venice, and how Baptiste – my father – sailed all the way to London with his five brothers, and was the greatest player in the King's consort – '

'And after he died?'

'Mother kept his recorder hidden in a secret place, but I knew where it was. And sometimes, when I was alone, I would get it out and play some notes upon it, and it seemed to me...' I hesitate, not sure if I want to say more.

'What?'

It had seemed that the recorder held its own music, and there were notes waiting for me, and the sound flowed upwards; so beautiful. This was the reason that I began to play the virginals, and would practise and practise. I was seeking those sweet notes.

'You are gifted,' says Forman, decisively. 'You are your father's daughter. And yet you didn't ask your mother why he was killed? Or who did this terrible thing?'

I shrug. 'Murder is common enough.' I do not say that I know it was bound up with the extraordinary beauty of his music, and with his being a Jew. I know that great gifts come at a price, and that not all talent inspires admiration. His was too much; it set him apart.

I know that I was happy, those first seven years. So much of what I remember is like a giant's eye view of people far below, and this is because my father was in the habit of walking with me on his shoulders. I remember tangling my fingers in his black, curling hair, and seeing the panorama of the streets and fields stretching out around me, and the sudden knowledge that this was a busy and various world, and that behind one thing lay another, and then another, and this roof-muddle and chimney-forest and mêlée of men and carts and horses was all around, on every side. The Jesuits say a child is theirs for life if they have him for seven years. I have often wondered if being carried on his shoulders in this manner made me see the world through his eyes. And perhaps it was his tenderness that gave me my reverence for love.

My memories have distracted me. Forman is writing in his book.

'And this great learning of yours,' he says, scratching away. 'How did you come to acquire it?'

'Through application, sir,' I say, stiffly.

'Someone must have helped you. Someone must have given you books, and their time, and the benefit of their knowledge.'

'When I was a little girl I used to play for the Queen, because she liked me. And this continued after my father died. One day, Lady Susan Bertie heard me playing, and talked to me, and asked my mother if I could join her household, down in Kent. My mother agreed, as long as she could come to see me. So from that time – two years after my father's death – I lived between the Berties' house and Court.'

'And who taught you?'

'Lady Susan. I would say she formed my mind, being of the unusual opinion that girls can learn as fast and as well as boys.'

'You are fortunate.'

'A fortunate freak.'

He is still writing, looking well pleased with our conversation.

'So can you advise me?' I ask.

'What I am dealing with is the higher magic,' says he, without looking up. He stops writing and looks at the nib of his pen. 'Which is the study of such sciences as astrology – the prediction of men's fate by making a study of the stars – and alchemy, in which base metal is turned into gold. Your wise woman, on the other hand, deals in what I like to call "household magic" – the stuff of life.'

'Of love and sickness and herbal remedies and the like. Simple enough. Any fool might understand the difference.'

'Of course, of course, it is very simple indeed, yet not all of my clients are as *knowledgeable* as you are. Let us say, to put it crudely, that the wise woman deals with magic pertaining to the body, whereas high magic is the magic of the mind.' He taps his forehead. 'In short, it is a wondrous thing. It is *science*.'

'Which leaves aside the simple fact that our enquiring mind is contained within our earthly body. Like all distinctions made within your "science", this is merely conjecture, a chosen supposition.'

'Dear lady, I could indulge my taste for dialectic with you all day, but we must get on.'

The doctor measures and reckons and mutters and writes, and takes books down from this bookshelf and puts them back again, and considers me from between half-closed eyes and writes down some further observations.

Finally, he looks up and smiles, showing exceptionally black and fetid teeth, and says, 'It's done.'

'So… what is my future?' I ask. 'What will become of me?'

'Too vague. Ask me a proper question.'

'Shall I be married?'

'Yes.'

'To one I love?'

'No.'

'Then I am doomed.'

'But you will truly love. Your love will be…' He looks down at his notebook. 'Your love will be the better part of you.'

I stand up. 'You have sat there, looking at me as if you could read every fragment of my existence like one of your queer old books, and you can't tell me anything that's any use at all!'

'No use? I thought I was being most informative.'

I toss a crooked florin at him. 'There's your fee – I'm not parting with a penny more.'

He picks it up. 'I wouldn't want more. It is a pleasure doing business with a lady of such passion. But you, on the other hand, should want a great deal more than this.'

'Of course I want more! Did I not just say so? I want to know… what will become of me.'

'But what of art? What of that clever mind of yours – all the Plato and the Seneca that furnishes it? There is something trapped behind that siren's face. You've as good as said so.'

'Could learning be my destiny?'

'Do you want it to be?'

I frown, uncertain. 'Could *poetry*?'

He beams, and dips his quill once more into the pot. 'How your eyes shone when you said that word!'

I feel a pang of hope and recognition. 'Then… what is your prediction?'

'You will be remembered.'

The room is getting dark. He lights a candle.

'There is one more thing you want to ask me.'

My mind says, *Ask him! Ask him, you fool!* But I do not know how to begin. 'I don't have any other questions,' I say.

'Then why did you come?'

'I could not settle.'

He leans forward and, to my horror, kisses me gently on the mouth. His breath is hot and sour. 'I'd ask you to stay with me… longer. But I fear you'd break my heart.'

I push him away. 'I'd break your head, sir, before I broke anything.'

He stands up, frowning, and fetches my cloak. As he puts it about my shoulders, he says, 'His name is Shakespeare. William Shakespeare.'

'Whose name?' But I know. Of course I know.

'The playwright you want so badly.'

'What…?'

'He will be your lover. At least I hope so, for if you won't have him he'll run as mad as Legion.'

'Possessed by evil spirits?'

'Driven insane by wild desire. Judging from *his* chart, that would be a national deprivation.'

I stare at him, finally astonished by his science. Forman fixes me with his weird gaze.

'Intense sort of fellow. It doesn't take an astrologer to see that.'

'You know him?'

'He was here this morning.'

'What?'

He opens the door. 'Be careful how you go. Those stairs are slippery.'

Scene III

My servant Alice rushes into my chamber all fly-brained and affected. She is a silly girl and I can see she has recently been conversing with some man she thinks important, or handsome at the very least.

'I have a letter, mistress,' she says, pink in the face.

I flinch. There is not a hair's breadth between what I most fear and what I want more than anything. Anyone who has loved two men at once knows that it's not an abundant feeling, but mean and sweaty and undignified.

'Give it to me,' I say. It is a long slip of foolscap, the colour of buttercream, folded and sealed with red wax. Alice stands, smiling, at the foot of the bed, as if she is expecting to watch me break the seal. 'Get out, you brainless creature!' I say. 'And...'

'Yes, mistress?'

'You are free for the rest of the day. Go to see your mother at Islington. The country air will do you good.'

'But... mistress!'

'Go on!' I throw the letter on to the table as if I were not interested in its contents. 'My lord is coming soon, and wants to see me alone.'

'But I thought – '

'Alice! Go!'

As soon as I hear the door to my apartment close I grab the letter and tear it open. It has to be from *him*. It has to be.

It is from Petruchio.

Madam,

I am writing to you on behalf of Mr W.S. on the matter of his play The Taming of the Shrew, *which sadly failed to please you. His thoughts are these:*

First, is he the only man to write a tale about the taming of a Shrew? (He is not: the tale is as ancient as old Ovid.) Second, is this the cruellest tale of woman-taming, or the crudest? (It is not: this Katherine keeps her dignity more than most of her fair sex, and speaks most ably, too.)

Further, if you recall the exact words of this tamed Shrew, you will know that she agrees to her husband's will and rule on the understanding that he is 'loving' – a fair bargain, would you not say? Therefore, she is making a truce. She is no scold, dumbed by a bridle.

And lastly, as this is an entertainment, laid on for the drunkard Sly, Mr W.S. had hoped that his audience would see this for a tale enlivened by his Wit. In short, a comedy of levity as well as form. So his wish is that it might amuse a Lady, learned as you are, rather than cause Rage.

I ask you humbly, as Mr Shakespeare's prattler, the voicer of his words, please do not judge the Poet by his Puppet.

With great respect,
Petruchio

What had I expected of this poet? Too much, it seems. He has sent this to me not out of admiration, or even lust, but only to convince me of the greatness of his Art. He does not see in me someone of fellow mind, as I had almost hoped, but as an audience member lacking in the proper perceptions, the fit response. The squibbling, shifty knave cannot even lower himself to put his right name on this letter, but must pretend his 'puppet' is writing in his stead! God's blood.

I confess, though I should respond with silence, I must reply. I can't let this letter, this preening, false-writ scrawl, be the last word in our discourse. I cannot let this 'playwright', some provincial chance-man, swelled with pride, put *his* words over mine. No. Katherine will speak. I write thus, with my left hand:

Petruchio,

I speak on behalf of one who was enraged to see a play so violent and ill-tempered, fuelled by cruelty and bile. If this is comedy, then take yourself to Tyburn and laugh with the mob who like jigs danced by corpses.

It would be easier to laugh at your foul 'jokes' if Women were not caged, and tethered, and made small. If they owned property, or goods, or their own skin. If they had gold, or land, or the respect of Men. If, unchaperoned, they could walk the streets and smell the bakemeats and the brew-shops. Or ride astride a horse, or put their plays upon the stage, or speak in Court, or choose their mate, or go abroad, upon a ship (in search of the Americas, or Oriental spice).

As for Wit, if you steal this from a woman, and make her call the moon the sun or darkness light, then she is done for. Because Wit is all she has. It's Wit that gives us life, or we have nothing left to nourish us. It is our sole possession.

Make a joke of all this if you will, put a play within a play, and say 'all's false'. You still make the bully smile to see himself reflected in your person. Greedy, preening, bed-smug Petruchio.

Katherine (and never Kate)

I dispatch this letter and time goes on its way, and I live my life as I must. I dissemble. I read my Bible. I eat my milksops and apricocks and drink my Madeira wine. I seem to have bewitched myself: this letter should never have been sent. I wonder if it found its mark. Was it lost in the Globe, where it was sent? Was it found by some other knave, and laughed around the theatre? Will it threaten my future (though nameless, and disguised)? If he read it, the Poet, did he frown or smile, or throw it on the fire? Did he turn from it without a thought, or brood on it, and go back to his pages, not so sure of them? Did he? I look inside my head, as if a picture of the world beyond these rooms was hidden there. And my life is just as it has always been: the life of a kept whore, the highest in the land. Dressed like a princess, a taffeta angel, a fairy in cloth-of-gold. But all I am is Queen of cunts.

And then. Then it comes, the answer, from the Pen. It is a different sort of letter altogether.

> *Katherine,*
>   *You truly own your wit, and no one can take it from you. Not this Petruchio, for certain. I would not seek to curb your headstrong humour, not in life.*
>   *Not if you were my Wife.*
>   *I do not believe there is a man in Christendom who could own you. You would put God Himself on his mettle.*
>   *Petruchio*

I read this several times.

This, then, is the way he wants to play it. He will lure me with his silken little lies, to tie me up with my particularity. There is no one like me, no, therefore I need not think of my gender, nor of any woman as my equal or my sister. I can be Chosen, and set above all others. Still the false princess, decked out in Sin.

I use my right hand this time, for speed, but none who knew me would recognise my furious scrawl.

Petruchio,

You deserve no more than a blank page, a blank stare for your blank verse. Husbands abuse their wives, and tyrannise them, and they are less than their equals. In spirit, virtue, soul, and body, Man is the weakling. The woman brings forth men, so SHE is the source of all life. And the Man, with his dangling, clownish wren-cock, puffs himself up to twice his natural size. (Twice, do I say? No, tenfold!) He makes the Woman small so he can spit in her eye.

Man must sing a weak, cruel song to comfort his cold nights. You don't fool me by saying I am different from the others of my sex. I am not different, I am the same but more so.

Katherine

There. It's gone, and this wild feeling is all spent. I have turned longing to gall, my dusk-dreams to white rage. I can read, I can dance, I can lie with a skilful lover. I can wear my new sleeves and my embroidered gloves and I can sip from a silver cup. I can watch the sun rise and see it setting, a blaze of Heaven. I am young, and I can savour all the daily miracles of life. Something happened, nothing happened; it is the same. It is all the same. Days pass. Weeks go by. I am forgotten. He is forgotten. His eyes watch me from the glass but they are my eyes; they are a trick of the light. The years will make sense of me again; it is not possible to fall so hard for nothing, for words and a hungry look, a moment in time.

Then, just as I am beginning to believe that I might be myself again, this letter comes.

Dark Aemilia,

I will not say 'Katherine'; but I do not know how to address you, meaning, with what form of embellishment, so let there be none. You find me churlish and insulting, even when my wish is only to entertain.

What do I want to say? I want to be honest with you. As you know, I have a wife, and, as you may not realise, also children. So.

I have walked the streets of London these past weeks till the very cobblestones cried out for me to stop. I have seen necromancers in search of the antidote to these violent, obsessive and lunatic cravings, a cure for foolish and forbidden love. I have been drunker than I had thought possible (I am generally given to sober industry and good fellowship). I have made myself so ill with this that I felt it must be a form of penance for a sin that I have committed only in my heart.

What do I wish to ask you? Not to exist? Never to have existed? To return to my mind and stay there? For I fear I may have conjured you from my febrile imaginings. I thought that you were locked up safely in my mind. I thought that in this actual, tangible world, women were just as women are. Which is to say, loud strumpets in foul taverns; dull ladies in fine houses; vain damsels waiting on the Queen. Or serving-wenches, or dairy-maids, or worldly widows... the common run of women in their place, with the qualities that place prescribes. But what are you? A scholar or a mistress? A temptress or a wife? An angel or a witch? I cannot say. And, as I cannot, I don't know what I want to ask.

But I do. I do know what I want to ask. But I cannot and will not ask it.

There is a fine play on at the Bel Savage Inn, off Ludgate Hill, written by my friend Kit Marlowe. The title is Dr Faustus. *I will be there tomorrow afternoon. I expect you are engaged in some palatial busyness already. I am certain that this will be the case. If you come, come alone, and dress plainly. It's not Whitehall Palace. It is not even as respectable as the Rose. I will be outside at half-past one. To take the air, you understand. It will be of no matter to me if you are not there, and I do not, indeed, expect you. Nor can I quite believe that I am writing these words at all, nor that I shall seal this note and entrust it to some messenger. No, I will take the thing myself.*

I am your most unworthy servant,
Will Shakespeare

I read this delirious missive in a state of trembling disbelief. Twice. Then a third time, hardly breathing. He writes to me, in my name, and he signs himself as... himself. No dissembling here, none at all. He has lost his reason. I have heard that this is sometimes the way with poets. Of course I cannot go. A royal mistress has a position to maintain, and her reputation to consider. And he is treating me like a common street-drab, truly. But my eyes keep wandering back to the looping words... *I fear I may have conjured you from my febrile imaginings... temptress... angel... witch...*

There is no question of accepting such a preposterous invitation. (To an inn, no less! To see a play! And 'alone' – what can he be thinking of?) If he isn't mad he is determined to insult me. There is a class of man who would as soon humiliate a woman as lie with her, and, again, those of a poetic disposition are often afflicted with this vice. And more – he is asking me to lower myself to this station, of tavern-doxy, behind the back of my protector, the great Lord Chamberlain himself. The words blur in front of me when I think of this. The affront to Hunsdon is even greater than the insult to me. All I have to do is show this little love-note to my lord and Will Shakespeare will be shut out of London's play-world and doubtless locked up in the Clink as well. The risk he is taking is out of all proportion to the pleasure he might gain.

I have seen necromancers in search of the antidote to these violent, obsessive and lunatic cravings, a cure for foolish and forbidden love.

Oh! He has felt it. He has felt the same. The same... There will be no other.

I sit down upon the rush-strewn floor, and command my body not to lust for something so ridiculous, command my skin to harden and my loins to... well. My mind not to summon up that profane word: 'loins'. Am I myself? Am I? What is this 'self', this pretty thing I have become? Was there another way? Another Aemilia that I could have been, could still be? I still care for Lord Hunsdon, and he has treated me with respect and sweetness for six long years. He is like a father to me, as well as a loving spouse. This longed-for letter is a vile temptation and a deceiver's snare.

And yet... I close my eyes, and see Will's face again. So I open them, blinking. Some speak of love as fever – if this is a sort of love, it is a vicious malady indeed. (*'And yet, who are you, to think about adultery?'* says the Devil standing behind me. *'You are no one's wife. Hunsdon's marriage bed is cold because of you. There is no virtue in your nature. You are just a whore – what's to stop you now?'*) If this is love, then it should be accorded some respect. There is not much love at Court, only place-men, and place-women, and place-fucking. If this is love, I need it. I must have it.

Will Shakespeare's letter has infected me with his insanity. My life depends on my destroying this unworthy note and forgetting that I ever saw it. I tear it into a hundred tiny pieces, go to the fireplace and toss the fragments on to the flames. One tiny piece of paper flutters down and falls among the ashes. On it is written 'Faustus'.

I try to distract myself with finery. I put on a yellow silk dress, and the new sleeves, and a wonderful ruff that makes me look like the Faerie Queene. I make a mouth at myself in the glass. Then I lean forward and kiss my reflection, blurring my own image with my hot breath. Lord, what is this yearning? Am I going mad? There must be sanity in Latin. In Plato, surely, so I call on him to help me. But another plain and lumpen English phrase comes to mock me, some words from Gower: '*It hath and shall be evermore, that love is master where he will.*' My mind is a mess of twisted things, like a squiggling heap of worms.

I reason thus. I may lose everything. I may gain everything. Life is a fleeting shadow. Death is eternal, and there is no fervid fornication in the charnel house. I have not known this thing before. I do not know what this thing is. I am not afraid.

I am not afraid.

Spring has forgotten us this year. Eddies of snow flurry from the cold grey clouds. My cloak is too thin, and my horse's hooves slip and slither on the hard ground. I am pretending to be more respectable than I am. I am used to that, at least. As he trots along Fleet Street, I shiver in the icy chill. Yet as the wind numbs my body I am grateful – for this distracts my mind. All I can think is how much I wish to sit before a roaring fire. If there is a poet there, so be it. If he is William Shakespeare, what of it? Or so I nearly think, as I crosss the bridge over Fleet River. The Bel Savage is, I know, close by. I have been there to see a new play with my lord. When I came before, I was borne upon a barge along the river, then taken in a private carriage from Blackfriars Stairs. This time I have only Frey to carry me, and, when I see the squat shape of the Inn and the clustering stables around it, I falter, and pull him to a walk. Even from this distance I can hear shouts and laughter, and the sound of an old ballad being belted out in chorus.

I am minded to turn Frey's head and ride back to Whitehall when I see a man, walking towards me along the road. Broad-shouldered, and with a countryman's gait, easy and long-limbed. It is strange to see the playwright in the open air. In my mind's eye he is always cooped up with his pages, or cheek-by-jowl with others of his sort, in some crowded City tavern.

He stops, and holds the bridle, and we look at each other for a moment, then swiftly look away.

'Is it really you, Aemilia?' he says.

'So it would seem.'

'The fevered champion of shrews and vixens? I can scarce believe it.'

'I am still their champion,' say I, 'fevered or otherwise.' But then realise I am addressing myself to my horse's yellowed mane. I wriggle my feet free of the stirrups and Will helps me down, and I feel the hardness of his arms through his thick sleeves. I dare not look at him, and sense that he dares not look at me. We must seem like two gaping fools, staring this way and that, as if the white sky and the cold street fill us with astonished wonder. My skin burns and my heart is pounding and I want to turn and run.

'I didn't think you'd come,' says he, patting Frey's nose. 'You seemed so angry with me.'

'Nor did I,' I say. 'Nor should I have.'

'Your letters were – '

'They were from Katherine. I have never written to you.'

He laughs. 'Katherine writes well.'

'I wish I could say the same for Petruchio.'

'He is a lost soul, my lady.'

'Lost?'

He shakes his head. 'Look, madam… I have a room…'

'Indeed! What do you take me for?' I turn away, ready to mount Frey again. 'I've made a terrible mistake, I'm not myself.'

Will turns me to face him. 'Aemilia – madam – please. It's my mistake… it's me who is not… myself. Please. I meant to say – a room where we can see the play. In private. Away from the crowd.'

I collect myself. 'Thank you,' I say. 'This meeting must indeed be private. That is thoughtful of you.'

We stand in silence for a moment. I have had dreams less dreamlike.

'I have a mask,' I say. I pull my vizard down, foolishly, so that my blushing face is hidden. In some mad part of my mind I wish I were Katherine, the True Shrew.

Will takes my hand most formally, and kisses the tips of my gloved fingers as if I were the Queen herself. I see that his own hands are ungloved. They are long, fine-boned and marked with lamp-black. Our eyes jolt together, and I feel something swoop and fall inside me.

'Come. Come inside... out of the cold.' A groom takes my horse, and Will leads me to the inn, my hand held firm in his. But he makes no other move to touch me, at which I feel a strange ache, the like of which I have not known before. It is the infection again, that disease that was carried in his letter.

Inside, the blistering March cold is soon forgotten. There is a warm buzz of talk and the glass windows twinkle in the firelight. The press of people gives off its own heat. There are young and old, men and women, drunk and sober, sitting in snug wooden booths, or gathered round the fire, house-dogs snoring at their feet. Will leads me up a narrow staircase, till we come to a small, oak-panelled room.

He closes the door and leads me to a table. Next to it is a curtained window. Drawing back the curtain, he nods to me and I see that it looks out into the inn-yard. Two hay carts have been backed together at one end, to form a makeshift stage. This is shrouded all in black, with a carved wooden chair and oak table at one end. A group of men are hammering nails into a trapdoor that has been constructed in the floor of one of the carts, and which seems not be to working as it should. Another man stands apart, dressed in black like the stage hangings, with a giant cross around his neck.

'Ned Alleyn,' says Will, opening the window.

'He is Faustus?'

'He is, and most excellent in the part.' He beckons me over, and I stand a few inches from him, not daring to go nearer. '*Too* excellent, one might almost say. Some of the players believe he wears that cross for good reason.'

I see that Alleyn's face is drawn and pale in the afternoon light. He looks anxious, and bends down to look at the trapdoor and consult with the carpenters. A cold draught comes from the open window, and the sound of hammering echoes in the frosty air.

'What do you mean?'

'When he summons Mephastophilis, the agent of Satan, he uses true magic. He uses words that good Christians would never utter, for fear of losing their immortal souls. The trap-door in the cart looks like a simple piece of stage-work now, but when the play begins it seems to have a different function, as if it can truly link the men upon the stage with the hidden fires of Hell.'

'Why draw upon such evil?'

'To make a wonder of it. To shock and amaze the crowd, so that they will speak of nothing else. To go beyond where tame and tedious playmaking has gone before.'

'Plays like yours?'

He laughs, his eyes hard. 'It's true. He has gone beyond what passed as "good enough" before. Romance, comedy, low-brow tragedy – only one step beyond a mystery play – each written with a paucity of pain and passion. We've settled for too little.'

'Or you have.'

He stares at me. 'Or I have, yes. But I am quick to learn.'

Ned Alleyn's posturing Faustus is a fool, but his descent is terrifying enough to grip me. He prowls and leers upon the boards like a staked bear at the pit, growling and griping against his mortal prison, and who but an idiot could not see where that would end? Mephastophilis, summoned by real magic or no, is just a tall player with a head slightly too large for his frame. Will is close beside me as I lean out into the cold air to get a better view. Then, suddenly, his breath is soft in my ear. 'Are you surprised that I set out to charm you with Marlowe's evil play?'

I turn and my lips accidentally brush his cheek. His skin is cold beneath the stubble. Something is sticking in my throat, and I have to press my legs close together beneath my skirts to halt their quivering.

'To charm me? Or tempt me?'

He steps backwards, raising his arms as if in innocence. 'Tempt you, Katherine? I wouldn't dare.'

'Perhaps you want to quell me. Scare me, with this diabolic stuff. Then I will fall…'

'Fall where?'

'To Hell, perhaps, or Limbo…'

'There is no Limbo now, my lady; it is forbidden.'

'Oh, this is Limbo, Petruchio, do not doubt it. I am caught between reality and poetry – and between…' I hesitate, not able to go on.

'Between what?'

He is closer now. How did he come closer? I am vapour, liquid, longing. I want to say, *Between two men.* Or even, *Between two lovers.* But they would have to crush me beneath a stone-piled door before I'd spit the words out.

'Why are you so cautious?' he asks.

'Why would I be otherwise?'

He pulls me round and looks into my eyes. 'I wanted you to see this. I knew you would understand it.'

'What do you mean?' The voice that comes from my stopped throat sounds sane enough, not strange. And this is most peculiar, for I could not say what's stage and what's sky, or my whole name, or any part of Plato.

The Seven Deadly Sins are on the stage, each a conjured demon brought forth by Faustus. One by one he names and dismisses them. First comes Pride, then Covetousness, then Wrath, Envy, Gluttony and Sloth. Then:

'What are you, Mistress Minx, the seventh and last?'
'Who, I, sir? I am one that loves an inch of raw mutton better than an ell of fried stockfish, and the first letter of my name begins with lechery.'

Lechery is the last sin, so why is there another demon, as yet uncounted? I stare hard, but I cannot see it clearly: the other devils are in the way, their bodies shift and shuffle around it so. I can make out a hooded figure, taller than the others, and motionless. Its face is shadow but from its outline rises up the faintest pall of vapour. The players around it falter. The demon lifts its head, and the cowl falls back.

I strain to look, yet cannot see it.

I hear a woman scream. 'God's death, the Devil himself is on the stage!'

Cries and shouting spread across the courtyard. 'Heaven help us, Judgement Day has come!' There is a terrible roaring and shrieking, and the next thing I see is a prentice-boy run on to the stage wielding a flaming torch, bellowing more horribly than a bowelled man, and the stage is alight and the players are running this way and that way, and the crowd has erupted and people are banging on the closed doors of the courtyard to get out. Through the smoke I think I can see the still figure of the demon, but the shadows flicker and I cannot be certain.

'What's this?' gasps Will. The shouts of terror grow louder, the flames higher… I cannot see… I crane forward. The courtyard is in shadow, the stage obscured by smoke. I blink, sure that my eyes are tricking me, and, when I look again, sure enough the figure has gone. But the awful screams and wails continue, and I see the prentice-boy convulsing on the ground before the stage, his legs kicking and his arms flailing. He has gone stark mad.

Will grabs my arm. 'Aemilia, let's go, let's find a place to – '

I pull away from him, and run.

I am halfway back down Fleet Street before I stop, remembering my horse, and then I double up, my chest heaving. I cannot think; I cannot breathe. The dreadful sound of the prentice-boy is trapped inside my head, and I can still see the weird jerking of his limbs. The gloomy, freezing afternoon seems haunted with floating spectres. Even my steaming breath is ghost-like.

A hand falls on my shoulder and I scream.

'Aemilia! Aemilia, it's me.' Will pulls me towards him and holds me tightly, trembling almost as much as I am.

'What *was* that?' I ask. 'Did Marlowe summon Satan? Is he *mad*?'

Will's head is buried in my shoulder. 'I don't know. I don't know what he is about. Something has possessed him, some desire he hardly seems to understand. But that is his weird fancy, not ours.' He straightens up and looks down at me. 'Come with me,' he says. 'There is somewhere we can speak, alone.'

My body still shakes with cold and terror. He wraps his cloak around my shoulders. We make our way off the road and along a muddy track. At the end of it, I see a ruined abbey, surrounded by a coppice of naked winter trees. Some of the buildings are half-dismantled, the stone doubtless purloined to build new homes for wealthy men. But the abbey house is intact. We follow an overgrown pathway that leads to a side door. Will opens it with a key hanging upon a hook. Inside, he lights a torch, and locks the door behind us. The house reeks of damp, and I can hear water dripping. He takes me up a flight of creaking wooden stairs till we come to a solar on the upper floor. It is still furnished, and someone has prepared it for us. I see that Will has been bold enough to hope that he might bring me here, and has laid it out accordingly. There is a bed in one corner, made up freshly with black silk bolsters and a white counterpane. And even logs in the fireplace. Will lights these, and his hands steady as he holds them to the flames.

'It was a stage trick,' he says, as he watches the fire grow higher. He seems to be returning to himself, making a pattern of what seemed unfathomable. 'Kit is ambitious. What better way to make his name?'

'What about that poor prentice-boy? What about the fire?'

'The boy could have conspired with him. What you see is not always the truth.'

'What else can you depend on?'

'It's not Satan that frightens me,' he says. 'It's Kit.'

He comes towards me, and helps me out of the cloak. 'I don't want to talk about this any longer,' he says, softly. 'One day, I will write a greater play than that. I wanted you to see it.'

'Why? If you are going to be greater?'

'Because I want you to know me.'

'Why?'

'Because I want *you*.'

I hold him at arm's length. I feel as if I have stepped into another world, as if this secret room is an enchanted place. What I do here is separate and different from every other part of my life. Time, too, seems twisted out of shape. And as for virtue... well.

'I want you,' he repeats. 'If you can forgive me for abusing Katherine.'

He has small white teeth. There is a blue vein snaking from his left eye to his hairline. His eyelashes are thick and black and make his eye-whites seem paler. There is a scar at the base of his neck, like a dagger-nick, in the same place that I have a black mole. If we lay together, they would fit quite neat together. He looks more Spanish than English. He looks more Jewish than Gentile. He looks like me.

'Aemilia,' he says. 'Are you listening?'

'Yes. You want me for your whore.'

'I want you for everything.'

'I am whored already. Shall I be doubly sinful? And what about your sin, your soul, your wife?'

'I can't help it. I can't... stop. This is not some fuck-led dalliance.'

'Not very poetical, is it? And if not fuck-led, what is it led by? You don't deny that you want me to be your little strumpet, and then – if you're minded – I must soothe you with some poesy when we are done? Is that the "everything" you have in mind?'

He holds my wrist. His long fingers easily encircle its narrow bones. 'I want *you*, Aemilia,' he says again. 'I want to know you. Because there is no one like you.'

'That's true enough. And I fear that there is nobody like *you*, or else I might be in some warmer chamber, with a man who's free.'

'Hunsdon isn't free.'

'But he is powerful. He does what he likes.'

He grips my wrist more tightly, staring at me till I feel the room recede and cannot think. 'My wife is far away from London, and I have had mistresses enough since we've lived apart. It's an itch, a thrill, a need.'

'Enough? How many?'

'Several. Plenty.'

'More than three?'

'I haven't counted.'

'More than seven?'

'I don't know!'

I yank my hand away. 'So, I'm the new diversion, am I?'

He takes both my hands. 'Please. Aemilia Bassano. My lady. I don't want you to be my mistress. I want you for my love.'

'Love! What about Hunsdon, and your poor neglected wife?'

'He has abandoned his own lady, so I shall not grieve for him. And my wife, as I've confessed, has been deceived already.'

He is clearly untaught in the art of disputation; his arguments are useless. But at least he can speak. I can't say anything.

Will stares at me. 'You came,' he says. He smiles at me, a pure, sweet smile. 'In spite of everything, you came.'

'I did.' A feeling of pure happiness begins to take possession of me. There are arguments; there are things I should say to him. But what are they? 'I had to.'

'You have risked your place – your station.'

'I have.' I begin to laugh, half-drunk with the madness of it. 'Such as it is. Do whores have a place in this Manworld? Have we been allocated a tier of Being?'

He leans down and kisses me for the first time, and I won't describe it because I can't. The world has shifted now; madness is closer.

'This room is ours, and secret,' says Will.

We kiss again. Madness, madness, it's at my feet.

'Will you come to bed with me, Aemilia?'

I stare at him, unblinking. I should say something. I should make him wait. This is what I have instead of virtue: the power to make one man wait. Only it seems I don't even have that false virtue; I can't play the Anne Boleyn game. Withhold and promise, promise and withhold. I can't do either. I am lost.

He draws me closer and unpins one of my sleeves. It is one of Hunsdon's gifts, patterned with angels. My naked arm gleams pale in the firelight.

'Are you an angel, too?' asks Will, eyes shining. 'Or a witch?'

I look at him, solemn as a virgin bride.

He lays the sleeve down on a chair by the bed and begins to unpin its fellow. I watch his fingers, my breath coming faster.

Scene IV

From that day on, we meet in that secret room as often as we dare, and our shuttered love flourishes. I was happy with the lovemaking of Hunsdon, but this is of a different order. Sometimes gentle, slow and almost sacred in its intensity. Sometimes raw and ugly, raging, screaming and obscene. I find that Will loves most what he hates strongly; that what I do to give him the greatest pleasure revolts him even as he comes, jerking and crying out my name. I, who have been fucking a man I saw as father-like since I was sixteen, have no shame. I see bed as a place to try every version of delight that a body might endure, and in Will I find a lover who does everything to please me. The more we do, the greater his desire, and the greater his desire, the closer I feel to a sort of ecstatic disappearance. I want that. I want to reach a height of passion of such a degree that I might never return to myself, but remain there, locked inside him, and he in me.

I like it best at the brightest hour of morning, with the shutters open and the sunlight streaming down upon us as we go at it, open-eyed. 'See this?' I say. 'See this?' He buys a heavy mirror at the Royal Exchange and carries it to our room one night, and it reflects all we do. I hardly sleep when I am apart from him, and cannot eat. My ribs stick out and my poor dugs have nearly vanished and my lord worries for me, fearing I have a tumour or some other malady. If it is madness, it is also the most precious and bright-hued time in my life.

* * *

I am lying on a riverbank, looking up into a cloudless May sky. Skylarks are singing and the Thames is lapping at my feet. I close my eyes. The sun warms my cheek. My chemise tickles my skin. A fly lands on my arm and waves its foremost legs at me. I sit up and look around me. Will is sitting beside me, clutching a wad of foolscap and reading intently. His shirt is unbuttoned, so that I can see the pale skin of his chest. I want to lean across and touch it.

He looks over at me, frowning. 'You haven't answered me,' he says.

I look at him, distracted. 'What was the question?' I say, smoothing down the sun-warmed folds of my chemise.

'The question I just asked you.'

'Ask it again.'

'You say you want to be a poet. But what sort of stuff is this? A bosom-brained Court lady could pen something like it. Where is your learning? Where is your wit?'

He throws the pages down. I remember what Simon Forman said, and pick them up. I can do better. I know I can do better.

'If I worked on them… so they were improved. What then?'

'I don't know. You could find a patron, and a publisher.' He leans over and begins to kiss my neck.

'A bastard concubine could be a published poet?'

'Why not?' He has lifted my hair and is kissing the hidden skin beneath it.

I push him away. 'You're making a mockery of me.'

'As you wish. Leave this Art to those who understand it.' He is laughing openly at me now. 'You are such a wondrous pretty thing – no need to strive for a life of the mind.'

I slap his face, slightly harder than I intended. 'A woman can do anything, if she has a mind to it. The Queen writes verse.'

He clutches his cheek in mock pain. 'The Queen, good lady, is a prince. No, no, you are quite right. Stick to your love ditties; true Art is quite beyond you.'

'What about you, the palace playwright? Everything you know, you learned at a country grammar school.'

'Whereas *your* learning…'

'Is of the Ancients, as you would expect.'

'Oh, indeed. A little of Athens, and much of Rome.'

'Much of both, sir. The trivium, of grammar, logic and rhetoric.'

'Ay, like a learned blade at Oxford.'

'Like the learned fellows everywhere. And also the quadrivium…'

'Of arithmetic, geometry, astronomy…' He hesitates, unsure.

'And music.'

'Of course – you are the lady of the virginals.' He seems to think this is a joke of some kind, so I keep silent. 'And this has fitted you for… rutting with an aged soldier, has it?'

I get to my feet and walk to the river's edge, hating him suddenly. He comes up behind me.

'It has fitted me for discontent,' I say.

'You see?' He pulls me close. 'We are two of a kind. Would I have written plays if I had known my station? Or would I have stayed in Stratford, making gloves for the gentry?'

I let him kiss me, but am still preoccupied. 'I know enough to be a poet, I have read enough to know how it should be done, but I don't know how to make my lines sing better!' I say. 'I can't turn thoughts to written words! There is some magician's trick to it.'

Will leads me back to the grassy knoll and spreads out his cloak so that we can lie down again. 'There is no magic,' he says. 'Treat words as if they were rubies.' He unhooks the beaded hood from my hair, so that it falls around me, curled by its enclosure. 'Choose the right one for each part of every line.' He undoes my stomacher and lifts it away. 'Write every line as though your life depended on it.' He opens the front of my chemise and regards my dugs quizzically, as if deciding whether or not to buy them. 'As if the executioner was standing by your shoulder, and this

45

was the last chance to speak that you would ever know.' With that, he pushes my chemise back, so my white shoulders are naked in the sun.

I do not smile, nor assist him in his task. 'That sounds like a kind of madness, I say. 'I fear I am too sane.'

He laughs again. The sun has browned his face. His eyes are full of sky. His lips are swollen red from reckless kissing.

'Do you want me?' he asks, very serious.

Oh, I do. I do.

And so we make love in the sunshine. Till at last Will calls my name, over and over. 'Aemilia! Aemilia! Aemilia!'

I need the skills of a player myself, in my dealings with Lord Hunsdon. It tears at me to lie to him, who was all in all to me for so many years. But I do so just the same, the whole summer long. And it scares me to think that, if he knew how I betrayed him, his anger would know no bounds. I once saw him kill a dog that turned. He beat the creature till it could not stand, and the ground was running with its blood. And that dog loved him, and had sighed at his feet with its great head upon its paws, watchful of his safety. If he knew how I lay with Shakespeare, and what we did, and how we cried out together in the boundless repetition of our lust, what would he do to me? I do not know.

But what I fear is not his power to hurt me, although I know that he could wield it, but that discovery would put an end to my deception. My true life is lived in those secret times with Will, which make the fakery of my Court life fade to nothing. Each time we meet, he gives me a letter, and I give him one in return. He says my words are his comfort when we are apart; his missives to me are more beautiful than I can say. These are not just letters which talk of love, but which talk of everything. (And if you think me a fool as well as a wanton, then let me say these letters are written in a sort of code.)

Today I am trying to put such thoughts from my mind, and I am reading St Paul's letters to the Corinthians in my chamber, disliking his view of women. But Hunsdon comes in, and says, 'Aemilia, are you tired of your life here?'

I put St Paul down, taking my time about it. 'Tired in what way, sir?'

He sits beside me. 'You know what I have spoken of. I am growing older.'

'Not to me,' I smile and touch his cheek, trying to read his expression. 'You are my lord in all things, dear Henry.'

He takes my hand and places it in my lap. 'What do you say to this – we go away from here?'

'Go? Where?'

'To Titchfield, where Wriothesley has his seat.'

The fear rises in me – is this a trick? A ruse to get me away from Will? I smile, and lean across to kiss him. 'Why, what shall we do there, my love?'

'The Queen is going on a progress.'

'But is this newly thought of?'

'Her Majesty has been out of sorts, and blames the parched and putrid drains. She wants fresh air, clean rooms, and some diversion. The players have a new piece, and they're to stage it there for her.'

The fear remains. 'Which piece is this?'

'*Love's Labour's Lost.* Wriothesley has commissioned it, Shakespeare has wrote it, and he assures me it is good. Some comedy or other. He claims it's better than the *Shrew*.'

'Mr Shakespeare?' I feel the room swimming around me. 'And... Mr Burbage? Will they be there too?'

'Most decidedly they will! Why would they not be? It will be an entertainment for us all. And much needed, before the nights draw in, and the autumn creeps upon us. Place House is handsome, and the country all around is green and pleasant. And it's not too far – no more than three days' ride.'

'But… are you sure you want me with you?' Hunsdon usually leaves me behind if he goes on a progress with the Queen. It is unspoken but understood between us that it pleases his wife better if I stay in my Whitehall rooms when he is gone from London, as if my body was a chance adornment of the palace and not a chosen pleasure. Travelling with his lordship is too spouse-like. So is this suggestion a sign of his growing fondness for me, or his burgeoning mistrust?

He kisses my obedient little breasts, pushed up tight and high by whalebone and fashion. 'But me no buts, my dearest chuck. We shall have the players to please us by day, and by night we shall have our sport together.'

Scene V

There is little sign of the countryside being green and pleasant during our journey, which seems to take three weeks, not three days. A great storm rages for the whole duration, so fiercely that I cannot ride, which I prefer, but instead must leave poor Frey to be ridden by a servant, while I am piled into a coach with a heap of scented, smirking ladies, all of whom seem party to some private joke. This conveyance bumps and trundles along, giving us all great discomfort, and the rain is so heavy that it trickles through the leaking roof, and soaks our cloaks, and the ladies declare that they will all die of the sweats, which sets them off again in the most hysterical and unpleasant-sounding laughter. I stare out of the window, watching the dark clouds flying and wondering at the amount of mud that churns along our way. We should have been better off in an Ark than a wobbling coach, for the wrath of God seems to be upon us and the heavens turned to perpetual water, as if the ocean has risen to the sky and must now fall down upon us, returning to its rightful place beneath the moon.

At last, the coach shudders to a halt, and I look outside. Through the falling rain I can make out a huge edifice, long and many-windowed, its lights blurred by the downpour. Stout towers reach up into the stormy sky, and it is neatly turreted, like a child's picture of a castle. Herded inside with my giggling companions, I am dazzled by the brilliant splendour of the great hall, so high and spacious as to rival that at Nonsuch, if not Whitehall. There are chandeliers and torches everywhere, casting their flaming light on many-coloured tapestries and golden panelling, so that I feel as if I am walking into a giant's treasure casket. The gallery above our heads is filled with musicians, who sing sweet and unfamiliar melodies as we come in – though of course these newly written tunes are not for us but for Her Majesty, whose entrance follows ours and we must push ourselves against the walls as she sweeps past, smiling with marble impregnability.

As I make my way up the great staircase, with Hunsdon close behind me, I see that Will is standing at the top. I never saw him look so handsome. He is dressed in black. He stares at me solemnly as he bows before the ascending procession of courtiers and I feel a sudden urge to weep. I have never wanted him so much, nor feared so painfully that I may not have him.

Hunsdon catches my arm. 'Aemilia, have you met our great scribe?'

I turn to look at him, chiefly so I can avoid looking at Will. 'What scribe is this, my lord?'

'Young Will Shakespeare.' Reaching Will's side, he grasps him by the shoulder. 'This is my sweet mistress, sir. As clever as she is beautiful, and quite as skilful in… every art as any man could wish.'

Will bows, unsmiling.

'Aemilia fancies herself a poet, don't you, my dear?'

I can only incline my head, scarlet with discomfort.

'I am sure that no poetry she could ever write would match the perfect symmetry of her face,' says Will. His voice is cold.

'Symmetry, sir! It's not the length of a lady's nose that keeps an old man happy. You poets! What a strange set of fellows you are! Do you slake your lust with symmetry, or with sport?'

Will bows again, as if to acknowledge Hunsdon's superior wisdom. 'Poets are poor lovers, my lord. We save our deepest passions for the page.'

Hunsdon laughs and takes my arm. 'Come now, Melia, forgive us for our idle talk. Let's go to our chamber and read some verse!' He makes a final bow to Will, the faintest inclination of his head. 'She prefers Sidney's *Astrophil and Stella* to your *Venus and Adonis* – what d'you say to that?'

Tonight, as luck would have it, my lord is in an amorous mood. Despite the fact that he has been a lusty lover for many years, in recent months he has been too tired or ill to fornicate with me, but this night he is keen to get to bed early, and undoes my bodice breathing heavily, showing every sign of wanting to have me as he used to. I confess, with Will nearby I can't bear the thought of this, and come up with the stratagem of reading my poetry to my lord, as a supposed preliminary to our love-making. In fact, as I had hoped, Hunsdon is snoring peacefully after three stanzas.

For a while I lie next to him, singing a lullaby and stroking his white hair back from his brow. And then I stop singing, and watch him breathing, steady as a rivertide. I pull the counterpane over him to keep the night chill from waking him, slip a shawl over my nightgown, and pick up a candle from our bed-table. I am an assiduous adulteress, and I noted where the players are sleeping. Will was given a small chamber to himself, while the other players were given a large room in the eaves. Will claimed he needed a quiet room to finish some writing. I don't know if this is true, or if he is hoping that I might find a way to go to him, at dead of night. Whether this was the case or no, I will do it. The thought of his look as I climbed the stairs with Hunsdon drives me on.

I close the door of my bedchamber behind me, and tiptoe across the dark landing. The house spreads all around me, like a village in the sky, with corridors and staircases leading in every direction. Shielding the flame with my hand, I make my way silently along, counting the doors and noting my way. I hardly dare breathe, and hate my own heart for its fulsome beating. Yet I swear to God I have never felt more alive than I do at this moment, fearing discovery, astonished at my own foolishness and longing to lie once more with my lover, skin to skin.

Just as I pass a grand, carved door to one of the great bedchambers at the front of the house, I hear a noise and stop still, a dribble of sweat trickling down my neck. I can hear voices shouting, and dare not take another step lest they burst out of the door. I can see nowhere to hide, so I stay, motionless, like a vole sensing the descending hawk. As I stand there, the voices rise higher and higher, and I recognise one of them: it is that of our boyish host, Henry Wriothesley, the Earl of Southampton. The other – a deeper man's voice – I do not know.

'Oh my lord,' says this voice. 'Oh my lord! Oh my lord! Oh my lord! Oh my lord!' Each cry is followed by a bang, like a board being struck in steady rhythm. I stand, terrified, willing myself to move, but unable to take a step.

There is a pause on the other side of the door, yet not silence. The two voices mingle to make the strangest noise, part scream, part groan. Then the deeper voice makes a peculiarly terrible sound, a wolfish howl.

Now comes Wriothesley's light and laughing tone, as if he had had no part in what had gone before. 'Say, "Oh my Lord God."'

'My lord?'

'Say "Oh my Lord God" each time I go up you.'

Then they were off again.

'Oh my Lord God!'

Bang.

'Oh my Lord God!'

Bang.

'Oh my Lord God!'

This time it builds and builds till the final scream is so loud that I am sure the whole household will come running. A drop of candle-wax spills on my wrist, and wakes me from my trance. I hasten along the passage until I come to a narrow flight of stairs

I had noted earlier. I climb them, breathless, and there, at the top, is a door, no bigger than the way into a priest hole. I pray to God that I have remembered right, and tap at it, three times.

The door opens immediately, as if the occupant had been waiting for me.

Will is wearing a nightshirt, but his bed, which I can see over his shoulder, has not been slept in. Close by is a table, on which a candle burns, cluttered with papers – he has indeed been writing. This is his habit at night: he is the only person I have ever met who sleeps as restlessly as I do. For a moment, we look at each other.

'What's this about *Astrophil and Stella*?' he says. 'Disloyal minx.' Then he smiles and pulls me inside.

Scene VI

Having deceived Hunsdon and borne silent witness to Wriothesley's peculiar sodomy, I am trembling with shock and fear. Yet once I am in Will's bed I forget all my terror, and what we do now is like no other love-making that I have ever known, such is its silence and its slow tenderness. As we twist and rock together, I feel my mind fill with a profound sweetness, and I smile as I kiss him, locked closer, closer till we finish as one creature, still soundless, deeply bound. There is such joy in me that I am shocked to find that we are soaked with tears. And when we both lie tangled in my loose black hair, Will whispers, 'We are married now, my love. I have no wife but you.'

We lie silent for a long time. Will strokes the round mole at my throat.

'What's this, my little sorceress,' he says, 'if not your third dug, where you give suck to your familiar?'

'Shall you be my familiar, then?'

'I would be nothing else, if it were possible.'

'Do you ever wonder if the creatures of the night are those that God did not get quite right?' I ask, dreamily.

He is busy kissing the mole upon my neck, but begins to shake with silent laughter. 'Such as what, my strange one? Such as yourself?'

'Well, both of us are wide awake when others sleep. So you are night-odd too…' I laugh myself, and twist my neck away. 'But I meant – badgers, hedgehogs, moles. Or bats. All the odd things that are queer to look at.'

'What of the owls, though?' says Will. 'An owl is perfect.'

'Perhaps he is the king of all nocturnal beasts,' I say. 'Unrivalled beneath the moon. He rules us too.'

His lifts his shadowed face to stare into my eyes with mock puzzlement. 'What *are* you, Bassano?' he asks. 'Where did they find you?'

'I found a bat once, fallen from the roof beams,' I whisper.

'Foolish bat, if it could not fly better!' says Will, kissing his way from my neck to my breasts.

'It was a baby, hardly bigger than two farthings,' say I, gasping as he begins to suck. 'I kept it in a little box and fed it with cow's milk in a thimble, and it grew to full size, though I never would have thought it possible.'

'Your witch's magic, I have no doubt of it.' His hands are creeping down, over the skin of my belly.

'Afterwards, it made its home in the eaves of my apartment, and I would see it at dusk, spinning around the roof beams with sightless ease. And it would still come down and drink milk from a saucer, like a tiny flying cat.'

'Fortunate bat, to sip from your saucer!' His fingers have found their place, and he begins to jerk them in a rhythm that I know and love, and for some time neither of us speaks, but go at it bat-like, knowing our way.

'I cannot bear to be without you,' I say at last. 'I cannot live like this, divided, like Judas.'

'What else can we do?' says Will. 'Where else can we go?'

'I don't know,' I say. I think of Hunsdon, pumping away with his old man's wiry passion, and feel the bile rise in my throat. 'I cannot bear to lie with Hunsdon! I am no better than a tavern whore, turning tricks for trinkets.'

'This is our world,' he says, with his arms around me. 'There is no escape, except when we are lost together, and it's those times that we must think of, and seek out, and keep safe.'

I kiss his ink-black, cunt-wet fingers.

'Why can't your words save us? Why can't we set up in some fine house, Lord and Lady Letters? Why must it be so squalid and profane?'

'Aemilia.' He strokes my hair. 'Before I knew this, I knew nothing. Nothing of love, and what I knew of life was book-learned, or filched from other poets, or sketched to please the crowd. My plays were martial, my poetry a forged confection, like a sugar-swan. No more. No more.'

'What – and you were married? And had little children? And this taught you nothing?'

'Nothing of this,' he whispers into my hair. 'Of *eros* and its wondrous madness. I love you, and, if that is wrong, so be it.'

Then sleep comes. I wake and hear the sweet song of the nightingale and see a faint light round the shuttered window. Sitting upright, I notice that the candle has burned right down. Will is fast asleep, curled into his pillow. I kiss his sleeping mouth, slip from the bed, pull on my nightgown and shawl and leave with anxious haste. I retrace my steps as quickly as I dare but, as I pass Wriothesley's door, it opens. A figure steps out and stands in my path. I am filled with horror. It is the young earl, in a splendid purple robe, like some Roman pontiff. In the half-light, I can only see his outline, slim and flimsy as a girl, and the pale aureole of his curling hair, which hangs loose about him.

'What's this?' he says, in a loud voice, more suited to the daytime.

I stare at him, in an agony of horror.

'It's Hunsdon's pretty mistress, if I'm not mistaken? Pert Aemilia, the bed-wise scholar.'

'It is, my lord.' He may speak as loudly as he wishes; I will whisper.

'What are you about, my swarthy little puss? Why are you not with his lordship, in his chamber?'

'I was restless, my lord.'

56

'Restless! Oh, my sweet lady. You should have come to me – and with me – sweet and stealthy restlessness of woman! I would have given you no rest at all.'

'I have been… walking in the garden,' I say. 'My mind was disturbed. I sometimes walk at night.'

Wriothesley comes towards me and kneels down. I see that the grey light is casting day-shapes on the dark landing – here a carved chair, there a great urn. Hunsdon might be waking up, and wondering where I am. He picks up the hem of my nightgown and scrutinises it carefully. He looks up at me, his blue eyes suddenly illuminated in a ray of morning light.

'No dew on your gown, I see.' He stands up and comes close, so I can smell the semen on him. 'But I daresay you are drenched… in some other place.'

I smile at him, desperate. 'When I came to myself I was standing upon the pathway, looking up at the moon,' I say, twisting my hands together. 'Sometimes my night-walks bring forth new ideas for poems.'

'Indeed!' He smirks, and kisses me lightly on the cheek. 'Perhaps one day you will write a poem for me.'

The performance is the cause of much excitement. The beauteous Rosaline has made a great impression on our host. Yet I find myself distracted all the way through. Will is playing Berowne, and his words make me ache. I cannot look at him. After it is over, the Queen announces that she must see the gardens and out we spill, out of the dark Play-Room, down the handsome staircase and out into the square of summer light. A storm has soaked the fields and gardens and disappeared without a trace, so that the dripping trees and heavy flowers have the brightness of spring, and yet are deep-coloured with summer's heavier hues.

The Queen and her ladies process along the wide garden paths, surveying the knot garden and fanning themselves as they talk and laugh. I fall behind them, so tired that black shards of night faze in and out of my sight. I feel sick and strange, wishing in one part of myself that I could leave all this spoiled and rotten life behind me, and enter some cool nunnery and pray my way slowly back to God. I am sick of Greeks, and Romans, and learning; sick of fine clothes and smart words and the ways of Court, in which everything is permissible if the Queen wishes or approves it, or does not deign to notice it.

Indeed, I am so worn out that I do not at first notice that Will has fallen into step beside me.

'How are you today, my love?' he asks.

I turn to look behind me, but no one is walking within earshot. 'I am well, sir,' I say.

'What do you think of all this?' he asks, indicating the wide garden which has subjugated Nature with such ruthless symmetry.

'It is very fine.'

'Could you see yourself in such a place? A country lady?'

'Certainly not! The life of a country lady consists mostly of praying, walking, Bible-reading and being unwell.'

Will throws his head back and laughs delightedly. 'God's teeth, you have a way with words, Aemilia! What a summary!'

'Ssh, do not laugh so loudly. Hunsdon will hear you.' I look across the knot garden to the far window. Hunsdon and his advisors are in an important huddle, discussing affairs of state. The Queen and her ladies have settled down in a leafy bower. A lute-player is hurrying towards them, as if anxious to stave off the spectre of boredom with his sweet songs.

Will is abruptly serious. 'At least a country lady has a place. A position.'

'Oh, surely. She is planted in her lord's estate, like an oak tree, and she must manage servants and clink with keys to all that must be locked and tidy. For variety, she may admire her fine linen or fish for trout.'

'A pleasant enough existence.'

'While her lord parades himself at Court, perhaps gaming, perhaps fornicating, and probably amusing himself around the town or at the theatre. Did I miss my vocation, in being too much the bastard whore to make a proper match? I think not.'

'You are a woman, Aemilia. You cannot rise above that.'

'Why not? If Our Lord rules over all the magnificence and violence of Creation, then why must his women be so timid and obedient?'

'Aemilia – '

'All of it is His – the wolves and roaring bears, the wild boar, the proud lion, the swift claws of the eagle and the kite.'

'Madam, if I may only speak – '

But I will have my say. 'Think of it all – the secret vastness of the great Leviathan that slides, lightless and unclassified, beneath the mighty ocean. And we placid little Marthas may have the hearth.'

'You are too clever for this old game. You should rule kingdoms, not that dotard Hunsdon.'

'Ay, that would be a fine thing. Except that our Prince is also the keeper of her own prison. She rules her own spirit quite as harshly as she rules any of us.'

We walk on in silence for a while, with a cautious space between us. Only my skirt touches him as it swishes along the path.

'What riles me is the littleness of learning,' I say, suddenly.

'The what? Is this more of your philosophy?'

'The facts and factions, the scholars in their ponderousness of robes and competition and self-display and mutual vilification.'

'Ha! Yes. Now this, I like.'

'How can any man know a little and not crave to know much more – the "all" that is the sum of what we have? To go beyond the walls of this fine college or that one, and be Godlike in his wisdom, so that the map of all learning is stretched before his gaze?'

'They are gentlemen. They have nothing more to prove.'

'I cannot credit it, the narrow, self-regarding focus of the scholar on his portion of Cicero and Seneca, his puffed-upness with it, his satisfaction with the verse he's stuffed whole into his empty head. For every Bacon there are a thousand lettered dolts.'

'Lady, what fuels this rage? You speak like no one else I know.'

'Oh, yes, I should calm myself. I am just a woman, accidentally and freakishly deformed by teaching which took no regard of my station, nor of my sex.'

Will stops and turns to face me. 'God above, you're like a maze, with every twist and turn taking me further from the sober world! Such anger and…' here he swallows '…such ardour. I never knew anything like the earthly joy you spun with me last night. I keep thinking of your soft tears in the darkness, and how they mixed with mine.'

'My love,' I whisper. 'We must be cool in daylight.'

'And of… Jesu. I am sick with love for you, Aemilia. I am ill with it.'

'Will, be quiet, don't speak of these things in this place! Be cautious!'

'I cannot be cautious and love you. I must be reckless, or give you up.'

'No, sir, you must be cautious and not give me up!'

'How does Rosaline compare to Katherine?' he asks, abruptly.

'How… what?'

'It is the man who is quelled in this tale, don't you see it? Who must cool his ardour and his arrogance to win his love. She is as far removed from that poor Shrew as I could make her. And she is darkly beautiful, like another lady that I know.'

I can't help laughing in spite of myself. 'There is a message in that play for me, is there?'

'It's a love letter to my own fine, clever Rosaline, who makes me think and makes me weep and will not let me have my way.'

'Oh, sir! Now you are playing with me! How have you been thwarted? Why, there is not a man alive who has got his way with me as you have, or for whom I've taken greater risks!'

A drop of rain falls heavily on my hand. I look up, and see the storm clouds have returned. The knot garden is empty, and we are standing at a stone gate, at the furthest side from the house.

He is standing closer now, and as the new rain falls he pushes me into the gateway and I see there is a tiny room within it, with a stone slit for a window and a cracked oak door.

'Will, I...'

But I move first, kissing him so hard I bite his lip and taste his blood, and as the storm breaks with a clattering roar of thunder we fall together in the garden room, and he kicks the door shut and somehow my skirts are undone and I am in my under-shift wedged halfway up the wall, and Will is tight inside me pushing higher with each shuddering breath, and I am shouting with each thunderclap, as nearly mad as I have ever been, and as close to Heaven as I'll ever come. Unless God is more forgiving than I dare to hope.

Scene *VII*

This is a fervent time, and I must remember it. I must keep it with me. I am writing notes on what we do, and how we love, all of them in Hebrew, which I know Hunsdon can never read. It is a sad fact of our lives that it is easier to convey pain and sorrow than pleasure and happiness – I trust that in the afterlife we shall find perfection more to our liking. This is a passion that transforms me, and a love that makes the world glitter. It is nothing like drunkenness, nor like witchcraft neither: it is like being reborn in Eden. And I have him: he is mine and no one else's. And I am his: no other man comes close. What happened to us before, and whatever sadness may come after – they cannot touch this period of our glorious rapture. Will belongs to me, and I rejoice in my dominion, and he is at once my equal and my lord.

We snatch at time together when we can, not just lustful but curious, and hungry to know each other's minds. We read together and write together, and laugh and weep and whisper in that secret room. And yet it's true, our wildest rapture is to *occupy* each other, in that modern phrase, and each time we lie together we count it a miracle, and wonder if a greater ecstasy could be reached than that which we knew in our last coupling; and each time it turns out that it can. Such is the way with new lovers when their bodies match.

The greatest miracle, I must say, is that for many months no child comes of all this exultant fornication. But Nature will have its way in the end, as Nature must. And there is no question: keeping two lovers makes me careless and distracted, for I have been a watchful, canny mistress for many years. I used to keep myself away from Hunsdon at my fertile times, and if my curse was late I would take a vile cure made from mandrake root. Which did its work, though each draught nearly killed me. I proceeded with these treatments with such success that I have come to think I must be barren, or that Hunsdon's seed is spent.

It turns out that, rather than being barren, I am like a mossy bank in springtime, ready to burst forth with new life. One day, soon after Michaelmas, I realise that my curse-blood is late. I cannot remember when it last flowed. Quite unconcerned, and confident that I can soon put this to rights, I say nothing. I take my usual draught of poison, pinching my nose to get it down. Then I wait for the blood to come, calmly enough to start with. But this time nothing happens, excepting only that my belly seems tighter than a drum. I take another draught, a heftier dose this time, which gives me fearful cramps. This time I am certain the brew has done its work, and wait once again. Again, nothing. Now, with mounting fear, I begin to pray for my deliverance, though it is of course against the teachings of Our Lord to ask for an unborn child to die. Night after night, I lie awake, dry-eyed. I know only too well what happens to a kept mistress who finds herself in this predicament. She is cast off, and sent away. I must free myself. I must get rid of it.

But who will help me? There is no one I can trust, no one I can turn to. Dr Forman might have a tincture he can give me, but I am not certain he would keep the secret. My dugs – so recently the size of winter apples – have swelled up so they seem ready to burst out of my bodice, and are painful to the touch. And I seem to have gained a layer of fat, even though everything I eat tastes like pewter. If I were a pig, I would soon be ready for the pot. I am nauseous and dizzy and can barely think. The pregnancy itself seems like a spell. I sleep in dream snatches, and see Will and Hunsdon fuck together, and wake twisted in the bed-sheets, crying out.

At last my head clears. Hunsdon has gone away, to execute some Catholics at York. And I hold Will off, writing a coded note to say I am too ill to meet him in our little room. Which is no more than the truth. If I am to do something to save myself, the time to act is now.

Alice, as luck would have it, is a stupid, unobservant girl, who lives most vividly in the looking glass. Thus, she sees nothing strange in my repeated bouts of puking.

'Dear me, mistress, what have you eaten?' says she, fetching me a cup of small beer as I empty my guts into the close stool. 'You've been ill for days! And yet you're no thinner – there's a marvel!'

'A marvel indeed,' I say, sipping from the cup. My mind is sharper after this last horrid spewing-up, as if I have rid myself of some internal confusion along with my breakfast. 'We must go out.'

'Are you sure you're well enough, mistress? You're very pale.'

'I am well enough to visit an apothecary,' I say. 'To seek a cure for this unpleasant malady.'

'Oh, but I could go for you,' says the girl, all eager. I know why: she will have the chance to prance past the law students at Middle Temple, showing off her pretty clothes, though they are like as not more interested in Aristotle's 'Refutations' than in her Spanish ruff. 'Oh – please let me!'

'No, Alice, we shall both go. Hurry up, and don't start messing with your cap. I'm well enough now, but may soon be worse again.'

Most of the apothecaries' shops are found in Bucklersbury, a narrow street which winds away from Cheapside. In the swirling City stenches this is a place which offers a rare delight to Londoners, for you can smell it half a mile away, such is the sweet scent of its herbs and spices. But, of the hundred apothecaries who trade in the City, I have heard that half are useless and the rest are cozeners. On most occasions I send a servant to see Ned Hollybushe, whose father has wrote an excellent book upon this subject. But today…

'Why here, mistress? Off the beaten way?' asks Alice. 'This is not our usual man!' We have arrived in a cramped courtyard, which reeks even more strongly than the busy street. The jutting storeys of the ancient houses make it dusk at midday. An open shop front stands before us, the counter folded out so that – in theory – we can see within. But all that is visible is the shop sign, which is a hanging tortoise. Behind this I can see nothing.

'Wait here,' I say.

'Oh, but, mistress…'

'Do what I tell you.'

And, with that, I push open the door of the shop and go inside. What strikes me first is its exotic scent, something between the smell of cumin and sweet basil. But as I look around me I see that the shop is very different from what I have been expecting. Though it is ill lit, there is a shaft of sunlight coming from a window set high in the wall, and I see that it is a larger space than had seemed possible from the street. The walls are dull red and lined with shelves, upon which are ranged pots and pitchers and drug-jars made of blue and white porcelain, painted with red and blue flowers and symbols and marked with the name of the herb or spice which they contain. On the floor beside the counter is a giant pestle and mortar, as big as a bucket. Everything is polished and clean, so that the falling rays of sunlight are reflected in the shining surfaces. So much precision and order, such neatness – I confess I am surprised.

Behind the counter stands the apothecary, Widow Daunt. She wears a white bonnet, and her face is sallow and deeply lined. Her expression is somewhat sour, as if a shop like hers might do very well if only she didn't have the bother of serving customers.

But there is no shortage of these. Joan Daunt is well known for her foul but cunning remedies.

Indeed, there are two people at the counter. A tall woman and her old manservant. The woman is wearing a fine wool cloak and her golden hair is arranged with great care. She turns to look as I come in, and I see that she has an old, shrivelled face, which is out of keeping with her good clothes and upright carriage. Her pretty hair must be a wig.

'Is that all you have to say?' she asks, turning back to look at Widow Daunt.

'All what?' asks the Widow. She has a surly manner, for a shopkeeper.

'That you can do nothing else for me?'

'What I have to say, madam, is that you came to me for an elixir to make you beautiful. Sparing your feelings as best I may, I told you no such thing exists, and gave you what I could, instead. And that was a potion to make a young man *think* you comely, at least for the space of one night.'

'Wine can accomplish that much,' says the woman.

'Indeed it can, and I told you at the time that there was wine in that mixture and by all accounts it did its work.'

'He loved for one night, that is true.'

'So our deal is sound.'

The woman draws breath deeply, and I realise that she is on the brink of tears.

'It is not enough, Mistress Daunt! I demand more! I want more from you!'

Joan Daunt leans forward across the counter. 'What more would that be, mistress?'

'I want him to love me!' wails the woman. 'I had him! I had him for one night – and what joy it was! And, when day broke, he looked down on me and fled the chamber. Make him love me! I demand you make him love me!'

'How shall I do such a thing?'

'Give me another potion! A stronger one this time.' She nods, and the manservant produces a money bag.

'Something to make him love you for longer?' asks Widow Daunt.

'I want you to make me young again. And beautiful. Forever. I have money. I don't care what pain I suffer, or how vile the treatment.'

Widow Daunt seems to find this a very good joke. 'Madam, I am an apothecary, not Almighty God. Take your business elsewhere. Or you could always pray.'

The woman nods to the servant and he takes the Widow by the shoulders. 'Do as my mistress says, or take the consequences,' he says. 'Do it, old woman, or you will suffer for it.'

'Get away with you, you buffoon!' says the Widow. 'I will not be spoken to like that in my own shop! Get out, the pair of you!'

Then the woman leans forward and slaps her hard, across the face.

This is quite enough. I throw the hood from my head and approach them. 'Kindly do the Widow's bidding and leave this shop, if you have no further business,' I say. 'I have waited long enough to be served, and you are wasting my time as well as insulting her. You can't bully your way to beauty, madam, nor bribe your looks back from Time. They've gone, and there's an end to it.'

The woman turns her tear-stained face to me. 'It is all very well for *you*,' she says. 'Old age comes to all of us, but *you* are still young.'

'Get out, the pair of you,' I say. 'Leave the Widow be, and go about your business.'

The servant keeps his grasp. I draw out Hunsdon's paper-knife and point it at his neck. 'This knife was given me by the great John Dee himself. There is venom in this blade. One prick from this and you'll fall stone dead, right on the spot. The last person to feel its point lived for just two minutes. It's not a sight I'd wish to see again.'

The servant lets go of the widow and leans away from me, his veined eyes full of terror.

'Who on *earth* are you?' shrieks the woman. 'Who is John Dee to you?'

'I am Queen Mab,' I say, 'for all it's got to do with you.'

The strange pair leave. Joan Daunt waits until the door bangs shut, and then turns to look at me. She seems neither alarmed nor grateful for my help.

'How can I help you?' she asks, looking me over. 'I see you have plenty of need for cures.'

'Do you, indeed?' A wave of sickness comes over me.

'You'll end up keeping it,' she says.

'Keeping what?'

'The child.'

'I never said…'

'You didn't have to.'

'Well, you are quite wrong. I do want rid of it..'

'Yes, but I just told you – '

'I need something strong. And I don't mind what you put in it. A hanged man's sperm is fine with me. It can burn my womb out, for all I care.'

'So that you could never have a child?'

'Why should I want one? All they do is bind you, and I am bound enough already.'

The Widow stares at me, and I see something unexpected: kindness. 'Sit down,' she says. 'I'll do you something. But you won't drink it.'

She collects together some jars and bottles, takes out a pestle and mortar – of larger than usual size – and fills it with leaves and fragments, which she begins to grind. Then she scoops a hideous little fish from a jar and scrapes the scales from its wriggling form. These she places into a clay burner and a most obnoxious perfume fills the air. What she has made – a sickly, semi-liquid paste, the colour of a dog turd – she squeezes into a tiny vial and stops with wax.

'Your remedy,' she says, handing it to me. 'Swallow it in one draught. The babe will come out in three spasms, whole and pulsing, but too small for you to see its face. It will be dead in five minutes.'

I open my mouth to speak, but she holds up her finger.

'Be careful. You are in a bad way. And your old life is over, have no doubt of that. And... when you need me, send word.'

'I have servants, Mistress Daunt. I am well cared for.'

'Nonetheless, I wait upon your word. And, when I hear from you, then I will come. Remember that.'

I look at the vial and its horrid contents, puzzled. The potion is not still, but heaves and oozes, as if in some low kind of pain. And the stench is such that I can smell it through its coat of glass.

Scene VIII

I will wait one more day, to see if my curse might start. Another night of prayer might see the unborn child bleed harmlessly away. The potion looks so horrible, and the thought of swallowing it is disgusting to me. But it is hard to wait for anything. I sit at my virginals in my parlour, and try to play a tune. It is a pretty piece called 'Giles Farnaby's Dream', which can usually calm my nerves but today it only vexes me: its brightness seems too far removed from the world I know. I look at the painted wainscot, the Turkey carpet which takes pride of place over the fireplace, the half-finished skirt that lies in a ripple of azure satin across my bed. Nothing seems real. I am like a child's toy, which is now broken and must be mended. My head aches. My eyes are sore. My velvet bodice digs into my flesh. I slam the lid down on the virginals, so that the strings let out a plaintive note. Snatching up my cloak, I rush down the stairwell and into the courtyard. I feel as if there must be a way out of all this trouble, if only I could clear my head and think. The gateway to St James's Park is open. I slip through it, and hurry into the darkening trees.

I put my face in my hands and moan. What to do? What to do? It is Will's child, I am sure of it – the fruit of all our hidden passion. I am not certain where the souls of unborn, unbaptised children are supposed to go, now that the Queen of England is our Pope, but in the old days they dwelt in Limbo. It does not sound like a good place for my unborn babe to be. Yet what else can I do but kill it? There is no way out. I should have kept away from Will. But I did not, I could not. Now what will become of me?

Just as I am racked with another bout of sobs, I find that I am not alone. Someone is by me. Someone's arms are around me.

'Aemilia – my love! What's wrong? You're cold – you're trembling!' Will's voice is soft and tender.

'Will!' I cry. I am almost afraid to look him in the eye, in case he can see what I am thinking. But I can't look anywhere else. How can he not know? How can I hide my knowledge from him? 'What are you doing here? What is the matter?'

'My love,' he says. His face is shining, as if he has found some new wonder in the world. 'I had to see you.'

'But... You know we must be...' I catch my breath. When were we ever 'careful'?

'Listen – listen...' He stares down at me. 'I came because there is something I must say.'

It is so sweet to see him, and look at his face, and hear him speaking so tenderly to me that I cannot help but weaken. Silently, I weep against his shoulder.

'What is it?' He looks down at me, eyes shadowed in the moonlight.

I struggle with myself, not knowing what to say. 'Oh... I am so unhappy that I can't be with you, and must live with Hunsdon, in the palace...' This is almost the truth. And yet, of course, I want to say, *Will, I am pregnant, and I cannot say for sure if it is yours, and yet I believe it is, and I've got a draught to get rid of it, and I thought that I could do this, and go on as before, but now I find I'd rather die. Please help me.* Even with his arms around me, I feel alone, and as if I have betrayed him.

He kisses me, and holds me tight against him. I can smell the leather of his doublet and the tavern stench of old ale and tobacco. 'Come, come, we can't stay here,' he says. (And how this sweet 'we' tears at me.) 'We must find somewhere warmer... there is an inn on the other side of the park where we can go. Here – look...' He pulls a stage mask from his sleeve, made of black velvet stiffened with bombast. 'You can be the mysterious lady and I will be your humble squire.'

When we are settled by the fire in an upstairs room, he takes my hands and holds them. 'Still cold, so cold, my love.'

'I am better now.' I stare at him, lulled by the fire and by a mute happiness that he is here.

'Aemilia, come and live with me.'

'Oh, Will! But what of Hunsdon?'

'I will care for you. You don't need him.'

'Don't be such a fool.'

'Leave him, and be *my* mistress.'

'Living how, exactly?'

'I'll be your protector.'

'And where shall we live?' I ask.

'I… have expectations.'

'Expectations?'

'My plays will make me rich. I am certain of it. How can it be otherwise?' He kisses my hand, and then reaches across and touches my icy cheek. 'You know that this is what should happen. You know that we can only be happy if we are joined together – think of it: to have each other in the daytime, in the open, instead of these furtive fornications and sneakings round at dead of night! To eat together, or stroll in the Exchange!'

He speaks as if he was offering me a chance to live with him in Heaven.

'I never heard such foolishness… how can this be possible?'

But he is determined. 'Listen, my love. There is a logic in the universe that goes beyond mere common sense – and this is the logic of our two lives, intermingling.'

'Will, I – '

'Our two selves, undivided. Don't you agree?'

'Of course, but – '

'Come with me! Come away with me, and who knows what will happen to us? Let's take our chance.'

'If only it were possible!'

'It is possible, my sweet Aemilia! It is possible. Just think of it...'

I close my eyes and see it.

He leans closer. 'Aemilia. You cannot deny me. You cannot deny yourself.'

Scene IX

Could I un-lord myself, and live with Will? I suppose I could. If there were no baby, and I had money, and I was sure I wouldn't starve. If there were no censure; if poets' mistresses were not seen as tavern whores. Should I drink Joan's brew, and end the baby, and live with my love – *be* that whore? At least my life will be a sort of whole; I'll be a common doxy, but I'll have the right man in my bed.

I pray for forgiveness, open that dread casket once again and take out the vial. The shifting, surging potion has expanded and mounted up the sides of the glass, like a semi-liquid fungus. My guts heave. I take the stopper out, and am assaulted by its appalling stench.

But what's that? I hear a sound and whirl around to see what it could be. It is – I could have sworn – the sound of a newborn crying. Plaintive, urgent, relentless. I turn full circle, startled. Outside the sky is grey and heavy rain is falling: a ceaseless rhythm is beating at the window panes. Of course, the noise must be a seagull's cry, echoing down the chimney. I raise the vial and tip it slowly towards my lips.

There it is again, even clearer than before. I lower the glass, trembling with nausea. I have never heard a seagull make such a sound. I replace the cork, open the window casement and the rainstorm rips into the room, drenching my dress and hair. Hardly noticing the sudden cold, I peer out into the storm, half-expecting to see an abandoned infant lying by the palace wall. It is not unknown for women to leave their newborn babies there, in the mistaken belief that royal largesse will ensure that they are well looked after. On this day, though, there is no baby. There is nothing.

I feel so sad about the empty, lonely gardens, and the fact that there is no crying child that I begin to weep. I think of those poor girls who bring their babes and leave them in this place, open to the elements: tiny, weak, milk-smelling creatures, unshriven, unbegun. And this in a city which pities no one, in which wealth is everything and penury the norm. Those poor children! Those wretched, abandoned souls! I weep silent, penitent tears. I cannot do it. I cannot kill this child. I hurl the vial out of the window. I hear a soft crack as it hits the ground and – in spite of the rain – I smell something sourly burning. I lean out and let the rain mix with my tears. And I know that, if I can't kill this unborn infant, then I can't leave my rich protector, furious and betrayed. Because if I am going to have this child I need him. No, let me be honest: I need his money. I do not know who has fathered this child, but I know who the mother is well enough. A penniless, bastard whore, half-Jewish, long orphaned. Nobody. I think of Will, expectant and full of love. If I could unmake everything so that I could be with him… but no. My thoughts fly to the four corners of the world, and then return, defeated.

The rain pelts harder and seems to wash some sense into me, and in the end I reach the conclusion that I like least and which pains me most. But I cannot see another way.

This next morning I wake early and lie still. I open my eyes and stare at the canopy above me. I have the whole bed to stretch out in, and I do so, pushing my warm feet into its coldest corners. The new day brings no hope, but in its light I know that I have made a wise decision. I have come up with a stratagem that will save my child, and keep us from the streets. It is not a design of any great cleverness or cunning. It is simply this: if Hunsdon thinks the child is his, he will provide for me. If he thinks I have betrayed him, he will cast me out with nothing. Therefore, my affair with Will must end, and never be discovered. As a loyal but careless mistress I might be married off to some lowly courtier – one happy to take the dowry Hunsdon settles on me as his bribe for taking on spoiled goods.

Hunsdon is due back from York at any time. Better to do nothing, and let my failure to appear convey its own message to Will. I curl myself into a ball, and pull the eiderdown around me, and wait for the time to pass. My head aches with grief, and I am filled with bitter anger that this must be my lot. If I am such a faithless whore, why am I disabled by scruples I can't afford? A depraved and desperate woman should be ruthless in the execution of her desires. There is no place for me in the hierarchy of mankind, and, to make things worse, my own character is wrongly put together. I have the mind of a philosopher, the education of a prince and the morality of a nun. The agony of my condition forces me to puke into a bucket with more violence than usual.

Spent and white-faced, I get up and dress and read the Bible with such fierce attention that I fear my eyeballs will drop out. Then I think again of the letter that I have not written, and this reminds me of those Will has sent to me, so I pull them out from beneath the mattress and throw them on the fire. I do not cry. I do not think of all those lost times, crumpling and burning to black ash. And yet, in spite of all this, and of all my determination to do nothing, when I look at the clock I find that just forty minutes have passed. I think that Hell must not only be a place of fire and punishment, but of clocks that tick and tock in an eternal present, where nothing ever happens.

I stand up, and pace up and down the chamber saying, 'It's Hunsdon's child. It's Hunsdon's child.' As if I were casting a spell. I can't be still. I can't stop my ceaseless walking, so I continue in this manner until at last, exhausted, I fall down senseless on the bed.

When I wake, Hunsdon himself is sitting beside me, his clothes still mud-splattered from his journey. He is looking down at me and stroking my hair, but he is not smiling.

He says, 'I have a gift for you.'

I struggle up on to my elbows and we kiss each other softly. I try to read his expression.

'A gift! You are so kind!'

'Not kind, my dear. It is only just that you should have it. I have loved you very well.'

A chill comes on me. 'Why do you say "have loved"?' I ask. 'I'm not dead.'

'No, my dear,' says he. 'Too full of life.' He pats my tight belly. His face is heavy.

I feel the world lurch, and look down at my body. 'You know,' I say. But I pray he only guesses the half of it.

'I shall build you a house, at Long Ditch. At Westminster, quite close by.'

Hunsdon is a soldier, not a politician. When there are decisions to be made, he makes them quickly.

'I... I'm sorry for it,' say I. 'So many years without falling pregnant, and then... it was my carelessness. My fault.'

He sighs and begins to pull off his boots. 'You can't blame yourself, my poor child,' he says. 'I put it there.'

I say nothing, at once relieved and quite bereft of hope.

'What shall I do there, all alone?' I ask, trying to keep my voice from rising to a wail. 'Like some dowager, pensioned off?' My mind says, *Do not question your salvation, Aemilia; take the house and keep silent.*

He leans across and kisses me gently. 'You are to marry,' says he. 'You won't be alone.'

My mouth is dry. 'Who shall I marry, my lord?'

'Alfonso Lanyer.'

'Lanyer! Oh, Henry! Whose thought was this?'

'He's always had his eye on you.'

'But sir – '

'Enough, Aemilia! He is one of your own.'

One of my own! This is a cruel blow indeed. Alfonso Lanyer is a prize fool, a womaniser and a gambler at the tables. Handsome enough, for sure. But as a husband! I want to cry out, to explain that this can never be, yet of course I cannot, in case my reluctance to marry one man suggests I might have a preference for another.

The wedding is all agreed. I stay in my room, reading and praying and seeking peace of mind. When Alice brings me letters, I make her put them on the fire. I know who they are from. I walk through my life like my own spectre, my heart and soul torn out of me, sustained only by the love-child that grows inside.

I do have one remaining hope. Which is that I might take with me, out into the cold world beyond the life of Court, a little of my learning. And that I might be allowed to write my poetry and to improve it, sustained by a patron willing to support me. This is a man's business, but I am as well educated as any man, and so, if any woman could succeed in such a project, it might be me. If the Countess of Pembroke is celebrated for her verse, is it so extraordinary an ambition to hope that I might be celebrated for mine? She has made her country home a supposed 'paradise for poets' – could I not make my own small house a place of industry and reflection?

The day before I am to leave Whitehall, I give Hunsdon some of my poems, which I have copied in my best script.

'They are pretty, my dear, thank you,' says Hunsdon. He sits apart from me, on a cedar wood chair, and seems preoccupied.

'You know me: I do like a play, and a good ballad that tells a tale, but… I'm not a man for sonnets and such fancification.'

'I wrote them all for you.'

'Indeed, I know it. And I am touched, very touched indeed. Now, tell me, do you like the house?'

'I like it very much. Thank you my lord. I am grateful – beyond grateful.'

'I think you will be very well accommodated. The solar, in particular, I have appointed to the highest specification.'

'The specification is quite perfect.'

'You will be married soon, as you know.'

'Yes, sir.'

'Good. Very good.'

I look down, so he can't see the expression on my face.

'He is a bloody fool, Alfonso, but they say the ladies like him,' says Hunsdon.

'They do indeed,' I say.

'He's always admired you.'

'Yes, sir. You said so.'

'So he'll be… good to you. You know. Shame for it all to go to waste.' He nods to me in a general way, which hints at our gaudy nights.

'Yes, sir.' I take a breath. 'Henry, I should like to have a patron.'

'A what, my dear?'

'A patron.'

He stares at me, speechless with astonishment.

'I know it is unusual,' say I.

'Unusual…? What are you talking about?'

'I mean… someone who has position, who might be interested in my…verse.'

'Christ's blood! These lines you've scrawled, you mean?' He waves my poems in the air. 'These funny little ditties?'

'They are poems, my lord. I know they need more work.'

'Good God,' he says. 'I fear that your condition has affected your faculties, poor child. You're barking mad.'

'No, indeed, my lord.'

'Whoever would have thought it? You always seemed so sharp.'

'I don't believe I am going mad at all, sir. I have always wanted to make more of my poetry, to learn how to improve it, and how to… apprentice myself to it.'

He shakes his head. 'I will tell you this, Aemilia, you're a strange one. The night-walking is just the half of it.'

This makes me want to weep. I think of the night-walking that had first made Hunsdon notice me, soon after my mother died. But there is no time to mourn the passing of his gentle but insistent courtship.

'Would it be possible to find someone, now that I'm no longer your mistress?' I say. 'I mean, there would be no disgrace attached to you, would there?'

He stares at me with his calm grey eyes, that only see what is solid and tangible. 'I never heard of such a thing.'

I let my words spout out, madly, in case I hesitate and never get them out at all. 'I don't want to vanish quite away. I'll cause no trouble, keep from the Court, not bother you or speak out of turn, or do anything that might displease you… but if I had some support, some patronage… as a man would…' I look at him beseechingly. 'Might anyone consider it?'

He seems dumbfounded, then begins to chuckle. 'My dear girl, how will I do without you? You are quite as entertaining out of bed as in it. Why not? Why not, indeed?' He laughs so merrily that I have to fight to hide my irritation.

'What would you suggest, sir? For someone in my situation? I have some verses – I could send them, if you are happy for me to do this.'

'To whom?'

'Whomever you suggest.'

'Lord above! I've no idea. Did you like the inlaid stools I gave you? Did you like the Aldersgate tiles, and the silver tankards? I have thought of everything, have I not?'

'Everything is there. It is perfect.'

He smiles, very pleased with himself. 'Of course, I did ask Lady Anne for her advice. I thought you wouldn't mind.'

I smile so hard my cheeks ache. It was logical for him to ask his wife's opinion, though hardly kind to either of us. 'Her ladyship has exquisite taste.'

He gets up and warms his back before the fire for a moment. 'I shall not see you again, after this conversation. I am sorry for it, and I shall miss you sorely. But a break has to be made, and I am afraid the time has come.'

I nod silently. My hands are very still. My heart beats slowly, slowly. I can control myself, no matter how the world might heave and lurch around me.

Scene X

God still being in his Heaven, though mightily indifferent to me, the morning before my wedding day I take myself off to the quiet of the abbey. I sit down on the rush-strewn flags and pray.

'When the wicked man turneth away from his wickedness that he hath committed, and doeth that which is lawful and right, he shall save his soul... I acknowledge my transgressions and my sins...'

'Aemilia!'

I open my eyes. My pregnant state makes my mind slow, my view of the world outside my body more hazy with each passing day. Is God speaking to me? But no, it is a white-faced Will. His eyes are set in dark rings; he is hatless and his hair is pushed behind his ears as if had just risen from bed.

'We must speak – come!'

He drags me down the damp passage to the high-walled abbey garden. At the far side of the quadrangle, an old servant is sweeping up dead leaves.

I stare at Will, shocked and yet for all my woe relieved to have him near.

'Is it true?' he asks. 'They say you're pregnant!'

I cover my face with my hands and turn away.

He pulls me round and prises my hands away. I am forced to look at him, and see that his eyes are wet with tears.

'Are you having a child?'

I can't reply.

'And are you marrying… Alfonso Lanyer?' He seems barely able to speak the name.

I look down at the muddy ground, licking the salt tears from my lips. Last night was stormy, and a fat worm is slithering in a puddle. Avoiding his gaze, I say, 'I don't expect you to understand.'

'Oh, Aemilia! Look at me!' He seizes hold of me and shakes me, gently. I don't want to look at him, but I am forced to. His gaze seems blacker and darker than it has ever been, as if it were a reflection of my own eyes. 'Have pity! I've never loved, never known what it was to love, never known such pain and wonder as I have known since I met you.'

I can't help myself. 'My love,' I say. 'My heart will break!' I take his face between my hands and kiss his eyes, his cheeks, his lips. We embrace as tenderly as we had on that strange and silent night at Titchfield. It seems as though a thousand years have passed since that sweet time.

He draws back and tucks a strand of my hair inside my bonnet. 'Answer me one question.'

I smile up at him, full of sorrow. 'I will answer it, I promise.'

'Are you having a child?'

I swallow bile. 'Yes.'

'Then – come with me! Be my mistress, be mine…'

'It isn't yours.'

His face hardens and his arms drop to his sides. We stare at each other.

'How do you know?'

It is all I can do to remain standing. I put my arm out and steady myself against the cold stone wall. 'I lay with Hunsdon, just as I lay with you.'

He winces and turns his back. For a moment I think he will walk away, but then he says, 'As you did for years before you met me, and nothing came of it.' There is no tenderness now; each word is hard and separate.

I go over to him, and turn him around to face me. I see, with a wrench of grief, that his face is contorted with pain. I want to embrace him, hold him close, and pretend that things could be as they were before. But I can do nothing. 'You can't protect me,' I whisper.

'He's marrying you off!' says Will, with a great sob. 'To a brainless knave who cheats at dice! A fine way to "protect" you! Are you grateful to him for that? Are you really such a whore as to be bought so cheap?'

'He has given me a dowry, and a house. He has bought me a place in the world. I will be respectable. With you, I would have nothing. Don't you see? We had a room, nowhere else. We were like conspirators, not man and wife.'

Now he weeps openly, shuddering sobs that seems to tear out of him. 'You would have everything. Everything! What is there, that is greater than our love? What in this whole world? Tell me! Tell me!'

My tears flow too, but all this weeping makes me angry. 'A lord may have a wife and keep a mistress,' I cry. The old man has stopped sweeping and is staring over at us. I lower my voice, but speak with desperate fury. 'A playwright can barely keep himself! Half of your noble profession are in the debtors' prison! I'm not living with my child, as a poet's whore, in some filthy ale-house! Or a back-street alley, like a pauper – how can you even ask me to think of such a thing?'

Will breathes deeply and closes his eyes, as if searching for the incantation that will change my mind and make me his. 'I can ask you because I love you. I can ask you because, without you, my life is a just a shabby, ceaseless repetition, and I don't believe there are two other people, in this whole great City, who have loved as we have loved. I can ask you because you are the woman I will always need, and look for, and revere. That is why I can ask you. And you, you speak of money! My God, has the Court so corrupted you? Is that all you can conceive of: the bald, material world?'

I shake my head. 'You cannot keep me, Will. You are being a fool.'

'I have my work to keep us.'

'Oh, yes! Play-making, and poetry! You're one step up from vagrancy.'

There is silence again. I think, *I cannot go on with this. I cannot keep pretending that I am strong enough to live without you.*

Will pulls his cloak around him, as if in preparation for departure. 'I thought you wanted to be a poet yourself? How can you speak of what I do with such contempt?'

'It's all words. Words, words, words. What are they? Flimsy, floating, fancy things, not real. You make it sound as if I expect a suite of rooms at Whitehall – that's not fair! But I do need a house, and bowls, and spoons, and chattels. And food and clothing and a safe haven from the streets. I've traded in my virtue, and now I'm trading in my love, so I can look after my child. If Hunsdon is marrying me off – so be it.'

He stares down at me, breathing hard. 'You'll bed that worm Alfonso, instead of lying with me? You'll let him have you, night after night? You'll do with him all those sublime and secret things that you have done with me?'

'You are not free! Will you keep the baby in a box of feathered hats? Shall it crawl across the stage-boards before it speaks? Will you feed this babe before you feed the ones that are already born, at Stratford? In wedlock? Leave me be! Stop torturing me with what you call love, and which is a sort of twisted lust!'

He stares at me as if I were at the bottom of an abyss. His face is as white as a winding sheet. Even his lips are pale. 'How can you say that? You know I love you.'

I close my eyes. 'I know it.'

'And you love me.'

He comes back and holds me in his arms and I hide my face in his neck. After a moment, I look up at him and say, 'I do love you. Will. If love alone could keep us, we would never part.'

'Then…' He hardens his grip around me, but I pull away.

'But love never kept anyone,' I cry. 'Did it? And we are joined to others. And we must survive and so must they. I am to marry Lanyer, and he will be my lord, and I will be his wife and his word will be my law. I will be tamed, like poor Kate in your play. See – how wise and prescient you were!'

'It's not possible. My darling, darling Aemilia. It cannot be.'

'It is the only way.'

And then, not able to bear another word of this, I turn and run across the garden. Will yells after me, 'It is not finished! I will not let you go! Hear me, Aemilia! We are not done!'

I look over my shoulder, my hands pressed to my mouth. Will has disappeared. The old man is staring after me, his broom suspended in mid-air.

Scene XI

For the first few weeks of my union with Alfonso, I try to pretend that he does not exist, and he pleases me by keeping away. I spend my days writing, sitting in the solar and looking down at the street, watching my belly grow. I soon look like a plum pudding.

A letter arrives for me one day. To my surprise, it is from Hunsdon. I tear it open, wondering if he might have changed his mind. Perhaps he wants me to be his mistress again. Perhaps Lady Anne has driven him mad with boredom. But no. It is a short note.

> *My dear Aemilia,*
>
> *I trust you are well. How do you like the set of Antwerp porringers?*
>
> *I had a thought, in answer to that odd question of yours. William Cecil is your man. Old Burghley takes a somewhat utilitarian view of the printed word, but the fellow has more influence with publishers than anyone at Court. He will know who – if such a fellow exists – might back a woman. (Though I warn you, my sweet lady, your ambition is quite absurd.) Good luck with him, dear girl.*
>
> *Your loyal servant,*
> *Henry*

Burghley House is on the north side of the Strand. It is a handsome brick building, three storeys high, built around two courtyards. I am shown into the library, which looks out over the gardens and the fields of Covent Garden which lie beyond. I can see two youths playing tennis on a paved court, and a servant working in the orchard. As I watch the young men, I reflect that I have about as much power as the leather ball that bounces back and forth between them.

It surprises me that Burghley has agreed to see me: he is known to be uxorious and upstanding, and has never approved of me. 'Utilitarian', Hunsdon said; could it be that Burghley has some use for me? I turn away from the window and look around me. The panelling is carved and painted, the floors newly strewn with sweet-smelling rushes and the air is hushed, as if in mute respect for all the learning in the room. It seems to me that Burghley owns quite as many books as his monarch.

'I see you are one who appreciates the beauty of learning.' The voice is silk-smooth, like the pages of a book. I look up, and my heart lurches. Standing in the doorway is not the austere, white-bearded Burghley but Henry Wriothesley, fair hair curled, dressed in peacock blue. He is regarding me with a knowing half-smile. He is one of Burghley's circle, but even so the sight of him is an unpleasant shock.

'Mistress Lanyer, how you have blossomed! Really… there is so much more of you as a Lanyer than there was when you were a mere Bassano!'

'I am here to see Lord Burghley, your lordship,' I say, coldly. 'Is he here?'

'Nooo, sadly. No. He told me to inform you that he has been called away on urgent business. But I bethought me…' He comes closer, smiling at his own affected speech. 'I bethought me – why waste this lovely visitor? Given that we have already met, and the lovely visitor is so… lovely.'

He walks around me, daintily, first this way and then that, and I smell the rich scent of his clothes. He smiles at my fattened face and sprouting breasts, seeming well pleased. He picks a book up from the table beside me. It is *The Rape of Lucrece*, by a Mr W.S.

'Dear Will,' he says, flipping it open. 'I've commissioned him to write a new comedy. Did you know?'

'No, sir, I did not. I am not... closely acquainted with Mr Shakespeare.'

He raises his fine brows. 'Really? You surprise me.'

'I have come to speak of my own work, sir.'

But he doesn't seem to hear me. '*A Comedy of Errors* – a noble title, don't you think? He is writing it at this very moment.'

'If I were to have a patron, sir, I might work upon my poems and make them... more than they are now.'

'Quill scratching fast across the page,' says the earl, apparently talking to himself. He looks up and smirks. 'Very well, you pretty pregnant thing, let's hear this verse of yours.'

'I was going to talk about my verses with Burghley. Your lordship.'

'So he told me. But I am a greater patron of the arts than he! You see – how fortuitous it is that I am here, instead of him! The stars are smiling on you.'

'I am not sure that I share your favourable opinion. Can you tell Lord Burghley that I would be happy to see him on another occasion?'

He smiles, shaking his head. 'He will not do it, my bloated chuck. It's not like you to be obtuse. Look at you! Hunsdon has cast you off, and you're the size of a cow-shed.'

'Then I must go.'

'Then you won't have a patron, will you? You will go back into the... outer darkness, whence you came. I hear he built a pretty house for you, which would fit into this library ten times over.'

He comes closer to me, smiling more sweetly than before. 'Forgive me. Forgive me. I would like to hear your verse. I see no reason why a lady like yourself – one well-known for her intelligence and learning – should not be a writer as good as any man!'

'You surprise me, sir!'

'I am young, mistress. I am part of the modern age. You are ill-served, and misunderstood.'

'That's true enough!'

'You see? I understand you. I know my reputation may be off-putting, but lay your prejudice aside. Let me hear your verses. Please.' He takes my hand, still smiling. 'Come and sit with me, and read your verse and I will see... what I can do.'

He leads me to the corner of the library and gestures towards a low bed heaped with velvet cushions. I pull my hand away.

'Isn't there somewhere else... more public?'

'Come, you're not afraid of me? A woman of your bearing? It is I who should be afraid! Look at you! God's blood. Almost too beautiful.' He pours out two glasses of wine and hands one to me. 'Almost. But not quite.'

I can hear two voices. But which is the angel, and which the devil? *'Run! Flee! Escape!'* says one. *'Stay! This could be your salvation! Prove yourself!'* says the other. He is smiling, smiling. I can feel the baby moving inside me. I wonder if, like me, it is afraid.

When I realise that I am scared of him, I force myself to step forward and take the glass, and sip it. For I am afraid of no one, and nothing, except Death itself. I will take this chance, and see where it leads. While I read, Wriothesley at first contents himself with listening 'raptly', which is to say, he acts out the role of one who listens with exaggerated astonishment and delight. His mock entrancement has the effect of making the shortcomings of my verse more obvious to me, and I vow that, if nothing else, I will make my poems better in future, even if I die in the attempt. And I also notice, as I read the stumbling, bumbling words, that his lordship is edging ever closer to me on the divan, so that, when I come to the end of the third stanza of the third poem, his breath is on my neck. When I finish, there is silence for a moment, and then he takes my face between his hands and twists it round so he can scrutinise it. Then he says abruptly, 'Your eyes are black, aren't they? Truly black. I have never seen such a thing.'

I stand up.

'The Bassanos are Venetian,' I say. 'My father was a Marrano, some say from Africa.'

He stretches out on the bed, with his head propped on his elbows. 'You know, I have had my eye on you since the night we met,' says he.

'Have you?'

'Do you want to know what I think?' he asks.

I say nothing.

'You are *greedy*. Greedy for pleasure, my glorious hussy. Greedy for men.'

'No!'

'Or should I say – for *poet*s?'

I stare, and he gets up and winds his arm around my waist. 'Standing by Will Shakespeare's stairway, in a dry nightgown with a wet cunt. Oh, don't look at me like that, sweet lady. I could smell it from where I stood.' He bends down, as he did that night, but this time his hand creeps underneath my skirts and I feel his silky fingers stroke the inside of my leg. 'He had you good and plenty, didn't he? Am I not right? I'll never forget the look upon your face. He fucked you all the way to Heaven, that gentle poet. Pumping like Beelzebub, I'll wager.' Now his hand is creeping up the soft skin of my thigh. 'Luckiest of poets.'

With a sudden motion Wriothesley forces me down, and I am lying on my back upon the low bed. I feel his weight upon me. He is heavier than he looks, and I scream out. 'My lord! My baby – be careful with my baby!'

'Ah, the poet's bastard, is it, lodged inside you?' He begins to laugh – a boy's laugh, hysterical and shrill. With a sudden force of effort I push him away and he falls to the ground, still laughing.

He stands up and shakes out his sleeves. 'Listen. I know you have been lying with William. I am a witness to it. If you want me to keep this information private – which I suspect you do – then I am determined to extract a fair price from you. If you wish to keep yourself from me – and that is entirely your decision – then I will let Lord Hunsdon know that his dowry missed its mark, and that he may as well have gone down to the Liberties and paid for any shilling strumpet to live like a merchant's wife.'

'No!' I see myself, clear and sharp. A street-walker, a doxy, a common whore. I see my baby, a harlot's brat, shrivelling in my arms.

He whispers, 'But if you want to keep your little house – with your little monkey in it – then I suggest that you sin a little and let me lie beside you.'

'I would rather die, sir. Look upon me! Have pity on my state.' The room is shifting; sweat is rolling down my neck into my gown. What can I do? What can I say?

'Think carefully, Aemilia. They say you are a woman possessed of a fine mind. Well, use it.'

Before I can speak, he has pulled me down so that I sprawl on top of him. 'No, sir!' I scream. 'No, I will not do it…'

He rips my skirts out of the way and, despite the swollen mound of my belly, he forces himself into me. His cock is a fire-poker and he is sucking at my sore dugs and then my senses are black.

When I look up, damp and trembling, Will is standing at the doorway, holding a book in his hand. His eyes are fixed on me with such an expression of disbelieving horror that I cannot speak, nor even think, but only stare back at him, my thighs spread and my soiled shift clutched between my fingers.

Wriothesley has his eyes closed. 'Oh, foul Jezebel,' he says. 'There is not a whore in London who is a better fuck. Come, I demand you kiss me.' He puckers up and points to his full red lips.

I look at Will. His face is pale and thinner than when last I saw him, with shadows beneath his cheekbones, and his eyes are black-rimmed from stage-paint that has not been properly wiped off, and his beard is new-trimmed and his razor must have nipped his skin, for there is a stab of scarlet on his left cheek. He is speechless; he is stone.

Wriothesley opens his eyes and looks at Will calmly. 'Forgive us, dear Will,' he says. 'Such scenes as this are hardly to be expected in a library. Patrons should be more sedate than this. I have my… position to consider.' He smirks up at me.

I pull myself up, and his lordship's limp cock flops down on to his white stomach. Will is gone. Liquid trickles down my leg. I pull down my skirts, pick up my slippers and run after him, tripping over my dress and sobbing without tears.

The library opens on to a wide landing. Everything gleams and glitters. I can't tell what is what, nor recall the names for things. Where is Will? Which way did he go? There is a stairway, sweeping downwards. He is not there. I run the other way, down a long gallery with sunlight sparkling through leaded windows. There is bright colour – Turkey carpet colour; there are high paintings of men with cruel faces. All are Wriothesley, sneering down. There is a doorway, between two carved chairs. There is Will, framed inside it, with his back to me, still as a statue.

I go through the door and close it behind me. We are standing in a small chamber, stark and plain. There is a table and a chair, and a riot of paper. A window looks out across a stableyard.

'Sit,' he says, without turning to face me.

'I'd rather stand,' I say, but then sink down on to the chair. My sight is wraithed with black vapour, like smithy-smoke. Will stares out of the window.

'Will …' I begin. 'This… thing. The thing you saw…'

He turns at last, but remains silent. His eyes are cast down.

'My love,' I say. 'My dearest…'

He will not look at me.

'I implore you, sir!' I hold out my hand. 'Truly, I implore you... Listen to me!'

At last, he looks at me, arms rigid by his sides. 'Listen to you?' he says. His voice is hoarse. 'Listen to you? What can you *say*?'

'That I was… I was tricked…'

'How did he trick you? Did he shape-shift, so he looked like me? Did he wizard himself inside you, with the magic of his mighty phallus?' He stares at me. 'Well? Did he?'

This time I am the one who is silent. I hang my head.

'I have seen Hell. I have seen a Beast with two backs. I have seen everything I loved and honoured made vile and evil. That is the thing that I have seen.'

'Listen, I – '

'There are no words, Aemilia. There is no "listen", and then some sentences that you can conjure which I will take into my mind, so we can be as we were. This is Death. This is the end of what I loved, and what I thought I knew, and what made my life bearable, for all its pain and sorrow. This fine woman, this great spirit, this mind beyond compare – a rutting strumpet!'

'I was reading him my poems and – '

'Oh, Christ Jesu!' He turns and throws open the window, as if the room is suffocating him. 'Your wretched poems! They are no good, my sweet. They are just doggerel, my lovely one. You may be the equal of all comers in the areas of algebra and astronomy and what you will, but let me tell you, a poet is not a learned man who pens out his learned thoughts in comfort and complacency! A poet is a madman, who knows nothing, and makes a world of his insanity. And you, my lady, may be a scholar and you are certainly a whore, but you will never be a poet.'

I can't weep. I can't think. I try to say, *He blackmailed me, he was going to tell Hunsdon all about you* – but I cannot see how to say this without making him even angrier, if that is possible. All I can think of is that I must go, away, and escape his burning eyes, and the hatred and contempt in his voice. I stand up.

'Goodbye, Will.'

'Goodbye? Jesu, is that it?'

'You said there are no words. And you are right, there is none. I have sinned and we are done.'

'Ay, we are done alright, for you have killed my soul!'

'I love you, Will.'

This seems to goad him more than anything I have said or done, for suddenly he is wild with rage and tears the pages on his desk and throws them round the room. 'Love me! Love me! God's blood, what do you do to men you hate? You are a witch – a witch; you have ensnared me and you are trying to destroy me!' He runs towards me, brandishing the torn paper. 'What can I say? What can I do?'

'If you think I do not love you, this is false, and what I did today was – '

'Oh – you say this is false?' He is so close now that his spittle wets my face and I see the blue veins jumping in his forehead. 'Look – I have a new phrase…' He runs to the table, takes up a quill and scribbles fiercely on one of the torn pages. 'Praise God – I am still a writer! Praise him, praise him, the poet lives! Look…' He runs back to me. 'See? See here? What I have wrote – you are still my Muse, Mistress Busycunt… see – "the bay where all men ride"! You see? I have made you into Art. That, that is poetry. Poetry is pain. Poetry is blood and hatred. D'you see?'

As he gets angrier, I grow colder. I am a prisoner in this place, and can only stare, round-eyed, at what I have made him. 'Will…' say I. 'Please, I beg you – '

'What, will you contradict me? How dare you contradict me? You came into my bed straight from Hunsdon's…'

'How could I do otherwise, when – '

'I saw the look upon his face when he arrived with you! Jesu, you whipped that old goat to a frenzy even as he edged towards the grave! As for Wriothesley – well, forgive me for my boldness! I just saw you, straddling the fellow, with your great-belly in your mother's hands as he shafted up inside you! God's balls, I'd sooner spit my own arse on Satan's cock than witness such a thing again!'

'I am no Jezebel. If you would only hear me!'

'Jezebel! What did she do to deserve comparison with you? I need new words for sin, for you have torn up decency and thrown it to the four winds.'

I stand at last, though I don't know how my shuddering legs can carry me. The babe is kicking, and I fear all this torment might force it early into the world.

'Farewell, Will,' I say. I go to the doorway, and turn to look at him. 'If you will not let me speak, if you will not understand...' But he is sitting at his desk, writing, his body racked with sobs.

Scene XII

Sometimes I read so hard and so long that when I close my eyes I see a million dancing letters, formed of white light against my own darkness. Sometimes, when I examine my face in the looking glass, my eyes are sore and bloodshot. Sometimes I think I see words falling down my cheeks, mixed with my tears.

My little house is made from seasoned Kentish oak, its heartwood turned outward to withstand the wind and weather. Thirty trees were felled to make it, sky-shifting branches fallen among wet fern. I first saw it when it was no more than a wooden skeleton, bare timbers sticking out of the mud, each one marked with a Roman numeral. It looked squashed and small, stuck between two older buildings. I could scarce believe that I was supposed to mark out my new life on so little ground. But within a week the carpenters added walls and floors and windows, like the lungs and belly of a man, and strangely it seemed to grow in size. Even so, my courage falters when I think of all the trammelled years I am doomed to spend inside it, a placid little Jill-in-a-box.

My space is this: six rooms in all, with the main door opening into a hallway, which is like a little version of the great hall in a great house, and is two storeys in height. A wooden staircase ascends from its centre. At the back of the hall is a door which leads to the kitchen, with its open hearth and cupboards, which Hunsdon has filled with the finest pewter. Around the fire is a fine array of pots, grid-irons, coal rakes and toasting irons, and from the ceiling hang pots, saucepans and frying pans. On one side of the kitchen is a low door, leading to the garden, such as it is, and the privy. At the top of the hall stairs is a handsome solar, an oak-panelled sitting room with a grander fireplace than the kitchen hearth, some heavy carved chairs and a long oak dining table. And on the floor above are two bedchambers, also brightly painted and well furnished with curtained beds and solid old chests. All are gifts from Hunsdon.

The gift I value most is the pair of Flemish virginals which have been placed in the hall. The elegant instrument takes up the most part of one wall. Most beautiful, its soundboards painted with flowers, birds and moths, all within blue scalloped borders. The natural keys are covered in bone, and the sharps are chestnut. The inside of the lid is embellished with a Latin motto: *Sic transit gloria mundi.* The notes it makes are soft and plangent and take me far away, back into a world of long galleries echoing with music and private laughter, of lush gardens overlooked by mullioned windows, of feasts and opulence and the giddy knowledge that the furled papers on my lord's table will govern the lives of earls and paupers, scribes and burghers, pimps and haberdashers, all across the realm.

At the very top of the house is a little garret, with straw-stuffed eaves coming down almost to the wooden floor. This is the servant's room, and has in it just a truckle bed and a three-legged stool. If I stand on this – though it wobbles badly – I can put my head through the window in the thatch, and see as far as the City with its Roman walls and mess of roofs and smoking chimneys, and above these the pointing fingers of a dozen churches, and the mighty Ark which is blasted, spireless St Paul's.

Act II

Prophecy

Scene I

Smithfield, Avgvst 1602

My hectic son is hardly able to breathe with the wonder and wickedness of it all. His eyes are everywhere: Bartholomew Fair, the greatest Fair in England. Such a press of people that you can barely work out where you stand. And what people – half the underworld is here: cutpurses from Damnation Alley, tricksters from Devil's Gap, vagrants from Snide Street. Everything muddled: stalls and sideshows, fops and ladies, apes and peacocks. As big a hotchpotch as the filthy warren of London itself. You can buy anything – oysters, mousetraps, gingerbread men; a hobbyhorse, a songbird or a bale of cloth. Pay to see a cockfight or a puppet show or join a game of dice and thimble. Everywhere is bother, jostle and noise. High fashion and foul breath, all pressed together: children and dotards, dogs and chancers, pigs and prostitutes. And the two of us – Henry leaping at my side, desperate to be off to buy a cheese-cake from Holloway or a Pimlico pie. Rattles, drums and fiddles rip into the air. The smell of roasting pork rises up from the eating-houses. One step too quick and you will fall upon a sweetmeat-seller or topple on the side-rope of a dancing tent. Here – a great, pockmarked head, ducking out of the crowd and leering at my chest. There – a glimpse of putrefying tumour, sprouting from a beggar's shoulder, tattered shirt turned down so the passers-by can get an eyeful and toss a halfpenny his way. 'Show! Show! Show' calls the crowd, all about us, pushing and shoving, careless of a small boy and a slight woman.

We are smack-bang in the middle of it all: besieged by every kind of mountebank and con-man, bawdy and punk. I try to side-step one way, thinking I see some open ground to my left, in front of the fish-scale virgin's stand, but a giantess blocks my path, stinking like Hound's Ditch and with a back as wide as a cart. So I twist another way, Henry's hand gripped in mine, but up loom three pissed prentice-boys, arm in arm, faces running sweat, eyes rolled back in their heads.

Henry is nearly ten. A boy who likes to throw himself to the ground, run, yell, eat. Hell-bent on everything. Big-boned, but pretty, with his flushed cheeks and fuzz of gold hair. Nothing like Alfonso, but we don't speak of that.

'Mother! Over there – can we see the baby with two heads?'

'No.'

'Why?

'I'll be sick.'

'The bearded mermaid?'

'No.'

'The pig-trotter man?'

'No.'

'The midget unicorn?'

'No.'

'Why? Why? All the boys at my school have seen the midget unicorn! Why can't I?'

I don't know why the thought of standing in a cramped booth, face to face with some freak – man-made or a slip of nature – makes me feel so weak and dizzy. I've seen it all before, and worse. So has Henry, come to that. He likes a good execution, that child; nothing lily-livered about him. Perhaps I'm pregnant again. My pregnancies ebb and flow in my body like the river tide. Few last more than six weeks. A good thing, as we live on next to nothing, and Alfonso is an idle dolt, barely able to put his doublet on the right way around.

'Buy my fat chickens!'

'Fresh asparagus!'

'Any baking pears?'

Now Henry's face is winding up into a baby-scowl. His curiosity amounts to a disease.

'You *said* I could come to the Fair, and now we can't *do* anything!'

'Henry!'

'Termagant!'

'Wherever did you – ?'

'Whore!'

'Obnoxious brat! How dare you!'

He slips his hand from mine and he's off.

'Henry!'

I look this way, and that. No idea which way to chase him. He has no money, will not go far. But I'm wrenched with fear. All I can see are the lurid banners: 'Giant Blackamoor'… 'Child Leprechaun'… 'Neptune from the Deep'.

'Henry!'

How will he hear me? My loud cries are lost in a multitude of voices.

'Posset for you, lady?' A skinny lad with a tray hanging from his neck.

'See the man who swallows fire!'

A blind girl thrusts her pouch at me. 'Sugar-pane fancies! Sweetest in Smithfield!'

'Henry!'

Then, the crowd pushes me forward till I am jammed hard against a wooden palisade. I can barely see through the spaces between the planks, but can just make out the back view of a fairground caller, dressed in scarlet like an alderman.

'Upwards of ten feet high!' he cries. 'His consumption of hay, corn, straw, carrots, water is that of twenty men! The Oliphant, the human race excepted, is the most respectable of animals! He has ivory tusks, four feet long, as sharp as swords! His trunk serves him instead of hands and arms! He can lift a man with it, or a mouse!'

The crowd surges forward behind me. Where is Henry? If the mob pushes at him as violently as this, he will suffocate in the crush.

'He remembers favours as long as injuries: in short, if you aid him, he will repay you. If you harm him, he will never forget...'

I have never seen an Oliphant, though I have read of them and seen a drawing. And at Whitehall Palace there was a monstrous tusk, among the Queen's objects and treasures, which were brought from all the corners of the world. It was heavier than any sword or musket. I don't believe this mountebank has an Oliphant in his tent – a great bull, perhaps, with an adder for its trunk, and dark hangings to keep the creature in the shadow. This is the Devil's marketplace, after all.

But Henry? Where is Henry? I turn, and begin to force my way out through the mass of people. And then a woman stands in front of me. Bars my way. Her face is almost touching mine. She is motionless; her face a mask. Looking into her cold eyes, I could not say her age, or type.

'Tell your fortune?'

'No. Go away. I'm looking for my little boy.'

'Oh, *he's* safe enough. For now, at least.'

'Where is he?'

'Tell your fortune?'

'Where's my son?' I try to push past her.

She sidesteps so she still blocks my way. 'Cost you nothing.'

'Where can I find him?'

'Not a penny.'

'I don't want my fortune told! But I'd give you five shillings gladly if you told me where to find him.'

'For nothing, I'll tell you this. You've a whore's past, and a poet's future.'

'Get out of my way!'

I turn, but now face a much older creature, shrivelled and black.

'Beware of slip-shod words,' she says. She looks into me with unseeing eyes. 'Words will make you, and undo you. You will aim too high, and fall too low.'

'What are you – lunatics? Or purse-thieves?' I look behind me. 'Are there three of you, a third to pick my pocket?'

'Beware of your own wit,' says the first woman, her voice whispering in my ear. 'Your human pride.'

'As for your son...' The crone's flesh reeks of piss and sweet decay.

'What?'

'The plague is coming.'

'The plague is always coming. No wonder your predictions cost nothing.'

'Not like this.'

And then – they are gone.

I spin round, full circle, hemmed in by the throng of fair-goers, the tricksters and the tricked. Then, stop. Another face. Smiling at me, all rouged and painted. A face out of place and time.

'Well, how delightful!' it says. 'Aemilia Bassano! I would not have known you.' A dramatic and unnecessary curtsey, and I have time to work out who this is.

'Lettice Cooper.' We were Court ladies together, ten years ago. She is flanked by two servants.

'*Lady* Lettice,' she says, 'to you.' She raises her eyebrows in disdain so that her manservant smirks to oblige her (odious palace arse-licker). If I have changed, then so has she. Always careful of her looks, she has plucked and powdered herself out of existence. She has taken Her Majesty for a model, and to no good effect, having made herself a doll-face of false surprise.

She hands her purse to her serving woman, and holds out her hand. I take it. Her fingers are silky, slippery.

'You!' she says. 'Who was once so beautiful! I would never have thought it!'

'Thought what? That I would turn out such a hag?'

'Oh! My dear, have you quite lost your mind? Why would I say such a thing? They say the natural look will be in next year. In France, the ladies are letting their hair grow quite low on the forehead. You will be all the rage.'

'Lettice...'

'*Lady* Lettice...'

'I have lost my son...'

'He is dead?'

'Only lost – mislaid...'

'It comes as no surprise. I've heard you spoil that bastard boy and he runs wild.'

'I had forgot the ways of Court.'

'Indeed.'

'Common people have better manners.'

A neat, malicious smile. 'I see Alfonso, from time to time, of course. In the distance. Quite the merry thing, those tunes from Mr Tallis. *Dear* Alfonso. With his little pipe...'

As she moves away, she seems to remember something. 'Oh – Aemilia. Oddly enough, I met a man the other day who was asking after you. That jumped-up fellow who used to be with the Lord Chamberlain's Men. With the awful *accent*, you know?'

'No, I don't.'

'Face of a clerk, but wears an earring. Arrogant, for a provincial.'

Arrogant is clue enough. And she would know his name in any case. He has been doing very well for himself of late.

'What did he say?'

'Mmm... can't quite think. Oh, well – it can't have been important...'

'If you see him again, tell him I hope he burns in hell.'

'What, the author of those pretty sonnets? He pleases everyone, they say.'

'Not all his sonnets are pretty, your ladyship, and he certainly does not please me.'

She bows her head, seeming delighted with our exchange. 'Do you know, I believe that his star may continue to ascend, even without your blessing?' She walks on.

Then, through a gap in the crowd, I see Henry, staring up at a sugar-plum stall. I catch up my dress and struggle through the mob, taking no notice of the shouts of annoyance as I elbow my way forward.

'Henry, for God's sake! I have been so worried! What were you thinking of, running off like that?'

He is crying. 'I'm sorry, Mother. I said bad words to you. The Devil tempted me.'

I hug him tight. His body is burly, already hard-muscled. He is growing up a manly man, the equal of anyone, if not their better.

'I don't deserve a sugar-plum, do I?' he says. 'Though they are so round and sweet to look at.'

'No, you don't.'

'Not even one. You must punish me, so that my character will be built up strong.'

'Not even one.' I squeeze him tighter.

'I'm a bad, rude, evil creature.'

'Bad and rude, Henry.' I bend down and kiss his hair. 'But never evil.'

The stall is heaped with sweets and fancies made from sugar and marzipan. There are animals, birds and tiny baskets. Wine glasses, dishes, playing cards and little flutes, all made as dainty and perfect as God's creation. I've seen such craftsmanship at Court, painstakingly fashioned for royal banquets. But never outside the palace. Even there, they were not as beautiful as this luscious, lustrous fruit. The sugar-plums are piled head high, a rampart of dark pinks and soft purples, frosted with sugar like a fairy shroud. I look at the stall-holder. She is as lovely as her dainty wares, fair-skinned, with yellow hair plaited tightly back from her brow.

'How many do we get for a halfpenny?' I ask.

She smiles. 'Two pocketfuls, mistress.'

'Go on, then, Henry,' I say, pushing him forward.

She fills his pockets and I give her the coin.

'One for you?' says Henry, turning to me with his best smile.

'One for me.' I choose a fat, mauve fruit. The sugar tingles on my lips as I bite into it. But my attention is distracted – I see the two witch-women, sitting on the ground just by the stall… I bite down, and my tooth cracks on the plum-stone. There is a sudden pain, a knife-jab in my gums.

I grab my jaw. 'See – there!' I shout.

Henry turns to look, mouth full. 'What? Where?'

They have disappeared. A trumpet band starts up. A troupe of acrobats is turning cartwheels. A bear begins to dance, its moaning growl like human words.

I peer distractedly. 'Nothing. Just… nothing.'

'Did you hurt your mouth?' says Henry.

'I think so.' I take the mush of plum, sugar and gore out of my mouth and look at it in my palm. There is a shard of tooth there. More than that. Half a molar.

'So much blood, Mother!' says Henry. He seems well satisfied. 'Would you like another one?'

Scene II

At first the pain is a hot, tender spot in my mouth, nothing more. My tongue keeps searching for it, poking into the fiery hole which had once been filled with tooth. All about it, my gum is raw and swollen. At breakfast time, I soak my bread in weak ale and suck down the brownish porridge like an infant. In the evenings, even though it is summertime, I sit on a stool near the fire, warming my naked feet as if soothing one part of my body would bring relief to another. It does nothing of the kind, of course. I force myself to think about something else. There is no shortage of subjects to think about, after all. Money, motherhood, the uncertain future, and the business of being married to a flimsy and improvident musician. And that isn't all. As well as the throbbing hole in my mouth, my day at the Fair has left me with a feeling of unease and dread, like a drunk's dawn gloom.

So I try to distract myself with reading. I once knew the great libraries of England: it is from these places that I have furnished the small library in my own head. And I have a few books still. I love to smell them and feel their pages beneath my fingers. They are kept in different parts of the house, so they come easily to hand when I have a moment to myself. I read with so much intensity that my head reels, for learning is there, and facts and a treasure chest of oddments of the world, trapped in ink. In the solar there is Foxe's *Book of Martyrs*, of course, and in the kitchen I keep Job Hortop's *Travels* next to the simples cupboard, being the tale of an old man who was press-ganged and sent on the Guinea voyage of 1567 and saw two of his company slain and eaten by sea-horses.

And his ship captured a most monstrous Alligator, which had a hog's head and a serpent's body but was scaled in every part, each scale the size of a saucer, and with a long and knotted tail and they baited it with a dog and caught it with their ropes.

As I stir the pot in the kitchen I feast my mind upon Hortop's wild tales, of how he and his companions fell among the Indians and were cruelly treated, but then discovered good Christian Indians (for such a thing is possible, it seems), and later found a sea creature who was half-man, half-fish, and his upper body brown as a mulatto. Then he went from there to Spain, where he was put to torture by the Inquisition (for good Christian Spaniards conduct themselves like savages) and two of his shipmates were burned, but he was sent to the galleys, which he rowed for ten years.

What I believe is that such a rollicking life of colour and calamity is the only kind a man should have, this life being a brief slit between two measureless eternities, and by 'man' I mean man and woman, for there would be no man alive today without the fairer sex and men are not half as clever as they think themselves and we are more than twice as strong as we let on.

Oh, and in my bedroom, to distract me from Alfonso's curtain-lectures about his great importance at Court, I keep Harington's translation of *Orlando Furioso*. Which tells the story of a man who – his wife being false – ranges over the whole of Europe looking for a good woman yet finds not one. This story so annoyed the Queen that she called Harington – who was her godson – to her Presence Chamber and gave him her harsh opinion. Of course, I agreed with Her Majesty that such stories are vile bawdy and not for Court ladies, yet, being no longer one of their number, I can both laugh at these naughty women and share a little of their forbidden lust, remembering my own misdoings and those little secret come-cries that we fist-muffle when we must. Such memories I will take as close to the graveside as I dare, and offer them up in exchange for Eternal Redemption at the moment of my last breath.

Some of my books have been wrote by women, too. I wish I could say these are the best of them, but this is not so. Compared to Hortop's terrifying journeys, reading the Countess of Pembroke's *Ivychurch* and *Emanuel* (translations from Mr Tasso) is like walking with a prelate in a country garden. Though her hexameters are handsome and there is no such thing as a book which is worthless. I have read her works with close attention, schoolboylike, and they are all excellently rhymed.

I pick up the *Martyrs*, and then Hortop, but cannot lose myself in them as is my usual custom. I am on the outside, and the worlds inside their covers are locked in. And I can't evict the memory of Lettice Cooper from my mind. Her talk of the poet and his sonnets disturbs me. My old lover has remade the form. He sent me a bundle of verses, written out in his own hand, full of bile and hatred for me and everything that we'd done. My only comfort is that they have not been printed. I have never thanked him for his poisoned gift, and prefer to think him dead. I should have burned them, but could not. In any case, each one has lodged itself in my mind, which keeps them stored neatly and for all time. I am the victim of my fine memory. All of them retain the power to hurt me, but there is one which is stuck fast, and goes round and round my head, day after day.

Stuck it is, stuck as a pig in dung. I sit in my room, and my head is full of it. The casement window has a high view of Long Ditch, and Camm Row beyond.

Th'expense of spirit in a waste of shame
Is lust in action, and till action lust
Is perjured, murdr'ous, bloody, full of blame...

This is the present moment, respectable. Actual. To the east, I can see the towers of Whitehall Palace; beyond that is Charing Cross, where Cockspur meets the Strand.

Savage, extreme, rude, cruel, not to trust,
Enjoyed no sooner, but despised straight,
Past reason hunted and no sooner had...

'No sooner had'! Oh, you had me, sir, right enough; you had me for a harlot and a fool. To the north are the fields of Haymarket and St Martin's, to the west, open country.

Mad in pursuit, and in possession so,
Had, having, and in quest to have, extreme,
A bliss in proof, and, proved, a very woe,
Before a joy proposed, behind, a dream...

'And, proved, a very woe'. That's me, the proven woe, the peerless whore, only enticing when unfucked; once fucked, I'm beastly, loathsome, ugly. A sly witch in a tale. You cannot see the river from this chamber, but if you stick your head out of the window you can hear the shouts of the wherrymen touting for business at the water's edge.

All this the world well knows, yet none knows well
To shun the Heav'n that leads men to this Hell.

You had me, Will, and you had no pity for me, and you have me still.

It is two days since my accident with the sugar-plum. Alfonso is standing in the downstairs hall, practising his monotonous tunes. His lips are pursed and his childish pipe trills out its familiar fluting patterns. The highest notes bore inside my jawbone.

'Alfonso?' Against my cheek I hold a linen bag, filled with burned and powdered rosemary wood. It has been prepared with great care by Joan, our old serving woman.

My husband lowers the recorder, a patient expression on his face. 'What, dear Aemilia?'

'When are you going to give me some money?'

'Quite soon, my love.' Off he goes again.

'How soon?'

An even more forgiving expression, worthy of St Peter. 'I'm a musician, not an alchemist, sweet chuck...'

'I don't expect you to make gold from base metal; I expect you to earn it.'

'When the concert is over.'

'Which concert?'

'The concert for the Queen's birthday. We get five shillings extra, apiece.'

'So till then we starve.'

He starts again, the notes in beautiful order, his life a mess of debt and deceit.

Joan is making her slow way down the staircase with a pail of rainwater. She is a narrow scrawn of a woman, and as she grows older it seems the years are scraping the flesh from her bones. Now Joan is a common name in London, but this is the very same Joan Daunt who owned the apothecary's shop in Bucklersbury. It was burned down by a mob the night that I summoned her to help at Henry's birth. And all its precious contents went up with it: the jars and vials and herbs and potions, the tinctures and the spices and rare ingredients from Turkey, China and beyond. Henry was a breech-baby. Born backwards, and would have died if it had not been for Joan.

'It's a bad do,' she says, throwing the water out of the door and into the street. The cat, Graymalkin, who has been sunning himself on the threshold, yowls and runs away. 'You can see blue sky through two holes now, each as big as a man's fist. We'll soon have the floor rotten, and that'll be the next expense.'

Alfonso has the recorder to his lips. He closes his eyes and blows, but no sound comes. He blows again. Nothing. He lowers his instrument once more, flushed with anger. 'I am the head of this household, and I demand silence!' he shouts. 'I must have… your wifely respect, Aemilia! And Joan's – servantly obedience.'

Pain's hot-poker twists in my gum. 'There is silence, husband,' I tell him. (A London silence, at least, which is to say that through the open front door swoop the city sounds of dogs barking, hammers beating, babies crying, couples fornicating, pigs snorting, cartwheels clattering and all the other Babel noise of people and creatures and buildings and shops and stews all piled together pell-mell.) 'At least, the only noise I hear is you. As for obedience…'

Joan lowers her eyes and coughs as she makes her way back up the stairs with the empty pail.

Alfonso looks at me, as if he is still trying, after almost ten years, to work out what he has taken on and whether he can survive it. He is a pretty man, I'll say that for him, with his dark skin and black coiled hair. The Lanyers have French blood, and this shows in the way he has of dressing himself. Even in his plain cambric shirt he cuts an elegant figure, and his dainty fingers hold the pipe as if it was a living thing.

'Why do you stare, Alfonso?'

'Why do you question me, wife?'

In bed, it is easy to feel lust for Alfonso, with his hard, lean body and his soft kisses. But in this house it is my word that carries weight, not his. This is in part because he spent all my dowry in a twelvemonth, gaming and dicing and showing off. Also because his musician's 'duties' – piping, gossiping and the wearing of a short mandilion – keep him at Court for long hours, overnight if there is a feast or a celebration. He comes and goes at odd times, like Graymalkin.

Yet there is more to it than that. Each time Joan reads my Tarot cards, a different pattern tells the same story – we are out of balance, my husband and I. If Henry is spoiled it is all my doing, because I decide when he is praised and when he is punished. Joan, too, listens to me, and not her master.

'Your face is swelling up still,' Alfonso says, as if deciding to withdraw from battle. 'You need to see the barber surgeon and have that tooth pulled, what's left of it. He should bleed you, too. There may be poison.'

Without replying, I go out into the bright morning bustle of Long Ditch, with its clustered wooden buildings. It is a street that does not know its place. Although it is close to the rambling sprawl of Whitehall, it is itself of no account. The dwellings were thrown up hastily, without forethought or symmetry. Some are no wider than their own front door, with four storeys piled above, seeming likely to overbalance and tumble down into the street. Others are hovel-high and no bigger than a cow-barn. And yet we are overlooked by Camm Row, and the calm and solid homes of great men like Sir Edward Hoby and the Earls of Hertford, Derby and Lincoln. Such great, commanding houses! Their casement windows glow bright with candles long after dark, and every house has a walled garden behind. Our mean dwellings are like birds' nests in comparison. All of us cheek-by-jowl, breathing the same smoke-filled air. The red kites, wheeling above, must see us coming in and out like little dolls, shaking our linen or stepping out in our fine gowns.

I look around me, thinking how much easier it would be to know my place if my position in the world had a little more sense to it. We know that God presides at the top, followed by the Angels, with Man below. And then Woman lower yet – above the animals, but a lesser mortal than her bed-fellow. By Our Lord's ordinance we are the weaker, lesser sex. It is a system, certainly. But where is my place in this ordered universe? I was first a bastard, then a lady (educated in Greek and Latin if you please), then a courtesan – on account of being a comely orphan. And now, a drudge. What few skills are called for to fill this station, I do not possess. Where is the divine plan there?

If I had less learning it might be easier to bear, but I am sure that few Court ladies know their Ovid as I do, could recite the Psalms in Latin or have the tales of Holinshed off by heart. In short, I have been tutored like a young lord, which is worse than useless to me now. If the aim of learning is a fitting-out to modern purpose, I say it falls far short, both for the young lords and for me. What has modern man learned from the Greeks – I mean in relation to his behaviour? Not enough, in my opinion. He is not the master of his passions. He is not wise. Men fight and tyrannise each other, and are given to extremes in blood and anguish, revelry and ribaldry. Great learning should lead to great lives – ha! Like the learned counsel at the Inns of Law, I rest my case.

So I am ill suited to being a City house-wife, married to a pile of wood and wattle-and-daub. Which pile, I must tell you, is not even my own. Within one year of our union, my dear spouse had spent my dowry, and within eighteen months he had borrowed money against my little house to pay his debts at table. So this place, fitted out with such care by my Lord Hunsdon (and in consultation with his lady wife) is no longer mine. It belongs to one Anthony Inchbald, an avaricious Dwarf and quite the greediest of landlords. I am surely married to the greatest fool in Christendom, yet I am his to ruin if he so wishes. I'm his possession: my whole mind and all its furnishings. Sometimes, I think of my mother and father. There was no ceremony to mark their union, saving only a handfasting, and yet they loved each other well. My own case is the opposite: it is a paper wedding, and all that joins me to Alfonso is expedience and the odd bout of merry fucking. (Forgive me, but I am only mortal, and the poor monkey has no other purpose I can think of.)

My mind rages, but here I stand in my drab dress, a creature half-mad with the tooth-ache. Wood smoke drifts upwards from the close-crowded chimneys of the houses opposite. The cat is still shaking his tail in angry jerks, ears flat to his head. He lifts one paw and shakes it singly, and little shining droplets of water catch the sunlight as they fall.

Widow Flood, my neighbour, comes out of her door with a full pot, and pours the foul-nosed contents into the reeking kennel that runs down the centre of the street. She is a plump woman, with a pleasant, open face, but she has an irksome weakness: knowingness. On all subjects she believes herself the expert. And she is an over-dresser, too, in keeping with this good opinion of her status. Even in the house she wears a white lawn ruff. Her face pokes out from the wired cloth like a pig's head on a platter, and she takes care to hold the pot well away from the wide bulk of her farthingale. So grand, and yet the ferryman of her own filth. You could not tell a baronet from a bee-keeper in the streets of London.

'Tooth still bad, Aemilia?' She puts the pot on the ground next to her and stands back, hands on her padded hips, as if ready to enjoy the sun. Noticing a dead rat lying near, she kicks it on to the dung-pile that banks against her house. Beneath her fine skirt she is wearing wooden pattens.

'Still bad.'

'The barber surgeon should pull it for you.'

'Indeed.'

'Should bleed you, too, for safety's sake.'

'You should join my husband's recorder band, since you pipe the same tune.'

She laughs. 'Pain can make you surly, Aemilia. It's good advice.'

Anne Flood was well-named. Good advice flows from her, and good fortune to her. Even her husband's death has been a sort of blessing, since he was a wintry old skinflint, a haberdasher by trade, who was more than twice her age when they married. Her son Tom has just been apprenticed to the Lord Chamberlain's Men, and will soon be prancing on the boards at the Globe.

But here is Joan with a bolster to shake out. 'There is devilment behind this, Mistress Flood,' she says, flapping it fiercely. 'I don't like it. The air is full of spirits and the streets are full of demons, preying on the unwary.' She folds the bedding against her chest and holds it tight against her.

'Spell-making?' Anne Flood's eyes glint. She is curious about my clever servant, whose knowledge of witchcraft far outstrips that of the other women in the street.

'Something wicked. And no village art, neither. Devil's magic. It was not by chance they met her. They were waiting.'

'Shush, Joan, don't speak of it,' I say. But the witches' words have stuck in my head. *The plague is coming.* And not as I have known it. *Not like this.* I feel the wisdom of Joan's words – there was some design behind our meeting, something I don't yet understand.

Anne nods. 'Speak of the Devil and he will appear. We should praise the good Lord, and pray for our immortal souls.'

'Amen to that,' says Joan, crossing herself. 'God have mercy. Let each of us know our place. That magic which can ease our suffering and help us along our way is well enough. That which seeks to harness Evil will always do us harm.'

I put my arm about her shoulders. 'It is a tooth-ache, my good Joan, that's all. I broke my tooth on a plum-stone; there was no fiendishness.' I push her gently towards the house. 'It's nearly twelve – go and prepare something for us to eat. Something soft that will swallow down easy. I could eat rabbit stew, on the left side. Or a little scraped cheese, with sage and sugar...'

She goes muttering into the house.

Anne is still pressing her case. 'All that is needed is a trip to the barber. I know of a man in the Shambles who is most excellent,' she says. 'Pulls teeth like eels from mud – you hardly feel a thing. See?' She grins, showing off her graveyard gaps with pride. 'He broke my jaw once, trying to gouge out a buried wisdom tooth. Almost too much even for him. But it soon mended.'

That night, my face swells fit to fill the bedchamber. Sleep twists pain into trumpets, drum beats, the drone of an afternoon recorder. The dreams I have are dense and dazzling; my head aches with the colour and busyness of them. I see the Queen again, not as she must be now, but as I used to know her, ten years ago. She is herself, and yet not herself: a tapestry in gold and green thread, a painted face on a wood panel, a straight-backed monarch sitting on a jewelled throne. Satan might send us pain; God soothes us with insanity to make a picture of it.

The rose garden at Whitehall, enclosed on four sides by high, crenellated walls. The heads of traitors all around, dripping fat-rot on to the pathways. Rose-heads rising ever higher. The Queen appears from the privet maze, fanning herself in the summer heat, face white in spite of the sun.

'Ay,' she says. 'Dark Aemilia, inspirer of our cousin's lust. We two – freakish black, and freakish red, would you not say?'

'Your Majesty?'

'Both of us midnight-weird.'

I curtsey as low as I can, as if my legs were liquid.

'For God's sake! Is this how you behave in the presence of other mortal beings? Stand up!'

She pulls me to my feet. She is shorter than me, face withered under the layer of white powder. Her fierce blue eyes are hungry for information, but flat, with nothing behind. Like a kite, looking sideways as it scoffs its offal. She takes my arm and sweeps me along the path beside her.

'You,' she says. 'Plaything of my Lord Hunsdon, yes?'

'Yes, Your Majesty.'

I look down and my child Henry is curled inside me, unborn, though a hefty boy of almost ten.

'Plaything, or his tormenter?'

'I – his tormenter, madam. Or both, by turns, madam.'

'He in charge? Or you, by any chance?' She waves a courtier away. He is carrying a galleon in full sail, ocean waves drenching the padded sleeves of his doublet.

'He is always in charge, madam. I am but a weak and feeble woman.'

The Queen's face is rigid with amusement. Her ladies come tittering towards us, carrying baskets filled with fiery sugar-plums, hitching their skirts so their beaded hems sweep clear of the wet grass.

Scene III

Have I woken? Or is this still sleep? Night-time, or day? I can see only darkness, but fancy there is sunlight too, coming at me from around Alfonso's head.

'Aemilia! You are awake! What a fever you have run – we have barely slept.'

Joan's face looms in front of me. She is holding a great wooden spoon, fit for a giant, which she forces into my mouth. There is some heavy, treacly substance on it, tasting of wine and hartshorn. Splinters of pain send more sunlight into my head; the morning rays seem to be breaking my skull apart. The scream which echoes from the walls might be my own noise, I suppose, listening to the sound with mild surprise. What tooth-ache is this?

'She must see the physician,' says Alfonso.

'Physician! What skill will he have, to cure such a condition?' asks Joan. 'This is more than tooth-ache. I said so before. More like the dropsy or the sweats.'

'The sweats! Don't say it! Unless we do something, she will die! I never saw such a thing – all from an ailing tooth.' His voice is breaking. 'I shall send for him now...'

'There is no physician on this earth that can give her the help she needs, master.' Joan speaks so firmly to her 'master' that if I weren't so ill I would smile.

'Then the barber surgeon can pull it out. She would hear none of that, of course. If she only would have listened to me...'

'It's too far gone.'

If I could speak, I would tell them that some vileness is eating me from within, and the cracked tooth has been an entry point for some evil poison, just as a viper's bite looks like a pin-prick and yet may kill a calf. I try to speak – but my whole body is frozen, although my mind is clear. My body, my limbs, my aching head – all are rigid and inert. I am like living marble, fixed upon my bed.

'Why can't you cure her of this, woman?' shouts Alfonso, sounding close to tears. 'She swears by you and all your tricks. Much use your cures and treatments are to her now!'

'I told you, sir, there is something far beyond my remedies here. I have the skill to know that, and the wit to let another cure her who has more knowledge than I do. If you ask me, someone has put a spell on her.'

'A spell! God's blood, who would do such a thing? That's nothing more than fancy.'

I feel a wet cloth soothe my head. 'It could be belladonna,' says Joan, as cool liquid seeps into my hair. 'But... I can't be sure. The antidote to that is worse than the poison...' Thin hands smooth my cheek. 'I need advice, that's what I'm saying. You can see the state she's in – look, try to move her arm. It's like a rock.'

'Very well, go to the apothecary.'

'I *am* an apothecary. I need a cunning-man for this.'

'Jesu!' Alfonso's voice fades away, as if he had walked to the window. 'I'm not paying for some mountebank to come sliding in here, mutter some incantations and then go on his way.'

'Then she will die.'

'No!' I am surprised to hear the fear in his voice. Has the fool grown to love me? But men are simple, even the clever ones. He has me where he wants and, even now he's spent the dowry, he still has a roof over his head and a woman in his bed.

'Forman,' says Joan.

'Who?'

'Forman,' she repeats. 'The man we need is Simon Forman. I've heard her speak of him.'

'That turd-faced lecher! Most foul and Satan-bothering necromancer! Over my dead body will she see this man!'

'It's her dead body we'll have to worry about, not yours, unless we find some cure. Forman may be a lecher, and he may be a necromancer, but he is wise. They say he cured himself of plague – who else do you know who has done such a thing?'

'You speak out of turn.'

'Forgive me, but I am all on edge.' Joan's voice is soft, but furious.

I want to thrash my head about, or wave my hand as if to say, *Not that filthy little chance-man, with his tricky hands and his ready cock, God save us!* But I can't move, nor even blink my eye. And it occurs to me that if it is a choice between being entombed by my own flesh and bone, or being groped by a ginger goat, I had better choose the latter. And, with that wise thought, my mind slips into darkness.

'Now, my dear, you can open your eyes.'

I open them, expecting pain and calamity, but nothing happens. The ceiling above my head is a familiar criss-cross of wood panelling. If this is Heaven or Hell, it looks remarkably like my own house.

'See if you can get up,' says a quiet voice. 'It's all done now.'

I struggle up so that I am propped on my elbows. My mind feels clear and sharp, more so than it has for many months. A bearded, elderly man is sitting next to the bed. Dr Forman is smiling. There is something complacent in his attitude, as if he has won a wager. And behind his chair stands Joan, all twisted with anxiety.

'Oh, Aemilia, praise God!' she cries. 'You are better.'

I put my hand up to my cheek, aware of a mild soreness, but nothing like the agony and madness of the last few days. 'My tooth?'

Dr Forman holds up a glass vial. Inside it is something bloody and rotted, tiny as a baby's little finger. 'I don't know what magic these crones put on you, but really,' he says, 'I have never seen such vileness. I am afraid your poor husband has had to go to a tavern. He did not have the stomach for it.'

'And my son?'

'He is downstairs. He's asked for the tooth, but I'm not sure it's safe to give it to him.'

I rub my face, and stretch out my arms, which are stiff and painful. 'Never saw such vileness, you say? I find that hard to believe. A man with your wide experience of all things unspeakable and horrid.'

'I know you have a sharp tongue, Mistress Lanyer, but within a few days you would have been dead from this infection, and lying in your grave. I won't take the conventional remuneration from such an old friend as you, but a little gratitude would be an appropriate payment, I feel.'

Joan looks at him, quizzical. 'Gratitude? Isn't her money good enough for you?'

'Mistress Lanyer is well known to me,' says the doctor. 'I would rather have her friendship than her gold.'

Joan pulls a leather money-bag from her basket and holds it out to him. 'Take this, and let us keep it strictly business. Gratitude smacks of debts that stay unpaid.'

'Joan, let it be,' I tell her.

She looks at me, her green eyes cold. 'There is some magic which is better measured by a pile of coin. Or else the scent of it will linger, like a sick dog's stench.'

'Joan!'

'It was a simple request for thanks,' says Dr Forman, bowing stiffly. He stares at me. I had forgotten the strangeness of his gaze, withdrawn and mesmerising at once. Last time I saw him, he was as ginger as a squirrel. Now his beard and hair are grey. He wears both long, as if styling himself a magus or a necromancer. And his robes are both mystical and splendid – his coat and breeches are purple velvet. Magic and medicine must have made him a rich man.

I sit up and swing my legs down to the floor. 'Thank you, Simon. I am sorry for my ill manners.'

'And so you should be, mistress,' says Joan. 'We'd given you up for dead.'

'You have skill in healing?' the doctor asks her.

Joan folds her arms across her chest. 'More than skill. It's in my blood.'

The doctor bows again, and smiles his sweetest smile. 'Then you have the better of me, most assuredly. What I know is merely the stuff of book-learning and weary application.'

'Will you like something to eat?' I ask.

'Thank you, you are kind. It is so many years since we have spoken. I have often thought of you, wondering how my predictions served you.'

Joan leaves to prepare some food.

Forman settles himself back in his chair. 'Well, well, Aemilia! If I were not a student of the constellations, I would call this a stroke of luck. As it is, I can see that the stars were in a most propitious alignment today. Which, if I may say so, marks a change where you are concerned.'

'I have not been blessed with great luck, except that I have my dear son Henry.'

He takes my hand and spreads out my palm. 'Dear, oh, dear. Hmm. What? You know full well the stars are not windows to the future, but perform a similar function to that which they fulfil on a dark night.'

'They shine, and they are mysterious.'

'Quite so, quite so.'

He looks at my palm again, frowning. 'Still scribbling at your verse, I see.'

'As often as I can. In the early morning, sometimes, or at the very dead of night.'

'Make time for those scrawled words. Make time for your mind.'

'I do, sir.'

He strokes his fingers across mine. 'I was hoping you might visit me for a friendly halek, dear lady, a little knee-trembler for old times' sake.'

I pull my hand away. 'Even though I have never fucked you in the past?' Forman is the only man I ever knew who had his own word for fornication: a clear sign of his dedication to that craft.

'Did you not? Ah, then, it is just that dreams and memories can entwine in the most confusing manner. In honour of many a merry skirmish, then, shall we say?'

'The answer is no.'

He sighs. 'You are cruel. But now…'

'Now, what?'

'Now, I feel that our time would be better spent looking, as far as we may with such feeble instruments as I possess, into the future. The possible, probable, potential future, as we astrologists like to say.'

He produces a pack of Tarot cards from a pocket inside his cloak. They are of ancient and arcane design. The pictures show men with the heads of eagles, and strange nymphs with gold faces and serpents for hair.

'Shuffle these,' he says, and I do so. He lays them out before me, face-down and with their edges overlapping. 'Choose three,' he says. 'Not in haste, but without too much thinking. Let your intuition lead you.'

I choose them, and he turns them over, one by one. In the centre is the glorious figure of an Empress, clothed in scarlet. On her left side are two Lovers, arms and legs entwined. And on her right hand is the mounted figure of grim Death.

'What does this mean?' I ask.

But he is silent again. Then he picks up the card which shows the Lovers, and puts it down in front of me.

'This is a most auspicious card. When you came to see me… before… there was a certain poet in your stars.'

'That was a long time ago.'

'He loves you still.'

'Now I know there are limits to your magic. He does not love me in the least.'

'We are speaking of the same man, I take it?'

'We are speaking of one who wrote me the most vicious, evil lines I ever saw.'

'That cannot be!'

'Some poets write pretty sonnets to their lady-love. Not he. If there is such a thing as a hate sonnet, then I have been presented with that very thing.'

'A passing mood, perhaps? He feared he couldn't have you.'

'A very sheaf of loathing. I am, in his eyes, such a Muse as you might encounter in the fires of Hell.'

He stares at the cards, eyes half-closed.

'So you are wrong,' I say.

'No. There is no mistake.' He pats my shoulder. 'Oh, my dear Aemilia. What travails you have had. I wish that I could tell you that they are over.'

I look at the Death card and shiver. 'So, what does it mean?'

'You must be brave, and resourceful, and bold, to cope with what is yet to come. Yet I have faith in you. And there is brightness, too, if you will only see it. There is love.'

From the same pocket which had held the pack of cards he draws out a pamphlet. The title reads '*Malleus Maleficarum, Maleficas, & earum haeresim, ut phramea potentissima conterens.*'

'*The Hammer of Witches,*' I translate. '*Which destroyeth witches and their heresy as with a two-edged sword*. This has nothing to do with me! Why are you giving me this book, of all books?'

'Not a particularly romantic gift, I fear, but you may find it instructive. And… well. There is something that you must do – of an urgent and peculiar nature.'

I look at the pamphlet, puzzled.

'What is done cannot be undone, but what has come in consequence… Well. I can say no more. There is no time now to do a proper reading. Let me just say that there is much to know in this field, much you do not understand, and that there is something evil here. Something beyond ill-wishing. Come and talk to me again.'

'I am not a fool, Dr Forman. And I have had my fill of aged lovers.'

'My dear! You quite mistake my meaning. I would like to help you.'

'Very handsome of you.'

He bends closer, and I see a glint of something like fear in his eyes. And yet, what is there to be afraid of? 'Aemilia, you have a good mind, and more than enough curiosity. I asked you once what you knew of magic. Do you know more now?'

'A little.'

'From that servant of yours?'

'She's taught me a few remedies, and I can make a potion or a poultice for most of the common ailments.'

'Yes, yes. That is useful enough – but what you need is something which goes beyond the household skills of women. Something to help you in the most severe and terrible adversity.'

'What sort of something?'

'There is no time to tell you now. If I am not mistaken, I hear your serving-woman's footsteps on the stairs. But be sure of this: there are dark days ahead of you.'

Scene IV

Today I rise early, with the words of Dr Forman in my head. What are these 'dark days'? Can they be avoided? There is no doubt that the old lecher knows what he is about. Not only has he cured the infection, and not only is there barely a scar to show where the cursed tooth has been – all my other little aches and torments have gone. Those besetting symptoms that all of us in London must put up with: soot-wheeze, ale-runs, head-gripe, back-ache, lassitude and dread-belly – not to mention sundry scabs, carbuncles and lesions of the skin – all such ailments have vanished.

I get up and sit at the little table by the window, and look at the books and pages that are stacked in order there. I have little money for paper, so I have taken to scribbling in the margins of my books, adding my own thoughts to those of Hortop and Plato. What was Forman's advice? *'Make time for those scrawled words. Make time for your mind.'* Make time – now there's an exhortation! If only I could. I would spin it, the way that other housewives spin their wool, and I would fill the house with it, the product of my labours. I would weave sheets of genius and sheaves of golden poetry, the harvest of my hours. Standing up, I stretch my arms upward, letting my mind's attention dwell on every inch of my body. Every inch is free of pain. My body is well; my mind still rages in its skull. If I wish to be well in my mind, then I must write, and there is no cure for my ambition, and thank the Lord for that.

I cross to the mirror. Has Forman's art restored some of my lost beauty? I see that I am not, as Lettice claimed, a woman old before her time. My hair is still black, without a single streak of white; my skin is unlined. My eyes, so much admired in the past, are dark, watchful, unblinking. When I look into them, I cannot tell what I am thinking. Perhaps I am still beautiful. Perhaps I might triumph over other matters. What is there to be afraid of? The plague? We have always lived with its comings and its goings. Fogs and dunghill odours bear contagion. Some say that Death is trapped in rugs and feather beds, and cover their faces when they pass a woollen draper's shop. Alfonso stuffs his dainty nose with herb-grace. Joan, with her store of soothing cures and potions, greets each new outbreak by hanging the house with rue. God will protect us, surely, until it is our time to meet Him. After all, there are ten thousand ways for Death to cut you down.

And so, in the days that follow I think, *Let God's will be done*. I can write my words, cross-hatched and cramped sideways in the margins of the works of great and famous men. I can gnaw at a chicken leg, delighting in the taste and texture of the meat, the greasiness of the bone. I am alive and well. The sun has forgotten us, the skies are dark and the streets and lanes are torrents of rainwater.

Yet what do I care if the sun shines, or the rain falls? I must go to the baker's, and the chandler's, to the cobbler and tailor, with my basket over my arm. And the mud and summer drizzle make me smile, even though my skirts are smeared with pavement mire, and I must barter for cheat-bread.

Do I think of Will? I will confess I do, for I see him every time I look at Henry, and even the touch of my own face reminds me of Will's skin. The Greeks knew far more of emotion than we do, and there is no English word for the feeling that I carry with me, shamed and rejected by the only man I ever loved. The Greek word is *pothos* – milder than wild *eros* but longer-lasting: a longing for someone unobtainable or far away. The nearest word we have is 'yearning'. I yearn for the Will I've lost, the Will who loved me, and who will never come again. But I can make my mind blank, keep memory in a little box.

A fortnight after my meeting with the doctor, there is a loud knock on the door. Anne Flood is standing there, dressed in her usual absurd splendour, head trussed in a new style of starched ruff – French, I dare say – which seems fit to throttle her. I let her in and return to my task: I am marking out a pie crust, pressing my right thumb in a firm pattern round its edge.

'Aemilia!' she says. 'I have an invitation for you.'

'An invitation to what, Anne?' I have a feeling this will be an event I would rather not attend.

'Oh, it's Tom's first big performance! He is in a new play at the Globe. We are off tomorrow afternoon, and should be so delighted if you would come.'

My thumb jerks and rips the pastry, but I don't look up. 'Alfonso is at Court.'

'Come yourself! Bring Henry. And Joan, too. You should be there, not only because you are my good neighbour and have known Tom since he was an infant, but because of the very part he is playing.'

Graymalkin, as if curious to hear more, unfurls himself from his position next to the smouldering fire, and comes grandly over, blinking and stretching.

'The very part? He is the leading lady?'

'Oh, no, he is too green yet for that. Only fifteen, you know, for all he is so tall! No, he is a second-ranking character, but one essential to the plot. Or so he tells me. I have only seen the pages with his lines.'

'I fear I am – '

'But wait, wait till you hear! His character is you!'

A coldness in the air, a north breeze. I put the pie in the oven and slam the door. '*How* is it me?'

'Aemilia!' Anne looks triumphant. 'He is a serving lady called Aemilia! It must be you. A friend of Mr Shakespeare's as you were. And I doubt he knows many Venetians, and the play is set in Venice. It's about a Moor.'

'Anne, I'm not a Venetian, I was born at Bishopsgate…'

'Yes, but your father was. And he named you. And this "Aemilia" is cynical and worldly, and has a speech making little of men! You! To the very life!' She seems to think that I should share in her delight.

'I…' But, before I can think up my excuse, Henry is here, all bounce and frenzy. He falls over the cat, who runs away, furious, to lay waste to some rats.

'Mother! You are in a play! How good! Can we be at the front? Can we be groundlings? Please! I want to be a groundling. John Feather and John Dokes have both been groundlings, and they saw a whore suck a – '

'We are busy, Henry; we must – '

'We are *not* busy, Mother. You were going to make me swot my Latin.'

'It is most historical,' says Anne, seeing how to play it. 'Based on the *Decameron*, says Tom. Mr Shakespeare translated it himself, he's quite the linguist. Though not as handsome as Mr Burbage, I have to say.'

'Please, Mother!' Henry grips my arm and squeezes tight. 'One afternoon of Latin is not going to make me an Oxford man. And Tom is my very best friend. I shall be heartbroken if you say no.'

I count it a small victory that I have not set foot in the Globe for ten years. Nor have I been to the Rose, nor the Curtain, nor the Swan, nor the Fortune. All London might be in thrall to the theatre, but not me. And yet. I can't lie: as we come up to the great entrance gate to the play house, part of a dense London throng, I am as curious as Henry, who is leaping and dancing and singing like a Bedlam boy. Joan has him by the arm, a grim set to her smile (she has no love for a play). I, meanwhile, am borne along by Anne, who is twenty times as giddy and talkative as my cavorting son.

'You see there?' She gestures at a portly nymph ahead of us in the line, with tight-curled hair and a tavern laugh. 'Breasts quite out – it's all the thing, they say, at Court. And yet, look, she's straight off to the pit, for all her gown is of silk taffeta.'

'A whore, Anne, as any fool can see.'

'Whore? Where, Mother?' comes from behind.

'Never mind that, Henry, you are here to see the play,' says Joan.

'What great big nipples has she, though! Half the size of her dugs! Mine are tiny beside hers.' Anne is frowning at the sight.

'Oh, yes, I see them now!' says Henry. 'Big as conkers!'

'Enough of this, in front of the child, Anne!'

'I quite forgot myself, forgive me.' But her expert eye has distracted her again. 'Is that Mr Burbage? Over there, with the gold and silver girdle? I am sure it must be him! Look at his actor's bearing – a true player, wouldn't you say?'

'That isn't Burbage. He will be in the tiring-house, waiting to go on.'

'It's him. Mr Burbage! Over here!'

'Not if he is the lead, which it says he is, on the playbill.' I flutter the bill before her face. 'Why would he be out here, gawping at the crowd?'

But Anne looks vague. She does not like me to draw attention to the fact that I can read.

Through the gate ahead of us, I can see the afternoon sun tilting down on to the pit, gilding the crowd that is gathering there. Eight-sided, the great Globe, like a Roman amphitheatre for our own day, the centre open to the air, the surrounding walls and galleries thatched. I have my pennies ready, to pay for a gallery bench, but Anne will have none of it: she pays for each of us. We push our way along, past the doorkeeper and into the bright 'O' beyond. Henry bouncing up and down, no matter what Joan does to try and quiet him.

The crowd is an unruly mix, with only beggars and the drunkest fools kept out. While all of London, and of England, may be divided in rank and importance, with attention to each man's smallest difference in wealth or status or the opinion of his peers, here is a place where no one quite knows where he stands – excepting only that he should have a good view of the stage. Court folk and well-bred dandies might dance around each other, puffing pipes and opining on the latest works of Dekker, Middleton and the rest; but they are perilous close to all who seek to fleece them; the knaves and tricksters, cozeners and coney-catching foists. And there are also plenty of the middling folk among them: cheery shoemakers, solid burghers and prentice-boys, daft with youth. The finery of the rich is half-hidden in the crush of sallow kersey, dun coats and rough-sewn jerkins, so that here you might see a flash of bright velvet, there a yellow ruff, so big it blocks the view of those behind, and there again an azure ostrich feather, nodding prettily above the rollicking crowd.

We climb the stairs and reach our place, and I look around me. I had forgotten how grand the inside of a theatre can be. It is like entering a great cathedral before they stripped out the gold and daubed lime over the frescoes, but better, for there is no homily to endure. The main stage, set at the far end of the pit, has vast pillars on each side, painted in a swirling pattern to resemble marble. Above the stage is a canopy held up by two smaller pillars: the Heavens, decorated with the sun and moon and celestial bodies. Gold and scarlet hangings cover the back of the stage, hiding the tiring-house, and green rushes are strewn upon the stage itself. Running out into the pit is a long, narrow walkway, so the actors might dance among the groundlings.

The musicians are already assembling on the balcony, blowing and strumming raggedly. A few young blades are taking their places on the edge of the stage, perched on three-legged stools, as eager to be part of the spectacle as they are to get a good view.

'Well,' says Anne, 'this *is* pleasant. I do so love a play.' She offers me a Seville orange, and I shake my head, nausea beginning to rise up in my throat. 'I don't for the life of me know what ails you,' she says. 'Why are you all on edge?'

'I am not well.'

She peels her orange with her squat white fingers. 'What is the matter?'

'I finished off a mutton pottage last night; perhaps it disagreed with me.'

Just then, something digs into my back. I turn, thinking it must be Henry. 'Keep still, child, can't you?'

But it is not Henry. It is a hunchback dwarf, bent over nearly double, so his head looks as if it is growing out of his chest. He is dressed well, like a prosperous guildsman. And yet this man does not belong to any guild. This is my landlord, Anthony Inchbald.

'Mr Inchbald,' I say. 'Good day to you, I am sure.'

'A pleasure to see you, as always, Mistress Lanyer. I suppose your husband told you I had called?'

'Sadly, no.'

'His mind seemed… occupied elsewhere.'

'I trust your visit was successful?'

He worms his way forward and settles himself next to me on the bench, legs dangling. He looks straight ahead, very calm.

'This will be a fine production,' he says. 'Love, and blood, and tragic death. What more can you ask for from a play?'

'What indeed?' say I.

'Though it's hard enough for a poet to keep pace with nature. I went to the bear garden yesterday. Saw the great beast Harry Hunks kill off four greyhounds, with a few claw-punches and much assurance!'

'Oh, sir!' says Henry, staring at Inchbald, wide-eyed. 'What joy!'

'One landed in the lap of the lady next to me, with two legs missing,' says Inchbald.

'By Our Lady! There could be nothing finer,' says Henry. 'I wish I could go. Mother keeps me from everything, I may as well live in a dog kennel for all the sport I see.'

'And there were rockets and fireworks, and hungry vagrants fighting for some bread and apples, and it all ended with an ape on horseback.'

'What are words compared to that?' I say, avoiding his gaze and staring into the crowd below, where I can see two cutpurses jostling their prey. One stuffs a purse into his doublet even as I watch.

Inchbald squints round at me. 'There was no success to be had.'

'At the bear pit?'

'At your house in Long Ditch.'

'I am sorry for that.'

He smiles. His two teeth are like twin pegs on a line. 'Nothing, in short, to be had at all. The cupboard, in a phrase, was bare. And yet you have the money for the Globe! I admire this, for I share your passion. A woman who would sooner be homeless than miss the latest offering from the Lord Chamberlain's Men. This I must applaud, even as I call the bailiffs to your door.'

'She is my guest, Mr Inchbald,' says Anne, leaning over me in a flurry of importance. Her house, too, belongs to him. 'We are all good friends here this afternoon. Your business can wait for another day.' She pats him playfully on the wrist. I am surprised she can bear to touch him.

'We have no business,' I say.

'Oh, I think we have,' says Inchbald. 'As long as I have your house, then we have business.'

'Ask my husband; he will pay you.'

'Your husband has air for brains. And his promises are worth less than a strumpet's virtue.'

'If he pays you, then who cares about his useless promises?'

'He has paid me nothing but promises all year.'

I look away, my face hot. What has my husband been up to now? Alfonso does not earn much, but it is enough to pay our rent. As long as he doesn't spend it first. But he can be trusted with nothing. I am like a widow with two sons, not a wife with one child. Lucky I keep a stash of Hunsdon's gold hid from him, to insure me against the debtors' clink.

'What can I give you? I have no money of my own. All I have is the idea for a pamphlet.'

'Words pay no debts. Give me deeds, Mistress Lanyer, give me money.'

'It's about the subjugation of Eve.'

'Hardly a subject to keep a roof over your head!'

'I also have a poem, a ballad, in the voice of Mary Magdalene.'

'Who will buy a ballad by a woman? I am as likely to purchase the tale of a tortoise, or the confessions of a crow.'

'Hush!' says Anne. 'The play is starting!'

Just as the trumpets and hautboys call us to order, there is a commotion in the pit. A fight seems to have broken out, somewhere near the stage.

I peer down, trying to get a better look. 'What's going on?'

'Some kind of disorder,' says Anne, standing up and shading her eyes with her hand.

'It's that freak Moll Cutpurse,' says Inchbald. 'They should lock her up for lewdness.'

There's a loud shriek, laughter, and then a figure seems to surge up out of the assembled mass, like a homunculus emerging from the mud. A young man is lifted on to the stage.

'Moll? A Molly-boy, from the stews?'

'A woman, if you can call it that,' says Inchbald. 'A blot on nature.'

137

The figure is sitting crookedly upon the boards, flat upon its arse with its legs splayed wide, face hidden by a wide-brimmed hat. Someone is calling from the crowd.

'A song, Moll Cutpurse! Give us one of your sweet songs!'

'An air, a dainty air to set the scene!' yells another voice. One of the law students on the stage gets up and gives her something. It is a lute. At the back of the stage I see a Fool, arms folded, laughing.

'Who's that?' I whisper to Anne.

'Robert Armin,' she says. 'Now, *he's* a saucy fellow!'

Moll Cutpurse sets the lute down with deliberation, then struggles, with great difficulty, to her feet. She throws down her hat and picks up the lute. She has a round, peasant face, and a huge red mouth, so that she is clown-like even without paint. Her hair is cut short like a boy's. In spite of this, and in spite of her doublet and breeches, there is something in the set of her shoulders and her way of strumming the lute which is pleasing. She bows, very low, as if she has already concluded a great performance. The audience claps and cheers. Some oranges are thrown on to the stage. She picks up two of these, and puts them in her shirt.

'You are most kindly, ladies, boys and men,' she shouts, bowing again. 'I shall repay this richness with some little ditty which I have made, adapted from thin air and the drunkish songs of bawds. If you are of a fribbling, foul-faced disposition, then close your ears. If not, kindly open them.'

'What else will you have us open, Moll?' shouts someone.

'Your purses, sir,' she calls back. 'Pull 'em back widely, at the lip.'

'Have you a sword, to entertain us?'

'No, sir, but poke me with yours and you'll get a shock.'

'I'll poke you any time!'

'Then you are in for fine sport. For I'm more wit-worm than wanton.'

Lots of screeching and guffawing at this.

'A wanton worm!'
'A worming wanton!'
'Wriggle-me-ree, Moll!'
'Wriggle with me!'
Then the shout goes up: 'A song, a song! Let's hear the bashful lady's song!' So she begins to sing, in a strong voice:

'There were three drunken maidens
Come from the Isle of Whyte
They drank from Sunday morning
Didn't stop till Saturday night.'

Another bow, and she begins to play her lute, not badly, though the notes do have a habit of sliddering around the tune. And then she goes on with her pretty ditty:

'When Saturday night did come, me boys,
They wouldn't then go out
These three drunken maidens
They pushed the jug about.'

Many people in the audience seem to know the words quite well, for there is much singing along and waving of caps. The song becomes a great roar:

'There's forty quarts of beer, me boys
They fairly drunk them out
These three drunken maidens
They fetched their sweet dugs out!'

Wild laughter and hooting follows, and coins shower on to the stage as well as oranges. Moll scoops these up quick: I see that she is not too drunk to forget her business, nor to sing while she gathers up her fee.

'O where are your feathered hats
Your mantles rich and fine?
They've all been swallowed up
In tankards of good wine.'

Now, the crowd goes quiet again, and Moll sings sweetly, seeming to have got her voice properly now, and she sounds like a perfect angel, sitting on a heavenly cloud:

'And where are your maidenheads
You maidens brisk and gay?
We left them in the ale house
We drank them clean away.'

Here is Armin, strutting his way along the walkway, smiling this way and that, his feet beating like drumsticks on the boards. He whirls Moll round, arm in arm, faster and faster, dancing around like a shittle-cock, till finally she flies off the stage and falls back into the crowd, roaring as she goes. (Though whether in sport or anger I can't tell.) So many arms are raised to catch her that she falls upon a feather bed of groundlings. She marches away, still singing. I watch her go, wondering if she is the first free woman I have seen in all my life.

The play begins. It is called *Othello, the Moor of Venice*. It is the worst and most lamentable tale, which makes you want to climb up on the stage and bang the players' heads together to set them straight. Othello, all talk and no sense, has the music of the language but no understanding of its hidden meanings. He chooses his wife wisely: she is a good and virtuous woman. (Though not sharp enough to keep her man in order.) His deputy, Iago, is recruited from the gates of Hell, being more or less a devil. Othello seems proud, but does not love himself well enough to trust his wife, and so he kills her. Murders her flat-out, in her nightgown. The thing he loves above all else, more than himself.

Well! There is no need. He is a Blackamoor, so it's a play to set the talk going, and he is mad in love with his fair wife. Could such a man exist? He is not half-beast, but demi-god. And his words have more tune in them than the oboes, lutes and viols that play between the acts. I know it is only Burbage who marches upon the stage, his face blacked, his voice mellifluous. But I believe he is the Moor. Then, my breath leaves me.

On to the stage comes bold Aemilia, serving maid to Desdemona, wife to Iago. Anne clutches my hand. 'Oh, Tom! The naughty baggage!' she says. Her boy is beautiful in his vivid scarlet dress (there is one of exactly that colour, hid away in my chamber in a cedar chest). His wig is black as a raven's wing, corkscrew-curled like Medusa's. (I touch my own black hair, as if to check it is not stolen.) He turns to Iago, hands on hips, saucy with indignation. I know enough of myself to know this is my own manner. He is an actor all right, this pretty boy! No wonder the company was so eager to take him on.

'He's good,' I hiss to Anne. But her hand is clutched over her mouth in disbelief.

Now Tom speaks, in his soft girl's voice.

'But jealous souls shall not be answered so;
They are not ever jealous for the cause,
But jealous for they art jealous; 'tis a monster
Begot upon itself, born on itself.'

My skin goes cold. Oh, Will, what treachery, that you would not believe me when I told you what was true! Your fine earl forced me; your jealousy was the making of your mind. *'Begot upon itself, born on itself.'* I had not put it quite so well, but the scene burns in my head. Wriothesley kissing me, seeking my screaming mouth and kissing me again, wet and slippy as a prentice-boy. How he grunted as he pushed his fat cock up inside me, and shrieked in ecstasy as he bounced and grafted.

The play holds us all; we are in its time and place, Othello is a grand fool, and his fear will be the finish of him. Aemilia, for all her spirit, will not save her mistress. And these words, too, are taken from the life.

'Why should he call her whore? Who keeps her company?
What place? What time? What form? What likelihood?'

In this play, it is the honour of the virtuous Desdemona that these lines defend. In reality, it was my own honour I sought to protect against the spite and jealousy of the poet himself, using, if not these very words, then something very like them. Will has retold another tale, it seems, as well as some old story by Cinthio.

The play is over. Desdemona, who was dead upon her bed, now parades before us in her white robes, hand in hand with Tom / Aemilia. We all stand to shout and cheer. Anne weeps. Joan grins – a rare sight, this. Inchbald dangles over the rail, waving his playbill, so fiercely that I think he'll fall and do us all a favour. And Henry whoops and yells, as if he were at the bear pit, dancing on the spot. Love, and blood, and tragic death. There is nothing like it.

'Oh, Mother,' he cries, 'what a miserable end! Can we see it again?'

'Once is enough,' I say. 'Wait till a new play comes; it won't be long.'

'And shall you bring me then?'

'I don't know. Perhaps Alfonso will come with you next time.'

'And shall we go to the tiring-house now, and see Tom?'

'It's no place for women,' says Anne.

'Or children,' says Joan. 'Unless they are players.'

'It's time to go,' say I, and, true to form, he's gone. 'Henry!' we cry, but off he runs, down the wooden stairs, nearly tripping an eel-man in his flight.

Inchbald, still leaning dangerously far over the balcony, says, 'There he goes, the young demon. Straight for the stage. Do you never think to beat him, Mistress Lanyer?'

I take no notice, but hurry down the stairs in pursuit and rush across the pit, weaving in and out of the boisterous crowd, till I come to the ladder at the foot of the stage.

'Henry!'

I hesitate. I should not, for form's sake, take another step. And yet, I cannot leave my silly son. I begin to climb, ignoring the cat-calls of the prentice-boys who stand behind me, and the shouts of disbelief from other, more respectable members of the crowd. At the top of the ladder, I look around. The people, down below, seem like one mass of watching faces. The pillars rise up on each side of me, like the gateway to Old Rome. In front of me, just a short distance across the stage, is the gold and crimson curtain of the tiring-house. A small foot – that of my son – disappears behind it.

'Henry, I shall whip you for this!'

More cheering. I can't go back; I must go on. I run across the stage, to escape those watching eyes as quick as I can. I hold my breath, screw up my courage, open the curtain and step inside.

Such a whirl of legs and arms and spinning bodies I never saw. All the cast are still in costume, and wearing the black masks of Court ladies. They are leaping and laughing, cloaks flying, skirts lifting, so I could not say how many there are, or who is who, except for Burbage, with his smudged and blackened face, and Desdemona, now wigless, in his gown. Stepping forward, hoping for a sight of Henry or Tom, I cast my eye around at the properties: there are banners and pikes propped against one wall;

before them, baskets and a coffin; beyond these, a table laden with books and platters and severed heads. But then my arm is caught and I am pulled into the middle of the spinning dance.

'Ho, mistress, step lively,' says one player, taking me by the waist.

'Fine ladies find themselves in strange places,' says another, spinning me round and passing me to his neighbour.

'No lady this – she's nearly as dark as the Moor,' says a third, turning me on my heels so I face yet another dancer. It's Burbage, the Moor himself.

'Aemilia, forgive us!' But he is laughing too, with an ale pottle in one hand. 'Nothing more sweetly comical than what's appalling, cruel and tragical. Oh, that poor, misbegotten Moor!'

'My son is here, hiding among – '

Then he is gone, too, so that I hardly have time to feel surprise that he recognised me after all these years. I am at the centre of a blurring circle, like the pole in May. I'm grasped once more, pulled through the crowd, the room dark and fast all round me, all men and boys, disguise and chaos. Then, suddenly, there is a voice in my ear. A breath on my neck.

'God's blood, I thought it must be you! Mistress Alfonso Lanyer, I can scarce believe it. What do you mean by coming here? I thought you loathed us players.'

I close my eyes. The sound of the players fades, seems to come from faraway. *He* is here. I knew he would be, but am still sick to hear his voice again.

I swallow, my eyes still shut. If I don't look at him, then perhaps I will be safe.

'I'm not here to see the players, sir.'

'Not the playwright, surely?'

Opening my eyes, I turn to face him. For an instant he is a stranger, and I see him as I would if I had never known him. A pale fellow, no longer young, but with an air of urgency about him. The instant passes, and I know him, as I know no one except myself. Deep, shadowed eyes, searching my face with an expression that is caught between laughter and rage. A twist to his lips that makes me wonder who still kisses them. The years have broadened him and lined his face, but he is proud and handsome, more so than in his youth. I had hoped to find him shiny-bald and run to fat. But he is Will, the Will I have loved, and more himself than ever.

I gird myself. 'Mr Shakespeare.'

He bows.

'I'm – I have no wish to be here.'

'And I have no wish to see you here.' He smiles with stately cordiality.

'My boy is hiding here, with your Desdemona.'

His mouth tightens. 'Oh... *your* son, is he? I saw a silly knave with Tom.'

'He *is* a silly knave, but I love him dearly.'

'Your son,' he says. 'I often...'

'What?'

'My own boy is dead.' He looks away, frowning. 'Hamnet.'

'Oh – the poor child! I'm sorry for your loss.'

'Yes.' Now he is examining his wrist, as if he had some lines wrote on it. 'My wife... They sent a letter, but he was buried by the time I got to Stratford. There was heavy rain and... the way was hard.'

'I didn't know...' Will still smells of ink, I notice, as a butcher smells of blood. 'God bless his soul.'

'He was eleven.'

'Henry is nearly ten. I mean... I would die if anything...'

'Of course,' he says. Then, 'Henry. Ha!'

Our eyes meet, then jerk away.

Will reaches out, and touches my shoulder with his finger as if he's making sure I'm solid flesh. I feel a breath of longing, as if a ghost had stroked the skin between my thighs.

I brush his hand away.

'Do not dare to touch me. I am sorry for poor Hamnet, but don't imagine that I will ever forget your foul words and accusations.'

He withdraws his hand. 'Your kind words about my son don't absolve you of your guilt.'

'My *guilt*?'

'You are a faithless whore.'

'There's not enough gold in all of Cheapside to make me *your* whore for a single night.'

He laughs. 'Who said I'd pay a farthing? You're not such a tasty morsel now, mistress. I can feast nightly on a prettier dish.'

I think, *He loathes me. I am repulsive to him. So be it, so be it; I shall not set eyes on him again.* Standing straighter, I look him in the eye. 'Oh, surely. The anointed sovereign of sighs and groans. What fortunate young women, to be sweated over by a lewd old versifier like yourself.'

'Fortunate indeed. I see your mind is still sharp, even if your eyes are growing dull.'

Over his shoulder, I can see the actors parading about the tiring-room, doing a mock pavane. I must find Henry, and be gone.

'You are too arrogant, sir. Putting yourself above me with your cruel words. You think that honest folk are like players, running to and fro at the command of your invention? No. We are living beings, closer to angels than your shouting, painted shams.'

'Honest? A bawd like you is honest? Most entertaining! Now you are after Armin's job: you aim to be a clown…'

'Yes, sir. Honest now, and honest since you have known me. A woman may not be a jester, but a poet may be a fool.'

'I saw what I saw. You were false to me!'

'You *saw* me with Wriothesley. But you are all eyes and no sight. No matter – it's nothing to me now. And you have more than paid me back, sir, with your wicked, poisonous lines. You turned your pain to wormwood poetry, and set every fibre of your genius to the task of breaking my heart!'

A shout goes up as John Heminge comes in with flagons of ale, followed by two boy players carrying trenchers loaded with fried collops, scented with frizzled fat, together with rabbit, humble pie, flat round manchets and other nunchions and snacks.

'Let us celebrate!' cries Burbage. He turns, and there's Tom, in his scarlet, and next to him I see my own son at last, who had slyly hid himself in the middle of the dancing men. Burbage waits till everyone has gathered round him, and quietened, and filled their cups. I stand quite still, hoping that, if I don't look at Will, he'll vanish into the crowd.

'This is a proud day for all of us, we merry Lord Chamberlain's Men, for we have two new triumphs to celebrate.' The whites of Burbage's eyes flash in his black face, which is streaked with dancing-sweat. 'We are, being players, part of one greater whole, with no leader, no prince to quell us, nor cunning-man to muddle us. We are brothers, and the success of one is the success of all.' I see that he is close to tears with the beauty of it.

Another speaker, smooth and cocksure. 'We are all as wise and foolish as each other, and in that lies our infinite wisdom. Till we reach the end of it.' It's Robert Armin. There is laughter, then silence. Everyone is waiting to hear what Burbage, the leader who would not be leader, will say next.

'First, we must celebrate our dear friend Will, and his new play, which is as sad and stately as we could wish. And which cannot fail.'

Hoots and laughter. 'Put money in thy purse!' calls someone.

'Most poetical and bloody,' cries Armin. 'The Blackamoor will get us gold.'

'And second – we have a new man among us, a beardless boy, but one who gave us a performance tonight that shows he is surely one of us. Tom Flood, you were a fine Aemilia!' There are more cheers, and someone makes Tom stand upon a stool. He takes off his wig, and twists it in his hands, and bows in mock-ceremony. His face is pink, his dark curls fall into his eyes.

'Speech!' calls Will, beside me, and I catch his eye, and am stabbed right through. It is the strangest feeling. I know him from my own mirror. Each time my face has looked out, it was Will I saw there. And now I look at him and see my own face in the glass.

I have to leave. I turn and make my way through the laughter and shouting, and Tom beginning to say something, and being drowned out by his fellow players. I find Henry, and clench my hand firmly around his arm.

'We are off,' I tell him. 'And for once you will be beaten raw for this.'

But Will stands before me when we reach the door. His eyes flash from me, to Henry, then back again.

'An entrance is an entrance, and so a turn must follow,' he says. 'You have a part to play, now you have returned.' His shirt is undone beneath his doublet; the dark hairs of his chest are caught in a thick gold chain. He did not have this chain when last I touched that hidden skin. Who touches him now? The Stratford housewife? A pert mistress, peachier than me? I hear a voice: *You are mine, mine. You are me. We are joined, for good or ill.* Did someone speak? I am sick and giddy.

'Goodbye, Will. This is your world, your "stage". These are your people. Make your riddles, strut your words – none of this can interest me.' I have my arm round Henry, who is squirming to break free.

'It is not finished,' Will says. His eyes seem to deepen. 'You know that, just as I do.'

'What is not?' asks Henry.

'The ale,' I say. 'They've not yet drunk the ale.'

Scene V

When we get home, Alfonso is out. I wait till Henry is asleep, then I go to my chamber and lock the door. With a great effort, I push the bed aside, then scrabble back the rushes. There is a loose board beneath. I lift it up, and thrust my hand into the dusty floor-space. There it is. A bulging leather pouch. I pull it out. This is where I keep the gold coins left over from my dowry. Hidden from my spouse, of course, who cannot be trusted with three farthings.

Spreading my skirts, I tip the contents into my lap. Yet what is this? The flat shapes that tumble out lie heavy on my skirts. But they are grey stones, pebbles from the river shore. Where is my cherished hoard of gold and silver? Where is my money? I feel inside the bag again. Empty. I shake out my skirts, letting the stones roll among the rushes, and plunge my arm inside the hole once more. All I find is a dried-up spider, in a winding sheet of its own legs, and a tiny, shrivelled mouse.

Then I think – perhaps the coins have fallen out? Perhaps they are hidden in the dust and scrimmage. I go downstairs, and fetch a fish-hammer and a candle. I take up another floorboard, panting as I work at the rusty iron nails. Then another, ripping it with my hands, tearing my fingers on the splintered wood. Blood drips on to my clothes. I smear the sweat off my face, light the candle and lower it into the floor-space. The flickering light reveals only dirt and floor-beams. The space is empty. But no! There, in the far corner. A small shape... I extend my arm, groping till I feel something with the tips of my fingers. I reach further, another inch, grasp it and pull it out.

It is a tiny pewter box, round and smooth. I prise open the lid and tip it up. Nine little dice fall into the palm of my hand. There must be a good reason why they have been hidden away so carefully. I examine them one by one. They are cheats' dice. Three are marked only with low numbers, three with high numbers, and three are weighted so they will fall the same way every time. They must belong to my husband. He has found my stash of money and gambled it away. But Alfonso is not just a fool, he is a trickster too. Not only has he lost my money, he has tried to swindle others out of theirs. Of course he is too stupid to succeed in such an enterprise. If he were any use as a cozener, he would have more than a bag of river stones to show for his dishonesty.

I sit hunched on the floor, not caring for my spoiled dress, thinking. I stare at the feeble candle-flame, the little light it throws on my little life. I see myself as I once was, listening as Lord Hunsdon talked, and, as the years went by, talking as he listened. He told me only the Queen had a better head for affairs of state than me. And that my Latin was a match for hers. He said I could have been an Oxford man, if I had been a man at all. And then he built me this boxed-in house and set me up with an addle-pate of a spouse.

It is true that Alfonso was pleased to have me, even though I was pregnant with another man's child. He saw that he was getting a handsome bargain. I would not have been kept so long by Hunsdon if I did not have a pretty face and a whore's skill in the bedchamber, and I came with a good dowry. He saw in me a lifetime of good fucking, and at least a year of good spending. And truth to tell, this is exactly what he got. To his credit, there is not an ounce of malice in the man, and he loves Henry as if he were his own child. In fact, such is his ability to see only what doesn't cause him pain, I believe he's come to feel that Henry is his natural son. So he is happy.

Only my poetry makes him angry. Property does not write poems. Property sits at home and puts her skill to churning butter. He seems to think my writing not only unwomanly, but also sacrilegious. 'What monstrous thing is this!' he cries, when he finds me scratching out a verse or scrawling down some passing thought. 'Play your virginals, if you want to show us how clever you are! Leave the words to the wits. God preserve us, get some food before me!' I hide my precious pages in the straw mattress, in case he throws them on the fire.

This is my lot. Wrong sex, wrong lovers, wrong place. The universe is neat as an egg, the layers held like white and yolk within its shell. I am neither white nor yolk, fish nor fowl. And now – what is my line of business now? If I could crawl into that hole, wrap myself in a death-caul like the shrunken spider and never be thought of again, I would do so.

But there is a cry from Henry's room. I put the dice-box in my pocket, unlock my door and hurry to his bedside.

He hugs me, as if he were still an infant. 'Mother!' he says. 'I dreamed that you were dead!'

I smooth his hair. He smells of smoke and sugar.

'My little one.' I kiss his cheek. 'Never fear. I'm not dead yet.'

'Nor me,' says Henry. He pulls away, wipes his eyes and looks at me. 'We shan't die for a while longer, either, shall we? God doesn't need us yet.'

'No, He doesn't.'

'And I am very sorry.'

'For what?' I have almost forgotten his flight to the tiring-room.

'For – all my bad ways.'

'You are just a boy, Henry.' I touch his cheek.

'I will stop all my running away.'

'Yes.'

'God would like that,' he says, sagely.

'Yes. You would make God very happy.'

I draw the counterpane tight around him before I close the curtains, making him a little tent, all snug.

By the time Alfonso comes home, it is midnight, and the trumpets have long since sounded the curfew at the City walls. I'm sitting outside the house, wrapped in a woollen cloak. It is a clear, chilly night and the crescent moon is an arc of silver, brighter than my missing coin. Alfonso is tottering and singing to himself, his recorder slung over his shoulders in its carrying case. I know the tune; it was composed by my uncle, Robert Johnson: 'The Witch's Dance', a favourite at Court. My husband comes slowly, slowly, weaving this way and that, whistling and humming and laughing, at one point almost falling in the town-ditch, at another sitting on the ground for several moments, tracing his own palm-lines in the moonlight.

When he sees me, he seems to be delighted, and not in the least surprised to find me waiting in the street.

'Aemilia!' he calls. 'Lady Aemilia! I am blessed in my work, yet even more so in my spouse.' He comes up and pulls me to my feet. 'Oh, wife! *Houses and riches are the inheritance of the fathers, but a prudent wife is from the Lord.*'

Alfonso is not devout by nature, and loves God most when he's in his cups. 'You have been at the Malmsey again, I see.'

'*May thy fountain be blessed, and rejoice with the wife of thy youth*!' he declaims, squeezing me tightly.

'Leave me be, husband.'

'*Let her breasts satisfy thee at all times and be thou ravished always with her love.*' He tries to land a kiss upon my lips, but I twist my head away and he slobbers on the doorpost instead. '*And why wilt thou, my son, be ravished with a strange woman, and embrace the bosom of a stranger.* Oh, woe is me!' He stares up adoringly at the door lintel.

'What have you done with it?' I ask, pushing him away.

'With what?' He turns, unsteadily, and puts one hand out to balance himself against the wall. 'Always questions, questions. Such a liveliness of mind. It doesn't augur well, my chuck. You should do more spinning.'

'My *money*, Alfonso. Where is my money? Did you lose it at the tables?'

'You have money?'

'Not any more.'

'Then how am I to blame for taking it?'

I grab him by the shoulders and shake him hard. 'Are you really so dull and brain-sickly? I *had* money, and now it is gone. Now all that remains is a pewter pot of tricksters' dice!'

'What are you saying?'

'That you are the cozener of your own wife and child, you worthless piece of scum!'

'Worthless... what? I know nothing of it.'

Disgusted, I begin pacing to and fro, too angry to keep still. 'What's more, I saw Inchbald today – or yesterday, I should rather say.'

'Oh! How is the dainty little fellow? Did you wish him well from me?'

'He told me we've paid no rent this year.'

'God's blood! The thieving scoundrel...'

'He'll be round tomorrow to collect what's his. Or else he'll take the house back.'

Alfonso closes his eyes as if making a difficult calculation. 'Hmm. Now, what *was* the problem with friend Inchbald...? Perhaps there was a misunderstanding in our transaction. A tenacious fellow, we must give him that.'

I thrust my face close to his, ignoring his filthy tavern stench.

'Husband.'

'Yes?'

'Are you not ashamed?'

'Ashamed?'

'Are you not a *man*?'

'I do all a man can do! Who would do more is none!'

'More? Who could do *less*?' I tear at my hair. 'Lord God! Help me! I am like an anchorite, walled in to pray and meet my doom!'

'Mistress Lanyer, you are raving!'

'Raving? The madness is that I walk about quite calmly, knowing I am done for! I will be a pauper, thrust upon the parish! I will end my days in public view, a starving creature locked into a cage!'

Alfonso, pale already from strong drink, takes himself a shade whiter. 'Calm yourself, wife. Show some respect.'

'Respect! I may have to kill you.'

'You forget, I went off to the Azores with Ralegh and poor Essex.'

'And so did many others. You are meant to be a courtier, after all. The task was to make a name for yourself and seek preferment. Though, in your case, hope was set too high.'

'I almost drowned. Your vaunting ambition will be the death of me.'

'But you *lived*. More's the pity. When I think of all the honest, proper men who go to their graves each day, while you continue with your doltish prancing.'

'I was shot through the shirt – and scared out of my wits.'

'The Queen should never have agreed to send you with them, you brought such evil luck. When they went the first time, without you, their ships came back loaded down with gold. But what *your* great expedition brought back was half a chest of bullion. And the Spanish all but landed at Penzance.'

His shoulders sag.

'I tried. Strived.' He frowns at the word, seemingly drunk enough to wonder if this is French. 'I *strove*. Wanted to be made a knight, but only four were chosen.'

'You are a worm, Alfonso. A liar, a boil, a plague sore and a turd.'

'I am a *musician*. It's my vocation...' His eyes swivel. 'My art, my heart... A musician can't be called to order...'

'To order? What are you talking about? All you had to do was pay the rent.'

'Which is what I wanted. What they said they could do. They said I would win a crock of gold worth twenty times your little hoard...'

'Who said?'

'The women.'

'*Women*?'

'The three women with the magic dice.'

'Save us! You think those dice have magic in them? You can buy them anywhere. They surely took you for the stupidest gull they ever saw.'

'It seemed likely enough to me. They are from Persia. I thought, since I had lost some gold, I had better win it back for you.'

I roll my eyes. Then a thought strikes me. 'Three women? What manner of women?'

'Just – women. Of the common sort.'

'Old or young?'

'Both – a mixture.'

My heart beats harder. 'But one was young and fair. Was she not? With yellow hair and white skin?' I see her, clear as I see Alfonso, standing behind her rampart of evil sugar-plums.

He frowns again, pulls his recorder out, and is about to put it to his lips.

I snatch it from him. 'Alfonso! What did she look like?'

'I can't recall.'

'Where did you see them?'

His eyes are closing, and I shake his shoulder. 'Where did you see them?'

He thinks for a moment. 'Tyburn. Yes, most delightful spot. They told me they had business there.' He closes his eyes, and recites, '*Who can find a virtuous woman? For her price is far above rubies.*' Then he tips gently sideways and falls asleep at an angle, like the fallen stone of a Roman archway. I take the recorder inside for safe keeping and leave him there, locking the door behind me. If the Lord is willing, my sotted spouse will roll into the ditch and drown in piss and offal before dawn.

I sit at the kitchen table, still wrapped in my cloak. The night deepens, the shadows fill the house and my cheap candle gutters as the tallow trickles down the shaft. But my thoughts and fears grow wild in the darkness. There is witchcraft behind all this. Something wicked stalks me. I must face down this dark magic with magic of my own.

Some women in my sorry state might sell their bodies. There are those who'd say my life with Hunsdon was a whore's contract, so I have only a short distance to fall. But there is a world between having a royal protector and being humped by stinking tavern scum. I still have my wits, undimmed by time. I'm not done yet.

Scene *VI*

It is a bright September morning. Joan is mending an old smock of Henry's, head bent over her stitching. The needle flashes in and out of the dark fabric as she works, so fast that I can hardly see it.

She doesn't look up, but says, 'He lost it, didn't he?'

'Lost what?'

'Your money.'

I break off some bread. I am used to her strange way of knowing more than she should. Sometimes it annoys me, sometimes it alarms me. Today, I just feel tired.

'Is *all* my business your business?' I ask, sitting down next to her. 'Are *all* my affairs of your concern?'

'I live here, don't I, mistress? Those that have eyes to see know what is all around them.'

'Yes.' I chew in silence for a while. 'But some of us see more than others.'

'Sure enough,' says Joan, biting off the thread.

'Joan...'

'Mistress?'

'I need your help.'

'You've had my help these last nine years and more. And I don't begrudge it.'

'I know. I could not ask for a better servant.' I swallow the last bit of crust and shake the crumbs from my skirt. 'This art of yours... this knowledge. Of herbs and remedies and... spells. How did you come by it?'

She looks at me, her green eyes bright in her lined face. 'I learned it. From my mother, and she learned it from hers. It's a trade, of sorts, the business of an apothecary.'

'And yet you know more than most, don't you?'

'How can I tell what's in their minds? I only know what's in my own.' She returns to her stitching.

'Could you teach it to me?'

She continues sewing, smiling as she works. 'Teach! As if it were the cross-stitch?'

'Could I *learn* this skill?'

Her needle stops in mid-air.

'What for?'

'I am afraid. We have no money – as you guessed – and Inchbald owns this house. Alfonso wastes most of his wages at the tables – we are all but on the street. And…'

'And?' She looks at me again.

'The women at the Fair – there was something wrong. You said so yourself. Something evil in them.'

'And then they gave master the trickster's dice.'

I stare. 'Were you listening to us?'

She gazes back, unabashed. 'Only in my sleep.' Putting her sewing to one side, she shrugs. 'What I can teach you, mistress, is knowledge of herbs and simples and suchlike. Some cures and some small ways to help yourself, and others. So you can ward off harm.'

'What about a small hex, here and there?'

She smiles. 'Who would you hex?'

'I don't know. Someone who deserved it.'

'I'll try my best for you, mistress. But you know I would do all of this for you. There's no need to trouble yourself with it.'

'But I want to know myself. I want to understand.'

'I know you do, mistress.' She touches my arm. 'Be wary. And be patient. Do what I tell you, and no more. In this, I am the mistress, and you are my apprentice. You are asking a great deal from me.' She gives me one of her narrow looks. 'That pamphlet Forman gave you – did you read it?'

'*The Hammer of Witches*?' There is no point asking how she knows of this, for she seems to have a better idea of my business than I do myself.

'You should read it. There are degrees in witchcraft, as in all things. First there is the wise woman, who knows of the lore that the Old Religion used to its own ends. Now that's all gone, and, as the new faith takes hold, more of us will suffer, I've no doubt of it. The next degree is occupied by Dr Forman and his like. They think experiments will help throw light on mystery, and who's to say – maybe they will? But the highest – and the lowest – form of witchcraft lies in wait for wise women and cunning-men alike. And that is the fatal knowledge that is possessed only by Satan and his familiars. This is a challenge to God, and will cost each man or woman who tries it their immortal soul. The spell those women put on you was of that order, in my opinion.'

I read this *Hammer* and think about this bolting-hutch of beastliness that is our world. Men hobble noble ladies with skirts and bind them with pearls. They snaffle scolds with bitch-bridles. They buy pretty maids for their bedchamber, from their fathers, or off the street. But those of us with nothing but our brains to keep us fare worst of all, as if the power to think was elvish-marked. Men will drown us and flay us; they will brand us and hang us; they will hound us from the light till we are the quintessence of dust. I read this book, and I think of this writer in his fine study, with the fire burning and his quill sharpened, his words scraping into the paper, into our souls. I think to myself, I am no man. But I can wield a pen. And I can learn to wield it well.

There are only four places in the whole of Europe that have become great cities. Venice, city of water and wonders. Constantinople, the gateway to the Orient. Paris, pride of France.

And London. In my own lifetime the City has grown, with tall new houses springing up, old ones split into different dwellings so that as many as a dozen families can live in a place designed for one. Outside the walls, and beyond the powers of City aldermen, builders and carpenters are free to do as they please. New buildings go up in unplanned confusion with no thought to how they fit in with what was there before. Haphazard houses block old thoroughfares, so there is no longer a way through. And side-streets shrink to rat-runs, too narrow for a full-grown man to pass. There are Roman ruins and pagan pillars; collapsed nunneries open to the sky; great mansions converted to spewing tenements; and newer, wooden houses, sprouting overnight. It is as if someone once planted the seed of a timber frame: a miller's son, let's say, in a fireside tale. The seed grew first to a house, and then a street, all neat and handsome, with windows well-set. But then, as trees sprout fungus, these streets gave forth their progeny. New rooms and chambers burgeoned forth. Little alleyways and cat-creeps were burrowed open, and dormer rooms grew upon the rooftops, like the sluttish baskets wove by nesting storks. (I knew a man who lived for six years in the belfry at St Margaret Lothbury. He was cast out only when they had to use the room for storing coal.) All is chaos, madness and clutter. Shouts and whistles, songs and ballads. French and Spanish, German, Russian. The accents of the Midlands, Wales, of Cornwall, York, the Norfolk flats. They are all here, filling the air. Babel is come to Albion.

How, then, shall a 'man' be heard? If the sound of words is drowned out, then let the people read them. Find a printing press, where each letter is placed with neat exactness in a frame, and your lines are blacked down on plain pages, like the Word of God. And if you want to see your thoughts made into books, and sold to Londoners, here, in the centre of the world, go to Paul's Churchyard. There, the dead lie close, in their eternal silence, freshly dug or grinning in the charnel house. And the quick shall make as much noise as we can before we go.

And so I make my way to this place of print and printshops. The sky is pale and piled with cloud. Kites are swooping and woodpigeons perch on the rooftops. I take a wherry as far as Paul's Wharf, holding a clove-stuffed orange to my nose to mask the stench of sewage and pitch. At the wharf, just by Burghley House, the scene of my undoing with Wriothesley, I pay the ferryman and go north between the Doctor's Commons and the College of Arms. It has rained heavily in the night, and the streets are muddy and foul. My pattens slither on the scree of shit from the overflowing ditch.

I cross Carter Lane, a yelling thoroughfare of rattling coaches, lowing cows and quarrelling prentice-boys, and finally reach the churchyard of the great cathedral, a towering Ark above the clustering streets. Our Lord may have thrown the moneylenders from the Temple, but he did not evict the ale-sellers, baker's boys, rooting pigs, pecking chickens, the football games, the beggars or the travelling players. On the left side is a row of houses: laundry flutters above the graves. And to the right, nestling close to the walls of St Paul's, are the open-fronted bookstalls, the object of my pilgrimage.

I am known to all the booksellers. They have all turned down my wares. Some call out as I pass.

'Good day to you, Mistress Lanyer. What is it this time, a pamphlet that says housework is a man's domain?'

'Mistress Lanyer, you are looking well. What do you have there, the secret of immortality?'

'Aemilia, over here! Let's see your fine words. I need a laugh this grey morning!'

'Get you gone!' I shout, over my shoulder. 'If men are so much to be admired and so high regarded in their dominion, how come crops fail, infants die, widows starve and the mad are shouting in the streets?' At that very moment, my eye falls on a Tom o'Bedlam, begging with his little kinchin-mort, a child of five or six years old. Her arms are withered like those of a sickly crone.

The very last stall belongs to Mr Cuthbert Tottle, who specialises in the rare and fancy. You might say he puts himself at the freak-show end of the market. The printing press itself is adapted from a wine press, among other such machines, and his folios and quartos are wine-soaked in their weird vagaries, written in the tradition of the ranting drunk. His religious tracts have the most gruesome woodcuts, such as a Jesuit hanging upside down, with two men sawing him in half between his buttocks. His polemical pamphlets have the rudest words about the Pope. And his pornography is the most salacious, with poses backwards, upside-down and sideways. His bestiaries tell tales of beasts I daresay never lived – the wild boar with a Cyclops head, the Tyger that suckled Dolphins, the mermaid that begat the Queen of Carthage and the Narwhal that swims the frozen oceans of the north, using its magic horn to cut a watery pathway through the ice. I like him for this, and he likes me (I think) for my sharp tongue, and the fact that I'm part-Venetian. His shop is always full of émigrés and refugees, and foreign words and noisy laughter.

Now I have something that I hope will appeal to Mr Tottle, with his love of the peculiar and extreme. It is the tale of Lilith, Adam's first wife. My father used to entertain me with this story when my mother was out of hearing. (She thought that Lilith was too wayward a creature to be the subject of a bedside tale.) Lilith was made from the same mud as Adam, according to old Hebrew lore. She thought herself his equal, so of course he threw her out and God gave him someone more amenable, made from his own rib. And this was Eve, the pliant mother of all mothers, born to take the blame for human sin. What my father did not tell me was that Adam and Lilith were estranged because, when they set to fornication, she refused to lie beneath him, but claimed her right to lie on top. For this, and this alone, she lost her place in Eden, and became a demon blamed for the deaths of newborn babes. (I found all this out many years after, from the Queen's conjurer, John Dee.) So I feel for Lilith, though I fear her name. But will Tottle like this story? We shall see.

I take a breath and walk in. The shop is crowded, as ever, and as ever I am the only woman, save for his wife, who sits silent at the back of the shop, working on a gold-leaf illumination. Tottle himself is a big fellow, jovial and red-cheeked, fond of the alehouse. And yet he drives as hard a bargain as anyone. Even in the throes of boisterous laughter, his eyes are watchful.

A group of Frenchmen haggle with him over a barrel of new books. Two law students, one tall and dark, the other squat and ginger, peruse a squalid chap-book with great interest. Tottle is pouring wine for the students, while refusing to give the Frenchmen a better price for their book-barrel. But when he sees me he sets the bottle down and hurries over.

'Mistress Lanyer!' He glances at his wife. 'The lady poet! Is this good news? Do you have new words for me? Something I can sell this time?'

'I hope so,' I say, taking his offered hand. 'I need to keep a roof over my head.'

He laughs as though this were a very good joke. 'Oh, you ladies! All the same! If you can't get starch for the latest Parisian ruff, you think yourself paupers.'

'You mistake my station, Mr Tottle. I wish that you were right.'

'Let us see, then, what you have.'

He brings a seat for me, and pours out a glass of wine. I give him my pages, and he reads them, smiling all the while. Occasionally he gives a little chuckle, as if especially pleased by some particular word or phrase. When he has finished, he is still smiling. 'Well, well. You certainly have a way about you.' He looks down at my writing, and laughs again. 'Let us see what this assembly makes of this.'

'The Frenchmen?'

'They speak English as well as you or I when they are not affecting Gallic ignorance of Anglo-Saxon prices.' He calls his customers over. 'Gentlemen, pay attention, I have a pamphlet here that you might like to hear. Wife, put your work aside. Listen to this.'

They all turn to hear.

'The title is *The Song of Lilith, first among women.*' He looks up and every one nods. 'A fair title?'

The lawyers shrug. The Frenchmen raise their eyebrows. His wife's eyes are downcast.

'A fair title, then. We are curious, I think. Well, here is a little of the text.

> *'I am that Lilith which Man loves to hate*
> *Night owl, screech-hag, black-eyed Fate.*
> *Before poor Eve was blamed for human sin*
> *I was Adam's wife, grown from mud like him*
> *Commanded to lie beneath, I told him no*
> *I cried the name of GOD, who made me go.*
> *Eve did his will, being born of his own flesh*
> *Till she bit the Fruit of Knowingness...'*

Tottle lowers the pages and beams at me. 'Oh, most fine, most fine! You have an ear for the drama, a gift for polemic.'

'Is this a joke?' says one of the Frenchmen.

'Is it permitted?' asks one of the lawyers.

Tottle smiles, and continues.

> *'Are women evil? Do we walk at night?*
> *A tribe of witches, addled by our spite?*
> *I say we are not, and you do us wrong.*
> *So hear this harlot tale, my siren song*
> *Open your ears to hear the old spun new*
> *Open your eyes to see another view.'*

He looks up again, and the lawyers begin to laugh, and the Frenchmen, seeing it is an English joke, laugh too.

'There is more,' I say, snatching the pages from Tottle. 'This is not the best of it.'

Tottle takes me to one side. 'Indeed, it is not the best of anything. This is not what the public is looking for. Look around you, see what sells!'

'What sells is mostly pap and nonsense.'

'Maybe so, but it is pap and nonsense aptly done. This work... there is no audience for it. It's slip-shod, badly phrased and – I hate to say this, Aemilia, but I speak as an old friend – it's really little more than doggerel. You must find a better subject, and you must improve your mode of expression.'

I hate him then, with his round, soft smile. 'You are making a fool of me.'

'I'm trying to make you more than the author of the unpublishable.'

'I will try another seller, Mr Tottle. I don't need you.'

He bends towards me, confidential. 'You are a woman; we don't expect you to do this well. The wonder is that you do it at all.'

'Go and piss in a puddle.'

'No, look, madam, I am trying to help you. Consider the market. Religion is good, but don't go off on some mad rant. Remember that you need to *entertain* us. Readers like martyrs. Blood. Decapitation. A breaking of the body on the wheel, or a long-drawn-out crushing with stones. This can never fail – what we call a crowd-pleaser. Who dies in your story? Who is disembowelled? Or, if God is not your fancy, histories will always sell. But don't shilly-shally. Skewer the reader with your sword! Find me a gentil knight whose story is untold, a fierce dragon, a brave battle on a field of gore.'

'Boys' twaddle.'

'Oh, come now.'

'This is fine work. Only a man could fail to see it.'

'You have a fanciful nature. This can work in your favour. So give me a tale from far away. A minaret, a monster. A traveller's tale will always catch the eye.'

'A story for a merchant to relate, or some loquacious seaman.'

'Or fashion. Have you an eye for fashion?' He looks at me uncertainly. As usual, I am wearing my old grey dress, embellished only with a ruff that Anne has loaned me. My hair is scraped back under my bonnet, and my cheeks are ruddy from the sun.

I hesitate for a moment, thinking of Anne and her like, and some of the strange outfits that Alfonso insists on wearing when he goes off to play for the Queen. 'Cunning ways with cross-gartering?' I ask.

Tottle clasps my arm. 'Oh, most excellent notion! Can you do a thousand lines on this? New ideas, Venetian styles, the courtly colours? I could pay you two shillings. One shilling now, one shilling when you bring it in.'

On the one hand is poor Eve, downtrodden since the dawn of time. On the other is a month's security, which might be purchased for this sum.

'Done,' I say, holding out my hand.

The dwarf has spies, no doubt, or the gift of second sight. No matter: there he is. Sitting outside the charnel-house, scoffing an apple cake.

'Mistress Lanyer. You have my money?'

'One shilling,' I say. 'A down-payment.'

He chuckles. 'I like a lady with wit. But this is not the bargain.'

I glare at him.

'You are still a fine woman, Mistress Lanyer.'

'And this means – what?'

'It's common knowledge that once you used your face to your advantage. Not to mention your other parts, which I'm sure are quite as sweet. Of course, no courtier would look at you now. But a humble landlord, like myself, might take a sup.'

'What do you want?'

'Some time with you might settle half the debt.'

'Some *time*?'

'These are the terms I have agreed with Mistress Flood: I visit once a month, and she pays me in kind. And very kind she is too, if I may say so.'

He beckons me over. Reluctantly, I draw nearer. He clasps my hand in his dry little paw.

'Yet nobody would call her fair. Her breasts are like sacks of dough halfway down her belly. Yours, I can see through your shift, are still sweetly rounded. Just the shape for sucking.'

I pull my hand away, not sure whether to box his ears or smack his arse. 'You aren't even tall enough to reach them, you lecherous little toad.'

'Two fucks a month would do me nicely. I should look forward to it, which, between ourselves, is more than I do with some of my ladies. With some it's a case of skirts up, cock out, and let's go about our business. But with your good self…' The little turd is ogling me as if he thinks we might go to it right away.

I have to laugh, even though the thought of Anne Flood giving herself to this manikin sickens me. 'Oh, Mr Inchbald! Most lascivious of insects! I would rather die, sir.'

He brushes the crumbs from his beard. 'You take a foolish risk, in speaking to me so rudely. Remember who I am, and who you are. Your grand ways edge you ever closer to the gutter. You are nothing but an ageing whore.'

'A plague on you, Inchbald!' I call after him, as he goes hobbling on his way.

The plague. I wish I could unsay it. Like the Devil's name, it's better not to mention this curse upon our times. And down on the harbour-side the busy ships are disgorging men and cargo from the furthest limits of the fevered globe. The wind picks up, the sky darkens. I feel the first sharp tang of autumn, and pull my cloak tighter around me. I look up, at the chasing clouds, knowing that what seems bleak now will soon look like Paradise.

'*The plague is coming,*' whispers a voice, and I look to see who speaks. But there is no one there. I stop: surely the voice was that of the old crone from the Fair? What do these creatures want, who stalk me with their foul predictions?

When I return home, I seek out *Malleus Maleficarum* and open it. I read till the candle has burned down and the words are scorched into my mind. We women, it seems, have a penchant for devilment, being so lascivious and lustful. A lecherous woman might lie with the Devil and become a witch in consequence. I remember my forced copulation with Wriothesley and Will's poisonous verse: this was how he saw me. '*All witchcraft comes from carnal lust,*' declaims the pamphlet, '*which in women is insatiable.*' And their device for recruiting new witches is to make something go amiss in the life of a respectable matron or young virgin, so that they consult a sorceress, and are tempted into witchcraft in their turn. I think about this for a long time, wondering if those fairground furies might have such a scheme in mind. But I am not like the other matrons, whose skill lies in the churning of butter and the fattening of geese. I am as clever as any man, and as cunning as any witch.

Scene VII

In my opinion, if we are made in God's image, it is God that we see dangling from the gibbet, and it is God's work to end a human life, not Man's. I know I am alone in this thought, as in so many others. But this scruple of mine about the executioner's craft has made any gallows-place a place of horror to me: I have no love for an execution. And there is no gallows-place more horrible than Tyburn Cross. It is a lonely, God-forsaken place, and the winds seem to sweep in from in all directions. The Triple Tree is a large triangular structure that stands upon the northwest road, in the way of passing traffic, so that the carters and horsemen can see what will befall those who break the English law. The ingenuity of its construction is that as many as twenty-four felons may be hanged at once, which is an expedient measure, as there is no shortage of murderers or cutpurses to keep the hangman busy. Beyond the Tree is an open field where soldiers are shot for their misdemeanours: I suppose this is of some benefit to them, as they die with their guts inside them, more or less.

When I was young, not long after I was married, I saw them execute poor Robert Southwell. He was a devout Jesuit, and tried to make the sign of the Cross with his pinioned arms, before quoting Romans: *'For Christ is the end of the law for righteousness to all that believeth.'* They wanted to bowel him alive, as they do all traitors, but Charles Blount and some of the other nobles jumped up and hugged Southwell's legs until his neck broke, to save him that final agony. He died so bravely that after his corpse was bowelled and quartered, and his blood flooded across the highway, the assembled crowd was silent. There were no cheers or catcalls, and no one shouted 'Traitor!' in the customary way. And that silence filled me with a fragile hope for all of us, that we could recognise true goodness and respect it, even as the hangman acted out his ritual butchery in the name of Law.

I think of that day as I walk to Tyburn. It was fitting that Southwell was a Jesuit, for they are often accused of idolatry and witchcraft. Healing relics and icons are part of the Old Religion, but they have no place in the new one, and Catholic priests are sometimes accused of 'Devil-conjuring' among their many other crimes. Devil-conjuring is not a skill I'd take up lightly.

I watch the heavy carts clattering along the centre of the pitted roadway, while parties of horsemen overtake them, trotting briskly. Not many women to be seen today – just one or two ladies riding side-saddle. It's a position both ungainly and undignified, as if riding a horse sensibly is the proper business of a man. Did Diana the Huntress ride all skewed over in her lady's saddle? I think not. For the most part, men ride, while women have nothing better than their own legs to carry them.

It's a pale, sickly afternoon, with a foul wind. I walk slowly, unwilling to arrive. Tyburn is an evil place – they say that Satan walks there, and I can well believe it. As I come nearer, I see there is a row of corpses hanging from the Tree. I do not look close, but notice that one is a woman. The poor creature's breasts are showing through her torn dress. A kite is perched on the Tree, proud and puff-chested, as if displaying its wealth. When I am a few yards away, I stop, looking first one way down the high road and then the other. Black clouds loom overhead and rain begins to fall. I take shelter under an elm tree and watch the travellers passing by. I think of the ships landing at the quayside, and the rats scurrying behind the wainscot, and the stench of the dunghills piled against each common house, and the wrath of

God and a thousand things besides, and wonder which of these is to blame for the plague. God surely has a gift for punishment. We are accustomed to horror and fear, and so Hell is easier to summon in a fresco or imagination than Heaven, a place of obscure cloud and blurred inaction. Job has many brothers (and sisters) in his suffering and pain.

Time passes, and I have the strange sensation of watching it go on its way, in the guise of carriages and horsemen and herds of geese. At last, I see that the road has emptied, and night has snuffed out the feeble sun. All I can hear is the swish of the falling rain. There are no stars, but the moon shines bleakly through the clouds. The silvery light gives the world a shifting luminescence, and most objects are silhouettes. A solitary carriage clatters by me, pennants fluttering. It rounds the corner, heading for Oxford, and disappears from sight. Once more, the road is deserted except for a troop of muddy dogs, sniffing and snapping at each other. Then the leader of the pack – a barrel-bodied mastiff – raises its head, listening. It howls, and runs back along the London road. The other dogs follow, barking fiercely.

Swallowing, I turn my gaze back towards the Tyburn Tree. Five of the corpses still dangle against the wet sky. But the sixth – the woman – is lying on the ground, beneath a severed rope. Three figures are crouching over her. One of them is sawing at her neck with a long knife. I gather myself and begin to walk slowly towards them. As I approach, I feel the air thicken around me, and the sounds of voices come through the rain's hiss, as if conjured from its pattering repetition.

'Bassano.'

'Bassano.'

'Aemilia Bassano.'

'No, she's Lanyer now; they tied her to the fool.'

'But it's Bassano that we know, my dears.'

'Aemilia Bassano.'

'Bassano.'

The rain falls in sheets, half-blinding me, and I can't see my way clearly till I am right by the Tree. The three dark figures are standing around a black cauldron that bubbles and steams upon a fire of blue flame, which leaps and crackles despite the downpour. One of them is scraping the eyeballs out of the dead woman's head, and dropping the scarlet mess into the pot. Another holds a severed arm, and is busy prising out its fingernails. The third – an aged, decrepit crone – watches me with hooded eyes.

'She comes, see, sisters. Bassano comes.'

I feel a wind rise, which seems to come from the ground below me, so I am enveloped in a screaming cloud. My cloak is torn from me, and the bonnet ripped from my head, so my hair streams out behind me and I am staring at the three women.

'What do you want with me?' I shout. 'What do you mean by creeping round me and whispering of dread things, and the plague?'

They are silent, and I listen to the rain.

I gather my courage and try again. 'You have tricked my husband, and stolen my money. What is the meaning of this? Tell me! I demand to know.'

'She challenges us,' says one of them.

'You don't challenge us,' says another.

'But you may seek our counsel.'

'I don't want your counsel!' I cry. 'I want you to leave me be!'

The three figures separate and walk slowly around the Tree, so that their slow footsteps mark out a circle. A spume of dark flame flies up from the cauldron, and the earth around it heaves, like boiling porridge.

'Hail, Bassano, bastard of Bishopsgate!' cries the First Witch.

'Hail, Bassano, strumpet of Stratford!' says the Second.

'Hail, Aemilia, spawn of the Equivocator!' says the Third.

'What do you mean? What are you saying?' I am shaking, my hands twisted together. Sky and earth seemed to have merged into one.

'He tricked us.'

'He tried us, sorely.'

'We gave him what he asked for, and he gave us nothing back.'

I pushed my wet hair out of my eyes. 'Who did? Who tricked you?'

The air seeps sound again, all around me.

'Bassano!'

'Bassano!'

'Baptiste Bassano!'

A spectre starts to form in the dark flames spewing from the pot. I see with horror that the face of my father is forming in the vapour. He is bloody and screaming, as I saw him in his final moments.

'What do you want from my poor father? He is dead, let him rest!'

'He would'st be great.'

'Was not without ambition.'

'But too full o' the milk of human kindness to catch the nearest way.'

'What do you *mean*?'

'Ah, yes,' say three voices. 'He is dead, but his soul escaped us. We are owed a soul.'

'A soul was promised.'

'The plague is coming,' whispers the air around me.

'The plague is coming.'

Another image begins to take shape in the flames. I see a bed with the curtains closed. As I peer at it, the curtains are slowly drawn back by invisible fingers, and I see a figure lying there, in that final stillness that is waiting for us all. It is a child, a boy, his eyes staring upwards, Heavenwards, at nothing.

'Henry!' I scream. 'No – never! You shall not have him!'

And then I am lying beneath the gibbet, and there are five bodies staring down at me, and the witches have gone. I stand up, shivering, my limbs stiff with cold. The rain has stopped and the clouds have blown away and the half-moon is reflected by the puddled ground.

Act III

Pestilence

Scene I

Weſtminſter, December 1602

The first sign is a giant comet which shoots across the sky soon after All Souls' Day. Like a wounded star, spewing its own brightness, it streaks across the heavens. The streets are full of staring citizens, squinting upwards. Children perch on windowsills. The boldest scramble up to the roof-thatch and cling there while the flaming star lights up the firmament, so that night is day and the City is ablaze with heavenly light. Then the rumours start. People have seen angels and coffins far above their heads. The graves at St Bride's Church crack open and the dead scream warnings from below. A phantom appears each night at Fetter Lane, bowing when the clocks strike twelve. The madmen at Bedlam break out and run into the streets, rending their hair and telling all who see them they must flee. 'Death is coming!' they shout. 'Death will come upon us!'

Winter sets in, and the sense of foreboding grows stronger, even though some say that cold weather dulls the power of plague vapour. Then one evening, as I am walking home at dusk, I see him. It is a clear, frosty night, with a full moon. There is a figure up ahead, a tall man in grey. At first, I do not mind him; there are others passing to and fro, and he does not strike me as strange or fearful. But as I walk I draw nearer to him; although I am proceeding at a normal pace, his steps are faltering, slow. Is it the slushy ground that holds him up? It rained heavily before the freeze set in, and the multitude of footprints have turned the path to mush. As I come closer, I think that I know him, but could not say where from. He is broad-shouldered and well-dressed, and his fur-trimmed cloak trails behind him on the ground. Then he staggers and cries out, falling to his knees. There is a note of despair in that cry which chills my blood. I stand for a second, not knowing if I should flee, but something pulls me forward and I go to him.

'Sir?' I say. 'Can I...' And then he turns his head. It is my father, as I saw him last. His eye-sockets are sightless holes; his mouth is choking forth a torrent of blood. I reach out towards him, but my hands are those of a little child.

'What did you do, dear Father?' I call out. 'What did you promise? Tell me, sir, I beg you!'

Then I am alone. The shade has vanished. Above me, the moon shines, and all is silver, silent. When I get home, I pray till dawn.

It is a long, cold winter. The Thames freezes over but the ice is not strong enough to walk on. A group of children think to test this out, and dance merrily upon the frozen surface, downriver from the Bridge. They fall through into the black water, and all are drowned. A few days later, one of them is washed ashore at Deptford. A little girl, no more than three years old, in a transparent coffin of Thames ice. She still wears her little bonnet and leather shoes. Her eyes are wide open.

And then, in the darkest days of winter, comes the worst portent of all. The Queen is dying.

'What do you mean, *dying*?' I ask Alfonso, as he shakes out his snow-covered doublet and hangs it near the fire.

He holds out his hands to the flames. 'What I say. She took ill, with a fever, then kept to her rooms. Now she is removed to Richmond.'

'With the Court?'

'Her ladies, favourites, a few physicians. She has no need of music now.'

Snow is falling against the window-panes. Outside, it has settled on the sewer ditch, making dead dogs ecclesiastic marble.

'Dear Lord!'

'She is old, Aemilia. She is not as you remember her. She has been low in spirits since poor Essex was executed. She weeps all day, they say.'

'I can't believe she's dying.'

'You thought that she would live forever?'

'Perhaps I did.'

The thought of the Queen's death makes me feel giddy, as if her presence in the world is a talisman against the Evil Eye and the worst that could befall us. This is a foolish fancy, of course. The Queen is a just a woman, now fallen into the sour humour of the aged. What's more, her reign has had its share of adversity. We have suffered bad harvests, lean winters, persecution, defeats abroad and the fear of invasion. Even the plague itself has afflicted us many times. But although the sickness has been foul, and many have died, it has never compared to the old stories about the Black Death, when the quick became the dead without warning, the Reaper took the living as they sat at cards, whole villages died and the streets were piled with corpses. Worse could come than we have known. Before her time there was blood and madness. After she goes – who can tell?

Alfonso is at home, listless and charmless, not wanted by the dying monarch. Nor by me, the hale subject. He plays his neat tunes, or goes off curled and oiled to the gaming-house, to gamble with money he doesn't have. While he goes about his business, Joan teaches me her craft. She takes me out walking in the fields and among the hedgerows, and tells me tales of faeries and hobgoblins, of the ways of spirits and the living demons who inhabit the air around us, and who watch us as we go about our daily round. Though I say it myself, I am a ready pupil. It reminds me of being a child again, when I was taken in hand by Susan Bertie and taught my Greek and Latin. Winter is not the best time to gather herbs and flowers, but we walk by the water meadows and Joan tells me all about them: how no two meadows are alike, how farmers will give each of them a name, just as they name their cows; and how pits and ponds have their own spirits. And how everything in nature has a name, a place and a purpose. She talks of beard grass, cat's tail and cock's foot, of crowflowers and salt marsh grass, which can grow underwater for many months. What I once saw as a barren place is full of life. And London, to me a place of wonders, is to Joan a brute invasion of the ancient land.

She teaches me about her apothecary's art: where each plant grows, the time to harvest it according to its governing planet, and when it can be pressed and stored. Nightshade grows under Mercury, and is an antidote to the power of witchcraft in men and beasts alike; cottonweed cures head-aches and infestations; while fleabane is the remedy for snake-bites and for gnats and fleas. Indeed, there is not a plant or simple growing in a single meadow in any corner of our land which is not a cure for some ailment, canker or distemper. I marvel that everything Joan knows is carried in her head, for she reads a little, but not easily, and prefers to store her knowledge in her memory.

I do not tell her about the witches: I fear to tell anyone what they said about my father. The meeting had the strange quality of nightmare, and the queer dreams I have when I walk in my sleep.

Joan's remedies mean that a trickle of money comes into the house, and we live frugally. Each morning, when the chores are done, I work on my cross-gartering pamphlet. This is proving an arduous task, as I have no interest in it. I have written some poetry too, but guiltily, knowing it will earn us nothing.

One night, long after curfew, when the streets are dark and only watchmen and spirits walk, there is a fearsome knocking. I sit up in bed, alert and listening. Was it our door, or the next one?

Could it be carousing players, come for Tom? Alfonso, at home for once, is whiffling next to me, too drunk to snore wholesomely. There is the knocking once again. I kick him in the balls.

'Husband, stir yourself!'

He yelps like a drowning pup and rolls away from me.

I kick his naked arse this time. 'See who wants us down below!'

Waking with a grunt, he looks around him, oiled hair perpendicular. 'Whassis?'

Bang, bang, bang. The whole house echoes with the sound. 'Who's within?' shouts a man's voice. 'I have a message from the Queen.'

Alfonso leaps up then, all right, lights a candle and goes running down the stairs half in his doublet, naked from the waist down. 'Yes, yes, yes! I come, I come.'

I follow him, shivering in my chemise, wondering who could want a drunken pipe-player at this hour. He pulls back the stiff locks and opens the door. A pale youth is standing there, thin-faced and blue-eyed with tiredness, wearing the Queen's livery and carrying a flaming torch.

'Her Majesty demands your presence,' says the youth, bowing. 'There is a boat on the river, ready to bring you to Richmond.' His rasping breath clouds the frosty night.

Alfonso stands erect, proud as a soldier. 'I will come now. Let me dress myself.' He turns to me in triumph. 'Aemilia, where is my best wool caster? And my mended doublet, and my...'

The messenger bows again, and begins to cough. Recovering himself, he says, 'Forgive me, sir, but it's *Mistress* Lanyer who is wanted by Her Majesty. Commanded to wait on her, this very night.'

Richmond! It was always the Queen's favourite palace. While it lacks nothing of Whitehall's grandeur, it is removed from the hurly burly of the town, and its magnificence seems all the greater amid the surrounding woods and fields. It is the greatest palace in the kingdom, high-walled and turreted, with a thousand chimneys and dozens of Arabian minarets. There, the Queen would receive foreign guests, flirt and fool us all, and then sweep off to the hunt. I remember how I used to watch the cavalcade departing. Elizabeth was always controlled, always cunning. She laughed hard, rode fast, and would return blooded and wet. What memories. They seem more actual than the icy wind that freezes my face as I sit huddled in the cushioned barge; clearer than the sound of an ale-house brawl that comes drifting across the water. In the boat, all is darkness. The sky is black and starless beyond the torch that flickers on the prow. But in my mind it is bright day, and I am at Richmond in a fine silk gown, looking down from the battlements across a landscape that is like a vista of the afterlife. The pale heavens are infinite, and clouds trail and shift above the distant oak forests.

As the oars dip into the freezing water and the barge slips quietly along the Thames, I feel as if it is taking me back to my youth. I remember the first time I was summoned to play for the Queen. There was a long walk from room to room; the scent of ladies and candle-wax and lavender. There were faces, all twisted and polished for looking at. And then a door opened, and there she sat, a blur of red and gold. I climbed on to the seat beside the virginals, and the keys were my friends and gave me courage, so I began to play.

When I had finished, she said, 'You are too clever, for such a little scrap of person.' (I think I was eight, or perhaps nine.)

Not knowing what to reply, I looked over at Mother, and she nodded to me to say something. I got down from my seat and curtseyed as my mother had shown me.

'I am not clever, Your Majesty,' I said. 'I work hard and...' I broke off, not sure if I should go on.

'Yes?' The Queen's smile was slightly colder. She found my hesitation irksome.

'And I wish to know things.'

She seemed to like this.

'Ah, child,' she said. 'We are the cleverest of all, those of us who have a love of study. The curious mind seeks nourishment. Our curiosity will make us wise.'

The messenger is silent, snuffling into his handkerchief. In front of us, a boatman rows, impassive. They seem no more inclined to talk to each other than they do to speak to me.

'How does Her Majesty?' I ask, at last.

The messenger sneezes again. 'Badly,' he says, seeming to do badly enough himself, since I hardly think this is a fit way to discuss the sickness of the monarch. He blows his nose. His face is ghastly in the torchlight. 'She is like to die within the week. She has seen no one but Robert Carey, and a few favourites. She has asked for the Archbishop.'

'Does she fear that she is dying?'

'So it seems. Richmond is a house of rumour. Some said she died weeks ago, we had seen so little of her. She keeps to her chamber, and will do nothing but walk and walk, never sitting, as if she could outpace Death himself. She will not go to her bed, but rests on cushions, on the floor.'

'I cannot imagine it.'

'She cannot imagine it herself, I believe.'

There is silence for a moment. Then, in a sudden passionate rush, the messenger says, 'Just a few weeks ago, she gave an audience to the Venetian ambassador. She was dressed in a taffeta dress of silver and gold, and a thousand gemstones. She was witty, spry, easily a match for him. Everyone said so. He came out of the throne room saying she had kept her beauty yet.' He sneezes again. I look at his sickly face in the flickering torchlight. Then, he points. 'Look, there – you see? They are waiting for you.'

And there is Richmond, a beacon in the darkness. I can see the windows of the state rooms dazzling bright, an earthly copy of the stars. Even the doors stand open, and I can see light inside, a gilded stairway, and darkly silhouetted soldiers, standing guard.

Scene II

Inside, all is blazing light. Torches are racked on every wall, lamps flame, and glittering candelabra burn above my head. Once I took this moon-dimming brightness for granted, and the world beyond it seemed a place of shadow. Now I have returned, blinking and stumbling, from the outer darkness.

I am still blinking when we reach the Presence Chamber and Lettice Cooper sets down her sewing and comes over to me. She is done up in black velvet and seed pearls, hard-faced in the midst of this abundance.

'Her Majesty is not well,' she says, somewhat needlessly in my opinion.

I curtsey, in the Court style, to remind her I am not some common housewife.

'Which circumstance requires that we do her bidding, even whilst we fear that her requests may not reflect her wishes when in her right mind.'

I curtsey again. After all, I can't spit in her eye.

'So I would ask that you do not take up more of her time than is needed.' She hands me a little silver bell. 'And you ring this when you are done.' Then she points to its companion, a larger bell, of solid gold, it looks like. 'Likewise, we will ring this if we fear that you outstay your term. Is that understood?'

'Of course,' I say, tinkling the bell, to test it.

She frowns. 'Hush. All our nerves are a-jangle.'

Another lady looks up. It's young Lady Guildford, who was a girl last time I saw her. 'They are jangled indeed,' she

185

says. 'The world is upside-down. The dead speak, and the living haunt us.'

'Hush, my dear,' says Lettice. 'We will not speak of this.'

But Lady Guildford takes my arm. She is a wisp of a woman, with a child's high voice. 'Her Majesty has been lying in her withdrawing-room these ten days,' she says, staring intensely into my eyes as if to make sure I understand the full import of her words. 'She is much afraid. She will not get into her bed, not even at the dead of night. She said to me, "If you were in the habit of seeing such things in your bed that I do, you would not ask me to go there."'

'What does she see?'

'She did not say. But there is witchcraft afoot.'

'Why do you say so?'

'Yesterday, I sat with her so long, praying and thinking, that my legs were stiff and cramping, and I went out to take a little air. I came out, through this chamber, and the throne room, and the next room, and came out halfway down the Long Gallery. You know it?' Her eyes are full of terror.

'I remember it.'

'Well. I walked along there, all distracted, thinking of the poor Queen and all her sufferings, when I heard a noise behind me, in the passageway, and I turned to see if someone called me back...'

She hesitates.

'And – did they?'

'At first, I could not see clearly. The candles were guttering, and the place was half in darkness. Then, I saw it was Her Majesty. I thought she had risen, feeling more herself. I thought she must have followed me. You can imagine my joy to see her so much improved. I went towards her, but then she vanished.'

'What do you mean?'

'In terror, for I knew something was strange, I ran back to her room. The ladies were all as I had left them. And the Queen lay in that same motionless slumber that I had seen before leaving her. I had seen an apparition, a spectre. Her spirit had left its place.'

Lettice frowns. 'That is more than sufficient,' she says. 'We are all sorely tired. There is likely nothing in it. These are heavy, dangerous times. Let's keep our wits about us.'

'My wits have not deserted me,' say I. 'Much else has been taken from me, but my common sense remains.'

Lettice frowns again, and proceeds towards the grand door to Elizabeth's withdrawing-room, the inner sanctum of her suite of private chambers, and beckons me to follow her. Her hand resting on the door, she speaks to me with quiet disdain.

'You are to enter her room alone, Aemilia.'

'Good.'

'You are to speak calmly to her, and take care that she does not become alarmed.'

'I shall do as you say.'

'You will find her changed.'

'Of course.'

'Remember, she is still the Queen, and in one thing she is as she always was. She will not submit. She will not die until she chooses to. She commands; she does not obey.'

The Queen is propped up with velvet cushions, half-upright like a wooden doll. Her eyes are cast down, and she sucks one finger. Her face is a mask of white ceruse, with a clown-mark of vermilion on each cheek. Below her chin hangs a great wattle of loose flesh, and this too is daubed with white. And she is wearing a splendid gown, a stiff and glistering carapace, encrusted with a multitude of gem-stones.

I stand just inside the door to her bedchamber – a room I have never entered before – not sure what to do next. It is hard to believe that we are quite alone. Every time that I saw her, in all my years at Whitehall, even when she had summoned me to speak Latin to her or play my virginals to soothe her mind, there were others present. Hunsdon, Cecil, Dudley, a clutch of ladies, a couple of ambassadors. She moved around in a throng of obsequious advisors and hopeful acolytes. Now, there is no one. Breathless, I look around the cavernous room, lit by silver sconces. After my little house I feel I am truly in the land of giants. A fire – great enough to roast an ox – crackles in the stone fireplace. The high bed, carved and gilded and hung with cloth-of-gold and silver, looms high in the centre of the room. It is as big as a stage; its closely patterned curtains remind me of the heavy drapes before the Globe's tiring-room. The valance is cloth-of-silver, heavily fringed with gold, silver and silken threads, and decorated with the shapes of beasts. The canopy is set off with feathered plumes. Beyond it is a painted mural, showing Our Lord as a child talking to the elders, then as a grown man preaching to the crowd, and finally kneeling in the Garden of Gethsemane. And above all this is the carved ceiling, vari-coloured in the flame-light, embellished with the likenesses of deer and boar, pursued by leggy hounds among the twisting trees and leaves. It is as if all the Queen's old joys and pastimes are here to taunt her.

Only Christ is left to her. But she is not looking at Him. She is looking at the floor, as if she made a study of the finely patterned Turkey carpet on which she lies. I stand for so long that in the end I think I must withdraw. What if these are her final moments? Or if she is already dead? I am not the right person to be present.

But just as I am about to leave the room, she speaks, though hoarsely and not in her familiar voice. 'Is that really you, Aemilia Bassano?'

'It is, Your Majesty. Except…'

I was never good at speaking with enough care for the Court.

'Except?' She takes her finger from her mouth, and looks at me.

'I am Aemilia Lanyer now. Your Majesty.'

'Oh, indeed. Married off for colour, with your misbegot.' She coughs and shifts her body. 'Come close, come closer. I want to look at you properly.'

I approach her. Her eyes, once shrewd and mocking, are faded and tired. She has a rank, rotting smell about her. Her shimmering dress with its armour of jewels seems to imprison her where she sits, in her awkward position. She is quite still. Only her eyes move, studying me. 'Aemilia,' she says, finally. Her hand comes out, fingers swollen now, no longer elegant, the cracked nails vermilion like her cheeks. 'You are the most welcome sight, most welcome. And still beautiful, for all you are dressed like some village drab.'

I bow my head. 'Thank you, Your Majesty.'

She sighs, and pushes my arm away. 'Not "Majesty", please, not now. Be sparing in your language. My own words tire me, but so do those of other people. There is so little time.' She stretches out her left hand, and shows me her wedding finger. 'Look. I am bone-thin, but my hands are swelled! They had to cut my coronation ring right off me – see? My wedding band is gone. I am divorced from Albion. I am lost.'

I can't think what to say, so I kneel down beside her on the floor.

We sit in silence for a moment, staring at the fire.

'Are you wondering why I have asked to see you?' The Queen shifts slightly in her robe.

'I – hardly thought it my place to question anything, madam. I am grateful that you have called me here.'

'No, Aemilia, no. I don't believe that this is true. You are always seeking to know the reason for things, and I have rarely seen you grateful. You know your own worth; I always liked that in you.'

I smile in spite of myself. 'I thought, perhaps, you wanted to talk to me because I am better-read than your ladies, and their Latin is somewhat poor.'

She nods. 'You understand more than most, Aemilia, and I learned from Hunsdon's good opinion of you that you are true, and loyal, and a keeper of secrets.'

'Thank you,' say I, sounding unlike myself.

'I see myself in that fire,' she says. 'My little person, burned by flames, but never consumed. I see myself burning in Hell.'

'No! It cannot be so. They are waiting for you in Heaven. They will have prepared a throne right next to God Himself.'

'I shan't get into that great bed,' she says. 'Death is in there, you know. I saw him, staring round the drapes at me.'

'A trick of the light, madam.'

'Don't humour me. For you, a trick of the light. For me, no. My time is near. I should know. I chose it. I have a heat inside my breasts, Aemilia, which will not go. And around my throat an iron claw. I cannot swallow. The appetites of life are past.'

'But…'

'But? But what? Do you question your Prince?'

'We still need you.'

'Ha! Carey waits on my death so he can ride off to Scotland. Even though I have yet to let them know whether my studious Scottish cousin shall succeed me.'

'The people love you.'

Now she laughs, an odd sound, like tearing paper. 'They are tired of me, as I am tired of life.' Then she stops, very sudden, and stares at something past me. I look over my shoulder at the empty room, flickering and glimmering in the light of flames.

'Do you know why I am here?' she asks. 'At Richmond?'

'Because Whitehall is too cold?'

'No. This is my warm winter box, but I would have kept at Whitehall longer, had I dared. No. John Dee told me to come here. Or rather, he told me to go from there. So off we all came, all the boatloads of us, but much difference it made.' She glances towards the closed door as if to make sure that we aren't overheard. 'I want to die, you see. I want to be gone. Whether

Heaven or Hell will receive my soul, I know I am all but done with this life. But the journey out is full of pain.'

'I am sorry for that.'

'Don't spend your sorrow on me. Your turn will come, and I doubt you will be lying on a Turkey rug, as I am, with a blazing fire to warm you.'

'I doubt it too.'

'My mind is not still; it keeps flitting hither and thither, the past is before me. And, as it flitted, it saw *you*. For all your learning, a restless spirit. Is that not so?'

'It is.'

'Like me. I always saw it in you.'

'Like you! I would not presume to think so.'

'A bastard, like myself.'

'A bastard, yes.'

'And mother to a bastard child.'

'Better a bastard than the child of Captain Lanyer.'

She shakes her head, very slowly. 'Ah, we are more like each other than you know. And you are not mellowed with the years?'

'I am not mellowed.'

'Good. Hunsdon would be proud of you. And how does the boy?' I see that her eyes have filled with tears.

'He is well. I love him dearly, too much. He is his father's son.'

'And who would that be, Dark Aemilia?'

I look down.

'I always wondered if Hunsdon could really keep you to himself. And you were a wild one, mistress. Don't imagine that it went unnoticed.'

I say nothing.

'Nothing about *you* could go unnoticed,' she says, quietly. 'I used to watch you. Sometimes I thought you could be my obscure twin, a dark shadow of my own self. It has been hard enough for me to use my mind – how must it be for poor Aemilia? If ever a woman was born out of her right place, it was you.'

I look away. In my mind's eye I see a child's hands spreading over ivory keys. They are ink-stained and the nails are bitten. I see a young woman in a yellow dress, glittering with jewels and borrowed pride.

'And there are more similarities between us than you know – more links between our two fates.' She pauses. 'And now... wife to a recorder player.'

'Yes, madam.'

'Is he a proper husband to you?'

'I couldn't say.'

'You hoped for more.'

'Wedlock is a narrow business.'

She laughs her tearing laugh again. 'Oh, Mistress Lanyer! You can still amuse me. Narrow, too narrow, you have it right. The bastards have the best of it.'

I hesitate again, not certain what to say. The Queen smiles, very thinly. 'It is an odd thing, but as I sit here, trapped in my own crock of bones, and as the world shrinks, as it must, something else happens. Do you know what that is?'

I nod. 'The world is far from you, so you see the pattern. I sometimes think of London the way a kite must see it. From above.'

'Sharp Aemilia. I should have made you Chancellor. If only I could have done. Yes. I see the world from far off, so though I am lodged here in my tiny room, propped next to my great bed of death, I see my life all clear, like the most wonderful tapestry of nonsense and pity.'

I watch her clown's face, lined with sadness.

'My esteemed brother-in-law, Philip, King of all Spain, of the Americas, the high seas, ended in a tiny room. No different, when he died in the Escorial, than the humblest of his servants. The world stretched from that palace, a great and grand dominion.

But in the end it was no longer his. He had to leave it.'

'And yet, it is a fine thing, to rule. You are not like other people.'

She flaps her hand, as if batting away the foolishness of this thought. She looks again into the corner of the room, and again I turn, wondering what she sees. As she speaks, her eyes are steady on this unseen presence. 'They cut her head off while she prayed. Did you know that?'

'I did not know that.' I do not even know who she speaks of, but I dare to guess.

'The executioner, hot from Calais, got his man to catch my mother's eye, and slashed his blade right through her neck, in that moment. Cut right through the muscle and bone. He did his job well. Her lips were moving even as her head fell down into the straw.'

Now, I truly cannot speak. I cannot breathe.

The Queen presses on, remaining curiously still, as if all her living was in her head. 'Was that mercy? Do you think? To smite her before she knew, but also before she had finished her prayers? Did she die in grace?'

'I cannot tell. I pray to God she did.'

'They said she was a witch. Will God forgive a witch? Is it a mortal sin? There is a place for every creature, for every leaf and blossom of the Lord's creation. Even beggars. A wild rogue has his position, and an Abraham man, who rants and preaches in his rags. So witches, too, they must have a portion of their own.'

'That must be so, madam.'

'I thought to learn the craft, from Dr Dee, but it is harder than Greek or Latin.' She sucks her finger again, childish. 'I can read the Tarot. Such pretty cards.'

'Evil's in them, madam, if you ask me. I always draw the Devil.'

'One day, Dr Dee prepared a chart for me. In my privy chamber, just outside this door, I will never forget. And then he refused to let me see. Later, I found out why. He saw it coming, this terrible duty. That I would be forced to kill my own kind. First Mary Stuart. God forgive me. I meted out to her what my father meted out to my poor mother.'

'No prince would have done otherwise.'

'And yet. That is not it... I killed my son. Robert Devereux, my dearest, bastard son. Not one clean blow for him, no! Three strikes of the axe. Mangled and bloodied, in an agony that *I* inflicted on him!'

'Madam, I – '

'Dreadful, most dreadful pain and suffering, that, but for me, he need never have endured! My little one, a traitor at my breast. Oh, I shall go straight to Hell! I am burning now!'

I fear·she is out of her wits. 'Your Majesty – madam – you should rest now.'

She looks around her, as if she is unsure of her safety. 'They say I rule England like a king. But my duty is a prison. Would that I had the other power, that hideous, demonic gift!'

'What gift?'

'The greater one. That which makes castles into air, and air into castles. I would have done some mischief then. Sunk the Armada with the foul gale of my hag's breath. Torn down the Tower walls, and thrown the scaffold to the winds so he could go free, my naughty, upstart boy! Opened up the seven gates of London so he could gallop forth, go anywhere, in peace and freedom.'

'Oh, madam...'

'I dream it is so, I still dream it is so.' She starts. 'Are we alone? Is Hecate here? She is a greater Queen than I.'

'We are alone. But, madam – '

'And did I summon you, or did you come by chance?'

'You summoned me.'

'Ah, yes. You live at Long Ditch. You are married to that ape Alfonso.' She pauses, and squeezes my hand again. 'I have a warning for you. That is why I have called you here. It concerns this thing, this matter of witchcraft. Dr Dee has told me something which concerns you…'

A bell tinkles. The Queen frowns. 'Tell them to go away. I am still their monarch, and I wish to speak to you for longer.'

I open the door a crack, and see Lettice Cooper's frowning face. 'Please leave us,' I say. 'Her Majesty wishes it.'

'Isn't Her Majesty done with you?' she asks.

'Done with me?'

'Address me as "my lady".'

'I have told you. My lady. She is not ready.'

'Would she not care for a drop of rose-water?' Her words are solicitous, but her tone is ice-cold. Before I can speak, there is an odd sound from the Queen behind me. I turn, and she is trying to rouse herself from her place, but is weighted down by the jewelled robe. One hand is raised, but, instead of words, all that comes this time is a strange cry, like the call of a gull. Lettice Cooper pushes past me, in a rustle of damask and velvet, and I stand back as she soothes the Queen, and offers her rose-water, which Elizabeth declines, turning her head away and pursing her lips tight shut. Then she points to me. Somewhat unwilling, Lettice nods to me. The Queen seems unable to summon her former strength, and stares at me for a moment, her eyes seeking mine as if I could explain a mystery that is puzzling her. She raises her hand again, beckoning me near. I stoop before her, obliged to lean over Lettice and her glistening skirts; she does not shift an inch.

'Wait…' The Queen stops.

I lean closer.

'Sa…'

'Your Majesty?'

She pulls me forward so that our cheeks touch. Her stench is overwhelming. Then she whispers, 'Save the boy. By fair means or foul. I could not save mine. Save yours. Guard him.'

Scene III

News of the Queen's illness has spread. London is silent, waiting. The ports are closed by government decree, and the dockyards stand empty. There is barely a sound along the alleyways and cat-creeps, or among the mean hovels in the east, or the grand courtiers' houses at the river's edge. The sound of hammering has ceased, the church bells have been muffled and even the dogs have stopped fighting. Only the sound of birds remains: the soft song of the woodpigeon, the peewit's cry, the seagulls calling and squawking, sometimes with the screams of dying babes, sometimes the chatter of Tower monkeys. The weather has changed, too. The snow has melted, and unseasonable sunlight floods the empty streets. Wild flowers have opened their petals, fooled by the early heat. The bluebell fields of Charing Cross are an azure wasteland.

It is a freakish spring, and these are strange days. I know we are willing Elizabeth to die. The golden time is over, and something else must follow. The old Queen seems as ancient as London Bridge itself, as relentless as the river tide, as long-lasting as a Sunday sermon. Now her life, like everything on earth, must end.

This is the subject of Father Dunstan's homily. He is a miserable, choleric old man, and he has taken the occasion of her illness, and the convenient deaths of several children of Long Ditch parish, as an excuse to ruminate upon the similarity of Flesh to Grass, and, by his religious logic, the need to obey the Word of God. He has chosen as his text, as is his usual habit, one of the *Homilies* most thoughtfully provided by poor Archbishop

Cranmer, who later plunged the very hand that wrote these words into the fire. The subject is 'Against Disobedience and Wilful Rebellion' and the method – again one our good priest is wont to use – the brute punishment of boring us to death. Father Dunstan's borrowed sermons, read out from his weighty book, are often two hours long.

So the droning progresses thus: '...*and as GOD would have man to be his obedient subject, so did he make all earthly creatures subject unto man, who kept their due obedience unto man, so long as man remained in his obedience unto GOD... in which obedience, if man had continued still, there had been no poverty, no diseases, no sickness, no death, nor other miseries wherewith mankind is now infinitely and most miserably afflicted...*'

He booms the words over the pulpit at us, daring us to daydream at the white-limed walls. I look down at Henry, who is scuffing his shoe round, making a circle in the strewing-herbs. I frown and pretend to cuff the top of his head, and he squints up at me, half-smiling.

'...*He not only ordained that in families and households the wife should be obedient unto her husband, the children unto their parents, the servants unto their masters: but also...*'

Alfonso, who was at the gaming tables last night, has his head bowed, his hands clasped before him, as if in prayerful thought.

'...*the root of all vices, and mother of all mischiefs, was Lucifer, first GOD's most excellent creature, and most bounden subject, who by rebelling against the Majesty of GOD, of the brightest and most glorious Angel, is become the blackest and most foulest fiend and...*'

Joan is standing a little apart from the three of us. She is staring at the priest, her green eyes giving nothing away. As I watch, I notice that she is rocking to and fro, to and fro, slowly, as if a gentle song were lulling her to sleep.

But then, as if he has observed that we are dozing through his tedious words, Father slams the book shut, and fixes the congregation with a furious gaze. 'When Death comes for us, we must make our reckoning. We cannot tarry, we cannot bargain, we cannot name the day we are ready to meet our Maker. We must go when we are called, and there is no way back from the gates of Hell.' He seems to be staring at me, though I know this is how each person feels in a great crowd, confronted by a lone orator. The priest isn't addressing me, any more than Burbage aims his monologues at one particular groundling in the crowded Globe.

'Which of us will live to see Midsummer? Which of us will light a flame for Candlemas? Who will see another winter? Hmm? I ask you? Who can say this?'

Mouths gape. Eyes open. A lap-dog growls. 'Death is coming – for you, just as surely as for the Great and Good. Do not feel your Prince is nearer to the grave than Thee. There is not one of us that knows that we will live to see another dawn…'

Oh, Lord preserve us. I hate this worship of the dead.

'They say the plague ships are come from distant places, the Indies, and the Azores. They are docked now, at the quayside, by East India House. None can know what causes us to die when the sickness comes. The barrels are rolled into the taverns. The sailors are gone among us. It is God who sends the pestilence, and only God can save us. Fear him.'

I notice a man on Joan's left side, at the end of our pew. He is a brown-skinned, wrinkled peasant, a stranger in the parish. He regards the priest with an air of confusion and unease, blinking as if he can't quite see. He takes a dirty napkin from his leather doublet and mops his face, which dribbles sweat and is mottled purple. Joan catches my glance, and looks at him. Even as she turns, I see the bubo on his neck, yellow as a head of corn. He drops down on his knees. 'Lord have mercy!' he shouts. 'Lord have mercy on us!' It is the plague cry, the words the doomed daub upon their houses. And he vomits a bellyful of bile right out upon the herbs and rue. The old peasant might have the sweating sickness or the clap; he might have eaten a plate of mouldy mutton – it makes no odds to me. I see that horrid image conjured by the witches: the dead child still in his bed. My skin goes cold. I take Henry's hand, push past Alfonso and run to the end of the pew.

'Do not run from Death!' shouts the priest.

'I run towards Life, Father,' I call over my shoulder. With Henry's hand clasped firm in mine, I run towards the back of the church.

'Jezebel!' he shouts. 'How dare you speak to your priest in this manner? Remember your place, and be silent.'

It's almost enough to make you laugh. What fools does God take us for? But I have no breath for laughing; I am turning the great iron catch on the church door, then pushing it open. Outside, it is a bright spring day. I look back and see all the rows of faces, turned towards me, and the priest, pale with anger, leaning over the pulpit.

I wake, suddenly. All is darkness: it is the dead of night. Aptly named. I know the Queen has gone. Did I hear a noise? A cry? A scream? A fired musket? Something has disturbed the blackest hour. I push back the eiderdown, and go to the window. Opening it quietly, I look both ways, up and down our street. The cold night air smokes my breath. There is nothing to be seen. All is silent beneath the stars. The only living creature is a house-cow, tethered opposite. She dozes by the water conduit, sleeping on her feet. Behind me, Alfonso rolls onto his back and sets to snoring louder. I crane my head to look westward, towards Richmond, but I am hemmed in with brick smoke-stacks and tight-sewn thatch.

The good news about the death of the Queen is that Alfonso is employed again. All the Court recorder players are summoned to Whitehall, to rehearse some new tunes for the funeral. They brought her corpse from Richmond in a lead coffin, and she is lying in state at Westminster Hall to await the orders of King James of Scotland, soon to be King of England. The bad news is that we are still in a state of anxious waiting. The Queen is dead, but where is this new Prince? Alfonso says he is processing down from Scotland in grand style, meeting his northern subjects along the way. So we are suspended in a nowhere place between two monarchs. And, just as spirits walk between Christmas and Twelfth Night, so idle and malicious talk fills up this space. For evil is about us and among us, evil acts are more common than saintly deeds, wicked men prosper and the good starve; angels are frailer in our world than night's black agents, and in this dark and shifting place of nightmare we must seek protection where we may.

Rumours spring up and run along the streets. They say Elizabeth never saw her own face in her dotage, that her cheating courtiers gave her a magic mirror that reflected only what she had been in her youth. That when at last she saw her true self, aged, unadorned and ugly, she died of grief. (This was false, I knew. It was a twisted version of the truth, which was that John Dee gave her an obsidian mirror, and that she knew most precisely what its powers were, and valued it most highly.) And they say that her body was so racked with vile disease that it swelled monstrously and exploded, bursting forth from her coffin. I think this must be falsehood too, but then remember her swelling fingers and the missing coronation ring.

My husband has had plenty of time to learn his new tunes. But now, the day of her funeral has come.

'Wife, bring me my tasselled stockings!'

'They are on the bed, Alfonso.'

'Wife, my trunk hose! Be quick about it!'

'You are wearing your trunk hose. Arse-brain.'

'Wife...'

'Silence, husband! Put your clothes on, which are spread before you. You may be the master of your music, but you do not command your spouse.'

Off he flounces in a sulky humour. I watch him go, his pretty steps all dainty down the filthy street. I wonder, as I do so, what Will is wearing to bid his Queen farewell, and who has helped him with *his* trunk hose, and found his shirt, and watched him dress. Such thoughts can still confound me, so that time seems twisted and love and hate are twinned. But then Henry comes up behind me. 'Mother, shall we go and get a good place now? Tom says he will stand in King Street, to get a proper view.'

'I may go to King Street, young man, but you will stay inside the house with Joan.'

'But Mother – '

'But nothing. In this, for once, you will obey me. You know what I have said about the plague. Two dead in this street already. In the parish, seventeen. You must stay at home, and learn your lessons from your hornbook, and behave.'

'But – '

I raise my hand to him. 'Henry, if you do not do as I say, I will beat you. I will.'

'But you are going – '

I slap him hard across his cheek and his eyes are hard and angry.

'I hate you.'

'Good. I am your mother. This is as it should be.'

Outside, the streets are filled with a fairground throng of watchers and mourners. The way is blocked with every manner of person, old and young, men and women, ale-wives and aldermen, cozeners and cripples, all herded together, head to head and cheek to cheek. Had I not wished to see her one last time I would keep indoors myself, for I can see that, whatever miasma or mist brings the plague, we are all piling together in a manner most favourable to its passing on.

Anne Flood bustles up, done out like a Venetian courtesan.

'Come along, come quickly,' she says. 'We shall miss the best of it if we don't make haste.'

I have been avoiding her since Inchbald told me of their arrangement. Now I can no longer hold my peace. 'What's this I hear, about how you pay your rent? No wonder you can afford such dainty ruffs.'

She rolls her eyes. 'Will you judge me, for wishing to survive? Since Mr Flood passed on, I have lived on my wits, and what little he left me.'

'But lying with Inchbald! Anne! Does he not make you retch?'

'Certainly.' She gives me a piercing look. 'I consider you my good friend, Aemilia. And you told me once that you think of another man when Alfonso fucks you, though you are too close to tell me who it is. If you had to suck a dwarf's tiny cock to keep yourself respectable, you'd have my pity, not my contempt.'

I shrug, and we walk in silence for a while. This other man, this secret incubus of mine, is Will, of course. My demon lover. For a while, my skin prickles with the memory of lust. Hot lust, cold words. That's my great love. That's his legacy.

Then, overcome with curiosity, I ask, 'How tiny?'

She laughs. 'I've seen bigger on a newborn hedge-pig. Here, take this.' She passes me half an orange, which I press to my nose to mask the street-stink as we hurry along.

We come to the bottom of King Street and we can see the palace gates. The procession is upon us. First come the black-robed bell-ringers and marshall's men, calling, 'Make way, make way!' and clearing a passage through the crowds. They are followed by a procession of poor women – and just a few poor men – marching four abreast, all in black, eyes cast down. Then come artisans, messengers and servants from the Queen's woodland and stable. Then follow empty carts driven by stable boys, and two of her horses, riderless. One is covered in a black cloth, the other in black velvet. And this is but the start of it. Trumpeters blast their horns at the crowd, to keep us back, and sergeants-at-arms pace along the line.

Now come the standard-bearers, with the great symbols of the Tudor house: the Dragon, the Greyhound, the Lion and the Portcullis. Then the fifty-nine musicians – and there's my sweet husband, quite the prettiest of them all. Then the apothecaries, physicians and minstrels of the Court. Parliament, the Privy Seal, the gentlemen and children of the Chapel Royal, all singing a mournful tune. Here is Lord Zouche carrying the banner of Cheshire, Lord Herbert with the banner of Cornwall. Next came the Mayor and aldermen of London, and the gentlemen pensioners, with their axes carried downward. On and on they go. Here is the Welsh banner, there is Ireland, and there goes the French ambassador. His train is carried by a retinue of page-boys. It must be six yards long.

Anne is weeping at my shoulder. 'I shall never forget this!' she says. 'The poor Queen! God rest her!'

I see a weeping widow cut a purse, and pretend not to. I see a wet-nurse slap a baby to keep it quiet. I look for Will. I long to see him – and dread the sight of him.

At last we see the hearse itself, a chariot pulled by four horses in trappings of black velvet. As if this were one of her great triumphal processions, the Queen is there in person, a life-size waxwork, as magnificent in death as she ever was in life. The painted effigy reclines upon her coffin, dressed in Parliament robes, with a crown upon its head, and a sceptre in its hands. Above the hearse is a canopy, carried by six earls, with a dozen lesser nobles carrying six banners alongside.

'I never saw such a thing!' says Anne. 'I never did!'

'It's a shame her waxen self can't rule us,' I say, 'rather than some Scottish prince who knows as much of England as I do of France.'

'Oh, what will become of us?' Anne cries out. 'The pity of it! The pity of it!'

I watch the chief mourner pass, Lady Northampton, her black train carried by two countesses. It looks like a procession from the Underworld itself. In my memory I see the Queen laughing, striding, picking up her skirts to make more speed. I see her drinking a glass of watered wine, accusing Blanche Parry of making it too strong. I see her straighten the gold circlet upon her curled red hair, when her beauty could still be faked for a grand occasion. And I see her face, that last time, fallen into a death-mask beneath the clown's paint.

As the hearse rumbles past, there is a general sighing, groaning and weeping.

'God rest Your Majesty! God rest your soul!'

'Lord save you, for all eternity!'

'Lord Jesu, save us all!'

Suddenly, there is a terrible scream and the plague cry: 'Lord have mercy on us!'

'Back, back,' shouts someone. 'See who comes – a plague-mort! Mind yourselves…'

A young maiden is pushing to the front of the crowd. The people fall back, more anxious to avoid her than to see the coffin of our departed Queen. Once, this girl must have looked a little like Elizabeth. She has the same bright red hair, crinkled and shot with gold, and the same fair skin. But her beauty has been blasted. Her eyes are sunken and bloodshot. Her face is swollen and purple with plague-spots. The skin of her bare arms and legs is covered in weeping lesions. She is half-naked, wearing nothing but a linen undershift, torn and bloodied and hanging from her shoulders. She cries out, and runs at the procession, but a sergeant-at-arms pushes her back.

'Leave off – away!' he shouts, shoving her with his cere-monial lance.

The distracted creature puts her head back and screams again – such a soul-sick sound! She tears at her smock, grunting and laughing, so it hangs down in front of her to show her white breasts, covered in evil sores, putrid and stinking. There is barely an inch of her that isn't riven and bleeding, as though she had been flayed with a whip. She turns to face the crowd. 'You should kill me!' she calls out. Her voice is soft and childish. She catches the arm of an old man, standing next to me. He shakes her off, white with fear. 'Who will kill me? Who will cut my throat?'

No one speaks. The procession moves on. Now the Queen's ladies pass by, in orderly completeness, as if they can neither see us, nor hear us.

'You would slay me if I was a dog!'

'By Jesu, what are you all? Will no one help her?' Father Dunstan forces his way to the front. He pulls the maiden to her feet, and wraps her in his cloak. 'Shame on you!' he shouts.

The girl is chattering again. The cloak hides everything but her bright hair.

'Will you slay me, Father? Will you throw me to the dogs at Bankside? Or shall I poison them? Shall I poison them, Father?' But then she begins to convulse like a hanging man, and her mouth foams. Father Dunstan drags her away, through the parting crowd.

Scene IV

London is my home. A horde of bloody prentice-boys shouting 'Clubs!' can make me smile. I love the filthy bustle, and would as soon hear the shout of the night watch as the song of a nightingale. But we breathe yellow, corrupted air that chars our throats. Even our snot is black with soot. The petty pains of daily life are cruel enough. So it's not always plain what is plague, and what is not. And the fear that every ague and pustule is the harbinger of certain death can haunt the best of us.

So. There is first a fever, but the sun is hot, the day is long; we may need no more to cure it than a draft of small beer. Then there is the vomiting – but who in London does not throw up their guts from time to time? We are careful never to eat raw fruit from the tree, but still the lurgy gets us. Every time we puke up in the chamber-pot, we think we are victims of a poisoner's craft. But there are signs, Lord help us, and, when these come, we know the end is near. God preserve us from the swelling, for that is a portent of the end indeed. And though there are those who live, they are few, and strong. It starts like a strain, a pain that stretches down an arm, or around the groin, but then focuses its evil into one place. Which place is fixed to be a bubo, a sac of heavy poison that will kill in moments if it bursts within your body. The ones who live are those whose buboes split outside their skin, so the fluid may be drained off. For whatever humour you may have – phlegmatic, sanguine, choleric, melancholic – none blends happily with this vile contaminant.

It is early summer. I am sitting at my hearth place, reading. Joan is standing at the doorway, looking out into the street, with that look of sour enjoyment with which she likes to greet disaster.

'It's a merry do,' she says. 'The dead outnumber the living all over the City. Heaven and Hell are bulging at the gate. St Bride's yard is full, and St Olave's. If it takes us off now, we shall be buried in the ditch.'

'Thank you for those cheering words, Joan. If you can't say anything more uplifting, go upstairs and tell your beads.' Rosaries are forbidden by the law, but I know she has one hid beneath her bedstead in a casket.

She takes no notice of me. 'The City pageant has been cancelled.'

'I know it.'

'Jack Mellor, that ran amok yesterday with his sores all out, was put to death this morning.'

'I know.'

'Cruel, I call it.'

'He would have died anyway,' say I.

'I was talking to the dog-catcher at St Margaret's, and he has killed more than five hundred hounds. Five hundred!'

'No wonder the streets are quiet.'

'Seventy-two parishes infected, Mistress Flood told me. And there are nine houses boarded up in Westminster, and eleven souls are newly dead. It stalks us close.'

I put my book down. 'For pity's sake, Joan! What do you want of me? Henry is kept from school. The house is full of onions and garlic. We have sweet herbs in every room: the physick garden is bare. And we pray.'

'I know it, mistress. We are taking every care we can.'

'What more can I do? Shall I lie down and weep in the fireplace? Shall I fill my hair with ashes? We are not dead yet. We shall sit it out.'

207

'Says who? Has the Almighty sent you word?'

'Don't be insolent. You are my servant, not my keeper.'

'Oh, and are the two so very far apart? Who would keep you, if not old Joan? Not your popinjay husband, that's for sure.'

This is quite enough. I get to my feet, ready to strike her. But she says, 'Mistress, you know I would do everything in my power to help you.'

I let my hand fall. 'Yes.'

'But what I can offer… my skills and remedies… they won't save us.'

'No.'

'There is something evil here.'

I have tried not to think of the witches, but they are never far from my mind. 'Joan – there is something that I want to ask you…'

Alfonso rushes in at this worst of moments. Back from the palace, and breathless with his own importance.

'The new King has called for the consort.'

'But the King is not here – not yet crowned…'

'Precisely. We are leaving London.'

'Praise be to God!' says Joan.

'Praise indeed!' I say. Is it possible that for once Alfonso has been useful? But – of course – there is a guilty look upon his face. I see how it will be without the need to ask. 'This *is* good news,' say I, falsely smiling. 'All the family will be saved. When do we go, husband?'

He looks down at his feet – fine shod in French boots, elaborately pointed. 'I… it is the musicians who are needed. At Cambridge, at the pleasure of His Majesty.'

'So be it,' says Joan. 'I will see to our preparations.'

'Preparations for what?' he asks, uneasily.

'Why, for the journey sir.'

'To *mine*. To my… preparations. Not to yours, Joan, or my wife's.'

'Nor to Henry's either?' I feel a surge of anger, even though this is no surprise. 'You will leave us, then. To live or die. And see what remains of us when you return.'

'This cannot be so, master,' says Joan. 'More people die each day. The pest house is full. They are digging graves out at Tothill Fields – graves as big as caverns... They lime the dead when their bodies are still warm... You could not leave your little son to that.'

Alfonso twists his hands together, his long, perfect fingers. 'It is not my choice, Joan. I am the master here, but merely a servant to the King.'

'Then you can pay for us to follow.' Her voice is quiet, but I have never known her so outspoken. 'You have gold, don't you? Or, if it is gambled, you have your fine Court friends, who will lend you a ducat or two to save your wife and child.'

'Get out!' says Alfonso. 'This is not a matter for you.'

Joan climbs the stairs, silent with rage.

I stare into the fire. I can see that this unmans him more than the tirade he was expecting. I watch the flames, thinking that each lick of heat is a like a human life, flaring up for an instant, and then gone for good. My calm is aided by my knowledge of my husband – expecting nothing is an excellent preparation for receiving it.

After a while he clears his throat. 'I am sure you will be safe.'

'Surely.'

'It will die out soon. Everyone says so.'

'Indeed. "Everyone" has such confidence that they are packing up their goods and chattels, boarding up their houses and heading for the hills of Kent.'

'The doom-sayers.'

'The wealthy. And the wise.'

'We have seen the plague before. Every year, it comes and goes.'

'Not like this,' I say. 'Not for years. If you insist on being a snivelling coward, then kindly have the grace to be an honest snivelling coward.'

'I shall be soon be back. With money. And preferment. A certain position, with the new King. I am doing this for all of us – for our future.'

'Alfonso?'

'Yes, my chuck?' He smiles, uneasy.

'Go.'

And so he does, with some clean linen in a bundle, and Joan's last impudent accusations following him down the street.

That night, I keep Henry in my bed, so I can will the plague away from him. His habit is to throw himself at an angle across the mattress, muttering and kicking, so the eiderdown comes off me, and there is no way I can lie straight. I lie there, sleepless. Much as I despise my husband, there is no doubt we are worse off without him. There was little hope of help before, but now no escape is possible. We can't flee the City like the wealthy and well-born. Money isn't all you need. Not only can the rich afford to hire carriages to remove their goods, they also have country estates to move to, with vast gardens, far from London. What's more, they have the legal right to run away. Each has a certificate of health, a pledge that they are clean of plague and not carrying the pestilence. Without this, if you flee, you may be hanged for your pains. When I lived at Court, we removed to Windsor Castle during one outbreak. The Queen had a gibbet put up on the village green. Poor souls who fled the City were put to death at her command. Horses supped water from the trough as these innocent subjects kicked their last.

At last I fall asleep, but I am prey to such dreams and nightmares! *I see them kill my father again, a circle of dark figures. I walk up behind him, and at first his steps are light and hurried, then slow and burdened, then they stop. Again he turns, and I see his silent scream. Again I reach out and my child's hands are in front of me. But this time they are botched with gore. I scream myself, but my screams are still silent.*

There is a voice.

'Yet who would have thought the old man to have had so much blood in him?'

Then I see Lord Hunsdon, as he was the very last time I set eyes on him, in the promenading crowd at the Royal Exchange. Old and frail, and half-turning in the square, as if he wants to speak to me, but then I am pulled away by his companion. It is Lettice, all got up like a Globe whore touting for a groundling fuck, breasts like twin peaches. But then I see, it is not Hunsdon, it is Will. And we are not in the Royal Exchange but on the stage, and the audience is buzzing below us, angry and unhappy with our show.

Then I see Death, peering out of the Queen's bed at me, laughing. The Queen is with him, and laughing merrily herself, quite back to her old form. Her forehead is blooded, as it was on the days she came back from hunting. For all I know, the stag is in there too, in a state of equal high spirits... but then I wake. Or do I? It is a moment before I know what must have happened. My old affliction has returned, caused by dreams so violent they drive me from my bed. Night-walking.

I am not wrapped in blankets with my son. I am outside, in the plague-ridden street, bare-foot in my nightgown. I slap my wrist and pinch my skin to see if I'm still sleeping, and the pinches hurt, and my feet are cold, and I can smell the stench of putrefying flesh from the plague-house that is boarded up next door. I am awake, that is for sure, and abroad. I turn, too quick, to get back to my house, but for a second my head spins and I fear that I will fall. I stop for a moment, and put my hand upon the wall of the plague-house. From inside, I suddenly hear a dread cry, like the shriek of the damned.

'God help us! Help us! Give us water, show us pity! I have children! I have a baby! Help me!'

Two sotted prentice-boys appear. Staggering along the road, laughing and doing a little dance. They are tossing a flat cap between them, and tussling to reach it when it falls to the ground. When they see me, with my hand upon the plague-house, in my nightgown and with my muddy feet, they take me for one of the unfortunates who live there.

'What's this – you have escaped to spread your pestilence?' says the first, a great big lad with a mass of black hair. 'Get back inside!'

'You disobedient witch!' says the other, who is smaller, and has a scuff of brown beard 'Go indoors, and stay there till the Devil takes you.' They grab my arms and began to push me towards the door, though how they intend to get me through it I don't know, as the boards are nailed down sound, and there is no way in any more than there is any way out. I try to speak, and wrench myself free, but cannot, and a nauseous dark descends.

I dream of my father again.

We are on the stage with his consort; the boards stretch away in all directions, to the four corners of the earth, which are trimmed with heavy wainscots. To the east, these are carved with Chinamen and pearl-fishers; to the west with natives with feathered heads; to the south with Moors and minarets; to the north with wolves and mountains. Father is sitting cross-legged, holding his recorder. His lifts the pipe as if to play it. There is a dagger in his chest.

I sit down beside him. 'Father,' I say. 'You aren't dead.'

He looks up. 'Why should I be dead?'

'You were killed when I was seven.'

He laughs. 'I never died,' he says.

'Then where are you?'

'In Purgatory,' says he. 'Playing all my sweetest tunes.'

212

Then I look up and see a demon standing next to him. Its head is a thousand charnel-skulls, grinning rottenly; its eyes are empty graves. It is wearing a magician's gown of cloth-of-gold. My father produces a vial of scarlet notes and throws them upward. And the air is filled with the music of rubies, ascending and descending in filigree formations.

'Father!' I cry. 'Father, what happened to you?'

But he has climbed on to a giant viol, which is a tomb.

Scene V

'What is – ?'

'Hush. Keep your foot still – Lord knows what you have stood in. Fox shit, most likely. It's the worst of all, unless you ever step in the leavings of a wild boar.'

I am in the kitchen. My feet are in a bowl of warm water, scented with rosemary and orange peel, and Joan is squatting down before me, rubbing at my filthy toes with a piece of cloth.

'Night-walking again! I thought you were all done with that.'

'So did I. It's been years… not since…'

'…Henry was born, God bless him.'

I have only the vaguest memories of that dreadful time. Left on my own with Alfonso, who was rarely in the house, I was at first content to watch my belly grow bigger and bigger, waiting to be delivered of my baby. I ate well, and had a good serving girl who baked me apple cakes and brewed small beer. But, as the birth-date drew nearer, I began to sicken. Gall rose in my throat and would not clear, so I had to sit upright every night. Then my whole body swelled up to match my distended belly: my face and hands were so round and tight they might have been pregnant with their own progeny, and about to spill forth little newborn limbs. After a few days of this, I was struck down with a blinding head-ache, and I had a violent fit.

I remembered Joan's words when she gave me the potion in her apothecary shop. So I sent for her, and she came and saved me. All through the howling horror of the birth I was blind with pain and my head seemed to be stuck inside a dark box. What kept me sane was the sound of Joan's calm voice, urging me on. And at the end of it, she gave my perfect son to me, with his blunt and folded face and his curled hands, and he opened his mouth and began to suck, and I would not have him taken from me, and I would not have a wet nurse, but fed him from my own breast and everybody marvelled at the way he thrived. When at last I emerged from my chamber, ready for churching, it turned out that Joan was now my servant, and my old one had vanished away. I never questioned this, being so pleased to have her there. Joan said little enough about it, only that her apothecary shop had been burned down by a mob, and they had stolen her herbs and simples before they torched the thatch.

She is looking at me now, her eyes bright. 'You're a good pupil, mistress. You have the makings of a wise woman, if not a sensible one.'

'Thank you.'

'So maybe you would like to help with a new concoction.'

'What is it?'

'An ugly brew.'

'What is it *for*?'

'It is a plague-juice.'

'An elixir? A cure?'

'No. For some, not all, it may work as a preventative.'

'How do you know it works?'

'I don't. But I made it once, long, long ago, and it saved my village.'

'From the plague?'

'We called it the Black Death back then. Only a few of the people caught it, but those that did all died.'

'Shame it's not a remedy.'

'Once you have the contagion, mistress, it is time to pray.'

'Pray? I do that every night. Dr Forman must know more than you do.'

Joan is quiet for a moment. 'If he has cured himself of plague, then he has bargained with the Devil himself. I told you – the Devil tempts the scholar just as he does the crone.'

'Perhaps he found a means through science and knowledge.'

'Maybe so. But all science comes from somewhere, and all knowledge has its price. All finished now – they're nice and clean.' I lift my feet out of the water, and she wraps them in a linen cloth. 'You aren't as strong as you think you are,' she says, drying them gently. 'The spirit is willing, I'll say that for you, but flesh is just flesh.'

'It's not my fault the plague has come.'

'No. But you are pitting yourself against it.'

I shrug. 'Who else can help me? Almighty God? I don't see much hope for this life coming from Him. All *His* promises are to be fulfilled when we are dead souls in Heaven. Then I shall be grateful. Now I am afraid.'

Joan ignores my blasphemous talk. 'That pamphlet for Mr Tottle,' she says. 'What'll you get for that?'

'Two shillings. I've given half to Inchbald, anyway.'

'Should you want another way to make a penny or two, you could always give him the recipe for my plague-juice.'

'There is a *recipe*?' I almost laugh. I think of plum pies and stuffed swans, of simnel cake and peacocks poached in wine.

'You need the brain of a plague corpse to make the paste, for one thing. A palmful of that. And a mandrake root. And various other – items.'

'What sort of items?'

'Gibbon blood can be hard to come by, unless you know the right apothecary. Not so difficult for someone with my history, of course.'

I watch her as she dries my feet, patting them gently with the towel. Joan can make a poultice of ointment flowers, read a urinal of piss, and brew up the most powerful of purgations. When Henry was teething, she soothed his sore gums with the brain of a hare, and knew a cure for shingles made from earthworms and pigeon dung. Once, when Alfonso had been poisoned by a rival at the gaming-house, she cured him with a potion of rue, figs, walnuts and powdered Narwhal tusk. No more and no less than you would expect from a good apothecary. Yet there is something truly sinister about this plague-brew. She is a wise woman, and a faithful servant. What else do I know of her? And what don't I know?

Her hair is loose and hangs around her shrivelled face. Her skin is dun, her hands withered like the talons of a bird of prey. As she works she sings to herself. I don't recognise the tune, or understand the words.

'How old are you, Joan?' I ask.

She is drying the skin around the great toe of my left foot. Her grasp is firm; the cloth is rough and ticklish. She doesn't look up. 'Five hundred years,' she says. 'Or thereabouts.'

'*What?*'

She folds the towel, and straightens up, using a stool to lever herself on to her feet. 'Five hundred years,' she repeats. 'Time enough to learn all I needed.'

I'm not sure Methuselah lived so long. 'Joan, are you a witch?'

'What does it matter what I am?'

'I want to know. I believe I have a right to, being both your mistress and your friend.'

'I am a cunning-woman, who knows more than most.'

'A woman? Just as I am? And you have lived to such an age?'

'Remember, mistress, you are still learning. You know less than little, even now.'

'Joan, I have something to tell you. I should have told you this before, no doubt, but I thought you would take it for one of my night-fancies. If I tell you about this thing, will you tell me, in return, what you really know of witchcraft?'

Her face is shrewd. 'I might say a little more, but not enough to put you in the way of harm. Tell me your story, mistress. Does it concern the witches? I can see them standing by the Tyburn Tree.'

So I tell her the story of the meeting, and what they said about Baptiste and the plague, and how they showed me the bed with Henry dead upon it.

At the end she says, 'We must pray.'

'Pray! Will God help us, who helps no one when the pestilence comes?'

Joan hangs the towel over a chair to dry. 'God bless you, mistress, and give you strength.'

'God bless us all,' I say, testily. 'Now, Joan, what is this you say about being five hundred years upon this earth? Did God play a part in that?'

She crosses herself. 'Do not speak lightly of Our Lord, Aemilia. I was a witch once, and I did many things that I cannot bear to think of, and I have lived for many years beyond my span through the use of my craft. But I have repented of it now. They shut me in a nunnery, and I escaped it, and resolved to do my penance in this world, not in some stone prison. And so I am here. I have come to you. So you must believe me when I tell you that some matters are the will of God, and His will only. I have some experience in these matters.'

'But five hundred years!' I say. 'That is not possible.' Anne says there are rumours that Joan is mad, and I have always thought this to be a foolish piece of gossip. She is strange, yes, and possessed of far greater knowledge than most wise women. But... perhaps she is out of her wits after all? She hands me a pair of woollen stockings and I pull them on. I remember the two young ruffians who threatened me.

'What happened to those boys?' I ask.

'What boys?'

'Outside. They thought I had escaped from the boarded house.'

'You were dreaming. I saw no boys.'

I go to the door. It is a dank day with a dull grey sky. A dead-cart has stopped outside the plague house. The carter is adding two fresh occupants to his load. But they aren't boys. They are street-hounds. Their grey tongues are dangling from their open mouths. One is black with shaggy fur, the other brown, a bearded collie-dog.

Even Paul's Churchyard is quiet in this time of plague. The shops stand empty, their open fronts showing here a solitary printer proof-reading a chap-book, there a determined play-buyer, scrutinising a bill. When I reach Cuthbert Tottle's shop and look inside, at first it seems deserted. All I can see is the monstrous printing press, filling the room almost to the ceiling. Then I see Cuthbert, sitting alone, head bowed, hands folded as if he is praying. He is dressed in black.

'Mistress Lanyer,' he says. 'I bid you a good day.'

'And the same to you.'

I stand, waiting for him to demand a cheerful pamphlet, or one with two-headed monsters or demon births. But, after smiling at me vaguely, he returns to the contemplation of his hands.

'I have the cross-gartering pamphlet that you asked for,' I say. I've little confidence in this. I have rarely seen a thing so dull. But I hand him my pages and he peruses them, pushing his little spectacles up his nose. I see that it is wet with tears, which set his glasses sliding down again, and what I thought was prayer is grief.

'How is Mistress Tottle?' I ask, as he reads. 'I don't see her in the shop today. I hope she is well?' Of course, I fear the worst.

'She died on Sunday.'

'Oh, God rest her!'

'It took her off in two days. I was away at Cambridge, or else I would be boarded in our house, to await the Maker with her. On Friday she sat over there…' he indicates her habitual place '…setting a psalter. She was as perfect… as perfect as… Well. I can't bear to see the half-done words.'

I frown. 'Mr Tottle, the pamphlet I have brought in is a very poor thing. I don't think I should trouble you with it any further.'

Grief has not affected his head for business. He hands it back to me. 'I can't find fault with your description. It's not worth sixpence,' he says. 'Nor even a farthing. At least your Lilith poem had some amusing passages, I seem to recall. I mean to say, they seemed amusing then…'

'I am sorry for your loss…' I hesitate. 'I do have something else. Something useful for these dreadful times.'

He rises from his seat and stands awkwardly, dwarfed by the printing machine. 'Hmm,' he says. 'If you can help us to survive the plague… I think I can vouch that there is an audience for that.'

'There is this,' I say, and give him a sheet of paper. It is Joan's recipe for plague-juice. 'It wards off the pestilence,' I say. 'It doesn't cure it.'

'Isn't that what we all want? Better avoid the smallpox than survive it, with the face of a pitted toad. Better avoid the plague than dance with death.'

'Then we might do business.'

He reads it, front and back. Then he turns it over, and reads it once again. His face brightens. 'Very interesting. I like this. I like it very much. It needs a little background – where you found this cure, why it works, why this is the best protection known to Man. That sort of thing.'

'I can do this.'

'When can you bring it to me?'

'Give me some paper and I will write more now.'

'Would that all the pamphleteers and poets could match your industry.'

'Would that I could match their sex.'

He brings me new paper, virgin-white. I stare at it for a moment, almost frightened to ruin its purity. But then I shake my head, sit down and write for two hours. I find that I can recall almost all of Joan's lore and a fair bit besides. Scraps of rumour, homilies from Anne, stories of strange cures and spontaneous recoveries. A little touch of Plato adds a scholarly flourish. When I have finished, Tottle takes the pages to the window and reads my words. Finally, he says, 'This is worth three shillings of anybody's money.'

He pays me in silver coins and I look down at them, not sure if I have been rewarded for words or witchcraft.

Scene VI

There is a rat on the kitchen table, bold as you please, eating cheese off Henry's trencher.

'Be off with you!' scolds Joan, thwacking it on the head with a poker. The creature barely seems to notice, but jumps off the table, a large chunk of cheese bulging out of one cheek. Its great earthworm of a tail flops into a bowl of small beer as it lollops on its way, finally disappearing into a hole in the wainscot.

'What's ailing Graymalkin?' I ask. 'Are we overfeeding him, or has he lost his taste for rat-flesh? There are more than ever this summer, I swear.'

'On account of the weather being so warm,' says Joan. 'It's not natural. I pray for rain, and a wholesome north breeze.' She fans herself with a pamphlet I had been reading to distract myself. (The title is *Jane Anger: Her Protection for Women to defend them against the scandalous reports of a late-surfeiting Lover, and all other like Venerians that complain so to be overjoyed with women's kindness.* Nothing about cross-gartering there, you will observe.) 'Flaming June indeed. We are burning up.'

'It's the sort of weather that makes a boy want to run out and play!' Henry is sitting at the table, grinding a knife into its side. 'No one else but me is stuck inside, with their old serving-maid, and nothing better than rats for playmates!'

'You stay here, where it's safe,' says Joan. 'There's another plague-house in this street, Lord save them. We must do all we can to stay away from the sick, Henry. It's a terrible illness, and a cruel end.'

'I don't care,' says Henry. 'If I did get the plague, I wouldn't notice any difference, seeing I am a prisoner already.'

Joan crosses herself.

'The difference would be that you would be purple-limbed, racked with pain and burning up with fever,' I say. 'Instead of missing the open fields, you would have a most sincere wish for Death. And stop sawing the table.'

'Well, I wish for Death now, if I can't go out,' says Henry, sawing harder. 'I want to watch the dead-carts! I want to see a plague-pit! I want to see them pour the lime! It's not fair!'

I smack his hand, and the knife falls to the floor. Joan crosses herself again. 'Dear Lord,' she says. 'There is no reasoning with the child. Say your prayers, Henry. You are tempting Providence.'

'I care nothing for Providence,' says Henry. 'I care for running and fighting and… falling over in the mud. And tree-climbing, and throwing stones at ducks and mallards, and making footballs out of dead frogs. And stealing eggs and blinding cats. All the normal things that boys must do.'

Joan shakes her head at him. 'These are not normal times. People are dying in hedges and on the highway. They say half the prisoners in Newgate died in one night, still chained to the walls. In any case, the bells of St Sepulchre's never stop their tolling. No wonder the new King is shut up at Greenwich and keeps out of the City.'

'Joan is right,' I say. 'And it's not just an illness, it's a madness too.' Sometimes the sick run mad through the streets, driven by witless spite to try to infect their fellows. They cast down their ruffs and cuffs and handkerchiefs as they go, wishing to spread contagion.

'I care for none of that. I am not a coward.'

'It is not a matter of cowardice, but of wisdom.'

'Then let me help you with the plague-potion. I am wise enough for that.'

'No, Henry,' I say, picking up the knife. 'It's as disgusting as anything you could get up to with those urchin friends of yours. We are using the brain of a plague corpse...'

'How good! Wait till I tell Tom!'

'Which is too much of a risk for a young boy. And tell no one. We came by it by means that not everyone would approve of, least of all Father Dunstan, so don't go blabbing on to Tom. Now, be off with you, and we will get on.'

'Stay in, but be off with me? Be off where?'

'Go into the vegetable garden. Or up the stairs.'

'You are a wicked gaoler. I shall go up to the attic and look out at the sky, and watch the kites and learn to fly.'

'So be it. Go away, you cheeky little hound.'

He runs up the stairs, in a great commotion of clumping feet.

Joan smiles wryly. 'You've made a rod for your own back,' she said. 'The child does as he pleases.'

'Yes, well, it's too late now. He is what he is, and I must take the consequences.'

We set to with the potion, and Lord above, it is a filthy business. When we have done, we scour our hands clean. Then we sit at the table, drinking ale. The plague-brew is simmering on the hearth, belching out its foul odours.

'Fetch Henry down for something to eat,' I say to Joan.

But she comes back shaking her head. 'He's hid himself somewhere,' she says. 'There's always something with that boy.'

'What's he up to now?' I sigh. 'I'll soon find him.'

But the bedchambers are empty, and he isn't in the wardrobe on the landing, or in the space under the eaves, or hiding on the balcony over the street. I climb the ladder to the attic. There is no sign of him there either. All I can hear is the rustling of rats in their nests, and the sound of their babies squeaking. Could he have climbed out upon the house-top, to look at the sky as he had promised? I open the window and see that a rope has been flung across to the open window opposite, above the narrow street, to make a bridge. The house belongs to Anne Flood.

'Henry! I call. I half-expect his head to appear at their window, but no. There is no reason for him to stay at Tom's once he has made his escape. He could be anywhere.

We search both houses, from top to bottom, with Anne exclaiming over Henry's bad behaviour, and assuring me that Tom could have nothing to do with it, as the players have been summoned to a meeting at the Globe, which has been closed due to the plague. 'I shall send word to Tom,' she says. 'Heaven help us! We must tell him Henry has fled.'

'He'll soon turn up,' say I. But I am sick with fear, for there is no denying it: Henry has disappeared.

'The Lord has taken him,' says Anne. 'Oh, my heart goes out to you, Aemilia!'

I turn away from her. 'He has run away, off to play somewhere. He'll be back by dusk.'

But dusk falls, and there is still no sign of him. Fear takes hold of my body with an uncanny coldness. My limbs are heavy with dread. Yet at the same time it is impossible to stay still for one second, and I pace the house, up and down, ceaselessly, endlessly mounting the stairs, searching each chamber, looking under the beds, climbing up into the attic and sticking my head out of the window. I even go to the outside privy several times, as if he might have found himself some cranny to hide inside that malodorous place. At last I can bear it no longer. I set out, torch in hand, leaving Joan to wait for his possible return.

In the City, bells toll, marking not the hour but the passing of the dead. The evening is close and airless. A raven flies over my head, giving out its strange, throaty call. *Prruk-prruk-prruk*. An ill omen, if I needed one. Where can I look? Where might he have gone? If Tom has been at the Globe all day, there is no reason to think that Henry is with him. In any case, the Globe is on the other side of the river. Going by the Bridge is too far round, and

225

he doesn't have money for the wherryman. He would be more likely to head for the fields and woods. But then, he also likes to frisk along the outer walls of Whitehall Palace, fencing with himself and shrieking out in mock agony when the invisible blade strikes home. I can almost hear his high voice. 'Ooh! Aargh! Have at thee, knave! I bowel you – dead man!' My little Henry, wandering alone in the plague-ridden City.

Oh, Lord! Curse the boy! Or rather, bless him, protect him, deliver him from harm! I walk, as fast as I can, along Long Ditch and towards Camm Row, my breath heaving in my chest. If this is God's way of punishing me as an unfit mother, then it is roughly in proportion to his other punishments – an eternity of hellfire for a life that mixes sin with sorrow. From time to time I call Henry's name, in an agony of rage and pain.

I hold my crackling torch high against the dark sky, and what I behold looks like one of the old church wall paintings of the Dance of Death. I see a blasted, empty place. Deserted houses, blind and shuttered. An old woman, on her hands and knees, puking into the stinking kennel in the middle of the street. A skinny boy, carrying a limp baby. Here is a dead-cart rattling by me, loaded with corpses. Some are bundled in sheets; others are naked, mouths gaping open like landed fish.

I call out to the carter, 'You haven't seen a little boy, have you sir? A boy of ten or so. Yellow-headed and skittish.' My voice sounds unreal in this weird place. I meant 'haired' not 'headed', and in my mind I see Henry-as-monster, skull gold-painted.

'Not if he's alive,' says the friendly fellow, hunched and faceless. 'I deal in Death. I don't see the living.'

'You might have seen him running along somewhere. You can't miss him. He's – bold and bonny. Noisy. You'd be sure to remember.' I'm smiling at him, as if this might encourage him to recall my child.

'Take a look in the cart if you've a mind,' he says. 'I've got all sizes in there. Might be one of about that age, if you're lucky.'

I turn away, too brimful of horror to answer back in my normal way. The house before me is boarded – not a plague-house, but a grand merchant's home, left in a hurry. A sack of flour is spilled across the doorway, evidence of the hasty departure of the occupants. Against one of the wood-shuttered windows, a pamphlet has been posted. It is a warning from the City fathers, recounting a litany of causes of the plague. The fault lies with *'runnygate Jews, thrasonical and unlettered chemists, shifting and outcast pettifoggers, dull-pated and base mechanics, stage-players, pedlars, prittle-prattling bawds, toothless and tattling old wives'*, and many more. I read the words in a trance-state close to despair. I can't stop looking. But where should I go? The very ground hungers for corpses and sucks them in, nameless and unshriven. I say a prayer, a wordless, secret prayer, for my mind is blank of proper thoughts.

Then, I remember Henry's words – he wanted to see a dead-cart, and a plague-pit. Of course he did. Though the streets are empty and the populace lives in terror of this cruel distemper, gawpers crowd round the rims of the mass graves to wonder at the twisted faces of the dead. So, as I have no idea where to find him, I will follow the dead-cart to its destination.

I walk some distance from the cart, keeping it in view as I follow it along the road. From time to time the driver calls out, 'Cast out your dead! Any dead bodies to bury? Cast out your dead!' But the houses are silent.

Then, behind me, another shout goes up. 'Have you any more Londoners to bury, hey down a down dery, have you any more Londoners to bury, good morrow and good day?' I turn to look, and see two fellows behind me. The first is shabbily dressed and with a beard somewhat wild and untrimmed. The other is thicker-set, and looks more prosperous. His face is shadowed by his feathered hat. I quicken my pace, even though all there is to protect me is a cart loaded with corpses.

'Madam,' a voice calls out. 'A fine night for barn owls, and cut-throats. Not so fine for the likes of you.'

I answer without slowing down. 'A fine night for finding my son, I hope.'

'You look to find him in a grave? You will be lucky.'

'I look to find him above ground. He is not ill, he is merely disobedient.'

'Ah, the disobedient roaring boys! London would not be the same without them. Myself, I pray they live forever. For if London's underworld is the map of merry hell, then they are the dancing devils sent to please us.'

'Shush, Dekker, shush!' says the other man, grasping his arm. 'It is she.'

I know that voice only too well. The cart has lumbered to a halt, and the driver has gone into a house. I stop and wait till the two men catch up with me, knowing now that I have nothing to fear from them. No danger to my life, in any case. And I realise, as they come closer and our three torches make a bright space in the night, that I know both of them. The first is Thomas Dekker, a boy actor with the Lord Chamberlain's Men when I was Hunsdon's mistress, who has now turned his hand to writing. An eager, lively fellow, who is smiling now even in this earthly hell. I know the other fellow better, even when he hides behind his cloak and keeps his head bowed in the guttering torchlight.

'This is a strange time to be out,' say I. 'Did you come to take the air?'

'Aemilia,' says Will. 'Forgive me, but Tom Flood told us your son was lost. And I wanted to… It seemed fitting to come to see where he might be.'

'I assure you, sir, I have no need of help from anyone.'

'You are white as alabaster,' says Will. 'The poor child! God bless him.'

'Indeed, madam, you do not look well,' says Dekker. 'We will escort you, and I am sure we shall find this naughty son of yours.

Why, the whole City is running mad, but there is no need to fear for one quick boy who can outrun the pestilence.'

I know this is untrue, but I'm grateful for his cheerful tone.

'We will search with you, whether you like it or not,' says Will.

The flames illuminate his dark eyes and I see his fear, and I remember how he stared at Henry at the Globe. There is no mistaking the similarity between them.

Dekker's spirits seem unaffected by our two drawn faces. 'It's a pretty place, indeed!' he says. He gestures around him, as if to include the silent houses, the red crosses daubed on the doors and the weeds that grow on each side of the kennel. 'I am tired of being a poet to whores and strumpets. So I am writing a pamphlet on the plague.'

'A gloomy subject, as I am sure Mistress Lanyer will testify,' says Will.

We walk on together. My mind is so fixed on finding Henry, and the fear of not finding him, that I accept Will's presence as part of the nightmare chaos that surrounds me.

'Never was a vile contagion so badly run,' says Dekker. 'The Corporation hires women to keep their eye upon the sick and dying, and insists they are all sober and ancient. But instead they are a bunch of blear-eyed, drunken night-crows.' He lowers his voice. 'As for the likes of that one up ahead – I swear they hire these carters from Satan's own stable-yard. Nasty, foul-mouthed breed. Too brute and slovenly to make recruits for hangmen.'

'How long has… Henry been gone?' asks Will.

'Hours past. Hours and hours,' say I. 'I thought he was in the house – he might have been running amok since midday.'

'He might have been among the plague-pits these last ten hours,' says Dekker. 'Boys do love these places.'

My voice cracks. 'Dear God!'

'Show some sympathy for this poor lady, will you?' says Will. 'For pity's sake, she's at her wits' end. Her son is gone!'

'Not gone,' I say, quickly. 'He is mislaid.'

Dekker smiles. 'There is no one in London who doesn't run the risk of catching this disease,' he says. 'And most of us will live to tell the tale. I certainly hope I shall, for there is money in it. I plan to call my pamphlet *A Wonderful Year*. Satire,' he says quickly, catching Will's eye and clearly wanting to avoid another reproof.

'Look, Tom, go up ahead and see where that cart is heading,' says Will.

Whistling cheerily, Dekker obliges. We watch his torch move forward in a jaunty fashion through the darkness.

Then Will says, 'Aemilia, the boy – '

'He will be near, and we will find him,' I say. 'Have no fear of that.'

'He has such a look of Hamnet.'

'It makes no odds to us now, does it? We are estranged.'

'I know he is my son.'

We walk in silence for a moment.

'You have eyes to see: so be it,' I say. 'But he calls Alfonso "Father".'

He turns to look down at me, and holds the torch higher so that he can see my face. 'Do you wish to punish me?'

'Who has punished whom?' I ask. 'What am I – a foul-breathed Lilith? A demon succubus, come to corrupt you? I still have those poems you wrote – some strange respect for Art prevents me from burning them to ash. If there is a distinction in inspiring a poetry of hate, then I can claim it.'

'Aemilia – those poems – the words I used against you...'

But then Dekker returns, breathless. 'I have found the pit,' he says, all levity gone. 'There's no mistaking it. God save us all.'

We have reached the end of the lanes of Westminster, and come to open fields. Ahead of us, on the brow of a hill, a bonfire burns, lighting up the shapes of a crowd of people. There are smaller figures – children – among then. The cart has stopped at the bonfire, and the driver is climbing down. Will pulls my arm and we step back into the shadow of a hay-barn.

'What a terrible place,' says Dekker. 'Jesu. I have seen nothing like it.'

'Aemilia – let Tom and I go up ahead and see if he is there,' says Will. 'You will be safe here.'

'It's not fit for a woman,' says Dekker. 'Truly, madam.'

'I would not think of staying behind,' I say. 'I would go into Hell to save my son. A plague-pit is nothing to me.'

Scene VII

The two men walk ahead of me and I follow, silently. I still carry my torch, and am at once grateful for the glare it casts on the rough and tussocky ground, and fearful that we will catch the attention of the watchers ahead. But no one notices us. And, when I reach the pit, I see why. The carter has backed his cart close to the open gash in the earth, so that it is hard up against the drop. Now, he stands beside it, like a showman at a Fair. All around the edge, illuminated by the flames of the crackling bonfire, stands a motley group of citizens such as I never wish to see again. They are like the walking dead themselves, battered and bedraggled beyond humanity.

'Show us your wares!' shouts one, an old man with bullfrog eyeballs bulging from his skull.

'Yes, do your worst. Let's see what ingredients we can put into our pot!' shouts a young bawd, pale and hollow-cheeked, with a baby at her breast and a small child clutching at her skirts with its skinny arms. The bawd is swaying, and shaking, and I suspect it will not be long before she tumbles down herself. I look into the grave, and at first can see nothing, for the pit is twenty or thirty feet deep, and the fire casts little light into its depth. But when I look closer I see that what at first seemed like gravel and stones in the shadows is a muddle of hands and feet and faces, piled and confused and tangled. The bawd is right: the grave is a cauldron, and this is human stew.

'Now then, now then, ladies and gentlemen, babes and children, all,' says the carter, clapping his filthy hands to win the attention of the crowd. 'This is a good night, and good business. Sixpence I get for each of these deadmen, which you are about to see before you. The more of them, the better my breakfast. The Lord God is truly shining his light upon me.'

'Praise God in his wisdom,' shouts some ague-addled fool.

The carter goes to his plague-carriage and fetches the first corpse. It is the body of a big, wide-set man, of maybe twenty years or so. It is hard to tell, as its face is grey and twisted, and corrupted with sores.

'Here's a fine fellow,' says the carter. 'Wave at your attendants, good sir!' He flops the hand of the deadman at the watchers. 'We all know that worms need no apparel, saving only winding-sheets. So – let us take off what needs to be taken off.' He drops the corpse down, removes the doublet, and feels inside the pocket. 'Oh, indeed, my Maker blesses me once more!' He waves a leather bag before us, and drops the contents into his palm. 'Seven pieces of silver! I am near as rich as Judas! Thank you, sir!' And, with that, he kicks the poor fellow into the grave.

Next, he produces a naked baby. 'Nothing to speak of this small fry,' he says, holding it up by one leg. 'And I can see it has no pockets.' He tosses it into the pit, grinning as he does so.

I glance at Will. His face is clenched, as if he is willing himself to stay silent. I think this wise. The dead are dead, and God himself will deal with this man when he meets his end.

But here is something different, and which seems to interest the fellow more than either of the first two bodies. He lifts a young girl from the cart, aged sixteen or seventeen years. She is a veritable Juliet, with long, pale hair, as dainty and beautiful a young virgin as you could wish for. And she is still dressed in a fine gown, the ruff standing half-off, like a torn petal.

'O-ho,' says the carter. 'O-ho, again the Lord has showed me favour! What form of patient goddess have we here? Death is greedy. He takes this plump peach for his own and ravishes it like any hungry lover.' And with this he turns the girl round, so her head and shoulders flop down and she is bent double before him, then he lifts her skirts and pretends to hump her from behind. There are calls and cheers from the crowd.

But he has not finished yet. 'Let's have a look at her fine titties,' says the carter, dropping the body down. 'Would she had been so pliant in life. Would that I could have tiptoed into her bedchamber, and fucked her while she breathed. Never mind, I'll have her now.' With this he begins to unlace her bodice, but, finding it stiff, he tears at the fabric, muttering to himself. After a moment, he hauls her to her feet, facing us, with her small breasts revealed. 'Who wants a lick of these fine dugs?' he calls. 'Come on, I'll make my price on this excellent bitch. Sixpence for one lick, a shilling for two. Or – '

Out of the night, out of nowhere, a figure comes rushing towards him.

'Aargh – you shall die, you stinking Devil!' screams a voice. I know that voice! I know it! There is a mighty roar from the carter, and the dead virgin drops into the pit.

'He bit me! He bit me, the demon!' shouts the carter, falling to his knees.

'Henry!' I shriek. 'Henry, in the name of God!' I rush round the edge of the pit, wielding my torch like a pikestaff and pushing the watching ghouls out of my way. But Will runs faster, waving his sword, and pulls the sobbing Henry away.

'Henry! Stop this at once!'

'Henry!' I scream, and catch him in my arms.

'Now fly – go!' shouts Will, and he and Dekker face the carter, swords and torches in hand. But the rabble, deprived of its sport, is shouting and coming closer. The carter lunges at Will, who thrusts the burning torch at his beard. It catches fire and flames leap up around the carter's blackening face. The crowd begins to run at us, and we all turn and flee towards the cart. I am clutching Henry's hand as we run. Dekker gets there first, and then we throw ourselves upon it and he whips up the old mare and she lurches forward. Before the crowd can reach us she has lumbered to a canter over the uneven grass.

Dekker laughs wildly and cries, 'My God, we've escaped Hell, my friends! We've seen Death, plain as a pikestaff, and cheated him!'

But Will says nothing. His eyes are fixed on Henry.

When I dare to look behind me, the bonfire is growing smaller in the distance, and the cries of the crowd are fading, and I hold my son so tightly in my arms that they begin to ache.

Scene VIII

Henry sleeps till noon the next day, eats some bread and drinks some ale, then sleeps again till evening. When I go up to see him, he is lying in my bed, eyes open, looking thoughtfully at the embroidered hangings.

'I shall be good from now on,' he says. 'Biting the carter is the worst thing I will ever do.'

'Indeed, I hope so.' My throat is dry – why is he such a madcap child? *Please Lord*, I pray. *There was goodness in his heart. He was avenging that poor girl.*

'I shall fit myself for Heaven.'

I shiver and close the window. 'You have plenty of time for that,' I say. 'Year upon year. You will be an old man, all bent, with a white beard hanging down to your knees.'

Further along the street they are closing up another plague-house. The carpenters are smoking tobacco pipes and leaning planks of wood against the house front. A topless cross of St Anthony is painted in red on the wall to the right of the front door. The carpenters work calmly and slowly, as if taking pride in their craft.

'I shall fit myself in any case.' Henry smiles at me, so sweetly. 'I would have killed the plague-man if I could, so it's good I wasn't able to, else I would be a murderer.'

'It was very good we stopped you. Now, would you like a gingerbread man? Joan has been baking.'

'I'm not hungry.'

A spasm of fear in my guts. Henry is always hungry.

'Just a little?' I say. 'Just a tiny bit? I could break you off an arm or a leg?

'No, I will sleep again now.'

'Good.' There are tears behind my eyes. 'Good boy.' I smooth his brow, and he closes his eyes.

When I go back, half an hour later, with a cup of small beer, I touch his forehead, the little scar above his eyebrow where he had fallen from the window while trying to skewer a raven on his sword. He is slightly warm. Perhaps he will be well by morning, running into the kitchen demanding bakemeats and a farthing.

I stroke his face, and kiss his closed eyelids. Not a single lash shall be harmed; not a grubby toenail. I will stand between him and all that could threaten his safety. I will turn the plague from my door. I will face down the spectre of the Reaper, and cast it out, and it will limp away down the road, dark robe flapping, till it vanishes. My head aches, and when I shut my eyes I can see the Reaper's crow-form, black on red. I get into bed beside Henry and begin to pray, mouthing the words silently so that only God will hear them. But something is wrong: my mind is blanked with dead walls, and the ache of my head beats against them. The prayer I want will not come, only the litany:

'*O God the Father of Heaven: have mercy upon us miserable sinners.*' And then the response from the congregation. A thousand whisperers in my head, beneath the bed, behind the wainscot like black rats: '*O God the Father of Heaven: have mercy upon us miserable sinners.*'

I try again, seeking the prayer against the pestilence. But only say, '*O God the Son, Redeemer of the world: have mercy upon us miserable sinners.*' And there are the voices again, but this time I can only hear the rats: '*O God the Son, Redeemer of the world: have mercy upon us miserable sinners.*'

The tears run down my cheeks. Where is God? How can He hear me, down among the carrion and filth? *'O God the Holy Ghost, proceeding from the Father and the Son: have mercy upon us miserable sinners.'* The rats are ready for me: *'Have mercy upon us miserable sinners.'*

I raise my head, and listen. Silence, all around me, save for the rasp of Henry's breath. There is another verse – what is the verse? I close my eyes tight, tight, so there is no space for the Reaper, and bunch my hands together so the nails dig into the backs of my hands. *'Remember not, Lord, our offences, nor the offences of our forefathers; neither take thou vengeance of our sins: spare us, good Lord, spare thy people, whom thou has redeemed with thy most precious blood, and be not angry with us for ever.'*

And then come the rats: *'Spare us, good Lord.'*

Then I sleep, and in my dreams I feel the flames of Hellfire, rising up from the plague-pit and licking the feet of the watchers. They flock like patterned starlings against the roaring sky. When I wake, with a start, the flames still burn me, and I shrink away from the heat. My hand touches Henry's arm – flung out on the top of the covers – and I gasp, for his skin is burning hot. I bend to look at him. His eyes are half-open, and his breathing shallow. I push back his hair, and it is soaking wet.

'Mother,' he says. His voice is clear but small.

'What, my little one?' I touch his cheek with trembling fingers.

'Take my head away.'

'How can I, silly boy, when it's stuck fast to your neck?' There are tears on my face, and a raging pain behind my eyes. Is it his pain, or mine?

'It aches me. It's grown too big. You could tear it off and take it to the Bridge, and spike it up high, and the wind and air would cool me.'

'Don't speak of such – '

'I could see all the orchards of Kent, and the village ponds, and the hop fields and the apple trees going on and on till they reach the sea.'

'Henry! My love, my little love…'

'And then I could see the wild waves, and mermaids, and then France, and Venice after that, and then Constantinople and Ethiopia, where the dragons are ten fathoms long. My head is no good here.' He looks at me, and starts. 'But you're not my mother.'

'Yes, I *am*, dearest chuck. For good or ill, you have no other.' I gather him to me, and hold his quivering form against my chest.

'But you are old,' he whispers. 'My mother is young, and beautiful.'

'My sweet boy, I am still your mother!' I wonder where my light tone comes from, when I am brimful of fear. I talk as if the fairyland he describes is real, and the open grave of London just a dream.

'No.' His eyes close. I rock him, as I did when he was a baby. For this child I have lost everything: Will's love, Hunsdon's protection and my place at Court. I have sacrificed wealth and position and the only life I knew. And I have never wished it otherwise, not for one second, no matter what befell me. He is my son, my only child. There is no transaction to be made with such a love. I wish I could pass all the goodness and strength in my own body through to him. Save him, Lord! Save him! I search again for the right prayer, and this time come upon the words, '*Deus, Deus meus*,' then the Latin fades to English and I cry out, '*My God, my God, look upon me; why has thou forsaken me: and art so far from my health, and the words of my complaint? O my God, I cry in the daytime, and in the night season also, I take no rest…*'

There is a blank, then I try again.

'*All they that see me laugh me to scorn: they shoot out their lips, and shake their heads, saying, She trusted in God, that would deliver her, let Him deliver her, if he will have her…*

O go not from me, for trouble is hard at hand, and there is none to help me!'

But my voice rises to a monstrous wail, a she-wolf howling at the moon. This is not the prayer I need. Where is the prayer I am looking for, the spell that will summon the Lord? I stare up at the carved roof of the four-poster bed, and the brightly coloured waves and fishes heave and shift.

Then I see that Henry's eyes are fixed on me again. 'I've learned my lessons, Mother, don't beat me!'

'My son, what are you saying? *Who* beats you?'

His eyes are blank and staring. 'I've learned it well, the lesson. That all things have their situation, and must remain in that place. All things in Creation, fixed, like stars.'

'Rest, sweet baby; it doesn't mean a jot.'

'Of fish: carp, cod, dace, dog-fish, shark, eel, gudgeon, herring. And then the porpoise.'

'Henry – '

'Of creeping things – worm, serpent, adder, blindworm, slug and snail. And then the lizard and the gilded newt.'

I open my mouth to speak, but can make no sound.

'Of flies… house fly, blue-bottle, flesh-fly, louse and sheep tick. And then the… merry flea.'

He closes his eyes and I kiss his fluttering lids. 'That is enough now. The schoolmaster will be pleased with you. All God's Creation. In its place.'

He sits upright. 'But Mother, I have not done the dogs! The dogs must take their places! Let me do the dogs!'

'Do the dogs, my child. Yes, please do the dogs.'

He lies down again, and speaks precisely, checking the words off on his damp fingers. 'First the three ranks: game dog, house-dog, toy dog.'

'Well said.'

'Of game dogs: spaniels and hounds. Of hounds, eight kinds: harriers, temurs, bloodhounds, gazehounds, greyhounds, lymnes, tumblers and thieves. Of spaniels, the water spaniel and the land spaniel, for falconry.'

Joan is standing at the doorway.

'You should have called me,' she says.

I scramble out of the bed and run to her, tripping and staggering. I put my hand on her thin shoulder to steady myself. 'He has a fever. That's all. A touch of fever. We must give him something from your physick store. A draught – to take away the heat.'

But Henry is not yet done. 'Dogs of the homelier kind. Are either shepherd's curs, or mastiffs, which can be...' He seems to drift, then comes back, his voice louder. 'Barn-dogs. Tie-dogs. And watchdogs.'

Joan stares at him, her eyes wide with sorrow.

'And then... the toy dogs. Of the sort which lick a lady's lips...'

His voice fades, till I hear the faintest sound of growling. 'The mastiff is a proud dog. Three can match a bear, and four can eat a lion.'

Joan looks at my torn gown and tangled hair. 'Lord save us,' she whispers. 'God help the little fellow.'

Her tone is kind, but I hate her hopeless words.

'*We* must help him,' I say. 'We must soothe the fever. Come now, you are the one with all the knowledge.'

'Mistress, I will help you all I can. But we must be brave. We must be ready. Half the people in this street have buried babes and children.'

I close my eyes, to will her voice away.

She grasps my hands. 'The Flemish family – four doors down – had fourteen girls and buried nine. You know this as well as I do. The plague is not even the worst of it. Sweating sickness, drowning, hunting-dogs, the pox. Five infants died in the baker's fire just one week past. You can't guard Henry against every danger, for all your care. But – God willing – he may yet live for threescore years and ten. Put your trust in the Lord.'

I pull away. 'Bring me what you have to cure him!'

'Willow tea might soothe him a little. But for the pestilence itself there is no physick.'

'God's blood, Joan, I thought you were a wise woman! What wisdom is this? What about the plague-juice, the recipe you made?'

'Mistress, your worry is numbing your mind. It's for *prevention*,' she says. 'Not for cure. Only God in his mercy knows how to cure the pestilence.' And – so suddenly that I first think she has fallen – she sinks down upon the rushes. She puts her hands together, ready to pray.

I run barefoot from the chamber and down into the kitchen. The still-room is next to the cupboard on which I keep what is left of my pewter. It is lined with shelves, and barely big enough for a single person to stand up in. There Joan stores not only her potions and libations, but clear cakes of gooseberry, rose-hip conserves, syrups of green quince and melon, pickled nasturtium-buds, ashen keys, radish-pods and broom-buds – all stored in pots and capped with leather. Every manner of thing, in short, which Henry loves. I search the shelves, my breath coming in queer sobs. Each pot has been labelled in his best italic hand: he and Joan work together, she calling out the name, and Henry writing it down. I grab at the pots and bottles, and fling them on to the trestle table. A jar of moss-powder rolls over the edge of the table, and smashes to pieces on the stone-flagged floor.

'Calm yourself, you'll do him no good that way,' says Joan.

I turn to face her, my head full of aches and murmurs. 'I thought you had given him up for dead.'

She takes down a jar of hemlock. 'That's not what I meant.'

'What did you mean, then?'

'There is always the hope of a miracle.'

But God does not love Henry as I love him! Other children are dying, so why should He save mine? I need some other power, some other lore. There is one man who might help me in this enterprise, and, if the price of his power is a so-called 'halek', then I will fuck him for his knowledge just as Anne Flood fucks Inchbald to keep a roof over her head.

'I'm going out,' I say, putting on my cloak.

Joan looks up, startled. 'What, and leave Henry at such a time? And where to, in Heaven's name?'

'I will find a cure for him. You will nurse him well, I know.' I fasten my shoes.

'You're going alone?'

'Of course. Mind Henry, and, if he asks for me, say I will be back before he knows it.'

She looks out of the window. 'I pray to God you are true to your word. Be careful, mistress, and be quick.'

Scene IX

As I hurry on my way, the sky is lowering and I pull my cloak closer round me. The silent streets are grey and cold. As I pass Foul Lane, I see a kite, pecking at the corpse of a turtle dove. Its beak is crimson with blood. When I approach, it rises up, squealing, and flaps its giant wings, and I shield my eyes as it flies over my head.

Simon Forman lives at Lambeth. I know the place – a handsome new house on the outskirts of the village. Fortunately, it is on the river shore almost directly opposite to Westminster. Unfortunately, both the weather and the plague are against me. At the riverbank, I stop, looking up and down at the silent boatyards. The quays are usually a riot of noise and activity, crowded with boatmen and eel-men, shoutmen and shipwrights, trinkers and mariners. But now the quays are silent, and the only noise I can hear is the wind rattling in the rigging of the empty ships. I hurry along to the stairs, where the wherrymen are usually for hire. There is a single boat moored there, and a figure humped in the bows, hood pulled down low. The rain is lashing down now. I stumble along to the stairs, and make my slippery way to the boat.

As I approach, the hooded figure looks up. It is a young woman, with a white face, perfectly beautiful except for her cheeks, which are holed and pitted with smallpox scars.

'I am looking for a wherryman,' I say, unsure what she is doing there.

'Then you have found one.'

'Is your husband…?'

'Dead, and my children will follow him unless I earn some coins. Let me help you in.' She stands up with the sureness of any boatman, and hands me into the craft.

We set out for Lambeth Stairs, and, as we go, I wonder about this woman, sensing that she is as desperate as I am. 'How many children do you have?'

She is rowing strongly with her thin arms. 'Six. The eldest cares for the younger ones. They are good children.'

'And did your husband die of the plague?'

The current is faster now, and she pulls for a few strokes before replying. 'No, mistress. He was murdered.'

'Lord above! I am sorry to hear it.'

'Not I.'

Have I misheard her?

'Not who?'

'Not I. It would be a false sorrow, and I am not a false woman.'

She rows in silence for a while. She is not one for the wherryman's patter. As the southern shore grows near, my curiosity gets the better of me. 'Do you know who killed him?'

She laughs, and looks me in the face for the first time. 'I should say so.'

At the steps, I pay her fivepence. She gives me another curious look and says, 'False, he called me. False, and I bore his children, and baked his bread and worked my life away for him. That great sotted oaf. If I'd lain with half the men he said I had, I'd be the biggest whore in Whitehall.'

'They see their own faults in us,' say I.

She stares, and I see a shimmer of insanity in her face. 'When I washed my hands, I knew it was all finished. It was just a little deed, and quickly done. It's only when I sleep that they are all dripping scarlet again, and I wash them and wash them – and the Thames runs red. I see the carp and salmon choking in his blood.'

She smiles. 'So I stay awake. I watch the moon go from one side of the sky to the other. Then the dawn comes, and blinds me with its light.'

The plague is driving us all mad. I turn and walk into the storm, barely able to see my way, slipping and sliding over the stones of the path. My rain-heavy cloak pulls at my shoulders, and my hands are frozen. I look around me, wishing I had a guide to show me the way. And then, I see it. A dark building looms out of the rain. It is surrounded by trees, waving and crashing in the wind. I wade through the mire and beat upon the door. The sound is unnaturally loud. A shock of lightning flames the sky.

No one answers. I look up at the black windows, hoping to see a light. I knock again, hammering louder this time. Perhaps the pestilence has reached Lambeth? Perhaps the doctor and his family are dead? No, no! I knock a third time, then stop and listen for the sound of footsteps on the other side. Silence. I go round the side of the house, half-blinded by the wet strands of my hair. There is a door in a high wall. It opens into an orchard. The high walls give some protection from the wind, but none from the rain: the neat pathways between the apple and apricock trees are flooded like Venetian canals. I squelch across the grass, mud sucking at my feet, till I reach one of the latticed windows. I pick up a heavy stone from the path and hurl it against the window. It crashes through the glass, shattering the stillness.

A moment later, there is a glow of candle-flame at the window above. The window opens and Dr Forman's voice calls out, 'Who's there?'

'It's me. Aemilia Lanyer.'

But the storm drowns out my words.

'What? Who? Be off with you!'

I shout louder. 'It's Aemilia! I have come to see you! I need your help – please let me in!'

Now he puts on a quavering tone.

'If it's Simon Forman you are after, he is gone to Cambridge. Go away, or I will call the Watch.'

'Then call them, you poisonous toad! If they'll come as far as Lambeth. Tell them a bastard whore is smashing up his house.'

With that, I pick up a second stone, as big as a fist, and throw it at another window. The leaded glass crashes into tiny pieces, and inside the room something falls. I pray it is the heart of a unicorn preserved in a pot, or some other precious item.

'Stop that! Stop it!' Now he sticks his head out, and his beard blows sideways. 'Come to the side door – see it? Down there, in the corner. Unseemly baggage! And come *quietly*.'

'Quietly? Satan himself can't hear me in this storm.'

'Shush! Shush! Lord help me! There is a price upon my head.'

Simon Forman looks thinner and yellower than he was when I saw him last, and he has exchanged his flowing necromancer's gown for a stout doublet and plain hose. He looks angry and ill at ease. 'Really!' he cries. 'House-breaking and wanton destruction! Whatever would Hunsdon have said?'

'I believe he would have applauded me,' I say, wiping rain from my eyes. 'He was a soldier, after all.'

'God's teeth! I shall send you the bill! Whatever is the matter?'

'Henry has the plague. I know you cured yourself of it. How did you do that?'

'Let us say I have strong nerves, and much knowledge.'

'Through necromancy?'

'I cannot say.'

'Through conjuration?'

'That is information that I will never share.'

'I need to cure my child, and I don't mind how I do it, or what I do to find the knowledge.'

The doctor seems to have no sense of urgency. 'No one knows how it is spread, though I, for one, do not believe it is the vapours,' he says, in a scholarly manner. 'I put my money on *Rattus rattus*, the common rat.'

'I don't care if it's spread by Gabriel and all the ministering angels. Please help me.'

He closes the wooden shutters over the broken windows before drawing the heavy curtains.

'Did you come alone?'

'Yes.'

'Were you followed?'

'I don't think so.'

'You told no one your destination?'

'Not a soul. Why?'

He pokes at the embers of seacoal till they spark into life. 'The College of Physicians is trying to murder me. They've hired assassins. They nearly had me – twice. I've sent my family out of London. I am leaving myself in the morning.'

I must say, this strikes me as ridiculous. The august body of good doctors, paying murderers to finish off this poor old goat! Men, and their precious knowledge. All the world is upside-down.

'I am sorry about your windows,' I say. 'But I had to see you.'

'Well. You certainly know how to put yourself in harm's way.' He draws up two chairs, and sits down by the fire. Reluctantly, I join him. I am anxious to find out what I need to and return to Henry's side.

'As to the power to stop the plague, did you read the pamphlet I gave you?' Forman asks.

'Every word. It is an account of the degrees of witchcraft. I understand what it is saying. And I know what I want to do. I need something more tangible – a spell for conjuring.'

'For the conjuring of what, precisely?'

248

'Of a demon that can help me – what else would it be?'

He looks at me thoughtfully. 'Are you really prepared to dabble in that Art?' he asks. 'To conjure evil?'

'Yes, I am,' I cry. 'If God won't help me, then I will settle for the other side.'

He thinks for a moment. 'It is true that it may be an efficacious way of dealing with the curse.'

'What curse?' I think of the witches, and the foul visions that they called up.

'That is what I saw in your future when you came to see me. I believe there is some old score to settle. An unpaid debt, something owed by your father.'

'Such as his soul – can you owe such a thing?'

'Each of us is possessed of that mysterious entity. When you see a man die, you see him shrink and lighten as it leaves. If a soul may be owned, *ergo* it may be owed. That would be the logic of the matter.'

I say nothing, my mind confused and all my thoughts on Henry.

Forman pokes the fire and watches the spark flare up the chimney. 'I have discovered something rather interesting. You were not the first person in your family to visit me, Aemilia. When I looked at my old case notes, I discovered this fact.'

'No? Who else have you seen?'

'Your mother, Margaret Johnson. A clever but unlearned woman, and not anything like as beautiful as you.'

'She came for your predictions?'

'She wanted my advice – she was ill and knew her death was coming soon. She told me all about your father, and his mysterious end. She said that when he came from Venice he was a good musician but not a brilliant one, and there were others in his family who had more virtuosity. He was the youngest of six brothers, and always felt that he was in their shadow. Then, he was lost in a storm one winter night, up Tyburn way. When he came home the next day, with his clothes torn and his eyes starting from his head, he claimed to have no memory of what had happened. But, after that, he played the most extraordinary tunes, composed, sang, arranged – his talents seemed God-given. And then, after one year – exactly one year – he refused to play again.'

'He stopped playing? Why did I never hear of this?'

'She told no one.'

'But… I remember him playing all the time! So well! So wonderfully!'

'That may be because he was murdered just one full moon after he'd ceased playing. Murdered in cold blood, by assailants who vanished like ghosts, and were never seen again.'

'Oh, Jesu!' I say. 'I saw it happen. Did he break his bargain with the witches?'

'Who can say? Murderers are skilled at disappearance, such is their modesty about their craft. They may have been as corporeal as you or me.'

'But my mother didn't think so?'

'She was afraid. She had him buried quietly, and told no one of his violent end. No one but myself. It's a strange tale, certainly.'

'What I do know is that these witches have some grudge against me, and have sought me out.'

'Perhaps they believe the debt has yet to be settled.'

'Can such things happen? One soul traded for another?'

'I have heard of it. But all these things are beyond our realm. It is hard to have an illuminating discussion with the dead.'

'And now my child has the plague.'

'God protect him,' says Forman.

'Supposing God has other business?'

Forman looks uneasy. 'Proceed with care, Aemilia,' he says. 'I've known men driven mad by demon-summoning. One student ran babbling in the streets, stark-naked, and when they went to his room they found a demon as big as an oak tree wedged inside, with its wings pressing against the ceiling and its tail up the chimney. Amateur necromancy is dangerous.'

'I'd die for Henry, a thousand times.'

He sighs and goes to his writing table and picks up a heavy volume. 'Cornelius Agrippa – now, there is an interesting fellow,' he says, opening the book. 'You have heard of him?'

'No.'

'He believes the woman to be – in *some* respects – superior to the male. He cites a great list of those favoured by God, from Eve to Mary Magdalene. Strange, strange views.'

'He sounds like a sensible man to me.'

I follow him to the table, my skirts wet and flapping about my legs, hungry to see this book. The writing is plain and clear, as if it were written yesterday.

'I'm sure he does,' says Forman. He turns a few pages. 'Now, were I to share such opinions, I could pass on what I know to you. All my knowledge, all my secrets. The wisdom of Paracelsus, the learning of Dr Dee. All over Europe, great men are lost in alchemical research, and I would appraise you of it, just as I tell a new maid how to lay the fire.'

'Does he know how to summon demons? Could he help me call down their power?'

'He may help a man who knows enough. If he has sufficient learning.'

'And a woman? As learned as myself?'

'I do not speak of women. I do not share his view of them.'

'Why? Because a woman is for haleking, and nothing more?'

'Now you are insulting me. You know I have always respected your intelligence. However, a woman can no more become a cunning-man that she can become a priest. It is not my doing; it is the natural order of things.'

'But supposing the natural order of things is wrong?' I ask. 'Supposing – with our God-given minds – we can see where nature can be improved upon? If we were to accept what *is*, without question, why cure disease? Why seek to better anything?'

The doctor looks irritable. 'It is a matter of degree.'

'Good. Because I don't want to be a necromancer. I only want to save my child – as natural a desire as anyone could wish.'

'I do not see how I can help you.'

'If you cannot, then who can? You are my last hope!' I twist my hands together. 'What am I to do? I loved a man who damned me for a whore. Where am I to go? I am not allowed to be a lady, nor a poet, nor free, nor safe from the plague. How shall I go on? I am not allowed to do anything, in this stinking City of ours. Where does that leave me? My sole treasure is my beloved son. I will go now, since my sufferings mean nothing to you.'

The doctor shakes his head. 'You always did get the better of me. So be it.' He takes a bunch of iron keys from a hook by the door, and leads the way out of the consulting room and across the stone-flagged hall. 'I will show you the secret of my cellar,' he says.

'What?'

'If you wish to interfere with life and death, then you must see what is at stake.' He unhooks a rush lamp from the wall. 'There is a reason why such powers are those of gods, not men. Carry this, and light our way.'

I take the light from him.

'No matter what you see, do not drop this lantern,' says Forman. 'Otherwise we will never get out. It's dark as the pit of Hades down there. And, to my knowledge, there is nothing to match my discovery west of Constantinople.'

He unlocks the cellar door with the largest key. The heavy door swings into blackness and reveals a flight of stone steps, descending into the void.

Scene X

I follow him down the steps, my bare feet chilled by the damp stone. The torchlight shines on the scuffs and stains on his old doublet, and on the looped cobwebs on the dusty ceiling close above us. At the bottom of the stairs, the cellar opens out. There is space around us on all sides. It is deathly cold. He places the candle on the ground, and opens the chest. I peer inside. To my surprise, it contains yet another flight of steps, hewn out of the earth. There is a soft, cool scent: the smell of turned soil.

'What! Do you plan to bury me down here?'

'I wouldn't dare,' he says. He climbs over the side of the chest, and begins to descend. 'Whatever do you take me for? Come along! Follow me.'

I scramble down quickly, slithering on the earth steps. When I reach the bottom, I find myself in a narrow chamber, barely big enough for the two of us to fit inside. It is cramped, and filled with so many glass jars and parchment rolls and brass instruments and all manner of weird objects that I am forced to keep my arms close to my sides. Unlike Forman's public consulting room, which is neatly furnished and handsomely appointed, this is slipshod and disordered, as if this is where he lets his mind run free. There are all manner of cups and vessels, made of metal, stone or glass; a round oven, topped with a brass alchemist's kettle; and next to it, suspended from the ceiling like a great globe, a cow's swollen bladder, smelling sickly-sweet.

The doctor goes over to a desk crammed against one wall and spreads out a roll of parchment, pushing sundry oddments out of the way. These include the shrivelled corpse of a half-grown mouldiwarp and what looks like the beak of a little duck. There is also a mirror, of polished black obsidian; a jar of loose teeth; a crystal ball, big as a smith's fist, and a dismembered thumb resting in a glass. (Quite pink, as if newly severed.) I hold up the torch and try to see what he's reading.

'Magicians are earthbound, human, lumps of clay,' he says. 'Ordinary beings, for all our talk of necromancy, all our books. Diseases – like the plague – can carry us off, just as easily as any other mortal. We might as well be stool-boys or dairymen. Yet… we can call on some higher state – call upon the planets and the stars – whose sublime powers might influence our sublunary world.'

'They could cure the plague?'

'If one were to find the philosopher's stone, it could cure all diseases, as well as transmute base metal into gold.'

'But you have not found it.'

'Not *quite*, no.'

'But a demon might do the same task? Don't they say so?'

'You wish to learn how to summon a demon. I am reluctant to give you the means to accomplish such an end.'

'I wish to save my son,' I say, again, dogged and determined. 'I will do what I must.'

'For a price, a demon might do anything you ask. But this is dangerous and difficult. You know what happened to Faustus.'

'Faustus was foolish.' I look down at the mass of signs and symbols. 'Show me.'

He covers the numbers with his hands, though he needn't be so cautious, as none of it makes any sense to me. 'It is perilous, Aemilia. There is devilment here. This knowledge is not like some simple tincture, applied to a seeping wound. Remember, we are going above our station. Entangle your spirit with an angel in the heavens, and you will be consumed in fire by their burning righteousness. Tamper with the power of demons

254

and God help you. Or rather, He will not. Such a direct contact would destroy your fragile body, and imperil your immortal soul.'

'So – all your studies have led to this conclusion? That it's dangerous to take a single step?'

'Quite the reverse.' He shakes his head, fiercely, as if my dullness is too much to bear. He closes his eyes and begins again. 'A man's learning is the distillation of the thinking of a great institution, the riches of the libraries of Oxford or Cambridge or Tübingen.'

'A man! So be it. Perhaps a woman may be more whole-hearted.'

'Will you *listen* to me, Aemilia? Will you *hear* me?'

'My son might die this night for all I know. I have no time for lectures on philosophy.'

'This is no lecture, mistress. This is the stuff of wisdom. Agrippa, that great genius, used the natural elements to tell the future. Earth, fire, water, air. The manufacture of objects – talismans, potions and rings. The summoning of angels and demons to work miracles on his behalf...'

'So summon me one! Quick! And I will bear it home to serve me.'

He sighs. 'There you are, you see? Your impatience is proof of your weakness. You grabble after small things, won't wait to be wise. A woman cannot think as a man can think. She is of her nature ruttish, light-minded, and with one eye on her looking-glass.' He points to the obsidian mirror, and there I am, staring out at myself, wild and woebegone.

My hand twitches: I would like to strike him. But I keep silent, watching as he rifles inside a wicker basket before producing another clutch of parchment rolls. He unfurls one, flattens it out on top of the other documents on his desk, and proceeds to examine column after column of tiny black calculations, intricate numbers piled one on top of the other, till they sprout more numbers and still more, like lamp-black frogspawn. Forman touches the numbers lightly, as if they might sting.

'Theophilis and Cyprian gambled with their immortal souls in the quest for knowledge of this kind,' he says. 'As you will know, being a woman of education and much reading. Death is not the worst we have to fear.'

'Don't lecture me as if I were an infidel! Hell is as real to me as a garden gate.'

He pulls out another page, and bends close to look at it. 'The ignorant seek miracles. Priests, in their expedient wisdom, seemed to bestow as much. There's many a country church with an ass-bone on the altar, said to be the lost rib of a broken saint. Before Good King Henry swept away such falsehood, this land was steeped in lies and incense.'

He seems to have found what he was looking for. He stares at a long calculation, takes two vials of liquid and pours them into a long glass retort, thin as a reed at one end and spherical at the other. The two substances seem to hold back, one from the other, till they mingle with a sullen hiss.

'There is scarcely a town in the realm that could not offer its good burghers a blood-weeping Virgin or a sweetly nodding martyr. No surprise to anyone that the little fish swam shorewards to hear the preaching of St Anthony, or that the Virgin at Saragossa could make half a leg grow whole again.'

He breaks off.

'Magic, you see, Aemilia. *Magic*. Whereas what I'm about is *science*. If I show you what I have hidden here, you must swear that you will never tell another soul.'

'I swear.'

'Good. Because nobody would believe you anyway. This is the last night my discovery will remain here.'

'Why?'

'You are asking me to help you summon a demon.'

'Indeed, I am more than asking you! I am begging you!'

He pulls a stout chest out from underneath the desk and unlocks it. Very carefully, he lifts out a long, narrow object, shrouded in a black velvet cloth, embroidered with a pattern of silver stars. 'The point is, my dear, that the giving of life is a heavy responsibility. Just as any mother knows.'

'What's this?' I whisper. Something prickles my neck, as if a spirit walked. I glance at his little alchemy oven. 'Have you turned base metal into gold?'

'Almost,' says Forman. 'Or, you might even say that this achievement is the greater, since there is one thing in this world more precious even than gold.'

He rests his trembling hands on the draped velvet.

'Diamonds? Rubies?'

'Life itself.' He pulls the cloth aside.

My hands fly to my face and all the breath goes out of me. The cloth conceals a tube of glass, about a foot in length, and no wider than my wrist. I strain to see – my mind is chasing its own horrors – I see rats in the roof-thatch, plague-corpses in the street, a young virgin falling into Hell's pit. My child, running through this Hell towards me. A child. Oh, Lord God! What is the doctor doing? I stumble closer, catch my foot and fall upon the ground, which flames with stars. I come to myself – the doctor is so absorbed by the sight before him that he pays me no attention. I struggle to my feet. My belly is cold. Forman's body blocks my view. But, in the glass, I can see liquid and a little foot.

'What foul sorcery is this?' I whisper.

'Not sorcery, though fools will think it so. It is the higher magic – the crown of an alchemist's craft.'

'You *made* him?'

'Indeed.'

'But... I don't understand how this is possible. You are either God himself, or you are... the father of this manikin.'

'As you say, I made it.'

I stare at Forman.

'It's monstrous – terrible. Who will rear him? Who will suckle him? How can this be the crown of *anything*?'

'This required great study, let me assure you.' The doctor is studying the newly mixed liquid as it shivers and shifts at the swollen end of the retort. 'The creature is the fruit of a mandrake root and the semen of a hanged man's last ejaculation.'

'So that's what you are: Satan's midwife!'

'The root was dug up before dawn on a Friday, by a black dog bred for the purpose. I washed it and kept it in a pot of milk and honey. Each day I dripped in the blood of a stillborn and the hanged man's seed. And the creature grew and grew – to this.'

'God above! Can he speak, think, pray? Is he a man?'

'It is a homunculus.' Forman lowers the retort. 'I feed it on earthworms and lavender seeds.'

'May heaven forgive you! This is your science?'

'I have my natural children, through the pleasures of the flesh, and now I have this, through the power of my thinking.'

I think of my little Henry, when he was newly born, his tiny wrinkled face and elvish hands. I fear that, being so new, he might go back from this earth to wherever he had come from, and stay there for another eternity. And now… now that eternity is perilously close.

'Oh, most noble and erudite scholar! Most respectable philosopher! The Devil himself could not concoct a more vile experiment than this.'

'This is my brain-child.' The doctor frowns, drawing down his ginger brows. 'My invention.' He is distancing himself from his creation with cold words.

I press my hands to my mouth, feeling bile rising in my throat. 'Dear Lord, what are you saying? This is wicked, wicked blasphemy!'

Forman's face is set into a mask of disapproval. 'Do not upset yourself, Aemilia, please. This is merely an experiment in knowledge.'

'An experiment, you say?' I turn to him, shaking. 'You call him your "brain-child". So you are his father, and his mother too.'

'Only in principle.'

'But he is your own son!'

'Who is it, Mistress Lanyer, that wishes to summon demons to do her will? Ah, I forget myself. It is you! You cannot affect such squeamishness as this.'

I swallow acid-tasting puke. 'I want to call up some power that could aid me, so that I can save a life!'

'Very modest.'

'No, sir, not modest, but rooted in maternal love.'

'There is no link between "maternal love" and my vial-grown manikin,' says Forman. 'You see – your female logic is askew.'

'Jesu, sir! If you made him, then you must take care of him.'

'No.'

'Why not?'

'I am neither mother, nor father, to this manikin. I am its Creator.'

'Dr Forman! Hear yourself. Do you put yourself so high? You'll bring damnation on your head.'

He tears his gaze from the glass and looks at me. His eyes shine with determination. 'No. I will not be damned. Your theology is even weaker than your logic. What I have made is mine to destroy.'

'Isn't our Lord the God of Love? *Amor vincit omnia* – isn't that what we were taught? Love conquers all. *Love*, not philosophy. Not science.'

Forman frowns, his face set into stern lines. 'It's all very well to speak of love. Latin can be quoted in any cause. I might just as well say – *vita incerta, mors certissima*. Which has the virtue of being beyond dispute.'

'Oh, brave philosopher! "There is nothing certain in life but death." What thoughts of genius are these! I believe my cat knows as much.'

'In this brute world, men die each day upon the street, faces black with plague. Infants die before they learn to speak their mother's name.'

'Yes – but you can save him from such uncertainty! You can be a merciful God, not a cruel one!'

'And risk my own safety, and that of my family? No, Aemilia. Don't you see? Those who accuse me of necromancy might find this little experiment interesting indeed. Now I know that I can create such a thing, I have no need to preserve it. My work is done.'

'You truly mean to kill him?'

'I want to show you that meddling with life and death has consequences. And they are immense and terrible.'

'If you kill him, you do so because you choose to. You are sick in your soul, sir. Why do such a thing?'

'If the physicians find out what I have done, they will have their proof that I am not a respectable practitioner of medicine but a cozener, a conjurer of spirits.' His face twists to a smile. 'In short, no better than a witch.'

He lifts up the tube.

'Like Drake, and Ralegh, I am sailing to the furthest reaches of what is known. But I have no craft to bear me; my craft is my cunning. Those brave explorers must contend with pirates, ice-floes, sea monsters and the raging oceans. I must fight with vain physicians, caught in their staircase world of weasel tricks and pompous place-men.'

'What torments do beset you, sir! This is all vanity, nothing but self-seeking vanity!'

'They will kill me if they can, do not doubt it.'

My head is spinning with all this. 'You wouldn't murder your own child! Listen, Dr Forman – Simon – I implore you! You should feed him buttermilk and sweetmeats, see where his tastes lie! What does he hear? He might make music the like of which has never been heard in all of time, not even in the Court of Solomon... Your discoveries are only just beginning...'

'Silence!'

He comes closer. I can see the blood-threads in his eyeballs. I take a step backwards, and press my body against the cold wall.

'Aemilia Lanyer, you come here, breaking my windows, assaulting my privacy, when I am in fear of my life. This is my warning to you. Challenge the natural order if you must, but expect to pay the price.'

'What price?'

The liquid in the retort shimmers against the glass. It is the colour of a cat's eye, yellow flecked with topaz. 'The high magic has its own logic. I gave the creature life…' He picks up the glass and tilts it, then empties the liquid out of the retort and into the open top. Eventually, the glass tube brims with the golden liquid. 'And I will take it away.' He thrusts a cork into place, sealing the tiny fellow into his translucent prison. I hear a dread sound, like the aching wind that shakes the house above.

'For pity's sake!' I scream. 'Spare him!' I lunge towards him, but Forman knocks me to the ground. Inside, I can see something which squirms and writhes, then beats against the glass bird-fisted. Crouching like a dog, I spew forth bile. There are no Bible words for this. The doctor uncorks the tube, picks up another glass jar, and tips in the contents. This time the brew is a dark porridge, noxious as the shit in a ditch. It has an odour of incense mixed with the visceral stink of humankind. As the sick brew swirls into the amber liquid, it gurgles and bubbles, churning into black vapour.

I snatch up a candlestick and run back up the first flight of steps – into the vast cellar – and then the second, stumbling over my wet skirts. I run into Forman's study. I can hear his footsteps coming up the stairway. Looking around me, I see Cornelius Agrippa's grimoire, snatch it up and hurry through the hall. Then I unbolt the door and run headlong into the stormy night.

Scene XI

When I return, I run up the staircase to Henry's room and fling myself down beside his bed. He is tossing and turning, with his nightshirt pushed from his shoulders.

'Mother! Help me! I'm burning. I'm freezing...' His face is flushed dark, and his breath is foul. He stares at me foggily before his eyes roll backwards and he faints away.

'Henry!' I cry. 'Henry! My darling boy!' I hold him tightly. The whites of his eyes shimmer under his lashes.

Joan pulls the sheets back. 'There, see? Top of his leg. Tucked in the crease.'

A boil, blood-red.

'Plague-sore,' says Joan. She crosses herself and picks up the grimoire, which had fallen to the ground. 'I have heard of such a book, but never thought to see it,' she says. Her face is still. 'I don't need eye-reading for this.'

'What do you mean?' I scramble up and take it from her. I see that the words which were as plain as day at Dr Forman's have now formed themselves into indecipherable squirls and curlicues. '*Eye-reading*? What other kind is there?'

She touches the words on the cover. 'It's called *Pseudo-monarchia Daemonum*. A Bible of the purest evil. Is this what you have brought to cure him?'

I lie down on the bed next to Henry and kiss his hair. The room is swaying; the walls are pale with fever. Sweat is running down my back and Henry's body throbs against mine.

'Death is here! Death is in the house!' Henry starts up, and is staring at something behind me, just as the Queen had done. I turn to look, half-believing that the grinning spectre might indeed be gazing down at me. There is nothing, except a wall-hanging showing good Susanna and the elders. The two old lechers leer at her over a garden wall. She is draped, white and naked, against the steps down to the blue water. I try to say, 'It's just a fever, my love. You will soon be well.' But I'm drowned out by the sound of a woman sobbing. I realise that the sobs are mine.

'He's come for me! He's come for us all!' cries Henry. And with that he vomits up all down his skinny chest and over my wet chemise, and such a stench I never knew. He rages and pukes, and soon there is nothing left inside him, only bile. We wash him clean, and lay him down again. I change into a clean nightgown, and I can't remember a single prayer, not one, beyond 'Our Father' and then silence.

I lie next to him, my eyes wide and dry now, watching, watching. I hardly know if I live or die, only that he is beside me, and I must guard him, hold him close to the earth with my eyes. Joan scatters rose leaves and bathes his body in sweet waters, and applies a poultice to his brow. She might as well sing him nursery rhymes and do a hop, skip and a jump for all the good it does him. He writhes and tosses and jabbers wicked-sounding words. I hold his hand tightly in mine, in case he runs mad and naked into the windy street. After many hours, he falls into a twitchy stupor, talking to himself.

At the darkest hour of the night, Joan gives me a cup of ale. I prop myself on one elbow and glug it down, wondering at its strange and bitter taste. She rests on a stool by the bedside and drains her own cup to the dregs. The blackness of the night seems to press against the candle-flame. I hear a mournful howling outside. Each long-drawn-out note seems more doleful than the last, and grows ever louder, till at last I say, 'Go and throw something at that hound, I cannot bear it.'

Joan gives me one of her looks. 'Don't you know what that is?'

'A dog, Joan, howling in the night.'

'There are no dogs left. They've all been hanged and skinned for purses. The creature outside is not a thing of flesh and bone.'

'Haven't we troubles enough, without these old tales?'

There is the howl again, most dreadful. It seems to echo inside my aching head. I run to the window and throw it open. There is a bright half-moon, and enough light to see the street by. The wind is blowing hard, flattening the weeds and grasses growing among the stones. But there's not a soul in sight. And no dog, either.

'It's a portent of Death,' says Joan, as I close the casement again.

'Oh, surely. With you, my bold and cheerful servant, everything is a portent of Death. The humming of a bee, a blossom laden tree, the scent of green apples. Death, Death, Death, every time.' But my sharp words tire me, and I lie down next to Henry once more.

Joan stands up. 'I'm going out,' she said. 'Since your errand brought us nothing useful.'

'What?'

'To fetch Father Dunstan.'

'That miserable old Papist! What for?'

'He knows the old religion. The old magic, that some would like to strangle with the law. He'll call St Roth to help us.'

I must have slept, curled round my son. When a great rapping comes on the front door, I rush to answer it, half-falling as I go. But it isn't Joan. It is a man, broad-shouldered, his face hidden in a black mask. He is dressed for a journey in stout boots, a leather doublet and a velvet cap. I know him even before he lifts his mask to look at me.

'Aemilia – Mistress Lanyer – you are safe,' says Will.

'I am alive.'

'And... the boy?'

'He lives too.'

He smiles and raises his eyes to Heaven. 'Thank God! Thank God!'

'What do you want?'

He is staring at me so intensely that he seems surprised to hear me speak.

'Can I come in?' he says, urgently.

'Why? What do you *want*?'

'To speak to you, and – '

'Then speak.'

He sighs. 'Come, let me pass.' And somehow he is in the hallway, standing much too close, and I have the sensation of the world falling backwards behind me. He glances around, with his familiar quickness, and more than his usual air of impatience. Taking in my face, my nightgown, the pot of plague-juice on the table, and the cat, gnawing at the hind legs of a coney by the smoking fire. I take a step, and stumble. He catches me, and I look down at the lampblack on his fingers, shocked by their familiarity.

'I hoped not to find you here. I hoped to see your house empty, and you and your brave little Henry gone to the country for safe keeping.' He speaks quickly, yet almost unwillingly.

'Henry is very ill,' I say.

'The King's Men are off to the country,' he says. His voice is rough and throat-sore. I have the feeling that he has rehearsed these words and is determined to say them to me, no matter what. 'To Coventry, Bridgnorth and then – as we hope – to Bath. We're touring the country till the pestilence is over.'

'Henry has a fever.'

'You can't stay here. You must come too.'

'*What?*'

He clears his throat and gives a slight bow, as if he was speaking from the stage. 'Aemilia – I beg you. I am afraid for you. I don't mean to… Our association has… I know what's gone before. But you would be safe with me. Come, quickly, out of London.'

If I weren't so anxious I would laugh at his confusion.

'We can rent you rooms, apart from the players, in each town that we visit. You'll be away from the infected air and filthy streets.'

'Henry is too ill.'

'No. We can care for him. He can come in a prop-cart. We will keep him warm.'

'I don't think so.'

There is a pause.

'You will both be safe with us,' he says. 'He will not die. You cannot remain in London.'

'It's too late, Will.'

'What?'

'For God's sake, Will! You are not listening to what I say!' I clasp my head in rage. 'Henry has the plague. The *plague*! The very contagion that the bold players flee from – how can I come with you? How can he? What is the purpose in leaving London, if you carry the foul contagion with you? I wish it were not so! I pray I am mistaken! But I cannot go. We must stay here, my son and I, and see it out together.'

He stares at me sadly. 'I see,' he says. He reaches into his bag, and hands me a heavy purse. 'Madam, please. Henry will be well again, I am sure of it. If you won't come, then take this. You might still find a carrying-coach and a man to drive it.'

I give it back to him. 'Don't insult me, sir.'

He looks down at the purse. His hands are shaking. 'When did he fall ill?'

I hesitate. Will frowns, and pushes past me. Before I can stop him, he is upstairs and in my bedchamber. I follow him, dizzy and confused. Henry is breathing painfully, propped half-upright on his pillows.

Will sits beside him and touches his cheek.

'He has such a look of Hamnet! I knew it. I knew it, when I saw him in the plague-cart. My God...' He strokes Henry's sweat-soaked hair. 'When Hamnet died, he was just...' He stops. He is staring at Henry with an expression of intense sadness. 'He was eleven, so he might have been... taller than I remember. I hadn't seen him for a year. Such a merry little soul. And bold, like this one...'

He leans over and kisses Henry on the forehead, crosses himself and rises to his feet. His eyes are full of tears. 'God protect and save you, child,' he says. Then he whispers harshly, 'I always knew he wasn't Hunsdon's.'

I can't speak.

'Those sonnets were written from my heart,' he says. 'With love and hatred entwined within them. To one who changed my life, and then destroyed it.'

'What's done is done,' I say. 'We are older now, and it's all long past.'

He stares down at Henry. 'For pity's sake, Aemilia, take the money. For the child's sake.'

'No.'

'I want to help you. More... Or, that is, I should rather say...' He wipes his eyes with his sleeve like a child. 'Aemilia... He is our son.'

'Please – go.'

Then, another thought seems to strike him and he unhooks a bunch of keys from his belt. 'Take these – the keys to my lodgings at Silver Street. The house is empty – my landlord has taken his family out of London. A friend of mine would be a welcome guest while we are away. You can go there.'

'I live *here*! Is this house not solid enough for you? Goodbye, Will.'

'The poor child has the plague,' he says, flatly. 'If the City councillors hear of it, you will be boarded in for forty days. You know this.'

'Goodbye.'

'I will pray for him,' says Will. He hesitates. 'And for his mother, too.' And then he's gone, leaving the keys upon the bed-table.

Henry makes a strange sound, halfway between a moan and speaking, and I crouch down beside him and my tears pour out at last.

Scene XII

It is the hour before dawn. Footsteps come skittering up the stairs.

'The *parson* is here,' says Joan, in a warning voice.

I don't look at her, but at Henry's matted hair. The word 'parson' strikes me as odd, but not odd enough to jolt me from my misery and fear. 'Then let him pray for my son. He is a good boy and will soon be well. He'll be at church on Sunday.'

'Then repent now of your pride,' says a strange voice.

I see this is a new man, a young fellow, not Father Dunstan. I realise that I had put some faith in the old priest's Catholic magic, and was looking forward to touching the beads of Joan's forbidden rosary and smelling incense.

'Where is Father?' I ask.

'Dead,' says the young man. He has a hard, high voice, which makes simple words sound like sermonising. 'The plague took him off two nights ago. I have come to oversee his parish.'

He is no more than a youth, thin-faced and vinegar-skinned. His eyes seem hollowed into his skull. There is no flesh on his bones and his robes hang on him like dying-sheets.

'And who might you be?' I ask, holding Henry tighter.

'I am Parson John,' he says. 'A Cambridge man, of Sidney Sussex College. I abhor Papism in all its incarnations and I bring the Word of God to the common man.'

I take against him straight away. So much so that a glimmer of life returns to me. It is not hope that renews my spirit, but anger.

'The Word of God was here before you,' say I.

'The Word can be misunderstood.'

'By some, Parson John, but not by me, you will find. I can read it in the Latin.'

'Then be fearful of the sin of pride.'

'Say a blessing for this child, if you will. But we need neither priest nor parson. Go back to your flock. Some of them might yet be grateful for your sour-faced sermonising.'

But then Henry's eyes flicker open. 'Mother!' he screeches. 'Don't let him take me! Death is here! Death is in the room!' And he lets out the most terrible cry, worse than a murderer crushed under a pile of stones.

'Hush, child! Hush!' I say.

The parson glares. 'There speaks Satan's voice!' he cries. 'You see? This pestilence is God's punishment, and evil-doers suffer. That child will go straight to Hell if he is not blessed before he dies.'

Henry frees himself from my grasp. In doing so, he wriggles right out of his nightshirt, and stands by the bed, naked and dribbling with sweat. Parson John raises his hands above his head. I'm not sure if this is because he is calling on his Maker, or because he fears to touch my fever-ridden son.

'Pray for him, for pity's sake!' I cry. 'Speak to God, and ask him to spare my child. It is not his time! Tell the Lord this boy is innocent.'

'There are many mothers who could make the same plea. I see them by the score, Mistress Lanyer. You must accept the will of God. Do you forget that he sent ten plagues down on the people of Egypt? And the last of these *alone* killed every first-born son?'

'Mistress, you must save his soul,' says Joan. I look at Henry, and see that his limbs are covered with a rash of purple spots, dark as blackberries.

'No!' I scream. 'No! It cannot be.'

'It is God's will,' says the parson. 'Say your prayers.'

'By God, I swear I will not give up my child!' I scream. 'Get out of my house, you prating fiend!'

The parson's eyes widen, and he presses his hands together as if in prayer. 'Woman! How dare you speak in this manner to the servant of the Lord? Do you *defy* me?'

But I can no longer stop myself. 'I do defy you, sir! Yes, I do.'

'Then you are evil.'

'I defy you, and all who deny us hope.'

'Mind your words, mistress. For this, you will burn in Hell, for all eternity, with your son beside you.'

'Get out of my house!'

'You will exist in mortal agony, blistered and contorted in the flames, but never consumed. Your throat will cry out for water, but will crack like a desert. On Judgement Day the Lord will cast you out once more, into the eternal emptiness that lies beyond our understanding. Is that your wish?'

'If you call my son a sinner, who must be punished by this dreadful death, then I stand by every word I say, Parson John of Sidney Sussex College. I defy God himself, and all his angels. My son will *live*.'

'O-ho, mistress! You are not in your right mind. Remember who and what you are. A slip-shake pike, sliding through the twisting Thames, is only slightly less than you. A lowing heifer, chewing her cud on Chelsea Green, is your dull sister. By Heaven! I never heard an honest woman speak so!'

'Then honest women are fools.'

'Do *you* determine who will live or die? Are *you* the architect of your earthly fate? Fie on you for a witch and a most unnatural whore! There is something evil in you, I swear it, and in your kind, and the Lord will only forgive you if you bow down now and seek humble and profound forgiveness for this vile rebellion, this pustulating canker of the soul.'

271

I bend close to Parson John, so I get an unholy whiff of boiled onion on his breath.

'Leave this house,' I say. 'Get out, you scripture-spouting, fish-cold arse-wart. Or I'll call down a curse which'll curdle the guts in your belly.'

'Witch!' he hisses back at me. 'Evil succubus! Hear the Word of our Lord – *There shall not be found among you anyone that burns his son or his daughter as an offering...*'

'Spindle-shanked God-botherer!' I shout. 'I want to save my son, not burn him – '

'*...anyone who practises divination, a soothsayer, or an augur...*'

'Would you like to know what I predict?' I cry. 'That you will die in mortal agony, grabbling the air in your final madness, and Almighty God won't give a farthing...'

'*...or a sorcerer, or a charmer, or a medium, or a wizard, or a necromancer...*'

'Such a one as me? The fair and feeble sex? A wizard *woman*? Whoever would believe it?' I shove him hard, towards the door. 'I'll broil your brain in its shallow skull! Mangle your preachifying words into Bedlam babble, and corrupt your skin into a thousand worm-infested sores! I'll make you pray for Hades as a respite from your pain! And I'll twist your mind to such distraction that you'll tear off all your limbs to find relief and sanity! Do you hear me, you pox-groined, foul-nosed turd-stain?'

The parson takes a step backwards, eyes round with horror. And then Henry, who has been staring at the parson all this time, steps between us.

'Cure me, if you are a man of God,' he says.

The parson turns his startled gaze to the boy.

'Cure me, I command you.'

'Hell's progeny!' cries Parson John. 'Vicious, misbegotten whelp! Thou shalt not command a priest!'

And Henry spits a great gob of phlegm right at the holy man, and it lands on his yellow cheek and slides down slowly, leaving a shining trail behind.

The fierce insanity which loosened my tongue departs, and all I can see is blackest pandemonium, till at last I am crouching down on the floor, in the hall downstairs, with Henry shaking and spewing all down my chemise. It is dawn. I look up, and there is the figure of Joan, towering above us, wrapped in her black cloak. She seems taller and straighter than before, and her face, shadowed by the folds of cloth, strangely ageless. Her eyes, fixed upon me, are sorrowful.

'I hope I have served you well, mistress,' she says.

I stare up at her distant face wondering, in my feverish state, why she stands upon such high ground. It seems to me that I must be in an open grave, while she is standing on turned soil above. But I realise that I am lying on the stone flags of the hall, prickled by strewing-herbs. I am in my own house, after all.

'Until today you looked after me well enough,' I say.

'The parson could have helped you, if you'd let him. For all he is a Puritan, he serves the same God.'

'Serve! Serve! Why use this word so often?' I shift Henry's weight, and wipe his face. 'I am finished with service. Catholic, Puritan, parson, priest – I don't give a pigwidgeon for any of them. I will *not* serve.' I pick up a stand of dried marjoram and smell it, thinking of quiet herb gardens and meadow daisies.

'Beware of this ungodly pride, mistress. For I must leave you now, and, next time I see you, I hope it's in a better place than this.'

I toss the marjoram on to the floor. 'Abandon me now, in this house, with my sick son and the beadle doubtless on his way to board us in? A loyal and faithful servant indeed! Shame on you.'

273

She bends down and gives me something cold which jangles: Will's bunch of keys.

'You will need these,' she says. 'Listen to me, Aemilia Lanyer. In all my life, you are the finest woman I have ever known, and the boldest. But you are not the wisest. I have loved you dearly, as I have loved your son. From the moment I first set eyes on you, all fire and no sense, I knew that I must help you. I was a penitent, but had not served my penance. In you, I saw a kindred spirit, someone who needed help, and yet would never seek it. A brave soul adrift in a cruel world. I burned my shop myself, so there was no going back, and I became your servant. And I am your servant still.' Her voice is softer now, yet there is nothing of the servant in it.

Outside, I can hear the distant sound of shouting. Unusual now, in streets which are normally so silent. The beadle, of course, with his merry men, summoned by the good parson. The boarding-up of houses often lures a crowd.

'Now, go,' she says.

'Go? What do you mean? Where shall I go?'

There is a knock on the door, and she opens it. Tom Flood is standing there, blushing in his finest velvet.

'Joan – Mistress Lanyer – I...'

'Hurry,' says Joan. 'Tom has a cart, at the end of the lane. Full of costumes for the tour. John Heminge is holding the horses but he grows impatient.'

Tom stares at her.

'Take my mistress to the Mountjoy house, and be on your way,' says Joan. 'But be careful. The boy has the plague. There is a hand-cart by the door.' Mysteriously, there is.

Tom looks confused. 'Mistress Lanyer...?'

'Help me,' I say, getting to my feet. Between us we wrap Henry in a bed-sheet and lay him gently on the cart. He is sleeping uneasily, and his eyelashes flutter as if disturbed by nightmares.

274

Joan follows us out. 'This is a brave deed, child,' she says, touching Tom's arm. Then she turns to me and hugs me tightly, and when we break apart she gives me Simon Forman's grimoire. 'You'll need this,' she says, 'if you are set on saving Henry.'

'But I can't...'

'But you will. God bless you, Aemilia. Now, hurry.'

We trundle the cart slowly forward till we are halfway down the street, the shouting of the crowd growing louder and louder behind us. There are yells and chants and the noise of pipes and drums. I look back, wondering again how Joan could leave me at such a time. She is standing with her back towards us, facing the oncoming noise. Why is she waiting? What is she doing?

'Hurry,' says Tom, face set with fear. 'We must get on.'

'Why did you come for us?' I ask, as we set to pushing the cart again. 'You could be halfway to Coventry by now! Such kindness, Tom!'

Tom is more flushed than ever. 'Henry is my dear friend,' he says.

'Pray God you are rewarded for your good heart.'

The end of the street is in sight, and there is the carriage and John Heminge, just as Joan had said.

'Thank God,' says Heminge. 'How does the boy?'

I can't speak. We lift Henry from the hand-cart and settle him in the carriage among the masks and head-pieces. The sound behind us has reached a pitch of fury and I am sick with fear for Joan. Then there is a hideous scream, long and piercing, followed by wild cheering. 'Wait,' I say. 'I will only be a moment.' And, before Heminge can stop me, I run back towards the shouting mob.

The crowd has formed a wall of backs, making a neat circle. I push my way forward, but my view is still obscured by those who have fought for a good viewing place. Even so, I can see a dark-robed figure is standing in the centre, its face obscured by a black hood. The ringleaders are cat-calling and shouting filthy names. There are sixty or seventy people in the rabble: plague-followers, apprentices, vagrants, beggars and idiots. All of them are ill-dressed and ill-favoured. Some have the dazed stare of passers-by who have been sucked into the fray. Others – with their shrivelled faces and tattered clothes – look as if they spend their life on the road. I examine their contorted, shouting faces, wondering at their rage and hatred. A thin boy with a drum is beating out a gallows tattoo. An old crone with a twisted mouth wields a pitchfork. A young girl with a fair white face and filthy, tangled hair holds a firebrand above her head.

A clod of earth falls on the ground followed by a rain of stones and pebbles. Most fall short, but some find their mark and the figure winces and trembles at each blow. Then a heftier stone hits home, the hood falls back and the face of the victim is revealed.

'Joan!' I shout. 'Joan!' But no one hears me.

'What – would you hex a holy man?' screams one worthy, a wide and burly fellow twice Joan's size.

'Would you curse a parson?' cries another voice.

'Unruly, venomous bitch!'

The young girl thrusts the brand towards Joan. 'You stinking witch, we'll peel your skin from your body while you still live, and pin it up on the church door! The wrath of God is upon you! We'll do His will.'

Cursing the parson? What does this mean? Are they torturing her for *my* crime? 'JOAN!' I scream. 'For pity's sake, why don't you tell them? Tell them who cursed the parson! Tell them it was me!' I turn first one way and then the other, to see a fat matron screaming gutter-curses and a young lawyer squealing with rage. 'It's me you want!' I cry. 'It's me!' But the thunder of their joined cries is deafening. No one hears me.

The mob shifts, and I have a better view. Joan is almost unrecognisable as the upright figure from the hall. Her cloak has gone, and her dress is torn and bloody, half-ripped away from one shoulder so I can see where her flesh has been torn. Her hair is loose and her arms are scratched and bleeding.

'Witch's blood,' calls the crowd. 'Witch's blood! Bleed the witch and save yourself from her sin!' A boy runs forward – he is no older than Henry – and slashes at her face with a knife. She makes no sound, just looks from face to face without hope or fear. A stone hurtles towards her, smashing her on the temple. Another follows, then another, and suddenly the sky is filled with missiles and the crowd roars with blood lust. Joan grunts as she falls to the ground. The crowd closes in.

'Joan!' I scream again. I force my way forward. The crowd is dancing now, in a fashion, stamping in unison, first with the left foot and then with the right, and clapping out a slow rhythm. It has become one creature, one deliberate, remorseless behemoth. 'My God! Help me! Joan!'

The mob yells with one voice, 'Kill the witch! Kill the witch!'

Another boy throws a rope over an oak tree. Turtle doves fly from it, and he makes a noose and puts it round Joan's neck. Her eyes meet mine, and, although I long to, I can neither move nor speak. I open my mouth to call her name, but something is holding me back. And a voice speaks inside my head. *'Aemilia. I told you. Go now, in God's name.'*

The noose around her neck is pulled tight, and she grasps at it, her eyes bulging. They drag her towards the tree. With a 'heave ho' and shrieks of laughter they lug her upwards, so she stands on tiptoe. A heavy stone is flung towards her, smashing her mouth into a bloody hole of broken teeth. Then a burly man runs forward, and slashes her across the belly with his knife, and she grunts again, and all her guts spill out of her. Inside my head, I hear such a scream as the damned must scream, and I pray hard, hard, asking God to take her. I remember how Charles Blount and his men had pulled at Southwell's legs when he dangled from the gibbet and how they broke his neck and saved him from his final torture, and I long to do the same, but am still spellbound. There is another banshee scream. And then the voice again, from inside that dreadful sound. '*Go, Aemilia! Go from here! God speed. My service is finished.*' Joan's voice is stern and powerful.

The crowd laughs and whoops to see the blood, and the pale girl holds her nose, making fun of the stench of Joan's snaking innards. I squeeze my eyes shut, willing her to die. They pull her up higher, and her arms flail and her bare feet kick thin air as she dances her life out. I think of those clever hands, that saved my son, of her good sense and acid tongue, that have preserved my sanity a thousand times. *God help her*, I pray. *God help us all.*

Then, suddenly, everything stops. All is silence, and Joan is still. The crowd falls back. I cannot bear to look at her dead face. Her cloak is lying on the ground. I pick it up, then turn and flee.

Silver Street is a good road, wide and well-kept, off Cheapside, in sight of St Paul's and west of the low arch of Cripplegate in the City walls. Like the rest of London, it is filled with a strange quiet, a plague-quiet. As we make our way inside, the silence rings in my ears after the noise of the crowd. I keep my gaze fixed on my son's face, and do not weep for Joan's sacrifice, but determine to make it worthwhile.

Heminge carries Henry to an upper chamber, and gently lays him on a four-poster bed. 'This is Will's room,' he says. 'He is praying for you, Aemilia. So are we all.'

I don't like the way he looks at Henry, as if all hope has gone. 'Thanks, Mr Heminge, for all your pains, and your great patience. Now you can be on your way,' I say. My calm voice sounds false to my own ears.

He takes my hand and bows, very grave. 'I wish you luck, and God's blessing.' Tom is watching with tears on his face.

When they have gone, I lock the street door behind them, and tend to Henry as best as I can. His whole body is raised and black with plague-sores, and they smell most horrible. It is the scent, I suppose, of poisoned blood. The nails of his hands and feet are of the same colour, as if he has rubbed them with dark river mud. Each breath sounds like a knife scraping on a skillet, and his chest trembles with the effort. Though sweat rolls from his body, his limbs are freezing to the touch.

I am swim-headed. The room swerves and shifts around me. I feel that I am flying through the air. Here I am, in Forman's little cell once more. I am on the floor, and looking up at the good doctor working at his bench. He lifts a cloth from a tube of glass. There, lying peacefully inside, is a little man. Not an infant, but an adult, full-formed male, well-made and (for his scale) well-hung. Naked as Adam in the Garden of Eden. His limbs are as pale as the moon, the little muscles of his body all most perfectly aligned. He is sound asleep, his head resting on the crook of one arm for a pillow. Then his eyes open, and he gazes at me. And he looks down at his naked dangling parts, and covers them with his hands, as I've seen Henry do when he was bathing and fancied Joan could see him. Lord God! I could not save him.

And then I pray – some words come to me at last – hoping God might yet turn his face in my child's direction, even though I am hell-bound myself: '*O God, the Father of heaven, have mercy upon us miserable sinners. Remember not, Lord, our offences, nor the offences of our forefathers; neither take thou vengeance of our sins: spare us, good Lord, spare thy people, whom thou hast redeemed with thy most precious blood, and be not angry with us...*'

I turn to look at him, weary and empty. Henry's eyes are half-open. But I know he can see nothing, not the carved bed-roof, decorated with bright, leaping porpoises, nor my face as I bend over him.

'Henry?' I put my hand against his cheek. 'Can you hear me, little one?'

His breath comes in a rasping sigh. I know that sound. When Death is near, the watchers wait in the eternity between each breath. In the end, they witness the final rattle as the soul departs. The waiting is over, and the mourning begins. That rasping sound has the rattle of death in it. *My little boy, my precious one. Henry Lanyer, my only child. All my world, in this small frame. What will I be without you? How shall I live? What shall I do?*

But no. He is not ready. I am not ready. His life still lies before him. I will not serve. God has deserted us. It is time. Time to set myself apart from wise women and cunning-men. Time to see how far magic will take me. If a witch must call on demons, then so be it. If demons are in the service of Beelzebub, then I am willing to take the consequences.

Scene XIII

I pick up the grimoire. My hands are stiff and trembling. I fumble with the pages, not certain what I'm looking for. A sign? A clue? There are demons hidden here, in these queer hieroglyphics and tables, figures like amulets instead of letters, pictures of chariots and scrotums, serpents and priestesses, the sage hierophant and inverted Hanged Man. How can I unlock a spirit from these strange inscriptions? I close my eyes and think of Joan, hanging from the tree. I see her eyes, fixed on mine.

When I open my eyes, the room is writhing and spinning. I can see Henry, but he seems far away, on a shore I can't reach. Black mists drift between us. I stretch out my hand to touch him. Pustules like bilberries cover my arm from wrist to elbow. *Holy God. Holy God. He has the plague and now I have it too.* I close my eyes again, but this time I see Joan's face close to, angry and accusing. It seems as if she wants to speak to me. But I don't know what she wants to say. What does she want to tell me? How can she help me now?

I grasp the bed-post and haul myself upright. Nausea and pain flood my body. I stagger backwards, then notice a tumble of darkness on the floor. I touch it – rough wool, coarse against my fingers. But there is something else – the slightest tremor, like a living creature. An animal would be warm – but this fabric cools my hot fingers. It is Joan's black cloak.

I put it on, and it falls around me in deep, whispering folds. I pull the hood over my head and the whispering continues, like the wind in the bulrushes, like the beating of a raven's wing. I can

281

hear Joan's voice, as if it is coming from a long, long way away. I can hear words – what is she saying? *I am a penitent witch. I am a penitent witch.* I see her putting a newborn child into my arms. I hear her words: *You'll keep it.*

Then I hear her voice say, '*Draw a circle.*'

I hesitate, not knowing if I have the strength.

She repeats, '*Draw a circle.*'

I find a lump of white chalk in the pocket of the cloak. Falling to my knees, I scrabble on the floor, pushing back the rushes with feverish hands. Then, breathing hard, I draw a great circle, nine feet across. '*Very good,*' says Joan. '*The space you have made is outside creation. Demons and spirits may enter it. You must stay on the outside. Do not cross the line. Do not listen if the demon tempts you.*'

I pick up the grimoire once more. My head is hot and heavy and I want to lay it down, to lie upon the frozen Thames in winter and become as one with that white cold.

'*Open the book.*'

I do so, and the mist slowly parts. First, I see only:

Τηεψ σαψ τηατ τηε ποωερ οφ ενχηαντμεντσ ανδ ϖερσεσ ισ σο γρεατ, τηατ ιτ ισ βελιεϖεδ τηεψ αρε αβλε το συβϖερτ αλμοστ αλλ Νατυρε. Απυλειυσ σαιτη τηατ ωιτη α μαγιχαλ ωηισπερινγ, σωιφτ ριϖερσ αρε τυρνεδ βαχκ, τηε σλοω σεα ισ βουνδ, τηε ωινδσ αρε βρεατηεδ ουτ οφ ονε αχχορδ, τηε Συν ισ στοππεδ, τηε Μοον ισ χλαριφιεδ, τηε Σταρσ αρε πυλλεδ ουτ, τηε δαψ ισ κεπτ βαχκ, τηε νιγητ ισ προλονγεδ.

But then the signs begin to wriggle and squirm, and I see that they are turning into words, the very words I needed to find.

They say that the power of enchantments and verses is so great, that it is believed they are able to subvert almost all

Nature. Apuleius saith that, with a magical whispering, swift rivers are turned back, the slow sea is bound, the winds are breathed out of one accord, the Sun is stopped, the Moon is clarified, the Stars are pulled out, the day is kept back, the night is prolonged.

This, then, is what I was after! What verse, though, what simple verse could unmake plague? I search back and forth through the incense-scented pages. Then I read these words aloud:

'Her with Charms drawing Stars from Heaven, I
And turning the course of rivers did espy;
She parts the earth, and Ghosts from Sepulchres
Draws up and fetcheth bones away from th'fires,
And at her pleasure scatters clouds i'th'Air,
And makes it Snow in Summer hot and fair.'

Is it snowing, or summer, now? My head is hot, but my hands have turned cold. I look down at them: they seem far away from me. I pull the cloak tighter around me, and feel a sick languor overwhelm me as I read the second verse:

'At will, I make swift streams retire
To their fountains, whilst their Banks admire;
Sea toss and smooth; clear Clouds with Clouds deform.
With Spells and Charms I break the Viper's jaw,
Cleave solid Rocks, Oakes from their seizures draw,
Whole Woods remove, the lofty Mountains shake,
Earth for to groan, and Ghosts from graves awake
And thee, O Moon, I draw – '

A Creature comes forth from the darkness, forming itself in the circle, so that shrouds and filaments of shadow are woven into a formless shape. There is a wind around me, and a terrible stench, of rotting flesh and plague. There are sounds, like twisted weeping and the screams of babes. Yet unlike, too. The stench and the sounds are relations of what I can recognise, but not their copy. A band of pain wraps itself around my head, tighter and tighter and tighter. I clutch my forehead, but I stay in my place, holding some inner part of myself quite still. I have summoned Evil, there is no doubt of that, and it is growing and twisting in the circle, burgeoning out of itself, deforming as it grows. I listen for Joan, but I can't hear her. The sound of rushing air and weeping fills my ears, my mind, my body. I lower my arms and lift my head and look directly forward, at the Creature in the circle. For it has formed now, and is folded and hunched within its allocated space, and it has fixed me with its yellow eyes.

Thunder and lightning. The light shrieks over a blasted heath. Rocks are piled like plague skulls; the ground is running with rain and stones. A figure, bent double against the gale, walks towards me, a blacker shape against the dark sky. I turn to run, but my feet are broken tree-stumps, rooted in the frozen earth. The shape comes closer and I open my mouth to scream; my cry is noiseless and the creature grabs my hand. Its hood falls back.

'Fair is foul, and foul is fair,' speaks a bloody hole of broken teeth. Two horsemen are galloping towards us, two soldiers, bloodied with the battle.

'All hail, Macbeth,' shouts a young virgin selling sugar-plums. 'Hail to thee, Thane of Glamis.'

'All hail, Macbeth. Hail to thee, Thane of Cawdor,' says the beak of a raven.

'All hail, Macbeth, that shall be King hereafter,' I cry.

The men have fallen to the ground; their faces look up at us, the faces of children.

Knock, knock! Simon Forman shuffles to the door, a great gate the size of St Paul's. He shudders and shakes, aping frailty. 'Here's a knocking indeed! If a man were Porter of Hell-Gate, he should have Old Nick turning the key. Knock, knock, knock! Who's there, in the name of Beelzebub? Oh, come in, equivocator! Knock, knock. Never at quiet! What are you? But this place is too cold for Hell. I'll devil-porter it no longer: I had thought to let in some of the professions, that take the primrose way to th'everlasting bonfire... Anon, anon!'

Over the battlements, the wind rips my hair from my shoulders. The castle is stone and sky. I watch and wait for my Lord Macbeth. I have the spells and potions set around me. Poisoned entrails, toad-venom, dog-tongue and blind-worm's sting. The finger of a birth-strangled babe, ditch delivered by a drab. A charm of fell-gruel, hell-broth – wolf-tooth and hemlock digged in the dark. 'Glamis thou art, and Cawdor, and shalt be what thou art promised.'

For I can conjure what God will not; if Fate is tardy, I am always to the clock. The child lies in the dark room; the curtains are drawn around him; I tear them back. His face is black; they are calling him. The merry devils dancing in the fire and snow. The sepulchre is opening by his bed; all it needs is a little tumble – so – and there he goes! Down, down, to the place we all must end. Heaven and Hell are pulpit words; our station is in the ground, where the worms are, where the bee sucks.

'Hail to thee, Macbeth! Thou would'st be great, art not without ambition, but without the illness that should attend it. Would'st not play false, and yet would wrongly win.'

Here are the daggers. I would have killed the King myself, if he had not resembled sweet Bassano as he slept.

His hand is warm in mine. He towers above me. The tunes are angel voices, curling and rising in the air. His tales open out the seas and skies; I float over the Grand Canal and see high-tailed boats decked out with cloth-of-gold, and masked princesses, their pale hands trailing in the water. Blood curdles the still reflections; their scarlet fingernails make the green one red. They come behind us, silent. I hear nothing, only feel the wind of their bodies as they rush at us, and we are falling, falling. His hand is torn from mine; his scream is pig-like. Fly from here! His dear body, riven with blood, the stench of it, on my hands, my face. Here's the smell of the blood still. Father! If I could call him back – would I? He would be a dead thing, then, the bloody and disfigured spectre of himself. If charnel-houses and our graves must send those that we bury back, our monument must be the belly of a crow. Dare I?

Glamis thou art, and Cawdor, and shalt be what thou art promised. Then screw thy courage to the sticking point, and we'll not fail.

I run along the battlements. London is on the one side: the plague-carts rattle, the ale-houses are singing, there are flames on the horizon and there, far off, I can see the King and all his courtiers, watching Twelfth Night. *See the boys upon the stage! Graceful Viola, with Tom's fine leg. Safe from me, from my contagion. But this is Scotland: see how the Viking sea rolls and storms, see the mountains and the mist and there is Scone, where they will crown you, my lord. Far away.*

The witch has black hair and the wings of a gryphon and the body of a serpent, twined around a tree. She is angry, and her forked tongue is made of fire. They strung Joan up; I could not save her. I held my hand out to her. I called her name, but no one heard me. She died for us. I will smirch their faces with the King's blood, if it helps this cause. There is no stopping-place for me, for there can be no punishment that is worse than this. Look – my hands are your colour, but I would scorn to wear a heart so white. What need we fear who knows it, when none can call our power to account?

The witch holds me with her woman's arms, and presses me to her breast. Her heart is beating, and her wings tear at the sky. The wind blows harder as she carries me higher, and I see it all below me, and it is a perfect pattern; I understand everything. I am GOD.

The Creature shifts and settles, malevolent and silent. It is a Winged Serpent, green and glittering, with the face and torso of a woman, white and cold. Is it female? I think it is. Her head is covered with black hair, which curls and coils to the ground. Her skin is bone-white and her arms are corpse-thin with narrow, spindle-fingered hands. Her yellow eyes have no pupils, merely snake-slits. There is no mercy in them. The great wings are folded; they are bone and gristle and cloud. They press against the ceiling and shift against the plasterwork as if the room cramps them. Fragments of white dust fall from above, and speckle the restless emerald tail.

'Who are you?' I ask.

'I am Lilith, Wife of Adam and the slayer of his children.'

Of all the demons of the air, I have called this one. Removed from Eden, she set out to kill one hundred babes a day. Of all the demons of the air, I have called the cruellest Serpent Queen of witchcraft. But she is in my circle, and I have the spell-book, and I must control her.

'I want you to save my son,' say I. 'You cannot have this child. He's mine.'

Her tail lashes towards the perimeter of the circle. 'He is dying,' she hisses, unblinking. 'He is at our gates.'

'You can have my soul instead of his.'

'The soul that's owed?'

'Yes. I will die for him, and gladly.'

'And burn in Hades? Until the Day of Judgement?'

'I will do anything.'

Lilith looks at me, full of poison to the brim. 'There is another way,' she says. 'There is a service you can do us, and keep your petty life.'

A cauldron forms from the air, and Lilith fills it with smoke-vapour and a vial of ruby liquid. She catches the light from the room in her fingers and presses it into her palms, forming it into a tiny orb, so the room is dark and the orb its candle. Then she drops it into the cauldron, and all is black.

'Do we have a bargain?' she says, in the darkness.

And I say, 'We have a bargain.'

'Go into the plague-pit,' she says, 'and bring me the head of a child.'

I see it is there before me – the pit and the stench and the human stew. Lilith gives me a stinking knife, smirched with gouts of blood. So I climb down into the plague-pit – down a flight of steps, carved out of the earth, smelling of soil and the ends of roots – and I find a homunculus lying in his glass, but he is a little boy. I carve his head off; the blade cracks through bone and sinew, and his eyes open to stare at me.

Across the rooftops I run, over the blasted spire of St Paul's, here I come, to Cripplegate, to my little one. Ah, my pretty boy! I have given suck, and know what it is to love the babe that milked me. And I am he, the dying child, and through my closed lids I can see infinity. I will lay my hand on my own forehead, so. I will call my own spirit back into itself. I am all things, and all people, all deaths and all life. Henry Lanyer, return to this place. Lord God, it is not his time. Restore him, Lord, restore him!

I open my eyes. I cannot tell if it is morning or evening, but the room is in semi-darkness. I look around me. My head still aches, but I no longer feel confused – the fever has left me. How long have I been here? Above my head, I see a blue ocean. Azure waves chase each other across the upside-down seascape, and whales and porpoises and swordfish leap among them. The water is every shade of blue from navy to bright turquoise. The fish are grey and green and silver, painted bright upon the foaming spray so I can see each neat scale. I lie still and look at these for a while, not knowing who or what I am.

Then I remember.

'Henry?' I cry out. 'Henry?'

And I struggle up on to my elbows, and look, and there he is, lying next to me. He is quite still. His gold hair is matted against his cheeks, and he is half-turned away from me, so all I can see is one pale cheek.

'My love!' I scream. 'My little one!' I grab his body and hold him. 'Do not go away from me! Stay with me! God help us! Help us!' And I sob bitterly, drenching his tangled hair with my tears.

'I *am* with you,' says a muffled voice.

I hold him still closer, stunned and confused.

'Mother,' says the muffled voice again. 'You are squeezing me to death. Why are you crying?'

If I live as long as Joan I will never know such joy again. Henry wriggles out of my grasp. He looks up at me, pale but smiling. He is Henry, exactly and completely Henry, my merry son.

'Look!' he cries, lifting his nightshirt. I see that the vile plague boils have shrivelled up. Some are half-healed scabs, others nothing more than faint bruises. 'I am cured!' he says, eyes shining. 'I am immortal, Mother. You can let me do anything now, for God will protect me, have no doubt of it.'

'A clever thought, Henry, but we will dispute this later,' say I, kissing him on his cheek and hugging him again. 'My angel boy! Oh, Henry! Praise God! Oh, praise the Lord in Heaven!' I look at my own arms, and see that they too are clear of the inflammation. Miracle or magic, some wonder has surely taken place.

Now Henry sleeps, a deep, rosy sleep, like the first settled repose of a newborn. I lie next to him, looking at him, still dazed with shock and disbelief. Finally, I begin to drowse, but am jolted awake by Lilith's voice. *'The pages,'* she says. *'You must go and find your pages.'* I sit bolt upright, eyes wide open, and look around me. I notice, for the first time since Henry's recovery, the chalk circle on the floor. There is no sign of Lilith: it's as if she was never there at all. I look up at the ceiling, and the plaster has flaked off in places, but there is nothing to suggest that a demon's wing was the cause.

Then I see that the floor is covered with crumpled pages. I scramble out of bed and pick up one of the sheets. It is covered with writing – my writing. I peer at it, confused. It appears to be a record of my weird hallucinations: the castle and the lady and the fires of London. *'This is our bargain,'* says Lilith. *'Write up these notes and make a play of them. Write a play the like of which London has never seen.'*

I get up early and sit at the table by the bedroom window. On the table are some sheets of clean foolscap, a quill and a glass of lamp-black, as if Will were just about to sit down and start work on his next play. My mind is at once disturbed and clear: both filled with images and memories and quite empty. I pick up the quill, and dip it into the ink. I think of the wild castle and the strange creatures who live in it, and the blood seeping across the stone floor. I write the words: *The Tragedie of Ladie Macbeth*. And below it I add: *By Aemilia Bassano Lanyer.*

And then my fingers close more tightly around the quill, and I dip it again and began to scratch across the parchment. My hands move quick, as if I had written all this before. My queer dreams fill my head, the poems I have struggled to form make new and easy patterns, and the words of Holinshed whirl around me.

The raven himself is hoarse, that croaks the fatal entrance
of Duncan under my battlements. Come, you Spirits that
tend on mortal thoughts, unsex me here, and fill me, from
the crown to the toe, top full of direst cruelty! Make thick
my blood, stop up th'access and passage to remorse; that
no compunctious visitings of Nature shake my fell purpose,
nor keep peace between th'effect and it! Come to my
woman's breasts, and take my milk for gall, you murth'ring
ministers, wherever in your sightless substances you wait
on Nature's mischief! Come, thick Night, and pall thee in
the dunnest smoke of Hell, that my keen knife see not the
wound it makes, nor Heaven peep through the blanket of
the dark, to cry 'Hold! Hold!'

I write all that night, with the wind beating against the
windows, till the sun comes up over the City walls and its clear
light fills the room.

Scene XIV

Henry and I live happily in Will's house in Silver Street. The months pass quickly. In the daytime, I must teach or entertain my son. He is Henry, just as he was, hale and happy and silly and full of life. My greatest task is to keep him from the streets. He is allowed to come with me to buy food once a week, as long as he keeps close to me. I suspect he could not catch the plague twice. But I will not take the risk, so we live like hermits. I pray and pray and pray, and offer up my thanks to God.

However, when Henry sleeps at night, I return to my pages and improve them, taking out dead words and putting in live ones. It's a candle-tale, put together bit by bit in the guttering half-light. After many changes, I see that I have indeed written something that might be called a play. It seems to have drawn on fear, and horror of the plague, as well as something of Lilith's diabolic craft. It is plague-play, I suppose. I am so happy and so blessed that my son lives that it is strange to have written something so dark and sinister. And yet it is a celebration too, of the darkness of the human soul.

Who can say which stories will last and which will fade away? Old women crouch together round the fire, their figures humped against the flaming logs of oak and apple wood. They tell tales. Anyone can stop and listen. The servant girl carrying an empty flagon; the hunter sweating from his reckless ride; a young boy leaning against a sleeping wolfhound. Beyond the listening circle, the dark night shrouds troll caves in the mountains and forest creatures half-seen among the clustering trees. Wolves, spirits, urchins, centaurs, satyrs, changelings and hell-waines.

This play may be one survivor. At the moment, I am its midwife and its mother. I must stay here, in this house, till London is safe again.

One breezy spring day, Henry calls out from his perch at the window. 'Oh, look, what a sight is this?' he cries. 'A horseman, at full gallop!' I can hear the sound of hoof-beats hammering on the road outside and a horse whinnying as it clatters to a standstill. 'He has a feathered hat,' says Henry. 'His cloak is scarlet – Lord above! Oh! Who is it? He is at the door, Mother. He is coming in! Who can it be?'

I hear the sound of footsteps pounding up the stairs. The door flies open and Will stands there. He looks at me, and then races across the room and kisses Henry. 'You are well, little man! You are recovered!' he cries.

'Unhand me, fellow!' shouts Henry, struggling out of Will's grasp. 'Of course I am well.'

I send Henry to play in the solar. Will is by the fire, pulling at the feather on his hat. I realise with a jolt of some emotion that he looks just like his son. I am used to seeing the resemblance the other way, but here is a grown-up Henry, fidgeting.

'You will ruin that feather,' I say.

'What if I do?' says Will. 'It is a feather, merely. It represents "nothingness" with such neatness that one might almost put it in a play to fill that function.'

'What function?'

'The representation of nothingness. Only its very neatness would preclude it. Surprise is all.' He pauses. 'Or... almost all. Audiences can be obtuse.'

'What are you *talking* about?'

He looks up at me, and his gaze is so intense that I look down at my open book, jolted by memory.

'I rode two days and two nights to get here,' he says. 'The rest of the party are some way behind me – as far as I could put them, making speed and almost killing my poor horse.'

'Why did you…?'

But he has come to sit beside me. 'We don't have long,' he says.

'We?'

'You and I. Before your husband gets here. That fool Alfonso joined the players! His consort accompanied our plays… He was carousing late into the night, not knowing if you lived or died! What kind of man is that? How can he be so ignorant of his great fortune?'

'Alfonso has no fortune that I am aware of. Unless he has been lucky at the tables for once in his life.'

'I mean, his great fortune in having such a wife.'

I stare at him, perplexed. 'You have a wayward memory, William Shakespeare. I have your written words, and those in here…' I tap my forehead. 'The words you spat at me the day you found me with that plague-boil Wriothesley.'

'Yes, I want to speak of this – '

'Love is not immutable. It can be stifled at birth, or slowly suffocated, or killed, stone-dead.'

'No! I – '

'And you killed my love, in those dreadful verses, which I did not deserve, and will not forget, even if *you* have put your wicked cruelty from your mind. Perhaps it was of no account to you, but it was everything to me.'

He takes my hands in his and looks down at them. 'It was this matter – this matter of Wriothesley that I wanted to speak to you about,' he says.

'I cannot think what you have left unsaid.'

'I wanted to… I have meant to speak of this before.'

I am silent.

'He asked to see me before the old Queen died.'

'Oh?'

'He said he had something to tell me.'

I nod, biting my lip.

'So I went to see him in the Tower.'

He stands up suddenly and walks across the room. For a moment, he watches his horse drinking from a trough below the window.

'He said that it was his fault. He said that he admired your looks, but not your manners. He wanted to get the better of you… He said that he desired and disliked you. He didn't see why a mere concubine should be so proud, nor why an old man like Hunsdon should monopolise you. So when he saw a weakness in your situation… that you seemed to like me – '

For a moment I forget myself. *'Seemed to like*! God's teeth…'

A flash of rage crosses Will's face: the rage I saw after he found me with Wriothelsey, all those years ago. Then he shakes his head, as if he is calming himself. 'Just let me speak, Aemilia, for God's sake,' he says. He searches my face with his dark eyes. 'Will you bear with me? It's not a pretty story.'

I am silenced, by his seriousness and my own curiosity. 'Very well. Say what you have to.'

'When I saw Wriothesley, Essex had already been executed, and the headsman had done his task badly. He'd slashed poor Essex across the shoulders, ripping bone from muscle but leaving his head still set upon his neck. The scaffold was a waterfall of blood, and he was screaming in agony when the second blow fell. That, too, failed to find its mark – it was the third that sent him safe to God. Wriothesley knew of this. His normal cheerful humour was gone. He knew his charm was worth nothing.'

'Charm! Ha!' I say.

Will seems not to hear me, his mind fixed in the past. 'His earldom had been stripped away and now he was plain Henry Wriothesley, his possessions confiscated, his estate set to be divided among his rivals. And he was ill: his legs were swollen, he had the ague and for many months he had been refused visitors. He was pale, and fretful, nothing like the cocksure young rake I once knew. He was very low in spirits, and still believed the Queen might have him put to death. He had been no favourite of hers, after all, while she had treated Essex like a son.'

I look down at my fingernails, thinking of my last conversation with the Queen. This is indeed a sorry tale, but I feel no pity. Wriothesley surely deserves such a fate, if any man does.

Will is staring over my shoulder as if he can see the scene before him. 'He mentioned your name almost as soon as I arrived. I know this may be no comfort, but he truly seemed to want to do penance of some kind, make an honest confession about the… the commerce that there was between you.'

I cannot look at him. 'Lower your voice, Will! I… these are things I never speak of. Think of the child.'

He drops his voice to a whisper but can't seem to stop. 'And of course, being pregnant and cast off, you were weaker still… He admitted this. He said as much.'

Outside, his horse is shaking its head and blowing water from its muzzle.

'I could hardly think or speak,' Will says, 'but I managed to ask how the… the act itself had come about. And he told me that he had blackmailed you, and forced you. It could not be called a rape, he said, but it could be called a "wilful abuse of power". Those were his words. A wilful abuse of power.'

'I'd call that rape,' I say. 'But doubtless I am alone in that, as in so many other things.'

'I realised… I realised that I never… that I… that I should have listened to you. The pain… your rejection had already made me partly mad. When I saw what I thought I saw, I thought I was just your fool.'

I feel my face flush scarlet. 'You saw what you saw, Will. As you have said quite plainly. I have no wish to talk of this now, with Henry close by. We are estranged – so be it.'

He searches my face, his eyes dark with feeling. 'Do you have nothing else to say about this? Nothing at all?'

'Only that I have tried to tell you, and you gave me no chance. And now it turns out you believe this cocksure braggart, when you would not listen to me! Do you think men are more honest than women, or that lords are more truthful than cast-off whores?'

'Aemilia, please listen to me. I see – perhaps because I am older now – I see I was mistaken.'

'Handsome of you, who damned my name to Hell.'

'I see that you were trapped.'

'Wise poet! Do you want a prize for such an insight? It was ever thus.'

'My prize would be your forgiveness, the greatest prize I can imagine.'

'I have lived my life trammelled in by circumstances. This is a woman's fate.'

'Forgive me, dear Aemilia. Forgive me for those sonnets, or that part of them which was bilious and vile. Forgive me for the things I said, when all the world seemed blackened and obscene because of what I thought you had done to me.'

'Blackened and obscene – good words. You should put them in a poem.'

'Please, my lady. I am sorry.' He takes my hands.

'You wrote as if our love itself disgusted you. Our great love!'

'I wrote what I felt then. It is not what I feel now.'

I pull my hands from his. 'God will forgive you, I expect.'

'And you?'

'I don't know.

'Aemilia! Please!'

'Come a little closer,' I say. 'This is what you think of women, sir.' Then I whisper these lines to him, from his own sonnets.

'Two loves I have, of comfort and despair,
Which like two spirits do suggest me still:
The better angel is a man right fair;
The worser spirit a woman coloured ill.
To win me soon to hell, my female evil
Tempteth my better angel from my side,
And would corrupt my saint to be a devil,
Wooing his purity with her foul pride.'

'Forgive my hot words!' says Will, twisting his arms around me at last. 'Madam, there is no cure for our affliction! Not in this life or the next.'

I push him away. 'Do not insult me, sir,' I say. 'Do not come creeping here, like a whipped dog, all sneakish and colluding, in the hope that you can fornicate with me in secret once again! Don't speak of love, when you have mashed my heart to butcher's pulp! Do not speak of "sorrow" when my love is cold, and spoiled and dead! What do you take me for? What do I care if an aristocrat, your mighty *patron*, cants his little secrets to you, so you want to lick his arse? Shall I lick yours, in turn? Shall I let you have me, once again, all addled and unmade, as once I was? I will speak of an affliction, sir, and my affliction is your company! Go forth, go from me, and never bother me again!'

'What's going on?' says a voice I know too well. Alfonso is at the doorway. One arm is resting on his sword. Henry, goggle-eyed, is beside him.

'Mother?' says Henry. 'Why are you shouting?'

Will and I spring apart, quite as guilty as if we had been naked among the rushes.

Alfonso smiles, rather coldly, but comes over and kisses me on the lips as if he has bought me at a fair. 'Come, Aemilia,' he says. 'You must quit this place. The plague is over.'

Act IV

Philosophy

Scene I

Weſtminſter, December 1605

It is Holy Innocent's Day, the fourth day of Christmas, and the snow lies thick upon the ground. This year the Thames has frozen over so thick and solid that people crowd on to it, making all kinds of sport. From Southwark to the Temple there are stalls, sideshows, merry-go-rounds, puppet plays and even donkey rides. (The miserable creatures trundle up and down the ice with straw slippers tied to their hooves to stop them skidding.) Fire-eaters and clownish acrobats slide this way and that, tumbling from their stilts. The City fathers have no jurisdiction over any of these frolics, as the river lies beyond old London's walls, and they view it all with much begrudgery. The prentice-boys are quick to fill their snowballs with sharp stones and all manner of disagreeable items. Pigs and swans are roasting over crackling bonfires, and songs and laughter ring sharp against the aching air.

From my stool by the fireside, I can see through the diamond-mullioned window. The stars are points of ice over the frosted roofs and twisted chimneys. Cold creeps through the walls of cob and timber, freezing my back even as I warm my feet.

Alfonso reclines in his coffer-chair, his shapely legs sticking out in front of him, his recorder resting across his knees. He contemplates the glowing Yule log from beneath his drooping lashes. Henry sits at his feet, quiet for once, stroking Graymalkin. The cat is purring as he stares at the roast goose on the table. By the hearth is a pitcher of winter toddy, bubbling pleasantly to a woolly white top. Our new servant, Marie Verre, has laced ivy into the idle spokes of her spinning wheel. She's a foolish girl, seventeen years old, brimming with crazy laughter and tall tales, mostly of old France. (For she is the child of Huguenots who came from Paris after that foul Massacre on St Bartholomew's Day.) In spite of her silliness, she is a quick worker, and between us we have put together a table that wouldn't shame Whitehall Palace itself – though we could not match the quantity laid out for courtly gluttons.

A tap on the window. Henry jumps up and yells, 'Tom Flood! Tom Flood! All hail, Tom Flood!' Outside, a clear voice sings:

'Lully, lullay, Thou little tiny Child,
Bye, bye, lully, lullay.
Lullay, thou little tiny Child,
Bye, bye, lully, lullay.
O sisters too, how may we do,
For to preserve this day
This poor youngling for whom we sing
Bye, bye, lully, lullay.'

'It is Tom! What a voice he has, finer than any fey chorister!' says Henry, running to the hallway and flinging open the door. And Tom it is, and Anne Flood too, and a blast of Christmas wind and snow. Tom carries on singing while his mother shivers in her fur-edged tippet, her eyes popping with pride.

'Herod, the king, in his raging,
Charged he hath this day
His men of might, in his own sight,
All children young to slay.
That woe is me, poor Child for Thee!
And ever mourn and sigh,

For thy parting neither say nor sing,
Bye, bye, lully, lullay.'

'Isn't it pretty?' says Anne. 'Robert Armin taught it to him. The mummers sing it at Coventry.' I must say, it doesn't strike me as a pretty carol, or a merry one.

I point to Anne's lavish ermine trim. 'Surely they can put you in the stocks for wearing that?'

I finger the mottled fur, and she slaps me cheerfully.

'It's just a bit of Yuletide flummery,' she says. 'But it suits me, do you not think? Besides, an ermine is no more than a winter stoat.'

'I'm sure you have royal blood in you somewhere.' I wonder how many times she's sucked off Inchbald to earn enough to buy such an extravagant gewgaw. Or perhaps he gave it to her in fair exchange, for services rendered. Oh, Lord, now I can see her lips, pulsing away at his groin! And the white crumbs of her face powder, dusting his curly pubes.

She gleams with gratitude. 'And you can see it in Tom. He's more of a gentleman than any of those preening clowns at the Inns of Court.'

'Most decidedly,' say I, though this is scarcely saying much. Cross-dressing Moll Cutpurse herself is more gentlemanly than most young men of the law. 'Come along inside, and let's eat.'

'Indeed, I am hungry as a winter wolf!' says Tom. 'Ravenous, Mistress Lanyer, and sorely ravaged by thirst.' Spending time with the players has certainly improved his feeling for the drama when he is off-stage.

'Really, Tom!' says Anne. 'Have you forgot your manners?'

'I agree with Tom,' says Henry. 'I am dead with hunger. Let's stuff ourselves with greasy goose and Christmas pudding till we burst like rotting gibbet-men!'

So we sit round the table and fall to with a vengeance, finishing off the meal with coffin-shaped mince pies stuffed with currants, cloves and saffron – thirteen ingredients in all, in honour of Our Lord and His Apostles. We only stop when our bellies stick out roundly, though I am pleased to say that not one of us bursts open.

The drink makes Anne maudlin. 'This day always makes me nervous,' she says, making moon-eyes at her empty cup.

'Oh, Anne, be more cheerful!' say I. 'Don't just sit there maundering on. You can be miserable for Lent.'

'Those poor Holy Innocents! I cannot bear it, the thought of losing a child.'

'Poor indeed,' says Tom. 'The young are not always lucky.'

'Indeed not,' agrees his mother, dabbing off a tear.

Tom flushes deeper, anxious to be understood. 'Not everyone is as fortunate as Nathan Field.'

'Why is he so fortunate?' I ask.

'Only because everyone says he is the new Burbage!'

'Is that so terrible?'

'First he is the Queen of France! Oh, ladies, sirs, bow down before him! Then mad Ophelia, then love-sick Juliet – all in a fortnight!'

'You are doing well enough,' I say, 'dressed like a jack-pudding every afternoon.'

'They don't take enough note of his talent,' says Anne. 'It galls me, but of course I am the last one who should speak up for him.'

'Well, you are luckier than I am,' says Henry. 'My life is a vale of suffering, I swear! We are whipped and tortured and forced to speak dog Latin. There is no mercy for a schoolboy. I would rather be at the theatre, even if I were playing a joint-stool or half a slug.'

'Henry, don't be such a clodpate,' I say. 'Without Latin you will get nowhere in this life.'

Anne's thoughts are still on Herod and his death-dealing soldiers.

'Such little children slaughtered so cruelly,' she says, as we gather close around the fire and Alfonso fills her cup. 'To think of it! The screaming and the grief. You would run mad, would you not?'

I pat her knee. 'Let's not speak of such things now,' I say. 'We have survived the plague. We are together, warm and well and safe from harm.'

'Amen to that,' says Anne.

'Amen, amen!' says Henry, sagely. He is growing into a boisterous, impudent boy, and some say my softness to him has made him wayward. He has a habit of blurting out memories that I had thought long buried, as if he's brooded on them till he is ready to unleash them on the world.

He picks at a mince pie with his fingers. 'Mother wrote a play,' he says. His voice is sly. 'I found it.'

Tom's eyes shine.

'What's it about?'

'Witches,' says Henry. 'Witches and kings.'

'Henry, what do you mean by this? Sneaking around and purloining my poetry! How dare you read my pages?' I am glad I locked the grimoire in my safe-cupboard.

He pops the piece of meat into his mouth. 'You can hardly blame me for wondering what comes of all that scribbling you do.'

'I don't "scribble" nearly enough, and thank you for making it sound like childish nonsense. Without my "scribbling" I'd go mad.'

'It's good,' he says. 'A most excellent piece of work. For a woman.'

'The King has written a book on witchcraft,' says Tom. 'I have heard them speak about it at the Globe.'

'Then he will find my story of blood and sorcery very foolish,' say I. 'Besides, Henry is wrong. It is not a tale of kings, but of queens.'

Alfonso begins to polish his recorder with his sleeve. 'Queens! God preserve us!'

'It concerns the tragedy of Lady Macbeth.'

'Lord, wife, will you never learn?'

'Don't "wife" me, sir! Did we not have the best Prince who ever lived, in the guise of our departed Sovereign? Is her Scots cousin even half the man she was? Drunk all day, and dull all night?'

Alfonso frowns. 'Hush, Aemilia! Mind that tongue of yours. They'd hang you, just like Guido Fawkes, for saying so much!'

'Oh, dear Alfonso!' shrieks Anne. 'How can you say so? They wouldn't *dare*!'

He ignores her and stares at me thoughtfully. 'But witches, now, that might...' He blows some notes, making them sound like the whistling wind.

'A little magic always pleases, on the stage,' says Anne, looking down at her ermine trim as if she were wearing Titania's gown. 'Does it not, Tom?'

'I heard tell that one Agnes Sampson, a witch in Scotland, told His Majesty of matters which only he could know of.' Alfonso's tone is light, but I can tell that he is delighted to be so well informed.

I look up in surprise. 'What "matters"?'

'Secret words of love which he whispered to Queen Anne on their wedding night, when they were newly come from Denmark. Which he swore all the devils in Hell could not have discovered.'

Now I laugh in good earnest. 'My dear husband! I had no idea you were such an authority. Is this what His Majesty confides in you, when you've done amusing him with jigs and ditties? He acquaints you with his pillow-talk and curtain-whispers, and describes his horror of the instruments of Satan? Why, soon you will be Duke of Long Ditch and we shall all be dressed in cloth-of-gold!'

'It is *said*, Aemilia, it is *said*. Of course I have not heard it from the King directly.'

'They say His Majesty is very wise,' Anne declares, sipping her toddy. 'He should be a doctor in a university, not a king.'

Alfonso shifts irritably in his chair. 'From this awful meeting sprang his interest in demonology.'

I poke the fire. 'What nonsense,' I say. But, as the flames dance, I can see Lilith the Serpent and her yellow stare.

It is true – I have hidden my play away, for what am I supposed to do with it? It could not be staged, being woman's words, so I can only put it from me, and continue with my verse. The party is over now, and everyone is asleep. So I read it by candle-light, safe in the knowledge that it would take all the fires of Hell to rouse Alfonso once he has had a bellyful of wine. I am surprised, if I am honest, that the words chill me to the marrow. When I have finished, I lock it up with the grimoire, to keep it from prying eyes.

Scene II

A serving boy comes knocking with a letter. To my surprise, it is from Richard Burbage.

> *My dear Mistress Lanyer,*
>
> *We have heard from young Tom Flood that you have written some Lines. There being a Hiatus in our Programme pertaining to some particular items that are likely to be pleasing to His Majesty, in brief, a thing which has some Occult infusion, some Conjuration in its design, and, further, which conceals about its person some reference to the union of the Scots and English, to make our Good King feel that the Scots and English are bed-fellows, we are seeking an engagingly Horrid drama. To cut it short, we are in need of some new Words.*
>
> *This being so, and knowing that you are a Woman of sound phrasing and a pithy way with Fools, we thought to ask you if we may see these Lines. In short, if you might give the bearer some notion of when you can fix to meet with us at this Theatre, we might arrange some Business to the benefit of all.*
>
> *Your most respectful,*
> *Richard Burbage*

Now, this puts me in a dilemma. If a woman's words can't put on the public stage, then what use can they make of my play? And yet... perhaps it could be performed before the King.

I would hardly dare to hope for this, but it does deal with a subject that I know will interest him. I haven't seen Will since the day he came to see me after the plague, and have heard little about him since that time, saving only that he prospers, which is bad enough. After all he has said, and written, he thought a brief explanation about Wriothesley's confession would be enough to make amends! Perhaps even sow the seeds for renewed passion. More fool him. What riles me most is his readiness to believe everything spoken by His Lascivious Lordship, and his reluctance to believe me. Or even give me a proper hearing. And, if he truly cared, surely he would try to speak to me again. I know Will well enough: that which he wants, he will strive for to the utmost. He has forgotten me, as his star has risen at Court. The Globe's players are the 'King's Men' now, and nothing seems beyond them. Why would he want me, in any case, ageing, penniless, stuck in my little house? I am no longer the 'Dark Aemilia' of his poetry, or his memory.

But these are scratching, irritating thoughts. Must I be humble? Must I be obedient and obscure? Am I just a housewife now, a dowdy work-drab? No. No one would ever say that of me. If Burbage has seen fit to invite me to the Globe, then I will go, and see what may come of it.

So I set off, alone, disguised in that old cloak of Joan's, which makes me look twice the hag I am, and get half the looks from passers-by. Its strange scents have faded, perhaps because Marie keeps it in the scullery, next to the hanging game, which gives off a pungent blood-scent as it ripens for the pot. It is February and still freezing: it's the hardest, whitest winter I have ever known.

When I go into the street, the air is full of cries of bewilderment and fright. I see that the neat tracks of a cloven-hoofed creature are marked out in the glistering snow. They seem to have been made by a two-legged being, striding like a man. It has crossed streets and gardens, dunghills and the frozen kennel. Looking about me, I see its tracks even march up the side of an old hay-barn and over its pitched roof. How is this possible? Has some Beast marched over all things standing in its way? I shudder to imagine some black hell-wraith, perched upon a roof-stack, seeing all. I summoned Lilith – God alone knows what other demons fly among the roof-stacks, called up by those who know even less than I do. They say that Hades burns bright red, the city of eternal flame, but supposing it is froze blue-white, like winter? I say Hell is cold, the furthest distance from the Sun.

There is no need to hire a boatman: I walk across the frozen Thames, which is as black and smooth as an obsidian mirror and so clear that I can see a vast pike, frozen solid, several fathoms down. The booths stand in a disorderly muddle, not yet open at this hour. Dogs run hither and thither, cocking their legs and sniffing at littered bones, while sea eagles skid slush as their talons hit the ice. An apothecary sorts bottles inside the first booth I pass. Close by, a cobbler is selling leather shoes from a basket. 'Stout shoes for the frost!' he shouts, waving a pair before me. But I press on.

It starts to snow again, and the white flakes blur my sight. There is a strange light, as if the sun were shining from the river's edge. For a moment I feel confused and unsure of my way. I think of the pages I'm carrying with me. What am I doing, stepping out alone to visit a theatre in the Liberties? This is madness. What would Aristotle make of this, who saw Woman as some error in creation?

But I'll have none of this. I straighten my back, and walk more boldly. There it is, ahead, set back from the south shore: the Globe.

I study it as I reach Blackfriars Stairs. It rises like the castle of an enchantress above the surrounding trees. Midway up the walls is an encircling row of windows, no bigger than the arrow slits of the Tower prison. To the west of the building is the gabled roof of the stage and tiring-house, and pointing just above this a little cupola. It reminds me of the minarets of Richmond and Nonsuch: an Eastern oddity among the common homes and stews. This fake opulence is of a piece with the gilt and foolery within, since every inch of this great palace is made from wood, not stone, and it has been carried, post by post, from its old home at Shoreditch. This temple of varieties has no more permanence than a widow's shack; yet it thinks itself well above its station. Over the entrance is a crest displaying Hercules bearing the globe upon his shoulders, and the dubious motto: *Totus mundus agit histrionem*: the whole world is a playhouse.

I knock on the door: no answer. I bang harder: but there is only silence. So I push it open, throwing all my weight against it. It groans as it yields, opening just a crack, and I wriggle inside. I'm standing in the dark passageway between the lowest tier of seats, facing the stage itself. There's no sound, save only the cry of the kites, flapping on the roof thatch high above me. I look around, bemused by the emptiness of the place, having only been there as part of a boisterous crowd. The pit, open to the grey, snow-burdened sky, stretches before me. The great stage is deserted. I walk over to it, looking around me uneasily.

Someone laughs, loudly, from far above. I climb the steps on to the boards.

'Hello?' I look up. 'Mr Burbage?'

Another laugh, very merry.

'Who's there?' I call. I narrow my eyes, scouring the entrances to the tiring-rooms, and the musicians' gallery which is just above them.

'She can't see us,' says a familiar voice.

'Aemilia!' This is a louder, richer accent. 'Aemilia, look higher!'

I look around me, flushing with anger. 'I can't see you,' I cry. 'Come out, and stop fooling with me.'

'Higher!' calls the rich voice. 'Even higher!'

Finally I spy them. Two heads, peering down at me, from the topmost point of the Heavens, half-hidden behind a painted wooden cloud.

The cloud-space proves to be a narrow platform, like a hidden stage, just below the cupola. It is reached by a series of steep flights of steps. Burbage and Will are bending over a chart on a small table. They present an odd contrast: Burbage short and stout, with his walrus nose and doleful eyes; and Will, taller, well-made, tapping his foot in time with some rhythm that beats in his own head. Both are dressed in heavy coats with black coney collars, and fine kid gloves, with long patterned cuffs. They could be two wealthy merchants, discussing a consignment of new kerseys from Halifax or a cargo of pepper from the Levant.

Burbage kisses my hand, bringing off his trick of being mocking and gentlemanly at once. 'Mistress Lanyer, we are honoured. And you are looking so *well*.'

'Thank you, sir.'

'I hope the climb did not tire you?'

'I am not in my dotage yet.'

'Indeed *not*. You have not changed one jot since the first day I saw you. Still as comely as a maid.'

I bow. 'I am sorry to see that you are busy with Mr Shakespeare. I had thought we had arranged to meet at this hour.'

'Oh, no matter, we will be done with this in no time,' says Burbage. 'It's just some hare-brained scheme of Will's.'

'It is *business*, Dick, I wish you'd give it your proper attention,' says Will, not looking at me.

'Business, man? Our business is the play, upon the stage.'

'Indeed,' says Will. 'I am aware of it.'

Burbage straightens his back, pushes out his chest and seems to grow a foot taller. Stepping back from the table, he declaims:

'Blow, winds, and crack your cheeks! Rage! Blow!
You cataracts and hurricanoes, spout
Till you have drench'd our steeples, drown'd the cocks!
You sulph'rous and thought-executing fires,

314

Vaunt couriers of oak-cleaving thunderbolts,
Singe my white head! And thou all-shaking thunder.
Strike flat the thick rotundity o'th'world,
Crack Nature's moulds, all germens spill at once
That makes ingrateful man!'

It is a splendid speech: he seems both aged and magnificent in the making of it.

'You see?' says Burbage. 'The words are all. Not dandling players like newborn babes.'

'I agree that they are *most* significant, since I wrote them,' says Will. He has not looked up from his study once.

'What do you mean?' I ask. 'What "dandling"?'

'Will sets out to make men fly,' says Burbage, extending his arm with regal generosity. 'As if he were Icarus.'

'Daedalus, if I may correct you,' say I.

Will looks at me for the first time, almost as if he is about to laugh. 'They've done it at the Fortune,' he says. 'Our competitors.'

Burbage makes another expansive gesture, as if dismissing Greek legends in their entirety. 'Ah, yes, Daedalus is the inventor. Of course, of course. Icarus is the son, who fell. As did two men at the Fortune, and broke their backs.'

Will appears to be making some sort of calculation on a piece of foolscap.

'Do you not think of that?' I ask him.

'I think of divinities and angels, descending from above,' says Will, after a moment. He seems to consider the empty air in front of him. 'I think of the heavens, riven by the radiance of a suspended goddess. Strapped safely in a chair.' Quite suddenly, he turns and flashes a glance at me. 'Come, Mistress Lanyer, look...'

I go over, lips pursed. The diagram shows a strange construction consisting of a pivot, a long arm and a chair. It reminds me of the Wheel of Fortune, that most double of the Tarot cards, which can foretell great luck or dire calamity.

'You see, this is the stage we stand upon.' He indicates the outline of the diagram. 'We have enough space for windlass, drum and strong cordage. And – here – for the player to be readied for his flying seat.' He is looking down again, pointing to the next diagram. 'And here – with some little refinement to the plan, the whole business will be done in one sweeping movement – just a slight upward thrust so the chair can clear the edge of the platform – and then forward and downward. On to the stage. You see?'

I make as close a study of the diagram as I would if I were the carpenter myself. I dare not look up. At last I say, 'What do you want with my play?'

Will sighs and folds up the chart. 'You must discuss all that with Dick. It is nothing to do with me.' He disappears down the stairs, his dark cape flying out behind him.

Burbage, on the other hand, is smiling, all avuncular. 'Come, mistress, sit down,' he says, coming over to the table. 'Don't mind Will. He has a sore head. He has been doing the accounts again – it's best left to Heminge.'

'I don't mind him at all. I do not think of him.'

He smiles in a manner which annoys me. 'Please – sit down. I have a proposition to make, which I think will interest you.'

I sit.

'Have your brought the play with you?' he asks. 'I should like to read it, if I may.'

I pull it from my bag, but withhold it when he tries to take it from me. 'Sir, I should like to know *why* you wish to read it? Since a lady's work cannot be played upon a public stage.'

Burbage beckons me closer, lowering his voice and rounding his shoulders in a stage approximation of urgent secrecy. 'Can we speak in confidence? Up here, where none can hear us? Might I depend on your discretion?'

'I would not be alive today if I did not know how to be discreet.'

'Quite.' He shifts his chair closer, so I can see the smallpox pits on his great nose. 'To be frank with you, we are looking for something new. Fresh ideas, to please and reassure the King. He is distracted, sees an assassin in every corner and fears the Catholics will try again. He is not a happy man.'

'He can't be blamed for fearing plotters. Since they came so close to blowing him to Heaven.'

'Of course not. Daggers, poison, even curses might undo him. Or, like his own father, he might yet be ripped to pieces by a conspirator's bomb.'

'So why can't... Mr Shakespeare turn his hand to this?'

'Will is busy. His daughter is to marry, his wife wants more money to spend on her fine house, and he insists his next piece will be set in Ancient Egypt. I cannot for the life of me see a Scottish theme emerging there. We've looked at other plays – including three from Dekker – but none of them will do.'

I have to swallow hard at the mention of Will's greedy wife. 'No, I can see that would be difficult.'

'The King is... well, he is a scholar one day, and a sot the next. In his books, he is the wisest man I ever met. In his cups, the most foolish. I don't know what to make of him.'

'You are the leader of the King's Men. The Royal company, in his pay. What's there to worry you?'

'We are his appointed company now, but, in time to come – who knows? We must work hard to keep his favour.'

'Doesn't he like what you have done for him so far?'

'Well enough, I'm told. Though he's not as fulsome as the late Queen. Scots, you see. Uncivilised.'

'So what did you do last?'

'Madam! How can you ask such a thing? It was my greatest part so far. My King Lear!'

'The foolish dotard Prince? I saw it done at Court, years ago. I never understood it.'

He frowns, offended. 'What, a woman of your superior understanding?'

'Must Kings be told to keep hold of their kingdoms? I should not have thought so.'

'You must see the new play! We are staging it again in spring. No one remembers that hoary elder version now – Will's telling is quite new, and vastly better.'

'But you haven't changed the story?'

'No. Why should we?'

'The King divides his kingdom between his three daughters, and suffers the consequences.'

'That is the sum of it.'

'What King ever lived who acted in such a way?'

'In Will's hands, how could it be otherwise than great? An instructive, yet crowd-pleasing fable.'

'Crowds are not always right.'

'He always does so well with the *words*.'

'I've no doubt of it.'

'Also, there are some scenes of excellent torture, his best since *Titus*.'

'Now torture *is* a crowd-pleaser, that I certainly recall.'

'But… I don't know. The King seemed distracted, low in spirits when he was watching it. *Tired.* At least he woke up for my great speech, on the blasted heath. Which I just gave a flavour of.'

'So now you think… a Scottish play, with hags?'

'Indeed!' says Burbage. 'Blood and hags! We need a play to please the King, and to please the King, it must have murder in it, as he was nearly murdered, and that murderer must be most direly punished.'

'I see, but – '

'We must include the intended destruction of a kingdom – '

'Which I have – '

'The undermining of the good by the diligent deception of the evil. As our King was undermined – d'you see it? – by the traitor Fawkes and all the rest.' Burbage spreads his hands. 'And we need plots – which can be woven in, don't fear this. And equivocation, but we can do that in one speech.'

'Assuredly.'

'But most of all,' says Burbage, taking my hand in his, 'most of all we must have witches.'

'Why?'

'Marston has them in his *Sophosha*, and Barnes has his *Devil's Charter*. And Dekker's done one, which comes as no surprise, since he works like a thousand demons.'

Will has returned, with more rolls of paper, which he spreads out upon the table, using pewter mugs to flatten the corners.

'And what is Dekker's play called?' I ask.

'*The Whore of Babylon*,' says Will, his back still turned. He speaks with peculiar vehemence.

'So you see,' says Burbage. 'What you have wrote is well-nigh perfect.'

'But what's my reward for this?'

Burbage crosses his legs as if to make himself more comfortable in his seat, then recrosses them. 'Well… it would partly be this much: knowing these were your lines, of course, performed before the King of England. Few men can claim so much.'

'Few men. And no women. I should like my name to be heard.'

'Heard?'

'If my play were done before the King, this might be possible. As if it were a noble lady's closet play, put on at some great house.'

Burbage raises his eyebrows. He looks at me as he might have done if a black rat had addressed him from the wainscot. 'Give me the play, my dear, and we will talk about the terms – if it is good enough,' he says.

I consider this. 'I suppose it would be foolish to say no.'

Burbage smiles, and looks down at the first page, on which I have written: *The Tragedie of Ladie Macbeth, A Scottish Queen.*

'An excellent title, certainly. Leave it in my hands, and I will see what shall be done.'

Scene III

Something ails Marie. Never the most sensible of serving girls, she appears to have turned quite mad since Christmas, and at first I cannot think what can be the matter. She forgets to do the linen on washday, so that Alfonso has to wear a soiled shirt to the palace when he is called to discuss a new trip to the Indies with Sir Robert Unwin. Yesterday, she moaned so much over the drying of ruffs on wood sticks that I was forced to beat her about the head, giving her a thick blobberlip. Which I regret, as I am somewhat tender-hearted. After that, she was in such a state of woeful discontent that she spoiled the soap, burned the bread, spilled the milk, dulled the pewter and cried when I asked her to comb out my hair.

Today brings the latest of her blunders. She has failed to brush my best wool dress, so a great moth flitters up into the air when I shake it out to wear to church. The blind insect has feasted till the cloth is full of holes, and now it is only fit for wearing in the house. When I tell her of this, she is half-crying, half-laughing, and so distracted that I fear I might lose her to Bedlam. In fact, I have ceased being angry, and am afraid of what she might do next: set the house on fire or jump into the river.

'What's the matter with that simpleton Marie?' I ask Anne as we cross the fields towards the distant spire of St Mary's Church. Marie is ahead of us, walking along with Henry. I frown as she falls over a running pig, which Henry had the sense to side-step.

'Can't you guess?' Anne looks at me queerly.

'If I could, I would have said so.'

She smiles, hard-eyed. 'It's love. She feels the pangs of *love*.'

'But whom does she love?'

Anne regards me as if it was I who were the half-wit, and not my silly servant. 'Why it's Tom!' she says.

I give a scream of laughter. 'But he is just…'

She lays her hand on my arm and I see that Marie has turned to look at us. 'Just a babe in arms, I know,' she whispers. 'No more than a child in his ways. And besides, when he is of an age, he will most likely marry into the theatre, not waste himself on some little drudge.'

'To think of it!' I say. 'Of course, he cannot love her in return. Such a useless dizzard of a girl.'

'Of course not,' says Anne, sticking her chin out. And I see from the jut of it that he is utterly enslaved.

'Oh, Lord above!' I cry. 'Whatever shall we do with our misbehaving children?'

Anne stops and looks at the calm steeple of the church, cutting into the sky. She is weeping. All around I can hear the bleating of sheep in the winter sunshine.

'Marie is going to have a child,' she says.

'Dear God,' I say. 'So that is what it's all about!'

Anne wipes her eyes. 'He doesn't even know who else she's been with. Why should he marry the little slattern? She threw herself at him the minute she set eyes on him.'

'It was ever thus.'

'He could be great, Aemilia. He has a talent, you know. Now he wants to tie himself to that shameless trollop, and her unborn child.'

'Let us go to church,' I say, 'and pray. You have your son's foolishness to burden you. I have my idiot spouse.'

Inside St Mary's, we lower our heads and pray, most devoutly. 'Please God,' I say silently, deciding not to trouble with the Scriptures. 'Let Marie's womb-blood flow tomorrow, and let Sir Robert Unwin take Alfonso on his next sea voyage. Let him go to the Americas, and preserve our fortunes. And my virtue, what is left of it.' I stand, head bowed, for some time.

'I do not want to fornicate with Inchbald, Lord, if this can be avoided.'

I stand longer, before my Maker.

'Forgive me, Lord, for being so bold.'

God answers one of these prayers, but not both. Alfonso is given a commission by Sir Robert that very day. Of Marie's womb blood I hear nothing, but she burns the bread each morning.

The letter I have been waiting for finally arrives. What I receive is not – as I had expected – a slender folded document. It is a bundle of messy pages. My pages, I see at once. And yet the note itself is brief enough.

> *Madam,*
>
> *We regret that these words, though Admirable in one of your Sex, are not of the Quality or Kind which will make a Show upon the Stage. For this reason, they did not inspire that Passion in us which we must feel in order to transform your Thoughts into Theatricals.*
>
> *Might we thank you for your Interest and wish you every Success with your future Experiments in Fabrication.*
>
> *Your most humble,*
> *Richard Burbage*

I do not breathe – I think I might not breathe again – but scrabble through the pages as if looking for reassurance, desperate to soothe the fizz and fury in my head. A speech springs out at me: Lady Macbeth, at full height.

> *Was the hope drunk, wherein you dressed yourself?*
> *Hath it slept since?*

And wakes it now, to look so green and pale
At what it did so freely?

I close my eyes, not needing to see the rest, as I could hear it clear. A voice that echoes between Lilith's and my own.

Art thou afeared to be the same in thine own act and
valour as thou art in desire?

I speak aloud, my eyes still shut. '*Would'st thou have that which thou esteem'st the ornament of life, and live a coward in thine own esteem, letting "I dare not" wait upon "I would"?*'

Cruel, duplicitous Burbage! To trip off this shoddy letter, when he has seen what I had put. I sink down to the ground, and the pages flutter around me, and I bury my head in my hands and I sob. I cry because I know now they will never hear me. This is it, and this is all of it, this house of thirty oaks, this board with its crooked stools, this fireside, the ham, the pots, the dirty skillet. I am hemmed in by walls of wattle, and by hours of life. There will be no breaking out, no second chance, no late reward. I am a spent whore, and that is the top and bottom of it. The best I can hope for is to keep the roof above us by licking Inchbald's little cock.

I cry till my throat aches, and after that there seems little purpose to it. For I have my son to think of. So I wipe my eyes, and look around me, and think. I can't sit sobbing here for ever more. What shall we eat? Who will do the shirts? And I pick up the pages and sort them into a tidy pile, in the order in which they were written.

That done, I begin to sweep the kitchen. I remember, looking at the uncleared table and the dirty wooden trenchers, that Marie has been gone from the house for the whole day. Since Anne told me she was pregnant, I have realised that I was foolish not to notice. She's fattened up like a cooped goose, week after week, so that even her little wrists are now thickened, and her swollen breasts rest upon the table when she leans forward to sop up her pottage with her bread. What's more, her belly sticks out plainly now. And she and Tom are always whispering, and conniving, when they get the chance. Anne can do nothing with Tom, and I can get no sense from Marie.

But here she comes! Has she grown bigger in a single day? She waddles in from the street, sweating and with her dress loosened, even though the wind is still so bitter. Looking at her, I wonder how many months she's gone. More than seven? If so she must have been already with child at Yuletide, the little minx. Her belly is bigger than mine has ever been, and Henry was a porker of a baby, the biggest Joan had ever seen.

'Whatever are you thinking?' I say, straightening from my work. 'Are you turning vagabond and stalking the highway? Do you shun your mistress, and run out among the common doxies?'

'What is that you say?' She wipes her forehead with her kerchief. I may as well have spoken Latin.

'Street scum, that's what they are, with no home to go to and faces brown as privy slop.'

'I can't run anywhere,' says Marie. This is true, given she can barely walk. She lowers herself slowly on to a stool, using the table for support.

I frown. 'Shall your babe be born under a hedge? Or at Tothill Fields?'

'I don't know,' she says. Her face is white and set with tiredness. I feel a stab of pity for her, in spite of myself, this silly girl whose lustfulness has led her to child-bed so young. What fools we women are. I pour her some ale.

'Thank you, mistress. You are kind.'

'Kind!' I have to laugh.

'You are to me. I have been a bad servant.'

'I fear you have.'

'But I will pay for it.'

'You will have a child. *Then* you will pay. But you will also have your reward.'

Henry comes in from school, as if summoned, and throws his bag on to the floor. I draw him in and hug him, then push him from me. 'Begone, Henry, our talk is not for you.'

'Nor would I want to listen,' says he. 'Women's idle chatter. Of dull babies and fine dresses and… stupid slimy *kisses*.'

He makes a face, picks up his catapult and runs outside again.

I sit down opposite Marie, and pour myself a drink. 'You will still be my servant,' I say. 'The child – it won't prevent you sweeping, I hope, or stirring the stew.'

She looks at me, her eyes great with tears. 'No, mistress.'

I set down my cup. 'Then why are you so miserable?'

She rests her head on her arms and begins to sob.

I stare at her. 'Marie? What is it? Thomas is no worse than any other lad! Marie, tell me. What is wrong?'

At first she says nothing, just cries and cries, till I think I must get on and turn the mattresses. Then she stops, quite suddenly. 'There is something terrible,' she says, her face hidden.

'What do you mean?'

'Something is wrong.'

'*What* is wrong?'

She raises her head. 'Something is wrong with the baby.'

'Oh, for shame! You are young! It will pop out like a plum from a pie. You'll have another dozen before you're done.'

She rubs her bloodshot eyes with her wet fingers. 'I have dreams.'

'Dreams.'

'Dreams such as… such as I have never known.'

I sigh and pile up some dirty trenchers. 'And what do you dream of?'

Her gaze fixes on me, her eyes grow wider and wider as if she saw her nightmares in my face. 'I dream of monsters. Horrid midnight creatures. Demons, misbegot, that stalk us when the sun has gone.'

'Nursery fears, which you must soon grow out of.'

'I dream there is a monster growing inside me. My mother used to tell me an old French tale, about this very thing!'

This child is too fanciful for her own good. 'Marie, you are trying my patience. There are a thousand tales like that one.'

'But why?' she says. 'Surely it's because such things are common? When monsters are born, I mean *really*, the midwives keep it quiet.'

I say nothing. The girl isn't quite as foolish as she looks. Many years ago, I attended a birth with Joan. It was a hard delivery, which lasted for two days and two nights. And after all her travail the poor woman had little enough to show for it. The babe – of no gender – was born with one great eye in the middle of its forehead. A sexless Cyclops. Joan swaddled it, and sprinkled it with holy water. But when the father saw his child he swore, grabbed it by the feet and bashed it against the wall till he had beaten out all its brains. The infant's screams were the worst I ever heard; no witch, nor gibbet-rogue, nor half-bowelled recusant, could make such a sound. Unshriven, that malformed babe went straight to Hell.

It's true, we kept it quiet, saying only that the child had died.

And of course, now that Alfonso is off cavorting on a ship somewhere, my landlord soon gets wind of it, and here he is. I am cleaning out the jakes when he comes up behind me, quiet as a river rat.

'Mistress Lanyer.' He removes his hat with a flourish. It is a new one, by the look of it. Bright scarlet, with a yellow ostrich feather: colours which are all the rage at Court.

'Mr Inchbald, shorter than ever. Good day to you, sir.'

'Your servant let me in, I hope I am not intruding.'

I make a lot of business of pouring a pot of piss into the maw of the privy. 'I fear I am somewhat busy. Hard at my chores, as you can see.'

'Such a lady as yourself should not be mired in… these matters.' He is looking at his feet. A turd has dropped on to one of them. I pretend not to notice.

'I am not fit for entertaining. Can't you come another time?'

He kicks the turd into the air with surprising skill. 'The rent is due, sweet lady.'

'Ah, the sweet rent.'

'I'll wait while you wash your hands, and perhaps we can share a glass of something from your larder.'

'Very well.' My mind is working quickly. I have one last item of some value, which might buy him off.

'Excellent. The workmanship is most careful. Quality, Mistress Lanyer, most admirable quality.'

The dwarf is examining a little silver pomander, shaped like a galleon. I am offering it to him in lieu of rent – and fornication. We are standing by the walnut cupboard in the kitchen in which I keep the few things of value that I have left.

'It's made in Nuremberg. See the mark?' I say. I point with a long arm, keeping my distance. 'The figures there are meant to be my dear husband, God bless him, and my good self.'

'Though they could be anyone,' says Inchbald.

'You can keep condiments and salt cellars beneath the deck.'

'Most… elegant.' His eyes have not left my bosom once.

I decide my attention should most usefully remain on the pomander. 'Fill it with rose-water, and you can use it to ward off foul vapours and disease.'

'Why, it's almost a shame to take it from you.'

'Almost, yes. But think on this – if you were a just a fraction shorter you could ride on it yourself.'

'Your wit is well known, mistress, but it can sometimes mar your perfect beauty.'

'Shame. Stop staring at my dugs, please, Mr Inchbald.'

He puts his hands behind his back, as if this was the only way he could stop them wandering towards my breasts. 'I'd still sooner have a suck, for all it is a handsome piece of work.'

'Take it, or take your leave.'

Disgruntled, Inchbald wraps the pomander up in a linen cloth and stores it in his leather satchel. He bows gracelessly, and I turn away and set about cleaning a candlestick, hoping he will leave. There is silence for a moment, then he says, 'It is a shame that you are so ill-disposed towards me, madam. I was intending to invite you to the theatre, as my most honoured guest.'

'Well, you do surprise me.' This is true. None of Inchbald's other ladies is taken out to town. It strikes me that Anne would think it most annoying if I were rewarded for my virtue with such a treat.

'There is a lot of talk about the latest work the King's players are staging at the Globe. They say they put it on at Whitehall and the Queen fainted right away.'

I have been standing with my back to him, scraping at a gobbet of dried porridge on the kitchen table with a carving knife, but now I stop and look at him.

'Queen Anne fainted?'

'Indeed. Quite the horridest play that she had seen in all her life. So I have been told. She thought there was black magic in it. Just like *Faustus*.'

I drop the knife. 'What is it called?'

He taps his forehead, tutting with irritation. 'Oh, do you know, I quite forget. Something odd-sounding. Something of the north.'

'Scottish?'

'Scottish! Yes! I have it now. It's *The Tragedie of Macbeth*.'

* * *

What's in a name? What indeed. Macbeth is a good one. Perhaps it is just the title they have filched. It is not feasible, not likely, that these seasoned players have stole my work. And yet I cannot sleep for thinking of it. The sun sinks, the night blackens, the sun rises again, and I do not so much as blink. For three days, and three nights, this is my rest. Would they do this, and say not a word about it? I can't face going to the theatre to see it for myself. No, I will ask Tom Flood.

I decide to seek him out at the Anchor at Southwark. It is a good spot for actors, for when the talk runs flat they can amuse themselves by watching the pirates hang at Execution Dock, and so learn how to make their stage-deaths true to life. A gaggle of prentice-boys is standing outside, laughing together and drinking ale from their leather black-jackets. They call out when I pass, cocky as you please. I stare back stony-eyed, and all three of them look nervously away. Inside, darkness and a roar of talking. Narrow booths contain half-seen groups of drinkers and bawds: a man kissing a white-armed girl; an old doxy, sitting astride a red-headed sailor-boy; a group of law students, opining in the Latin.

A thin man with a twisted lip comes hobbling towards me. 'Mistress, can I be of help?' He speaks with false gentility.

'I don't think so, thank you.' I look around the crowded inn.

'We don't see many married ladies here. Who do you seek?'

'Tom Flood, a player.'

'Ah, well. He is engaged. Occupied, or *occupying*, if I am to be precise.'

'I see. We are speaking, if I am right, of fornication?'

'She's not the youngest, nor the comeliest, but she is the… well. She *accommodates*.'

'A gamesome old jade, I am sure.'

'Else he'd be throwing away a good sixpence.'

'Indeed. Take me to him, will you?'

'Are you sure you wouldn't like to wait? We have the finest apple cider, the old Queen's favourite tipple.'

'Drank in this doghole often, did she?'

'Slept here, mistress, on each progress.'

Of course she did, and feasted on broken hog meat. 'Then by all means bring me some cider.'

When he's gone, I hasten up the stairs. I knock on the first door I come to. 'Tom Flood?' There are little panting shrieks from within. Yelping, rapid, rhythmic. It reminds me of the time I heard the old rogue Ralegh at his game of forest hide-and-fuck, a sport he was most fond of. I heard him having Bess Throckmorton against a tree. At first she was all coy decorum: 'Sweet Sir Walter, will you undo me? Nay, sweet Sir Walter!' But as her pleasure and excitement grew all she could squeal was, 'Swisser swatter swisser swatter.' And the branches shook as if brave Sir W. were pleasuring the trunk itself.

This is a seamier setting by far. I bang on the door once more. 'Tom?' I try again. But the bullish roar which rips out next sounds more like the come-cry of the Beast himself than any sound that Tom could make. I try the next door. A Blackamoor opens it a crack, and peers out at me, suspicious. 'Is Tom within?' I ask.

The Blackamoor disappears. 'Are you called Tom?' I hear him say. He returns. 'No Toms here.'

At last I come to a door at the end of the passage. I bang on it with the flat of my hand. At first there is no answer. But I can hear the gentle rattle of a snore. Pushing it open, I see Tom, sleeping softly. Next to him sits a raddled whore of at least my age, with dangling naked dugs. She is eating from a little dish, and red wine streaks her chin.

'Who might you be?' asks the whore, mouth full. 'Not his mother, are you?'

'What's it to you if I'm his wife? Get out, you filthy drab!'

After she has gone, I sit down on the bed and look at Tom, with his white skin and his curling, matted hair. His breath rises and falls sweetly with each snore. The stench of ale comes off him like a river fog.

'Tom,' I say. I touch his hand. 'Wake up.'

He makes a noise like a puppy nosing for his mother's tit, a hungry little whimper. Then he opens his eyes. With a cry, he sits upright, clutching the covers to his groin. 'Aemilia! Mistress Lanyer – Lord above! What is the matter?'

I fold my arms. 'I have a question for you.'

'God's blood!' says Tom. 'Has my mother put you up to this?'

'You've been drinking.'

'A little, madam.'

'And whoring too, it seems.'

'Well...'

'No way for a leading lady to go on. But that's not the worst of it.'

'What?' Now there is panic in his eyes. 'Marie! Is she ill? Has it come? I must go to her...' He leaps out of bed, naked as an earth-worm, and begins to dress himself.

'Tom – stop. Marie is not ill. And I doubt the baby's ready – though it's twice the size it should be.'

He stops, half in his shirt, and looks at me. 'What, then? Why do you pester me?'

'Pester? *Pester*? And your mother thinks it's *Henry* who is spoiled! I've come here for some information. Some facts. No *equivocation*, please. I know you have the answer.'

He starts buttoning his shirt. 'I don't know what I know which is of any use to you, but ask me what you like.'

I stand up and walk to the other side of the room, trying to set my mind straight. 'What's this about a Scottish play? The next one you're doing at the Globe?'

He frowns, as if trying to remember lines. 'It's a secret. They've told us to keep it quiet. This play will startle all the town.'

'Why so secret?'

'I don't know.'

'So who do *you* play?'

His fiddles with his shirt.

'Your *part*, Tom, what is it?'

'Lady Macbeth,' he says, looking at me with a sudden glint of pleasure. 'Later the Scottish Queen.'

'I know who Lady Macbeth is, you buffoon.'

He smiles, uneasy. 'Nathan Field is only Lady Macduff, and then a serving woman with hardly any lines. He was most put out when Burbage told us.'

'Is yours a little part, or long?'

'Littler than I would have liked. But the greatest boy's part, by some way.'

'How long?'

'Long enough.'

'What kind of woman is she?'

'What do you mean?'

'What is her nature?'

'In some scenes, she's a better man than her lord.'

'She leads him into wickedness?'

'She eggs him on, to kill the King. Then falls into a most excellent madness, walking in her nightgown like an unquiet spirit. This part is worth a thousand Juliets.'

'So.' The tale was written down by Holinshed, but some of this is mine. I breathe deeply, imagining Will's head, and that of Burbage, high above the Bridge, upon a spike. Par-boiled with cumin seeds, and dipped in tar. 'Do you happen to have your pages with you, by any chance?'

Tom takes a wad of paper from his doublet and hands it to me. 'They are brutal lines,' he says. 'But bold.'

I read them, and the blood beats in my brain when I see how they have cheated me. 'Who wrote these?' I ask, as if even now all might be somehow mended.

'Why, Will Shakespeare, of course,' says Tom. He is dressed now, and looks around him, then picks up his hat. 'Who else would it be?'

333

Just as he has finished speaking, the door opens, and who should walk in but Will himself, neat as a character in a play? He too is buttoning his shirt-front. I wonder if it was his voice I heard, roaring his pleasure a few moments ago? The room sways as if we were all at sea, and I recall how he would look at me when it was me he rode, and loved, and rejoiced in.

He is saying, 'Tom, we must go, for it's…' Then he catches sight of me and turns pale. 'Aemilia!'

I bow my head.

'What are you…?'

'A woman, sir, more's the pity.'

'I mean – what are you doing in this place?'

'Business.' I look him up and down. 'And you? Pleasure, I if I heard you right.'

Oh, God! It is a summer's day again. I'm in his arms and he is fucking me in bright sun. When he comes he throws his head back and calls my name: 'Aemilia! Aemilia! Aemilia!' We are born again, one flesh, one love.

'Business?' He is staring back, then looks down at himself in dismay. 'I am on business myself, though I expect you will think otherwise.'

'It is no business of mine where you go a-whoring,' I say. 'I have other things to think of. I heard word about a play.' I nod towards Tom. 'From my young neighbour.'

'Of course. The play.'

'What is it called?' I ask, keeping my voice innocent.

Will smoothes his hands over his hair. 'It's – well. The title is *The Tragedie of Macbeth*.'

'The King's story, rather than the Queen's?'

'Quite so.'

'And therefore, different from the play I left with Burbage, which fell sadly short and which he returned to me. As you will recall.'

'Oh – very different! Utterly different! An India to your Kent, as it were. A chasm of difference between your… musings and this finished work. Yes.' He looks unhappier still. 'That is the way of it. Plays are adapted, from many, many sources.'

'And yet – here are Tom's pages, and nearly all the words are mine.'

'Yours? Surely not.'

'I wrote them, and I know I'm not mistaken. And what about the witches? And the murder of Macduff's wife and her little ones? All thrown out – or some of this included?'

'All are there, aren't they?' says Tom. 'It's a fine, dark thing, and will set an audience trembling.'

'These things are there,' says Will, blinking. 'And more besides. I mean – new things, beside these… others. Come Tom, let us go.'

I step into the doorway, so they cannot pass. 'I hear it is highly thought of, this great, new, secret production.'

'There is no secret – we waited till it had been approved of by the King,' says Will. 'And now he has seen it, and admires it, and all is well.'

I look from Will's face to Tom's and back again. 'It's a poor business,' I say. 'Is this greatness, or littleness, I wonder? Is this genius, or common theft? Tell me, sir, you are a man of many words.'

'We call it poetry,' says Will. 'We call it Art.'

'Oh, shame on you,' say I. 'You and your kind.'

'What "kind" is that?'

'Filthy players, sir, and twisted poets and your frilly little helpmeets in their skirts.' Tom looks behind him when I cast a look in his direction, as if I could not possibly be referring to him.

'Aemilia, listen to reason, will you – ?'

'Reason? Heaven help us! Reason? Is this the best that you can do? You… men! Cock-heavy, brain-light, and brimful of your own importance? The apex of Creation? God aimed too low!'

I turn and hurry down the stairs, through the crowded tavern and out into the street. The sun is low over the roofs and chimneys, and it will soon be nightfall. My head aches; my heart beats fast. What hope do I have of getting anything, in this City? I will end up starving in the Cage with the other drabs and vagrants. But I have not gone far when someone seizes my shoulder.

Will is breathing heavily. 'Aemilia – there is something I need to say to you.'

I shake his hand away and keep walking. 'What is there to say? Unless you will admit that you have robbed me.'

He half-runs, half-walks to keep up with me. 'I will *not* say so, because it isn't true.'

I look along the street and cross over, heading for the Bridge. 'You have played me false, you and your conniving tribe.'

'Not false, Aemilia – this is how it is done. No play is made by one man alone. You don't understand this world. You mistake your place in it. Look, mistress, slow down, please…'

'My place? Would that I had one!'

'Aemilia, no, you are mistaken…'

I try to outpace him but he matches me step for step. I skip over a dog turd and turn to face him. 'Don't you see it? If a man had written that play, and it were put on with some changes, and he were one of your company or a tavern friend, like Dekker, all would be well.'

'So… what is the difference?'

'Lord save us, Will! I am a woman! I will get nothing if you don't acknowledge what I have done. Nothing. I'm not Mary Sidney, or some other clever lady of the manor, who writes her hobby-lines and is fêted by her little retinue. I am alone. I am that turd.' I point at it. 'I am nothing.'

He takes a purse from his belt and holds it towards me. 'Here is gold, if it will help you,' he said. 'Once, you said that you could not be with me because of my lowly station. But now I am a gentleman. I have a coat-of-arms… and houses.'

'Always trying to pay me off! I don't want your cursed coin. I want to be a poet myself.'

'The world is not run according to my wishes, any more than it is to yours! You are confusing me with Almighty God!'

'Oh, go and play bare-arses with the rest of them! Every one a cozener and a cheat.' I push past him and walk on.

'Aemilia!'

I keep walking.

'Aemilia!'

I quicken my pace.

'Aemilia!' *Oh, Lord, there is that scene again: pale flesh, bright sun; his rapt face; the white light in my head.*

'My love...' His voice breaks upon the word, and stops.

I look back. 'Your... *what*?'

'I must see you! I need to see you!'

'Well, here I am. Solid as a dead sow.'

'What I mean is... I must talk to you! We must... God! Where are all the words, the *words*, when I need them most?'

'They cheat you, sir, as you have cheated me. Perhaps there is some justice in Creation after all. Your words came easy enough when you wanted to strumpet me, and whore me and harlot me, and falsely accuse me of fornicating with all and sundry. "The bay where all men ride"! God's blood, what a phrase! From your so-called love to those foul insults. How great was the distance? You made the change quicker than a viper slips its skin.'

'Jesu!' He stares at me hopelessly. 'What have I done?'

'What?'

'I thought that I could exorcise you, if my lines were cruel enough. But...'

'But... what?'

We stare at each other across the muddy street.

'I wanted to believe the worst of you. If you wouldn't have me, then, in my madness, it was easiest to call you whore.'

'Ah,' I say. 'Now we have it. Now I believe you.'

'But, even in the midst of writing those lines, I never could destroy the passion that tormented me. That is the essence of them. They are love sonnets, from my heart.'

'Oh, Will,' I say. 'You are such a fool.'

He smiles, a strange, sweet smile, and says, 'And now... now I fear it is too late.'

The sun is low in the sky. 'I fear so. Henry will wonder where I am.'

'What are you doing tomorrow morning?' he asks, abruptly. 'There is something... I must tell you something.'

'I'm praying at the tomb of my lord Hunsdon,' I say, flushing.

'You still pine for that old place-man?'

'He was kind to me. None kinder.'

'I'll meet you there.'

I laugh. 'What a fitting arrangement! Perhaps his lordship will rise up from his grave and beat you round the head for leading me such a dance.'

'I cannot bear this...'

He looks so woebegone that I almost pity him. 'I'm going to the Church of St Peter early,' I say. 'Six of the clock, when it's still quiet.'

'I'll be there.'

I'm startled by his burning eyes. 'I must go,' I say, like some awkward, untried maid. 'My son...'

'Say that you will meet with me tomorrow.'

I stare.

'Say it, Aemilia, I beg you.'

'I...'

'Please, sweet lady.'

'If you want.'

'I do want. I want to see you more than anything.'

'Then I will meet you.'

Scene IV

For the rest of the day I run hither and thither like the silliest virgin, to stop myself from thinking. I swear, the house was never half so clean, before or after. Marie and I fetch water, scrub floors, air counterpanes, scour knives and clean plates with shave-grasse – what would normally take me three days takes three hours. She complains at first, but she soon gets to it, and while I do the hardest tasks – such as sweeping out the green rushes from the floors and casting down new ones – she toils away with a good grace. Too good a grace, as it turns out.

At last, she comes into the hall, where I am folding linen and placing it neatly in the great oak chest. I look up, and notice Marie's drawn face. 'For Heaven's sake, sit down, girl. You have done enough.'

She sits down on a hall stool, and rests her head against the wall, eyes closed. 'Truly, I am dog-tired,' she says. 'And the babe is jumping.'

'A good sign,' say I. 'It is when they're still that there is cause for worry.'

But when I look up to see why she hasn't replied. Her face is contorted with pain. 'Marie – what is it?'

'A feeling like the curse but stronger,' she says. 'Oh, mistress, it is like a knife! I couldn't stand it worse than this! I am not ready! I am not strong!'

'It is likely just a false alarm,' I tell her. 'Go and rest, and it will ease.' But I have to help her up the stairs and into bed, for she is heavy with fatigue.

As I turn to go, she grabs my hand. 'Did you see him?' she asks.

'See who?'

'Tom. When you went to the Anchor.'

I hesitate.

'Did you, mistress?'

'Yes, I saw him.' I think of telling her about the whore, but find I can't. 'He was snoring and in his cups. You are better off without him, child. Don't put your trust in players.'

'He loves me. He says he loves me.'

'I am sure he does, my poor Marie.'

I wake at the dead of night. Did I hear a scream? I open my eyes and stare up into the thick dark, listening hard. Silence loads my ears; blackness presses upon my eyes. A dream, a night fear. My mind at its old tricks again, and now there's no Joan to guard me. I am lucky to find myself safe and warm under my eiderdown, instead of out in the cold streets in nothing but my smock.

Then I hear it again, a scream that rips into the night, tearing the silence, louder, louder, then collapsing into agonised sobs. I push back the bed-clothes, light a candle and wrap myself in a woollen shawl. Then I climb up to the garret. Shivering, I open the door.

'Marie?'

She is naked, kneeling on her bed, with her head hanging down. All I can see is her loose hair, which hides her face. It is swinging to and fro as she rocks in pain. Then I notice, in the shifting orange of the candle-flame, that the sheets are smeared with blood.

I set down the candle. 'Dear Lord! How long have you been like this?' But she only grunts. 'Marie?'

'Umbstone. Umbstone.'

I throw off the shawl and kneel beside her. 'What? What is it?'

'Umbstone.' She lifts her head and points to the amulet which hangs around her neck. It is an eagle stone, a talisman to ward off miscarriage. The baby will not come till she takes this off. I unfasten it and set it down on the straw mattress where she can see it.

'I must fetch the midwife,' say I. 'I won't be long.'

But then she grips my hand. There is a look of terror in her eyes. 'Don't leave me, mistress. Stay!'

'Marie… I have no skill in this!'

'*You* will birth my child. *You* will save me.' Her grip tightens. 'Please.'

'What foolishness – you need someone who knows how to aid you in your travail…' But then I see myself, as Marie is now, as clear as if a mirror had been held up in which I could view the past. The night Henry was born and Joan saved us both. I see myself, crying out and clutching the birthing stool, and I see Joan, gentle, patient, always calm. While she was with me, I helped her with the births of several children in the parish. In truth, I can remember what she did: how she rubbed the women's flanks with oil of roses, fed them with vinegar and sugar, and eased the pain with powdered ivory or eagle's dung.

'If you want me, I'll stay, but don't forget I am not a midwife, nor do I have anything to recommend me.' The night watch calls outside – one of the clock. 'Do not lie down when the throes come; walk gently about the chamber. Keep warm, but don't take to your bed.'

I bank up the fire, so it gives out a good heat.

'I don't have child-bed linen or anything else for my poor baby!' she wails through her fallen hair. 'I thought it would be weeks from now!'

'Hush, calm yourself, I will see what I can fetch. I have a store of linen downstairs. Don't fret yourself. There is not a man or woman in this world who hasn't come into the world this way. Think on that, and breathe easy.'

I run down the stairs and rush into my room. Sure enough, I have a neat pile of forehead cloths, caps and belly-bands. And some open-fronted shifts which Marie could use for breast-feeding when it is time. Then I fetch the birthing-stool from the kitchen. I also get a pound of butter, a bowl of lavender water, some juice of dittany and my sharpest knife. Returning to the garret, I help the whimpering Marie on to the low seat, so that she is leaning against the back, legs wide. Then I stop up the cracks in the chamber walls with rags and blow out the candles, so that the roaring fire is our only light.

'Too much brightness can drive a mother mad,' I tell her.

She says nothing.

'Here, eat a knob of butter,' say I, cutting her a slice.

She groans and dribbles, but most of it goes down.

'I cannot bear it, mistress! I cannot cope! I swear there is an Oliphant inside me.'

I give her a drink of dittany juice, and then feel carefully inside for her cervix, and discover that she is beginning to open. Pressing against the widening space I can feel a round shape, covered in a waxy layer of vernix. Pray God it is the top of her baby's head and not some other part of its anatomy, for I cannot recall what to do if it is a breech birth, or there is some other mischief.

'I can't do it, mistress!' shouts Marie. 'I can't do it! I don't dare to, and I'm not strong enough! It will tear me in two. I can feel it. Oh, God, help me!'

'You'll do very well, a fine girl like you,' I say. I soak a cloth in the lavender water and wipe her brow. 'Keep cheerful! Don't waste your strength by calling on your Lord, when He has better things to do than mind a child-bed. Do you hear a mare in the field lamenting and crying as she pushes a gangling foal into the world? Save yourself for what must be done.'

'Lord help me! Our Lady, save me!' screams Marie, and her hands clench around the arms of the birthing-chair as another spasm takes hold of her. She is not an apt pupil. Poor creature, I am beyond my own knowledge and experience, but not so much as she. I cannot see how such a flimsy thing as she can bring to birth the great protuberance that she's been carrying inside. I rub the tight barrel of her belly with butter, speaking soothing nonsense to her all the while.

'I will help you all I can,' I say. 'But you must also strive to help yourself.'

But now another seizure is upon her, and she screams and writhes in the chair, and it is all I can do to stop her thrashing in the rushes in a fit like Legion. When she has done, there is a great pool of blood all around her, so the chair is an island in a scarlet lake, but there is no sign of the baby. The limits of my scant knowledge being already reached, I mop up the blood with the bed-clothes and say my own prayers to God.

'Mistress,' whispers the child. Her eyes are tight shut, and her breath comes shallowly. 'Will my baby come?'

'In its own time.'

'So it could not stick inside for ever?'

'Of course not.'

The watch calls out again. Two of the clock. Time enough, time enough.

But then time contorts to nightmare, and it is as if some demon comes down and takes possession of Marie. The throes come faster and stronger – as they will – but her fear is greater with each contraction, and soon it isn't God and Mary that she calls for, but the Devil and his minions instead. I find myself shouting back at her, afraid that this can do no good, yet shout she will. To my horror, she leaps up from the chair and runs against the walls, tearing at the bloody shreds of her nightgown, roaring and yelling all the while.

And I swear she sounds more like a damned soul than a serving girl. 'By Satan! By the Devil in all his names! By Apollyon, Beelzebub, Diabolus, Lucifer, the King of Hell! Did I ask for this?'

I grab her by the shoulders. 'Marie! Marie! Stop it!'

'The walking spirits of the Earth do not feel pain as I do!'

'Come back to yourself...'

But it is as if she is in another world. She puts her head back and howls, then spouts the vilest gibberish, which sounds like the language of lost souls.

'Marie!' I cry. 'Stop this terrible noise! Do not speak of Satan at such a time! Say your prayers!' Still she rages on, scratching her own flesh with her nails.

I pray for her, hoping to limit the power of her wicked thoughts. She seizes my arm and, using me for purchase, pushes and screams, legs half-bent, eyes rolled back into her head. Then she falls down on the ground, and a torrent of blood comes belching from between her legs and there is the most fearful stench, and I am afraid that she has died. But when I feel the pulse in her neck the blood is still beating fast, so I take some more old sheets and press them between her legs, and mop up all I can of the blood and matter. Then I see that a baby's face is sticking out.

'Marie!' I say. 'Your prayers are answered! The child is coming.'

Marie only groans, and speaks more of her strange language.

'Be quiet now, and don't push out for a little while. Let it come gently.' I cradle the little head in my hands and gradually a tiny shoulder follows. Then comes the other, and then the top part of its body. I feel in its mouth, scrape out the dark mess that is there, and it coughs and splutters and begins to cry. 'It is good Marie, it's good, you have a child...'

I bend closer, wanting to release its legs, but they are stuck fast. I try to ease the infant out, but can't. So I grease my hands with more butter, and feel inside her, to see what ails it. I feel a rounded shape, a blockage. But then, with a terrible wail, Marie begins to push once more. Blood oozes out around the half-born baby.

'Don't push too hard now; let the child take its time,' I say, though I don't know if she can understand a word I say. There is another contraction and out slips the baby's legs. Yet there is still something wrong. The baby seems stuck to its mother's body by some hidden protuberance, and I can't free it. Its cries grow faster, and I look around me, wondering what I should do next. I see the sharp knife lying on a stool. I had thought to use this to cut the cord, but I know that sometimes Joan would cut the woman's skin to ease the progress of a birth. (It is part of Eve's punishment that babies are born with large heads, so that the agony of birthing is more severe.) I grasp the knife, and screw up my courage. Then I cut her taut skin, so that she is ripped wider. Thick gore gushes forth around the baby's protruding head. It seems Marie is indeed being torn in two. And then… a second pair of legs comes kicking out, a mirror copy of the first. Then slithers forth another child, a perfect twin. But then I scream myself, hardly able to believe what I see before me. The two infants are one flesh. It is a double-child, a hellish freak, joined at the hip. I shrink back from it, trembling, and the creature wriggles and mewls, crying out with its two mouths and flailing its four legs and four arms in the air. Creature? It? I must say 'they', for there are two souls here, two mortals bound together for eternity. Separate but whole. I cry out and take a step backwards, turning away, my hands clutched to my head. Turning back, I see the malformed creatures squirming and crying in a sea of blood. A hellish punishment indeed. A blot on nature, hideous and misbegotten. I think of the father who smashed his one-eyed child against the wall, and, looking down, I see that I still have the knife clenched in my hand.

I walk slowly back to the birth-bed. Marie is lying still, eyes shut. Her babies are crying with double force. Praying all the while, I cut the cord and tie it, then wash the infants with milk and water and wrap them tight. Then I put a biggin-bonnet on each of the two heads, with a compress under each to protect their soft spots. Then I swaddle the poor things on a board. And there they lie, in an unbreakable embrace, arms locked around themselves. The two heads match exactly: black-haired and fairy-faced. Sweeter, prettier monsters you could not imagine. I hope that they will quietly die, and bless them, wishing I had holy water instead of just my scented bowl.

Of their mother I have little hope. Her breaths are shallow and uneven and she is deathly white. I fear she might not last till daybreak. The linen cloths that I have used are turned bright red, and my hands and dress are of the same colour: I feel like a murderer, not a midwife. I strip the bed and change the sheets, then begin to sweep the scarlet rushes from the floor. Outside, someone calls out the time. But I can make no sense of it.

Marie is stronger than she looks. After I have washed her and sewn her wound as best I can, she wakes. Her eyes blink open, and I see that the madness has left her.

'Where is my baby?' she asks, looking round the room. 'Does it live? Is it a boy or a girl?'

I hesitate.

'Mistress, is my baby well?'

'You have two babies, Marie,' I say. I lift the swaddled infants from their cot, and place them in her arms.

'Two babies?' She smiles down at the two faces, which are pressed tight together. 'Twins!'

'Twin girls.'

'What a wondrous thing.' She stares down at them.

'Every birth is wondrous,' say I. (This is lying, plain and simple.)

'But why are they swaddled to each other? Don't they need their own bands?'

I want to find a way to tell her why they are bound together, but I can't. She sees it in my face. 'What's wrong, mistress?'

I turn away.

'There is something terrible! Please tell me. What's happened?'

I shake my head sorrowfully.

Her voice rises up to a wail. 'Tell me what it is that ails them! I beg you!'

'I cannot say it. I am sorry, but I cannot say.'

With shaking hands she undoes the linens so that her malformed babies are revealed. Four-legged, four-armed, two-headed... two bodies linked by flesh and bone. She screams and flings them down upon the bed, and they wake, and wave their freed limbs in the cold air and wail with her. 'Alair! Alair!' Such a sorrowful sound that it tears at me; the sound that Henry made when he was tiny, and Joan put him in my arms for the first time. And I feel such pity for them.

I pick up the joined infants, and wrap them tight once more. Their cries quieten. Marie's do not. She screams and screams and screams, half in English, half in French. Sadly, I understand both languages: her words are more evil in that foreign tongue than in our own. Wilder and madder and louder she shouts, calling for the lynching of Our Lady, an end to Time, the emptying of Hell and sundry other changes to the proper order of things. Until at last she spews green bile upon the floor – a dreadful stench. I clean it up. I am starting to tire of skivvying for my own maid. After that – silence. The rage has passed. It is as if Marie has puked out some evil in herself. She sits hunched up in the bed, a shawl pulled round her shoulders, staring ahead of her, contemplating nothing.

After a while, she wipes her mouth with her long hair and says, 'I have committed a mortal sin. God has sent this to me.'

'We are all sinners,' I say. I sit down beside her. 'What you did with Tom is no more than a thousand girls have done before you. A thousand thousand! You fell into bed before you made a marriage vow. You are more fool than sinner.' I take one of her hands in mine. 'I will fetch a wet nurse.'

347

'What wet nurse will suckle *that*?' she says. She nods in the direction of the cradle. 'She'll run from the very sight of it.'

'Yours is not the first freak born in Westminster, nor will it be the last. It is "they", not "it" – and they must be fed. Just like other children.'

'But they are not like other children,' she says. 'They are joined! They are doomed!'

'We don't know what their fate will be. There's an old tale of twins joined like these two, who lived in Kent, in Biddenham, and were born to a good family. They lived for more than thirty years.'

She isn't listening. 'What shall I tell Tom?'

I shake my head, pick up the infants and begin to feed them with a horn of watery gruel.

After this I must have slept. I wake to find that I'm curled beside Marie on the bed. I rub my eyes and look out of the window. The sun is high in the sky. The hour to meet with Will is long gone. I stand up, unsteadily. Marie is watching me. Her eyes are calm. The joined twins are fast asleep, snuffling in their cot.

'Give them to me,' she says.

'What?'

'My babies.'

I gaze at her, confused. 'I was going to fetch a wet nurse.'

'I don't need one. Give them to me.'

I stumble to the cot and pick up the joined twins. She takes them from me. And she sticks her little finger into the mouth of one of them, waking it, then gently probes her teat into its mouth. I've seen many women struggle with this first suckling, and their babies fall away from the offered breast. But this child knows well what it needs and drinks greedily, eyes creased closed, one hand clasped around the white orb of her dug. The second infant rests its cheek upon it.

348

The door opens a crack. Henry's face appears in it, bright and curious. I hurry over to block his view. 'Is she alive?' he asks. 'I heard such screams I thought she must be dead.'

'Of course she is alive, you dolt!'

'And is the baby born?' He cranes round me to get a better look.

'It is... all done, yes.'

'In that case, praise to God,' says Henry.

'Indeed.'

'And hurrah!' says a loud voice, and in bursts Tom before I can stop him. For a moment he stares at the frozen scene: the pile of blood-soaked rushes, the disordered bed, Marie, clasping the tiny freaks. One head feeding from her breast; the other waiting, round eyes fixed upon her face. Though they are swaddled again, it is clear that something is strange. But Tom, young as he is, seems puzzled rather than afraid.

'Marie – you have your – children!'

'Oh, Tom – go away!'

'Don't you want to see me?

'I do – but not now. Get out please, Tom, my dearest love.'

'But – *I* want to see *you*!'

'Not now, Tom, no, you must go.'

Henry, with his skill of slipping where he isn't wanted, has made his way to the bedside.

'Why don't you put one of them in the cradle,' he asks, 'while the other feeds? Doesn't it get tired of watching?'

'Is it – twins? Our children?' Tom's voice is uncertain.

'You heard what Marie said to you – get out,' I say. 'This is no place for you, and beyond your understanding. And Henry, come away from there!' I seize his arm and pull him roughly towards the door.

Tom looks at me, suddenly frightened. 'What is there to understand? She is my love, and we will marry – and these are my children! There is nothing strange in that.'

'Marry? What's this? No one is marrying without my consent.' Anne bustles in, bare-headed and wearing her shabbiest dress and oldest ruff, which droops down at one side.

Tom wheels round. 'Mother, you cannot forbid me to wed Marie. We are promised to each other already. Burbage oversaw the handfasting.'

She glances at the bed, seeming to notice the twins for the first time. 'Handfasting? Handfasting? How dare you even use such a word to dignify your sport? And with such a common little bitch as this? Handfarting, more like. She is a servant girl, nothing but a silly strumpet. There is no more reason to believe these… twins are yours than that they are the spawn of any other Tom Fool who came knocking.'

'Mistress Flood,' says Marie, 'please stop.'

'Stop? Why should I take note of you, that's laid a trap for my dear son?'

'Forgive me, but I think I can put him straight. These aren't your babies, Tom. I had a strange dream one night, and I believe I was ravished by some demon.'

Tom laughs. 'What? Marie, you are mad.'

'She's lain with another man, is the truth of it,' says Anne. 'More than one, I'm sure. Half the prentice-boys in the City have been up those skirts. She's a skittish, shameless doxy.'

'Marie, is that true? Have you been with another man? If so, tell me now.'

She looks up at him. Then she unwraps the twins. Anne screams and prays to Our Lady. Tom stares, as if the demon she had spoken of were sitting right in front of him.

Anne is still praying, eyes tight shut. 'Lead me from this place of sin,' she says. 'Lead me from it, and do not ask me to return.'

'Anne,' I say. 'This is cruel! Such things do happen, in the normal way of things. No demon needs to creep into a virgin's bed. God's creatures aren't all perfect – you can see that every time you walk down the street. Have pity on the girl.'

'Take me from here, Tom,' commands Anne, blindly holding out her hands. But Tom is still looking at his lover, as she quietly fastens one of her babies to her breast. Her movements are small and neat, and she has never looked so pretty. He kneels down and bows his head in prayer.

'Tom?' says his mother. 'Tom?'

'It is my fault,' says Tom. 'Get down on your knees, Mother, and pray to God to be merciful.'

'What?'

'May God forgive me, I have lain with whores. I have not been true to Marie as I should have been. This is my punishment. Pray for her, and pray for me. For we are man and wife, and nothing will divide us.'

I close the door and run, my head bare, hair flying. I am too late to meet Will, of that I am sure. But this is the only thing that I am certain of. It is as if all the times we ever met, or lay together, or quarrelled, have been broken into tiny pieces and tossed into the air, and mixed up with all my dreams of him, and his sonnets, and his burned letters. Everything has always conspired to keep us apart, and now this. Yet how could I have left that child, in her dark labour? I am human, after all. And what was it that he wished to say to me that has not been said already? Words joined and divided us. Words and the world. I think of Wriothesley and feel sick with rage. The great lord. His word against mine. I think of my play, that tumult of wild emotion, put to work at the Globe without my name upon it. I think of that wife, sitting Stratford-smug, counting his money.

But... there was once such a bond between us that it seemed that we could best them all, make our own world, and let them keep their lesser one. And there is still Henry. Oh, Lord. If Marie had given birth the day before, or the day after, all might have been... What? My mind is so full, it seems it must break open. All I can see is that last look I had from Will. My memories swirl; my thoughts are frantic – I can't tell truth from tale. I run full-tilt, heading for the Church of St Peter, my breath tearing at my chest. When I see the great stone structure rising up ahead of me, I stop and hold my side and weep, because I know there is no reason for this hurry. Too late! The bells are ringing. Twelve tolls. Twelve knells. I walk up to the church door and push it open.

This is the church where I worshipped with Lord Hunsdon every Sunday, unless the Lady Anne was visiting, which was seldom. A royal church, and royally magnificent as befitted the rulers of England. They have dissolved, destroyed and cruelly disfigured much of what once was, yet this great building seems as permanent and vast as any fortress. In the lofty nave the air is cold and still. Sunlight shifts in through the jewel-coloured window panes, illuminating the flat glass faces of the saints.

Unsteady, and still breathing hard, I make my way down the passageway towards the chapel of St John the Baptist, where Hunsdon has been laid to rest. I look around me, filled with wonder in spite of everything. I have been excluded from the majesty of Whitehall and the other palaces, but not from the splendour of this House of God. The gold and silver working of the high altar and the rich embroidery of the altar-cloths are bathed in soft light. Behind the altar at the far end of the nave, a polished brazen screen glows brightly. Above my head, the stonework has been carved with such marvellous skill that it seems to hang in the air, as light as cobwebs.

The chapel of St John the Baptist opens off the north transept. It is a little enough space, fenced off from the main church with a high grille. Anyone entering is confronted by Lord Hunsdon's vast tomb, which takes up most of the space on the wall opposite. I pause and look at it now. Such a monstrous and ungainly lump of marble-work you never saw. There is no sleeping statue of my Lord Hunsdon here: no, it is as if he were a guild rather than a man. His sarcophagus is decorated with black and white cheque-point, surmounted by what looks like a colonnaded fireplace. The man I knew is trapped behind a prison wall of weapons, armour and prancing bulls. It was his proud wife who built this hideous monument in his name, with money given to her by the Queen. No woman who loved her husband truly would erect a tomb that looked like Nero's privy.

My lord died in debt. Some say his taste in mistresses added to his woes. They used to say that I had put up with his aged passion for the sake of my fine gowns and the suite of rooms I had in Whitehall. There was a joke that I would make him hump me three times nightly in the hope that it would see him off. They did not know what we were to each other. He was a tender lover and a true friend, and I was happy with him. Until I fell in love with Will.

I sit down and rest my head in my hands. Twelve of the clock. There is no reason to expect that he would wait so long. I try to pray, to calm myself, dizzy with images of two-headed infants and splurting womb blood. Like a Puritan, I address myself direct to God, as if he were sitting next to me on the chapel step.

'Oh, Lord, please show me what should be done and give me the strength to see it will be...' My mind trails off again, seeing the knife slashing at poor Marie's pudenda and a face peering out from within.

'Oh, Lord,' I start again. 'I am sorry for wishing that Will would come, and I thank you for giving me the chance to help Marie and her baby. Her babies...' Now a vision of Will as I last saw him comes to me, and I stop again. It's not a prayer I remember now, but lines of Marlowe's: *Come live with me and be my Love...*

How beautiful these lines are! Why have I never lived straightforwardly? *And we will all the pleasures prove...* Why has my life always been such an unseemly muddle? I am blighted, like Eurydice, who died from a snake-bite on her wedding day, and was followed by faithful Orpheus into Hades. But there is no Orpheus for me.

'Oh, Lord...' But this time I can think of nothing else, excepting only, 'Why?'

I open my eyes and look around me. The silence in the high church, with its sunlit windows and its soaring stonework, is complete. *That Hills and Valleys, dale and field, and all the craggy mountains yield.* If my passion could have found its true expression, I would conjure Will now, and bring him here before me. Solid flesh. Ink-stained fingers. Leather doublet. And his questioning, relentless gaze. To see him, to feel the weight of him, to sense his fingers touching mine. My hand flinches, as if he has reached out from my mind.

The pews gape. Empty, empty, empty. I feel my feebleness and littleness as I never have before. *You are old, Aemilia,* I think. *You are weary.*

And then I think, *Will. Come.* I summon all my passion, all my woman's power, and wish him, wish him to come before me. I close my eyes and plead with him, so hard that my head aches. He has slandered me, and dishonoured me, but that was long ago. Can I forgive him? I don't know. But I yearn to hear his voice.

When I open my eyes, for a moment I think that someone is standing in front of me. I look up. 'Will?'

But there is no one. I can conjure evil spirits, but I cannot conjure my lost love. Yet... I do notice something, lying on the raised shelf at the bottom of the huge sarcophagus. A book – a little book, prettily bound. With a strange feeling of apprehension, I pick it up. It is a collection of sonnets. The title reads *Sonnets to the Dark Lady.* I stare at in horror. I know full well who this Dark Lady is. And I now know why Will was suddenly so eager to talk to me. He has a guilty conscience. He knows of the existence of this vile thing. He probably commissioned it himself. I open it, and look at the title page, and sure enough: his name is on there.

Oh, Will. As if you hadn't done enough. Is this the 'love' you spoke of, when you called after me? My God, what duplicity! You even believe your lies yourself.

Turning the pages, I read one of the verses, one I already have by heart, and which is now for sale in this foul City, for anyone to see.

> Past cure I am, now reason is past care,
> And frantic-mad with evermore unrest;
> My thoughts and my discourse as madmen's are,
> At random from the truth vainly express'd;
> For I have sworn thee fair and thought thee bright,
> Who art as black as hell, as dark as night.

Then I notice that the book fell open at this page because there is a marker in it. A letter. I unfold the single sheet, and read these words:

Aemilia –

You did not come. I told you that I could not bear this, which is the truth. I will not be tortured by your lies, and double-ways, and cunning. My desire, my dreams, my waking thoughts have been distorted by your image for too long. I have a life, a wife, a place, a future, and no space for you within it.

I tried to apologise to you, seeing that Wriothesley was lying when he bragged about his conquest of you, and that the sight I had – which haunts me still – was not all that it seemed. But you would not forgive me. You are too proud. Perhaps your pride is all you have. Your pride, and little Henry.

These poems are my finest work. I see no reason why they should be hidden from public view, as you have spurned me and still spurn me, and keep me from my son. You have him. I have my Art. To spare him, your name does not appear in this little book. There are those who will speculate about your identity; there are some who know. It is an ending, in any case. An end to my last hopes that we still loved each other even slightly; that there was something left to say. I wanted to warn you, but I have given up hope of any kind of commerce between us. So there you have it.

Do me one last service, if you will, madam. Do not come to me, or tempt me, or beguile me with your look. Do not bewitch me with your words. Do not think of me again, and I will not think of you.

Will

I fold up the paper, this way, that way. Again. And again. Dry sobs rack my body. I feel hatred and anger roaring through me; my veins are boiling with bad blood. Now the letter is shaped into a point as sharp as any dagger. You can kill with poetry. You can murder with a pen. I have been grievously injured, in the past, and in the present moment. I have been cast out, and ridiculed, and made invisible. My gender is nothing of itself – we are sought by men, loved by them, fucked by them; we are made pregnant with their seed, we mother them and then we die. In these functions, we may be solid. In any other, we are insubstantial as thin air. Give me the crow-scragged garb of witchcraft any day. Give me a witch's power; give me her ill-wishing, her night-spells, her terrifying potency. Give me the work of Hecate and of Lilith. As black as hell, am I? As dark as night? Well, I will take him at his word.

Scene V

The Tragedie of Macbeth rules all of London. There is talk of it everywhere, in the streets and taverns, at the docks and cook-shops. Prentice-boys run wild along the riverbank, affecting to be Macbeth in pursuit of Duncan. A chap-book is printed, which apes the play and puts King James in Macbeth's garb. A quick-thinking pie-man has starting baking Macbeth pies, pricked with an 'M' for Macbeth and for Murder. The streets seem transformed into the Globe's dominions, so each corner rings out '*I come, Graymalkin!*' and every window shouts, '*Out, damn spot, Out I say!*' The worst of it is that Henry's head is quite turned with it, and, far from thinking that this has anything to do with the play I have written, he is entranced by the Globe and the players and the genius of Mr Shakespeare. It is madness. It is Bedlam. It must stop.

And now I have a plan. Simple in its conception, though not in its execution.

For the plan to work, I must have solitude and secrecy. So one balmy day, I set out across the river. The water laps and gleams in the fitful sunshine. Flimsy clouds hasten across the sky. The waterman sets me down just by Deptford Creek, and I look around me. I am standing between two worlds. Down the river are the flags and cupolas of Greenwich Palace. Across the water is the Isle of Dogs, where thieves and cut-throats lurk among great banks of mud and stranded river-filth.

After asking the way, I walk along a dirt road passing through Deptford Strand. Much of the land is taken up with sheds and store-rooms, but open fields still stretch away to one side. At last I reach the place I am looking for. It is a sturdy, stone-made building, most unlike the top-heavy wooden houses that line the London streets. Sheep graze on the sward of smooth grass before its front door, and next to it is a pretty garden, dense with medlar and rambling rose-bushes and bordered with sweet william. Beneath the trees there is a row of straw beehives, sheltered by a stout roof. No one knows me here. No one will comment on my coming, or wonder at my going. I can wreak revenge in peace.

I have taken an upper chamber in this quiet inn for one night. It is a small chamber, but large enough for my purpose. I set my bag down. My hands are trembling, but I know what I must do. First I take out my Geneva Bible, noting its holy weight. Heavy to carry, but I dare not be without it. Next comes an equally weighty book, Cornelius Agrippa's grimoire. And a piece of chalk, taken from Henry's toy box. Last of all, a vial of holy water. I range them on the long oak table, in a tidy row. My heart is jumping in my chest and my throat is dry.

I cross to the window and look out. Fragile rose petals drift past the window in the quickening breeze. The sun lights up the patchwork view of roofs and fields, paths and dock-sides, stores and timber yards. Shaking violently, I lie down on the bed. After a while I doze, and dream of Simon Forman. He is following me down a steep stairway into Hell. I wake with a jump, as if I have missed my footing on the stair. The room is growing dark, so I light a candle and open up the grimoire.

Sweat is sliding down my neck as I sprinkle holy water and make a sign of the cross. It is so dark I cannot see beyond the flame.

I wait. There is more noise outside: men are shouting at the fighting dogs. I hear a woman's gurgling laugh. A cart rattles past, wheels squeaking unevenly. I lick my lips, wondering how long to leave it before I give it up, read some good words from the Bible and tumble into bed.

The night is growing colder. Though I would not have thought it possible, the darkness deepens, and with it comes a weird silence, muffled by a thickness that was neither mist nor solid. I hug myself, trying to quell my ague of trembling. I can barely remember how it was when I summoned the demon before. I remember Joan's voice: was that my imagination, or did she really help me? I listen hard, trying to hear her. But there is silence. Before, I was fevered, desperate: Henry was dying in front of me. This time I am fuelled by cold anger. Yet one thing is the same: I have no choice. I must do this thing if I am to keep my sanity.

Lilith is the female demon of the night. Lilith was Adam's true equal, his twin soul. This was how we started – man and wife; woman and husband. Lilith was cast from Eden because 'she would not lie beneath'. She demanded that Adam should treat her as his equal: in their sexual dealings and in their life. She demanded this because she *was* his equal. If there is any demon, in any firmament, who will understand my plight, it is this evil Lilith, this snake goddess. The one who wanted me to write this turbulent play.

First I draw the chalk circle on the ground. Then I pour the holy water into a glass and place it by me, for my protection. I know the rules – the demon must stay within the circle. The circle is a place outside creation. If the demon stays within that place, then all should go well. I open the grimoire and turn to the summoning pages that I used before. I read them loudly, then shut my eyes and summon all my courage. 'Lilith!' I cry. 'Lilith, I call on you!'

There is silence, but I feel it listening. I feel the evil more sharply now. There is no plague in me, only fear.

I screw up my courage once again. 'Lilith, I call on you to do my bidding!'

A rustling now, fainter than my own breathing. A change in the layers of the air. Someone laughs, far, far away. A thick band of pain begins to grip my head, just as it did before, but this time it is stronger and my nausea is overwhelming. And this time there is a shifting and heaving within my belly, a movement of my innards that causes me to lose my breath with sudden shocks of pain. The voices and screams that gather come from outside me – from cold air, from distant stars, from the riverbed. But they are also deepening and thickening and strengthening inside me, and I let out a mighty scream and a flying shape vomits from my mouth. It is as big as a dragonfly. It has landed in the middle of the circle, and the night air seems to feed it, and it grows and grows and grows. It is assembled from bone and shadow, from the webs of spiders, from my own saliva, from the sex-cries of the people in the next room, from a catfight in the street, from the keening of a beaten child, from the night-sounds I cannot hear. And yet, it is like a blurred reflection, steamy and half-seen. There is a vastness in front of me; the circle is filled, but the Entity is vapour and vacuity. This is the best description I can find for something that has never, I think, been fixed with Christian words.

Then I hear a voice, cold and distant, like the memory of ice.

I clench my sweating hands.

'Who calls Lilith?'

It is a physical voice this time – not human-sounding, but my ears can sense it.

'I do – Aemilia Bassano Lanyer.'

'Mother of the plague-child?'

'Yes.'

'Daughter of the recorder player, he who bartered his soul for greatness, then turned back to God at the last, defaulting on his blood-sealed bond?'

I feel a chill go through me, top to toe. The truth I have sought, revealed. 'Yes.'

Silence. I am straining so hard to hear the demon's strange unvoice, and make sense of its murky shadow-tones, that I feel myself swaying and try to control my movements: I must not fall into the chalk circle.

'We have done your bidding,' says the voice. 'Why call Lilith twice?'

'I have been wronged.'

I listen again. I can hear a cruel sound now, many-voiced and violent, like a great crowd shouting at a bear baiting.

'We asked you for something,' says the voice, a little louder now. 'There was a bargain. Are you an equivocator like your father?'

'No! I wrote a play. I wrote down all the odd things that I had written in my... my malady. In the madness of the quest to help my son. Lady Macbeth and the witches and all the rest of it. I wrote it all down, and I made it into something, and they stole it from me.'

The figure in the circle is now full size, and looks as solid as the nightstand by the bed. Lilith's yellow eyes are fixed on mine, and their black slits look like the cracks of Doom. I don't want to look into those eyes, but I cannot look away. Her voice is so loud in my ears now that I wince when she says, '*Who* stole it from you? Who did this?'

I lick my lips. 'It was Shakespeare – William Shakespeare and the King's Men... Dick Burbage and – Tom Flood.'

'Men,' says Lilith. 'Men took it from you.'

'Yes.'

'It was ever thus,' she says. 'And so it shall be for many years to come. But they shall pay. We shall have revenge.'

'I...' My words must come, even faced with an agent of the Beast. 'I don't want... I just want you to unmake the play. To stop it. You helped me write it; I wanted to call you so that you would stop it... To see if you would *end* it.'

Lilith's eyes seem to have swelled up to the size of the circle, to the size of the room. Through those snake-cracks I can see Hell now, and the people in it. Little ant-ish figures, consumed in flame. In Hell, there are no half-measures. 'We shall have revenge,' says Lilith, beginning to shrink again. 'Have no fear of that. The play is cursed.'

The room is colder than ever. I fold my arms, shivering, as Lilith begins to fade from sight. But then I notice that the holy water is red and bubbling in its vial. Then I see for the first time that the ground around her feet is strewn with tiny corpses – the bodies of babes and little children, still and rotted and wormy-eyed. I scream and stagger, and I lose my balance. Then I fall into the circle.

Scene VI

Henry is playing chess with Tom by the fireside, their faces drawn and intense. Tom's joined twins sleep beside them in their cradle. I am washing my face in a pail of water. The cold liquid seems more real than demons, and is washing away the black mist that is blurring my brain after my night in Deptford. Then, for an instant, I see Lilith watching, sitting in the shadows.

'Out – spectre!' I cry, and the two boys look at me in surprise.

'Mother?' says Henry. 'Whatever is the matter?'

'Nothing!' I say, turning away. And indeed, there is nothing there. Only Tom's cast-off jerkin and plumed cap.

'You will wake them,' warns Tom, pushing the cradle to a gentle rhythm with his foot. 'Hush now, Mistress Lanyer.'

'*Hush now. Hush now,*' says another voice, inside my head. Lilith's voice. '*I will do your bidding. Never fear it. I am to Silver Street, this night, to fix that thief Will Shakespeare for good.*'

The house is ordered and familiar. The pot simmers on the skillet. The goose hangs, waiting to be plucked. There is dust on the mantelpiece and the milk is on the turn. These are ordinary things with actual substance. The spirits haunt my mind, not the dinner table, nor the haberdasher's, nor the cowshed. But then I recall that voice, that nausea, the folded succubus before me. My own ignorance of these matters makes me more afraid. I do not know what I have done, or what the outcome might be. Like

Lady Macbeth, I have rushed to action, and must now deal with the consequences. But Lilith's voice and promise make me ill with fear. I called her once to save a life; this time I only wanted to save my feelings. This was wrong. I must go to Silver Street, and warn Will.

I slip through the Wall at Cripplegate just before the trumpets sound the curfew. As darkness falls, I make my way along Silver Street and towards St Olave's Church – a neglected, lichen-covered building – which is close to Will's lodgings at the Mountjoys' house. I still have the set of keys he gave me. Should I go in? Or should I knock, and ask to speak to him? My legs are heavy, and my heart thumps. I sit on a stone bench, my mind chasing round in circles. I can hear the calls of children playing in a nearby garden, and the shouting of the watch as they begin their patrol of the City streets. A fox slinks between the gravestones, with a chicken clutched in its black muzzle. The stone bench chills me through my skirts, and the grass beneath my feet begins to dampen with night-dew.

At last I stand up stiffly, and make my way across the street, taking the keys from the pocket inside my skirts. This must be done. As I approach, I see that the windows are dark, and not a chink of light shows anywhere. I knock on the door, and the sound echoes in the dark house. There is no one in. Still, I knock again, harder this time. Shall I return home? The curfew has sounded and the watch are doing their rounds. No, I will go in and wait.

I unlock the door and step inside. It opens on to a costume workshop. Of course, this is his landlord's trade. I light a wick-lamp and stare around me, distracted, in spite of myself, by the bales of satin, taffeta and gauzy lawn, each glowing with bright colour, the piles of silvered silk. When I came before, they had fled the plague and all this was packed away. Lifting my lamp higher, I see baskets of seed-pearls, glimmering on the shelves around the room, and golden gauze like fairy wings. Oh – what's this? A dark mass of human hair spilling across the workbench? It looks like Lilith's snaking tresses. But it is only a headpiece, set upon a workbench, made of coloured beads and pitch-black feathers.

Protecting the lamp-flame with my hand, I tiptoe up the stairs, and cross the solar to Will's room. I enter, and close the door silently behind me. I look around his chamber, breathing sharply. It is quite empty, and exactly as I remember it. In the centre is the great curtained bed, its heavy velvet hangings drawn shut. Piles of books sit on the desk, and on the floor around it. There is a walnut chest by the fireplace. I raise the lid, wincing as it creaks. It is filled with neatly folded shirts, and two doublets, arms crossed.

Just then, I stiffen. Something has fallen, downstairs, in the empty house. I pick up the lamp, and go to the door, listening. I hear a soft voice: '*Men have taken it. We shall have vengeance.*' Lilith! Oh, Heavenly Father! My hand flies to my mouth, and perhaps the gust of air this makes extinguishes the candle. Or perhaps it blows out for some other reason. I stand for a moment in darkness. Then, almost without knowing what I do, I draw back the curtains and climb on to Will's bed.

I listen, as hard as I can, from inside the curtain, and I can hear the sound of whispering, and the swish, swish, swish of a Serpent's tail. After a moment, I notice how warm it is within the drawn curtains. Then I catch the gentle sound of breathing. I stare into the dark, my own breath still. I notice a familiar body scent. Once it would have had me reeling with desire. Then, sightless, I stretch out my hand, and another warm hand grasps it.

'Aemilia?' The familiar voice is taut.

'William.' What else? What else can I say? Here I am, within his own bedcurtains. I wonder he does not strike me. To say 'Lilith is here,' seems a strange beginning.

'What in God's name is going on? Am I dreaming?'

'I fear you are awake.'

'And you are in my bed? In plain fact? What *is* this?'

'It is I. It is Aemilia.'

'Christ's blood.' His tone is as harsh as any blow. 'What kind of witch are you? First you haunt me in the whore-house…'

'I was looking for Tom Flood.' My lips are blunt with shock.

'Then I wait all day for you, and you don't come…'

'My servant was in labour.'

'Your servant? You think more of her than you think of me?'

'She nearly died.'

'And, when I give you up, you come!'

'I am… I wanted to see you,' say I. For what else can a woman say who has crawled into an old lover's bed? And God forgive me, it is true.

'You have maimed me, woman. I told you to stay away.'

'Maimed you! What have *you* done to *me*? Have I written slanderous verses? Have I damned you with false accusations, lies and abominations? Have I stolen your words, and claimed them for my own? Have I done any of these things to you? Or have you done them all to me?'

'I have loved you,' he groans. 'Loved you to madness and beyond.'

'Ay, madness is the word!' I cry.

'I wanted to make amends. I see now that it cannot be done.'

I feel the night's cold at my back, and begin to shiver. 'Will – there is something that I need to tell you…'

He squeezes my arm. 'You have bewitched me, Mistress Lanyer. So much so that I can't untangle what is actual from demons and nightmares.'

The black night seems to bind us like a spell.

'Will – it's that matter of a demon that I…' He holds both my hands now, so tightly that they hurt. As I look into the blackness

I hear the bedroom door creak open. 'Who's there? Who is at the door?' I whisper.

'There is no one. Have you never done?' His breath is on my face. 'Your scent, lady – what is it? I remember it so well, like the musk of old Egypt.'

'Will…'

'Are you corporeal, or spirit?'

'I'm Aemilia, real and breathing…'

'Then let me have you once again – and again and again – as I have each night in my dreams and nightmares! Oh, my lady! Let us stay together, in the darkness, and have done with words forever. Let us be flesh, flesh, and nothing but.'

He lets go of my hands, and I feel his fingers unlacing my bodice. A wave of horror and delight rushes over me. 'Oh,' I whisper, trying to control myself. 'Will – you must stop…'

He has pulled the laces apart, and I can feel my under-smock coming loose about my breasts. Now our bodies are pressed together in the fug of warm air within the curtain. My breath shudders, and my legs are running sweat.

'I have done something evil,' I say. 'I fear it cannot be undone.' But, even as I speak, I run my hands over his unseen form. With joy and nausea I feel his naked shoulders. I tear my shift down further, and take hold of him in my bare arms.

'What are you, Aemilia,' he says, 'but Circe, the enchantress? I am ensnared, and lost, and yours.'

Sightless, I find his hard belly, his soft neck, his salt lips. 'I summoned a demon,' I whisper, too scared to say her name. 'I drew a circle.'

'Then draw another,' says he, winding his arms tightly around me. 'And let's go to it for an eternal night.'

There is a tearing sound as I rip myself free of my skirts and wrap my legs around him.

'You are a mystery,' he says, as the bed begins to heave beneath us. 'You are my witch.'

'I am not a witch, Will. I am a woman,' say I, as the night writhes. But I am not sure if he can hear me, or whether I have really spoken.

The night rears up, within us and around us, and we seem to leave the chamber and fly high above the roofs of London and dive deep below the City to the Underworld beneath. There is no sweetness, but there is ecstasy and pain so pure that it seems close to God. And there are no words, just flesh and lips and hair and panting, and wetness and darkness and a desperate pounding in my head and everywhere, till I hear him cry, 'Aemilia! Aemilia! Aemilia!' and there is a great violence inside me and my mind fills with perfection and white light.

We lie together, afterwards. Do I hear something? Is it the sound of the door closing? I raise my head, listening and wondering what I have done, and whether Lilith has played some part in it.

'What is it?' asks Will. He holds me closer. 'What is this supposed evil that you did?'

'It was, indeed, a sort of witchcraft.'

'To punish me?'

'To put an end to that *Macbeth*.'

I feel his body quiver. He is laughing.

'Don't you believe me?' I ask.

'I believe that you believe it, but I don't believe the Devil walks among us. There's evil enough in what men do.'

'What did I see, then?'

'That I cannot tell, my love.' His hand is stroking my face. 'I should have married you,' he says. 'A long, long time ago.'

My breath stops.

'Marry?'

'It should have happened. Fate did me wrong.'

'It was not God's will, so there's an end to it.'

'And yet we are twin souls, lady. There is no woman on this earth, not anywhere, who is a match for me, as you are. There is only you. A freak of beauty, and mind, and learning.'

'A freak! A fine compliment! Only the old Queen was allowed to call me that.'

He catches hold of me and we begin again, rocking in the bed in our rage to have each other and make darkness light.

Scene *VII*

It is dawn. Will is still sleeping, and I look down at his face. Just as I used to many years ago, when I was someone else. He is quite beautiful, so pale. I don't kiss him. I dare not. The room assaults me with its stark reality, all boxed and tight and quotidian. I get up, and pull my dress on. There are some papers on the desk, and I pick up a quill and dip it in the lamp-black. For a moment, my hand hovers over the page, but I don't know what to put. In the end, all I can write is: *I have loved you.* Nothing else makes any sense.

When I get home, I go up to my room and fetch down Forman's grimoire. I page through it, breathless, looking for guidance. Is there a spell, a form of words, which can undo a summoning? I have a nagging, sickened feeling. I am not sure what anything means. I hardly know myself. I poke the fire, seeing Lilith in the circle. Did I really summon her? Did it matter that I tumbled into the circle? Nothing seems right; nothing seems to be in my control.

With the cooking-pot simmering on the fire, and the cat sitting hump-backed by the scuttle, reality seems too solid for such wild fancies. I have not been in my right mind. I have walked at night, and my febrile nature has always been at odds with my strong will. This sudden night with Will is thrumming in my head, each touch, each cry. Perhaps my passion for him has broken some dark spell? I tip sea-coal from the scuttle and my spirits lift. I will have him. I will have my lover, every inch of him, night after night. Why should I not? Henry will not suffer from my lying with his natural father. I can forgive Will for the sonnet book; I can forgive him for the play. What was I thinking of? Is God my master, or Lucifer and all the crones of Hell? I must go. I must go to the Globe, and see that play for myself, and hope to God that all is well.

Henry comes rushing in, bouncing a ball.

'Where have you been?' I ask, hiding the book in my skirts. 'Just because I am out on business, and Marie is resting, it does not mean you are free to run amok.'

'I have been playing football all around the town. You never saw such sport!' says Henry, sawing off a hunk of bread. 'We made the length of Long Ditch our pitch, and took on a score of prentice-boys and beat them soundly, though they bragged they'd trash us! What weakly, flap-eared knaves!' He stuffs the bread into his mouth all in one go.

'Those prentice-boys will stab you as soon as look as you, some of them. They're vile, rough creatures, who can't even spell their names,' said I, taking the ball up and keeping it. 'You should be safe at home, with Ovid and your hornbook.'

'Ovid!' says Henry, or something like it, through the bread. He pulls a goblin face. 'What does Ovid know? I saw a Serpent with a woman's face – where's *that* in your Ovid?'

'*What*?'

'She is not real, Mother, don't stare so! A fellow had a stall and charged us two farthings to have a look at his Lilith, Queen of Death. She is part woman, part Serpent. I touched her wings,' he says, modestly.

'Dear God! What "fellow" was this?'

'I don't know. His stall had "Lucifer" painted on the side, but I doubt that's the name he was born with. What is the matter, Mother? You are looking queer.'

I stand up, my head reeling. 'I am much put out and barely know which way to turn.'

He swallows the bread and pours out a glass of small beer.

'Because of Marie and her joined-up twins? Shall they always be such monsters? They are loathsome as all Hell!' He glugs back his drink with relish.

'No – because of… other matters. Things which do not concern you.' In truth, of course they do concern him. *I have just come from your father's bed, in which we fucked like werewolves.* How would that seem? Or, *I summoned the demon you saw today. Do not go out at night.*

Henry takes the ball deftly from me and begins to bounce it once again. 'Anyway, you need have no fear for me this afternoon. I am off to see a play.'

'What play?'

'Why, *Macbeth*, of course. If I miss it now, it won't be on for another month, and everyone else at school has seen it, and it's steeped in blood. And Tom says he will tell the doorkeeper to let me in for nothing.'

'*No!*' I say, startling even myself, such is the violence of my tone. 'No. You shall not go. I forbid it.' I must see this dark drama alone and Henry must remain here, safe from harm.

'But why? It is a most amazing play – everybody says so. And it's got fighting in it, and even some history, too.'

'I don't care. You must stay here and help Marie and her poor children.'

I pounce on him, catch his ear between my right thumb and finger, and twist it till he cries out. In this manner, I drag him into Marie's chamber, where she is sleeping, cradling her nuzzling twins. The spring sun is warm and heavy in the shuttered room, and a bee is buzzing drunkenly around her ale-jug.

'Mistress!' She jerks awake. Her face is drawn and tired. The babies begin to cry. 'What is it?'

'Henry will help you,' I say. 'Do you have need of anything?'

'No. Thank you.'

'Then will you lock the door when I am gone, and sit upon the key? And make sure he stays with you till five?'

'Till five?'

'Until the play is done,' says Henry, sulking. 'Mother, why do you persecute me so? I am not a child.'

'Is Tom playing today?' asks Marie. She picks up the twins and settles them into the cradle. 'Did he tell you, we are to marry next week?'

'That is good news,' I say, though my mind scarce takes this in.

'Don't tell Mistress Flood, lest she run mad in the street.'

It's hard to believe that I live in the same world as weddings and celebrations. How I wish that Will and I could begin again, stow away on some great ship and cross the ocean to a new world, far away. I would take Henry with me, but no other mortal, and we could be happy, somewhere, in a forest of tobacco trees. There would be no playhouses or print-shops, and no demons or deceived wives.

'Here is the key.' I give it to Marie, and wait outside till I hear it turn in the lock.

Why does my belly twist at the mere mention of the name 'Macbeth'? I'm not sure. But I suspect that Lilith might do us all most dreadful harm. I can see her yellow eyes so vividly, and, though I pray to God to let her sleep once more, I have no other power to rid myself of her foul presence. Yet I fear that God has matters to attend to other than righting misbegotten spells.

As I step out of the door, who should appear but Anne herself? All done up as usual, like the Queen of the May. She has a new ruff, all silvery like a fairy wing, and her eyebrows are plucked to nothing. Tom's misalliance has not distracted her from Fashion.

'My dear Aemilia,' says she. 'You are coming too? Well, then, we must hurry if we are to catch a boatman! All of London will be there.'

'Will be where?' I ask in confusion, with a sinking feeling.

'At the Globe, to see *Macbeth*! I would not miss this for all the world.'

'I thought you were angry with me.'

'I can't blame you for Tom's cock-brained foolishness! I am sure he will forget that girl in time. Now, come, quickly! It's a shame you look so poorly, but you will have to do.'

And so I consent to be dragged towards the river on her arm. The summer sunshine is bright and warm when we set out. But the weather changes suddenly. The sun disappears and rain is falling by the time we have climbed aboard a wherry, aided by an aged boatman. I throw my cloak over the two of us, for fear that Anne's finery will be washed away. When we reach the Globe, the storm is gathering strength. The wind crashes in the trees and rain is falling as if from a tipped bath. We sit in the second gallery, but it provides little shelter. Water streams between our feet, falling on to the heads of the groundlings below, who are slipping and falling in the mire. The covered stage, too, is awash with rain, blown inwards by the furious wind. I look up at the black sky and hear the first roar of thunder. No need for stage musicians for this performance – Nature is providing her own malevolent effects.

'They must call it off!' I shout to Anne.

'No, no,' she insists. 'If it is on the playbill, you can be sure that they will put it on. They have the public to consider.'

A dagger of lightning splits the sky. Three figures come on to the stage, and the trumpets blast out, calling for our attention. The trio gathers around the trapdoor in the stage, and up comes a black cauldron. I look hard at these three players – where have I seen them before? They are gifted boys indeed. One looks like an ancient crone, another like a middle-aged matron, and the third appears to be a beautiful young girl with a plait of yellow hair wrapped around her head. I narrow my eyes. It is hard to see anything clearly in this rain.

'When shall we three meet again?
In Thunder, Lightning or in Rain?
When the hurly burly's done,
When the battle's lost and won...'

The voices of the witches change, so that what first sounded like the newly broken tones of boy actors is first a keening banshee cry, and then a heavy-throated growl.

'Who *are* the witches?' I ask Anne. But she only grips my hand.

A heavy fog has rolled in from the river, and torches have been lit and set upon the stage, where they hiss and splutter. The crowd, subdued by the downpour, is silent. In place of heckles and cat-calls there is watchful quiet. In contrast, the voices of the three witches carry with a clear echo like words shouted into a courtyard well. There is a peculiar cold.

Lord Macbeth appears upon the back of a black destrier. The storm has upset the beast, and it is clattering round in circles, tail lashing, showing the whites of its eyes. Its hooves slip waywardly on the wet boards. Macbeth (who is Dick Burbage) is about to speak, but there is another flash of lightning, a livid fork above us, and the stallion screams. It rears up, pawing the air, and Burbage comes crashing down on to the ground. Dropping its head, the beast gallops from the stage, sending the players scattering. But none of this daunts Burbage. Not for one moment does his performance falter, and he gets back to his feet in an imperious manner, and regards the crowd calmly, hand on his sword.

And here is Lady Macbeth! You would never guess that she is only Tom, declaiming such evil words in her robe of gold and scarlet, crow-black hair hanging round her narrow face. Tom speaks his words with passion, and their meaning chills me more now than when they first spilled from my pen.

'I don't like this,' whispers Anne. 'It is unnatural.'

'That is the point of it,' I hiss back. 'Macbeth should know his place.' But, as I speak, there is a tightness in my head, as if the dead-cold of the theatre has clenched my skull. Whether through Will's alterations or because of this storm which is making night from day, my play now has a surfeit of evil in it. But I know that I *have* to watch it, for there is some rhythm in the story that draws me further and further in.

The scenes are rapid and the drama bloody – Duncan the King is killed, Macbeth takes his place, then murders Banquo and (as he hopes) his young son Fleance. Now the stage is set out for a banquet, with a trestle table, joint-stools and long benches. King Macbeth (as he has become) begins to speak of 'Noble Banquo' and to express the dissembling regret that his friend cannot be present at the feast. (Though he knows full well he is dead, having paid two murderers to slay him.) I know what's coming next, of course. The ghost of Banquo will appear, and Macbeth's posturing as King will be sorely tested.

It would have been simple enough to have the ghost walk out from behind one of the pillars. But of course they must use their latest effect: the crane. From above the Heavens, in the uppermost corner of the space above the stage, I hear the groan of the new contraption. Now is the moment for the flying chair to prove its worth. It cranks out into the audience's view, a suspended cradle with a seated figure strapped in place.

'Will Shakespeare himself is playing the Ghost,' says Anne, still gripping my hand. 'He will do it fearsomely, you can be sure.'

The creaking arm swivels slowly round. The figure is wearing a black cloak, and its face is hidden. There is something odd about its stance, something less than human.

'He always does the ghosts,' says Anne. 'There is almost nothing to it. He never had enough voice for a major part.' Her voice is tight with terror. Slowly, slowly, dangling in its seat, the chair creaks down towards the smoky stage. Macbeth's courtiers carouse among the flaring lights as the cloaked form descends. Then there is a cracking sound, like stone breaking, and screams from the stage.

'What?' I say, trying to see more plainly. '*What*?' I stand up, in spite of the hisses and the cries of annoyance from behind me, and begin to push my way along the row. I can't see anything but the heads and shoulders of the audience; I can't see anything.

I reach the stairway and now the stage is spread before me – yet all is chaos there. Burbage is standing with his mouth wide open. Where is Tom? Where is his Queen? I stumble, amid a rage of protestation. The crowd roars. Everyone is standing. Something has happened. There is another terrible scream – I push this way and that way – I am blocked wherever I turn. What is wrong? What is it? At last I break through, hurry down into the pit and run squelching through the mire, shoving my way through the mass of people. A child cries, an old woman falls. But I keep on pushing till I reach the front, then force my way to the steps up to the stage. Panting, I reach the wet boards where the lights flare and the fog drifts. I'm half-expecting Heminge or another player to bar my way. But everyone is frozen, spell-bound. A dozen courtiers, faces mask-like in their paint, stand motionless. The crane has fallen: the great arm must have broken off and is lying across the stage. Burbage is bending over a figure in a scarlet dress, lying stretched out on the ground in a pool which is also scarlet. Tom. His wig has fallen off and his hair is splayed out all around him on the boards. His eyes are wide open, staring upwards. The arm of the crane has smashed into his chest, and pinned him to the ground.

Will appears, dressed in spectral black, his face daubed with stage blood, and kneels beside him.

'Help him, in God's name!' I say. 'What happened?'

'The crane fell – I didn't see… He is still; he isn't breathing!' cries Burbage.

'Fetch him wine!' calls Will, and a Scots lord hurries off.

But who's that, standing by the empty chair? A cloaked figure, immobile, head bowed. I look closer. I take a step towards it, and then it lifts its head. The face is bone-white, and translucent, fading in and out of my vision. There's no skill with stage paint that can ape such an effect. This is the creature I have summoned, cloaked in fog and falling rain. Lilith's yellow eyes regard the scene without expression, but her mouth is twisted in a smile.

'Thou, demon!' I shout. 'By God, why don't you go back to the place where you belong?'

The demon shifts, still looking straight at me, but doesn't speak.

'I did not want this! I didn't say that anyone should *die*!'

There is a voice in my head. '*I am Lilith. I am the taker of children. You said they stole your play – now you have your vengeance. This play is cursed.*'

'Go down to Hell, and leave us,' I scream. 'You have done your evil now.'

The spirit starts to move slowly towards Tom and I run between them, hands outspread. 'Leave him alone! Fiend! Leave the boy alone, and get thee back to Hell!'

Dick Burbage is sitting on the stage. He is weeping and stroking Tom's hair. Field is shouting, Heminge is running into the tiring-room. And Will is staring at me, eyes livid through the streaks of painted gore.

'What – Aemilia? What is this? Why are you shouting at thin air?'

The spectre moves slowly across the stage. Not walking, but moving like sea mist. It stops by the dead boy, and stares down at him.

I push Will away. The spectre looks at me again.

'Lilith!' I roar, so fiercely that I scrape my throat. 'Thou foul demon! Thou evil, hungry, wicked monster! Quit this place, quit it, I command you!'

'Tom? My Thomas?' There's another figure now, running across the stage, her fine clothes soaked and torn. 'Oh, my child!' she screams. 'Holy Mother! Mary! Spare him! Spare him!' She collapses on top of him, sobbing out half-lucid prayers. There is a crack of thunder and a spike of lightning and then I hear the shouts of the audience.

'What evil has been done?' cries one voice.

'The Devil is in this place!' calls another. 'Who called on Satan?'

Lilith is smiling.

'There she is!' I cry. 'Satan's agent! She killed Tom! She murdered him!' I look at Anne, weeping, prostrate, and at the dark crowd that heaves below me. I point at the shadowed figure. 'She – Lilith! Look! She has brought this curse upon the play!'

'*Lilith*?' says Will. 'A hag in a fireside fable? Are you *mad*?'

'What?' Anne's head swivels till she sees me. 'Why do you speak of black magic, over the body of my son?'

'She saw the demon!' shouts one of the voices from the crowd.

'That woman there – she spoke to it! She sees it still!' The dark faces are turned towards me.

'She conjured a demon!'

'Conjured Death!'

'Conjured the Devil! Foul, unnatural witch.'

'I did not call the Devil!' I turn to face the crowd, but can see only darkness and rain.

Anne leaves Tom's side and walks unsteadily towards me. 'What evil have you done, Aemilia? You saw it – you knew something was wrong! You saw it before Tom fell!'

'I saw Lilith.'

'Saw a *demon*? With my son?'

'I drew a circle,' I say. 'At Deptford.' As if that mattered. 'I made a spell.'

'What *spell* is this? What *circle*? Are you God Himself now, that can take a life at whim?'

'I meant no harm!' I scream, but Lilith is moving steadily towards me. 'Get thee behind me! Get thee behind me!' I shout, and I grab a flaming torch and lunge at her, but Will snatches it away.

Anne runs at me, her face riven with grief and rage. 'You killed him! With your wickedness and witchery and pride! You called on Satan and it was my son who took the punishment!'

'Anne! Listen to me... Anne! I beg you...'

'I'll kill you for this, you demon-loving bitch...' With that she claws my face with her nails.

An almighty roar: thunder, or the crowd? I fall backwards, down into the dark.

Scene VIII

There is another flash of lightning. All is white light for an instant, and I crawl on all fours into the crowd, scrabbling through the filthy mud. Above me I hear voices shouting. The air is raging, and the mob has rushed forward, lured by the scent of death.

'Where is she?'

'Where is the witch?'

'She has turned herself into a bat!'

'She has made herself invisible!'

As soon as I dare, I scramble to my feet, drenched and slimed with mud. Out. Out. I must get out. Blindly, I make my way away from the noise.

'Seek her!'

'Find her!'

'Burn her!'

For a few moments I think this fury might work in my favour, for the crowd is shouting at the stage, as if expecting me to reappear at any moment. But as I reach the doorway the gatherer looks up from his pot of entrance coin.

'She's here – the one who called the demon!' he shouts, lunging towards me.

I slip past him, and pull the catch back on the heavy door. I feel a hand upon my shoulder, and bite hard till I taste blood. There's a scream of pain; the door opens. Rain and lightning. I kick off my pattens and I run. Helter-skelter I go, slipping in the mud, wading through deep-rutted puddles, my skirts clutched to my chest.

'She has called the Devil!'

'She is a witch! Catch the witch!'

My feet move faster, and I run as I have never done in all my life. But how can I outdistance a horde of burly men? I think of Henry and Marie, waiting for me. Oh, Lord God! What have I done? What have I done to Tom? Someone catches my skirt and it tears away; I run on in nothing but my soaking undershift. My hands and feet are bleeding. Sharp stones and brambles snare me as I run. But I will *not* die. I will *not*.

The ground is firmer when I reach the harbour, and the street that borders the river's edge. There are houses here, of the common sort, and candles burning in the windows. I smell the river-stench. The wind blows keener than before. I run down an alley and beat as loudly as I can upon the first door I come to, screaming and wailing, for no words will come.

A head appears from an upstairs window. 'Who's there?'

I find my voice at last. 'Aemilia Lanyer, a poor housewife! The mob are after me – please let me in!' I look back and see flaring torch-light at the far end of the alley. I run on, and beat upon another door.

'Away, witch!' shouts somebody inside.

I knock again. But there's no answer, just the rain. I run till I reach the end of the alleyway – the voices are louder, I can smell the torch-pitch as they gather in a crowd behind me. Then my hands meet a rough wall, and my torn fingers feel upwards and sideways. The wall is high and wide – it blocks the way. I look round, and see the faces in the spluttering firelight. My breath comes in shuddering sobs. This is it. This is Death.

For a moment the mob is silent. The people are afraid. Then a man as tall as a birch tree, a veritable giant, marches forward and says, 'Witch! You killed that boy! You called that demon!'

And the accusation is repeated by the crowd behind him, and a rain of heavy objects falls down upon me – rotted carrots, rat skulls and jagged stones. I shall die like Joan, with a cave mouth for a face. I cover my head with my arms and turn my back, and hear my own scream as the missiles find their mark. A slippery rope is slung around my head; I feel it screwing tight into my neck as they pull me back with them along the alley. I walk silently, thoughtless, speechless, pissing with fear.

'Find a tree!'

'A Judas tree, and string her from it.'

I am pulled and shoved from all sides. Someone punches my belly, and when I look down I see I am wearing nothing but torn rags. Blood is pouring from my wounds. I feel nothing; I do not know what I am. The earth? The sky? The Beast? Looking up, I see the bright upper windows, and the heads of the watchers set black against the glow. There are little children calling questions and a babe in arms, dancing.

I see my father's face, bending towards me, his black eyes and his curled beard. I hear the sweet harmony of his recorder, making patterns in the air. I see my mother, laughing, in Lady Susan's garden. A swan, retreating from the green bank, creasing the silver image of the sky. Will, turning from a knot of players, smiling at the sight of me. Henry, bouncing his ball along Long Ditch in the sunshine. Tom Flood, lying dead upon the stage.

I call out, 'Lord forgive me! Lord forgive me! I have sinned and I repent of it! Mea culpa! Mea culpa!'

There is a sound. Deep in the earth, far above in the heavens, inside my head. What is it? I seize the noose with my hands, and struggle to loosen the rope around my neck. What is that sound? I know I have heard it before. Louder now, louder, like drumming.

'Here is the tree!'

'Here is the place. Hang her here.'

The rope pulls again, and I gag as it grips my throat. The sound is not drums but hoof-beats. *Those hooves are coming for me.* A rescuer, or the Black Huntsman and his storm-dogs, sent from Hell? *I want to know.* I work my fingers between the wet rope and my neck. And then I find my voice, dry and sore.

'Why are you doing this?'

The giant speaks. 'To punish you for murder.'

Someone else says, 'To punish you for witchcraft.'

'For conjuring and evil.'

'Then take me to the King, and let him try me.' I cough and retch. My tongue cleaves to the roof of my mouth. 'He has studied witchcraft... Let *him* try me.'

'The King won't want to be bothered with the likes of you,' says the giant. 'A common witch.'

I can hear the hoof-beats more clearly now. Not of the air, or in my head, but on the ground. Yet between me and this sound there is a wall of bodies. In the rippling light of flares and shadows I see faces of every kind, some comely, some deformed, some scored with wrinkles. Each is distorted with the same murderous intent, more hobgoblin than human. Reason will not work with such a mob as this.

'If you kill me, what good will that do?' I ask, coughing and retching again.

'The good will be your death; no more is needed,' the giant shouts. 'String her up, there! String her up!'

But the rope stays slack. They are watching me. Words swim into my head, and I close my eyes and shout them out. *'Come, you spirits that tend on mortal thoughts, unsex me here, and fill me, from the crown to the toe, top-full of direst cruelty!'*

My voice is a raven-croak, sounding strange and terrible even to myself, but I am afraid to stop in case this breaks the spell.

'Make thick my blood; stop up th'access and passage to remorse, that no compunctious visitings of Nature shake my fell purpose, or keep peace between th'effect and it!' The words seem to warm me, and with each syllable, my strength grows.

'String her up!' shouts the giant again.

And someone says, 'I dare not!'

I grow taller and bolder as I speak. '*Come to my woman's breasts, and take my milk for gall, you murth'ring ministers, wherever in your sightless substances you wait on Nature's mischief!*'

'Slash her! Slit her open!'

'Use her guts to gag her!'

'We are afraid!'

I throw my head back, and scream at the sky. '*Come, thick Night, and pall thee in the dunnest smoke of hell, that my keen knife see not the wound it makes – nor Heaven peep through the blanket of the dark, to cry "HOLD! HOLD!"*'

The crowd falls back, and I hear sobbing.

'God protect us!'

'God save us, this is Beelzebub himself.'

With a roar of rage the giant leaps forward. The rope jerks and someone drags my hands away. The rope is pulled tight around my throat. 'Let it be quick, Lord,' I pray. 'Let me go quickly!'

'Ready, ho! Haul her up!'

My feet are lifted from the ground and all is agony and blackness. But the hoof-beats still come. There is a clap of thunder and screaming all around me. A horse squeals, men shout, there is a great crack, then the noise begins to fade.

Darkness, nothingness.

A swish of air above my head. I am falling. I am on the ground coughing and puking. I look up. The severed rope is dangling from the hanging tree. The black destrier from the Globe is rearing up against the bright house windows. There is a hooded figure clinging to it.

Satan has come to take me down to Hell. He lifts me from the ground and sets me on the saddle before him, then holds me tightly as the snorting horse gallops headlong through the mob. There are shouts and screams, hands clawing at me. The beast's back rocks beneath me as we charge into the storm.

Scene IX

Is this the road to Hades? If so, it's lined with the great houses of Camm Row, and the messy rooftops of Long Ditch. I look down, at the black-clad arm of the horseman who has saved me. It is the arm of a living man. We reach a small house, and the horseman halts his mount and jumps down. He reaches up and helps me to the ground.

Will's face is daubed with stage blood, and his eyes are rimmed with black.

'By God, Aemilia, what have you done?'

'I summoned Lilith,' I whisper. 'I drew a circle. I had a book.'

He wipes his hand across his eyes. 'Why, in Christ's name? Why dabble in such nonsense?'

'To stop the play! To end it! But not – '

'For pity's sake!'

'Not to do harm to anyone! Not to Tom!'

'What lunacy was this?'

I hide my face.

'What manner of falling off from what you were, and what you could be?'

'May God forgive me.'

Silence.

'Do you hate me so much?' he asks.

'No. It wasn't hatred that drove me to it.'

'What else could it have been? It surely wasn't love!'

'How do you know?'

'God in Heaven,' he says. 'If this *is* love, then we must leave it. Once and for all, and till we die.'

'Will...'

'You have driven yourself mad,' he says. 'You see what is not there, and are blind to plain truth.'

'No!' I cry. 'Lilith was there – upon the stage. She killed Tom. I swear it.'

'God rest that dear boy's soul!' says Will. 'He was the merriest, sweetest fellow I ever knew.' He pauses. 'The thing that killed him, Aemilia, was the falling crane. The crane *I* had constructed, so that we could have the best effects in London. If anyone is to blame, it's me. In this actual world.'

'Yes, but she was there! Lilith made it happen! She is the child-taker, and I called her, and she killed Anne's son!' I begin to weep, hopeless, tearless, grating sobs that hurt my chest.

Will puts his arms around me and holds for a long while. Then, very gently, he pushes me away. 'Let me say only this...' he begins.

'Don't twist the knife! I couldn't bear it!'

'Aemilia. Calm yourself. You are not a murderer.'

'I cannot calm myself! I cannot! Because I *am*!'

'Look at me. Look at me... Every evening, every morning, every moment – my love, my sweet girl. Aemilia, I think of you.'

'Will, no...'

'You have read my plays.'

'Yes.'

'Come back to this world. Come back to your true self. Didn't you see how it was? That all my heroines are versions of my Dark Aemilia? Black-eyed Rosaline, clever Portia, the Egyptian Queen who drove poor Anthony to madness – all you! All you. Each one.'

'Don't... don't say this.'

'I never was so happy, never so much myself, as I was when I was with you. When I loved you.'

'Will.'

'And you loved me.'

I hang my head. Rainwater swirls around our feet.

'Henry,' says Will. 'The boy – he is the two of us. I live in him, with you. It's only this that has sustained me. Only this, and writing. The recreation of my sweet lost lady in my words.'

'There is no… future for us, is there?' I say, my tears flowing from the sky. 'Only your words are left.'

Will says nothing. We embrace, and I know this is for the last time.

Act V

Poetry

Scene I

Aldgate, Spring 1611

I am a sinner, steeped in evil that is past, and I can never make amends. So it is now my habit to go to St Botolph's Church at Aldgate every morning for the matins service. It is a simple building, despite its gold-tipped spire. Today I feel ill and restless, and believe that the end of all this might be the madhouse. I have passed a disturbed night. The house echoed and stirred with malevolent spirits, and the air I breathed seemed odorous and distempered, infected by the demons that dwell among us. I could hear them whispering and gibbering in my ears, so I wrapped my head in the bed-sheet, sweating with terror. In the end, I crept up to the garret and sat upon a joint-stool by the window, waiting for the first rays of sunlight to drive the evil spirits away. Only when the rooftops and chimneystacks were gilded with the dawn did I dare to drowse a little, head sagging. I dreamed of Will, as I do most nights.

The last I heard from him was a short letter, sent to explain that the second publication of the sonnets was done without his knowledge. A volume was printed two summers ago: his hate-verse and the fulsome words he wrote to please Wriothesley. His note was polite, but there was no love in it. I keep it, with his poems.

Now I am sitting in the church, I feel as if I am lost in a dark mist, and the voices of my fellow worshippers seem far away. I sit among the other women, head bowed, ignoring their chatter, waiting for the service to begin. Our usual prelate is not here. I don't see the new man when he enters, as I am busy with my prayers. But, as soon as he begins to speak, something in his voice and manner catches my attention.

'It has come to my notice,' says he, 'that this City is as full of Sin as Sodom, and as riven with Bawds and Strumpets as Gomorrah. There is a not a homily that addresses this Disease of London, so this morning I have written you my own, in plain words. May the Devil in you hear this, so you can cast him out.

'And you may ask yourselves – how did we come to this pass? And you may ask yourselves – how did we come to be cast out of the Garden of Eden, we whom GOD made in his own image, to have mastery over Creation and over all the beasts of the field, and all the birds in the air, and all the fishes in the sea?'

I shift my position. My knees are growing stiff. Where have I heard that rasping tone before? I clasp my hands tighter, and try to pray harder. But the voice is insistent.

'I can tell you how. I can tell you why. I have studied in the greatest universities in all of Europe, and I have looked most carefully at the cause. I have found our culprit, with GOD's help. It is Woman who has ruined us. First in the person of that weakest of vessels, Eve, and since then in the frail form of every woman born.'

I bow my head. 'Lord, forgive me. Jesu, have pity. *Mea culpa. Mea culpa.*'

But it is hard to concentrate on my own sin when there is so much of it about. And most of it the fault of my ignoble gender.

'St Thomas Aquinas has warned us of this wanton, wayward sex. "*A male is the beginning and end of woman, as God is the beginning and end of every creature.*" Man is made in God's image; Woman is a thing distorted from Man's rib. Her Latin name is "softness of the mind", but Man is called "*vir*" which we translate as "strength or virtue of the soul". Compared to Man, the Woman is an imbecile.'

It is no good. I open my eyes. The man standing at the wooden table in the centre of the church is my old adversary, Parson John. I stare at him, blinking, forgetting my own misdoing for the first time for many years.

The prelate is warming to his theme. 'What is lighter than smoke? A breeze. What is lighter than a breeze? The wind. What is lighter than the wind? A Woman. What is lighter than a Woman? Nothing. And yet, even in this lightness, she gushes most detestably, sullying all she touches with her womb-blood. Fruits do not produce, wine turns sour, plants die, trees lack fruit. The air about her darkens. If a dog should eat her vile blood, it will run mad.'

Lord above! Is this truly the Word of God? I glance around me, at the bowed and reverent heads of all the women.

'A woman is the cause of all our ill. Adam was deceived by Eve, and not Eve by Adam. The Woman summoned him to Sin. She lied and tricked him, and the whole of Creation was overthrown. So the female must pay. She must yield to the man as a reed bends in the wind.'

His words work a curious magic on me. They rouse me from my torpid, grief-stricken state. Dismissing Eve as being both weak and wicked has always seemed foolish and unfair to me. She was subordinate to Adam, more obedient than Lilith. And yet, she ended by looking beyond the life of a child, fenced in by our Maker. Her existence as a naked animal enthroned in flowers was not enough. She sought out Knowledge. Was that a bad thing? *Should* mankind be stupid? The Serpent may have been the agent of the Devil, but in truth human beings contain the impulses of Hell as well as Heaven. We are not angels. In order to defend Eve, it is necessary to think beyond the version of the Fall that Parson John proclaims. Must all women bear this burden of limitless guilt? Must we spend all our lives accusing ourselves of sin, and despising ourselves as second best?

I sit upright. I am thinking of the Cornelius Agrippa book that I stole from Simon Forman, and the thoughts that this wise philosopher expressed. He was a good Christian – just as much so as our revered parson – and yet he saw women in a very different way. Supposing that the Old Testament God of rage and plagues was not the God of Jesus and his disciples? Supposing Eden had been, not a paradise, but a prison from which humankind had to escape? With knowledge came freedom. I blink hard.

The service is over, and the parson stands outside the church, addressing the congregation with an air of chilly discontent. I walk past him, with no desire to speak, but can't resist giving him a sharp look I pass.

'I see we have a Jezebel among us, a copy of that wilful Eve,' he says.

'Do you remember me?'

'You are the termagant whose pestilent son was possessed by demons.'

The other churchgoers look at me askance. I must admit, I have not made it my business to be neighbourly, and they are already suspicious of me.

'I trust he died soon after,' says the pleasant parson.

The fear and self-loathing fall away from me. 'He lived, sir,' I said. 'And he is living still, praise God!'

'Then a miracle took place. God is good; he will save all sinners, even your diabolic son.'

'Yes. A miracle. And I would like to tell you that your view of women is quite mistaken. Eve is not the mother of our undoing. She has been much maligned.'

'It is not my *view*, mistress,' says the parson. 'I do not invent the Word of God. I am the mouthpiece of the Church.' He bends forward slightly, as if to direct his spleen more precisely. 'Ask forgiveness, and it may be that Our Lord will spare your soul.'

'I will not.'

'Will *not*, madam?'

'The Church is wrong.'

'Heaven protect us!' cries an old man.

'May the good Lord strike you down!' says his companion.

Parson John regards me coldly, a pillar of furious contempt. 'If you wish me to refer you to the City fathers for sedition, then I would be happy to oblige you. I will leave it to our Maker to offer a more long-lasting punishment, and broil your flesh for an eternity in Hell.'

'Punish me when I am printed, sir,' I say. 'Punish me when I set down the true story of Eve and Eden in a chap-book. Punish me when I have made a poem of it. Then I will be quite content.'

Scene II

My night fears have diminished. My wakefulness gives me time to write, and to think, and the shadows keep to themselves. I write and write, referring to the books upon my desk, and using the thoughts inside my head. I look upon the guilt and grief of other women, and I conclude that we have been the cursed receptacle for all the ills of mankind. In failing to be the Virgin Mary, we are Serpents every one.

It comes to me, as I write by candle-light and consider the darkness, that it is possible that poor Eve did not sin at all. She was not wicked. She was curious. I set out the words, and this time they are clearer and sharper than before. I see not only Eden; I see the truth.

> *Our Mother Eve, who tasted of the Tree,*
> *Giving to Adam what she held most dear,*
> *Was simply good, and had no power to see,*
> *The after-coming harm did not appear:*
> *The subtle Serpent that our Sex betrayed,*
> *Before our fall so sure a plot had laid.*

And if Eve is free of blame, then Adam must take the consequence. Now the words flow. I break a goose quill in my haste to get them down, and dip a new pen, greedy for the ink.

> *If Eve did err, it was for knowledge's sake,*
> *The fruit being faire persuaded him to fall:*

No subtle Serpent's falsehood did betray him,
If he would eat it, who had power to stay him?
Not Eve, whose fault was only too much love.

From the suffering of Eve came the suffering of the rest of us. Of guilty women, who must pay eternally for the Fall of Man. I remember the lines that had haunted me when Tom sang his sad song at Yuletide: of Rachel, crying for her children 'because they were not'. What is 'not'? The empty cradle. The folded nightshirts, put away for other babes. Tom's laughing face, his joy and foolery. So I write of that too, the love of all mothers, of which the love and grief of Our Lady is the highest expression.

Yet these poor women, by their piteous cries
Did move their Lord, their Lover and their King,
To take compassion, turne about and speake,
To them whose hearts were ready now to break.

I write at night. I write in the daytime. I write when the pottage burns. I write while the soap congeals. I write while the house-mice nibble the fallen cake-crumbs at my feet. I write.

It is a work of many months. Back and forth I go, repeatedly, until I have made a poem which praises the Bible women and puts their case, as if I were a lawyer at the Inns of Court. And, when I have done, I sit down and think of all the women of influence to whom I might dedicate it, and who might now give me patronage, and I write them all my thanks. I start with Queen Anne, and end with virtuous ladies in general. (Of which there are, as you will know, a substantial number.) Redemption is sweet. I find a printer and a seller. I do not go to Cuthbert Tottle, who has died of dropsy, but make a contract with Mr Valentine Simmes, a most enlightened fellow who sees no harm in women writing verse, and believes there is great merit in the case for

Eve. My book is sold in the bookshop of Richard Bonian in Paul's Churchyard.

I send a copy to Will, with my good wishes, but I hear nothing from him.

Scene III

Stratford, March 1616

Time passes not as a river flows, smoothly and ever onward, but as a mob seethes, wild and unpredictable. First walking, then running, then slowing to a stop, then starting to speed up again: faster, faster. Or this is how it seems to me. So I am standing here, on this bright, blustery spring day, and cannot believe that I am so old, or that the things that live in my memory happened so long ago. My chest aches with the pain of times past and loves lost. But I have Henry still, and my penitence, and this good hour.

Alfonso is dead, and I miss him more than I thought I would, though it is pleasant to have the whole bed to myself. (And to know how much money I have in the house from one day to the next.) I have a widow's freedom, to walk the streets and go about my business. The Globe was burned down, and then built up again, in brick. All were saved from the fire, and I hear the King's Men are doing well. Will is no longer with them – he retired after the blaze and came here to live the life of a fat gentleman with his wife. It is this wife – this Ann Shakespeare – who wrote a curt note to me. Summoning me here, to speak to Will. I would have ignored her message if I could. Why should I be told to jump to it by this queening country wife? But I have longed to see him for so many years.

Stratford is a busy, noisy place. Outside the inn, there is a bustle of carts, livestock and crowding townsfolk, blocking the thoroughfare completely. There are plenty of beggar-folk as well, just as vile to look upon as their city cousins: doxies, vagabonds and all manner of hard-eyed beggars, displaying their deformities to tempt money from passers-by. And yet it's but a village compared to London's great smoking tumult. Around us is a rolling landscape of green hills and pleasant pasture. The trees that line the market square are beginning to put forth new leaves, and their branches whisper in the breeze. Stratford's most pungent odours are of the shippon, not the jakes.

I stare at the shop-fronts and at the cheery, bartering housewives, trying to imagine Will buying a joint of lamb or a bolt of cloth. The houses are modest, built tight together, so that each shop counter, which juts out into the street, buts on to the next. A master tailor is sewing a shirt; a barber smoothes a linen cloth over his customer's chest; a baker flaps her hands at the flies that buzz around the sugar loaves.

'Somewhat small,' I say to John Heminge, who has come with me from London. 'Too small for *him*.'

But Heminge isn't listening; he is paying the horse-boy.

'Is New Place in this street?' I ask

He frowns, looking at his change. 'Close by,' he says. 'You'll have to wait, Aemilia. We don't know when he will see you yet.'

'Did *she* not ask for me to come?'

'Be patient. He is not the man he was. And speak fairly of Mistress Shakespeare. It was good of her to ask you here.'

That night, sleep deserts me again. I sit in my room, watching shadows, and light one candle from the next to stop them from haunting me. I think of my past, and wish that I could be a better sort of person. I think of my poems and wish that I could have made those better too.

I finally sleep, bolt upright.

I am a child in Bishopsgate again, walking with my father. The air is full of music, and we are walking past the walls of Bedlam, listening to the mad singing their angel songs.

My father tells me not to listen, and not to look through the keyhole of the great gate we come upon, which is so high that it reaches the clouds. I say I will not, and then he goes away. Then I look through the hole and there is a yellow eye.

I look at the yellow eye, and the yellow eye looks at me.

A voice whispers, 'Little girl.'

'What?'

'Little girl. I have been watching you.' It is a woman's voice. It has a sibilant hiss.

'I didn't do anything.'

'You have come here for a reason.' Now there is a wheedle in the voice. It wants something.

'I must go now. My father told me not to look.'

'You came because I called you, little girl.'

'I didn't hear you.'

'That is because I did not need to speak.'

New Place is built from solid brick and sturdy timber. It is a long building, which stretches along one side of Chapel Street, edged by a high brick wall. It has three storeys and five gables. Much of it is raw-coloured, where new bricks or wood have been used to patch and mend it. There a gate in the wall which leads to a grassy courtyard.

A great deerhound lopes across and welcomes Heminge as an old friend, wagging its tail and gently butting him with its head. Then he leaves me there and enters the house, pressing my hand before he goes.

I shield my eyes and look up at the plain glass windows, set in lead, wondering if Will is behind one of these, and whether he might be secretly studying me, as I am trying to catch a glimpse of him. Nausea grips my throat. What will we say? How shall I meet his eye?

After a while, Heminge returns. He looks unhappy.

'Will is worse,' he says.

I frown. 'Worse than what?'

'He is very ill, Aemilia. I hope you understand that. It was no one's wish but his that you came all this way. Ann only tries to please him.'

'Then I must see him.'

'I don't know if he is well enough to see you today.'

'I am not going away till I have spoken to him,' I say. 'Even if it's only for five minutes.'

'She had better come in,' says a voice from the doorway.

I turn to see a woman standing there. I'm not sure what I expected in a neglected country wife, but it was certainly not this. A tall, upright woman, older than I am, but with fine, pale skin. Her eyes are grey, with long black lashes, like those of a young girl. She is dressed in a green velvet gown. She looks at me for a long moment, as if she was fearing the worst but I have exceeded it.

'I am Ann Shakespeare,' she says. 'The wife.'

'I am Aemilia Lanyer,' say I.

'The mistress.'

I nod.

'Come inside,' she says. 'I have been meaning to speak to you for some time.' I follow her to the foot of a wide oak staircase. It leads up to a long gallery, hung with bright tapestries. Behind her, a door stands open. I can see a physick garden, and hear children laughing.

We stand for a moment.

'We are alike,' she says, at last. 'I have heard that is often the way.'

'Yes, Mistress Shakespeare.'

'With some differences, of course.'

'I would expect as much.'

'Such as scruples, with which, I imagine, I have been better endowed than you.'

'I have scruples enough.'

'I dare say even a murderer has his limits.'

What has she heard? What has he told her?

'I won't stay long, Mistress Shakespeare, and I want to say how grateful I am that you have been kind enough to let me come. Ever since I heard about the fire at the Globe I have been anxious…'

'It was not your place to be anxious. He has people here who are anxious enough.'

'Of course. And then, I heard that he had left for good…'

'Not left. *Returned.*'

'After which, I heard that he was ill…'

'He *is* ill.'

'And then… then you invited me to Stratford.'

'He has become much concerned with giving things away. His books, for the most part, though I would like to read them myself. But, never mind – he had too many of them. I believe that he has something of this sort to give to you.'

A servant comes, and Ann speaks to her at length about drying malt, as if I were not there at all. Then the girl disappears. Ann stares at me in silence for a moment. 'You were beautiful,' she says, finally. 'I suppose there is at least some dignity in that.'

She takes me up the stairs, and leads me to a closed door. 'Here you are,' she says. 'When I open it, go inside and sit in the chair by the window. Keep your eyes down till I close the door again. Don't move from the chair till he has finished speaking to you. Do not go near him, and do not open the shutters. You will get used to the darkness when you have been sitting there a while.'

I go obediently to the chair by the shuttered window in the light of the open door. When it closes, I can see nothing. The room smells of woodsmoke and peppermint. But after a while I realise I can hear the sound of unsteady, rattling breathing coming from the far side of the room. I think of the last time we lay together; the hot night in that other darkness.

I keep my eyes on the shutters and their cracks of daylight.

'Your wife told me that you asked to see me,' I say.

There is a break in the shuddering breathing and then it begins again. It pains me to hear it, and I find I am taking deeper, slower breaths, as if this might help. I want to touch Will again so badly that I grasp the arms of the chair to stop myself from flying across the room. 'I have come to pay you my respects, sir.'

Silence.

'I am very sorry that you are unwell.'

The breathing becomes faster, accompanied by the creaking of a chair. At length, a rasping voice says, 'Not unwell, Aemilia. Not unwell.'

'Then I am glad.'

'Dead, rather.'

'No! Do not say that!'

'Yes, for I am stuck here, away from the world, and I am not of it any longer. That is death to me.'

'The fire…'

'Ah, yes. The fire.'

I wait for him to say more, hardly daring to breathe myself, as each word seems to cost him so much.

'Did you hear what caused it?' he asks, then wheezes and coughs.

'No.'

'The effects! In *Henry VIII*. We launched a stage cannon outside, to mark the King's majestical entrance, and the thatch caught fire.'

'You over-reached yourselves.'

'Yes, we over-reached ourselves. Indeed we did. I should have learned my lesson from that cursed crane.'

There is another pause.

'I wanted to ask you about Henry,' he says quietly.

'He is well, sir. Clever and handsome. A fine young man now.'

'And… what I want to ask is… does he know me?'

'What do you mean?'

'Does he know that he's my son?'

I close my eyes. 'Yes. I have told him.'

'And…'

'He is glad. He is proud to have such a father.'

'Does he… what does he do?'

'He plays in the King's consort.'

'Ah.' He breathes heavily. 'My wife has a doublet and rapier downstairs for him. I have told her that he was a player at the Globe. I mean… she has no idea of his connection to me. It is a good doublet – I hope it fits him. She doesn't know the value of the rapier, nor that the grip and pommel are solid silver.'

Silence once more. I wait, listening so hard that my ears began to ache. 'I am sorry, Will,' I say at last, able to bear it no longer. 'I am sorry for all the pain and suffering I caused you. I am sorry if I was ever faithless, and I am sorry for doubting your love. But I am sorriest of all for summoning that evil demon, all because of my jealousy and spite, and my rage about the play.'

'No, no,' he says.

'Yes, it was my fault! I wanted to put a stop to it. I wanted to be avenged on you, and Burbage, and all the others. All the poets and players who are men, and look me up and down, and either see a strumpet or nothing at all. And then Tom died for it – for my revenge! I can never forgive myself. I am damned for it, damned for all eternity, no matter how much I pray for redemption. And so I should be, for I deserve nothing less.'

'Ah, my Aemilia,' he says, his voice faint. 'You are troubled with thick-coming fancies.'

I smile sadly. 'My words, or yours?'

405

'Yours, I believe. Poor Lady Macbeth.'

'They are thick-coming, certainly. But are they fancies?'

'Aren't they?'

I wait.

'I have read your poems,' he says. 'Or I should say, Susanna has read them to me. For I am… weak.'

'Your daughter?'

'Yes. She doesn't approve of your opinions. She thinks they are seditious.'

'And you?'

'I think it's excellent work. Most… polemical. You are right about the mistreatment of poor Eve. I saw… I saw how it might be. The other side of it. To be shut out because of your sex, by men and boys. And, *de facto*, by all the world. Not all maids can storm the Inns of Court by aping Portia.'

'No.' I am so happy to hear his words that I can think of nothing else to say.

'I once said – among many other cruel and angry things – that you would never be a poet.'

'You did, sir.'

'Well, you have proved me wrong. You *are* a poet, Aemilia Lanyer, and you are a good one, too. And you taught me much – remember that!'

'About Italy, and the ancients.'

'Ay, and about love.' Will is breathing heavily again. 'You must go soon.'

'I am so thankful to you. You are so… gracious.' These words are so feeble that I burst out: 'No one else's opinion is *anything* to me. No one else's words *exist*.'

'Think nothing of it. You have worked hard at your Art, and deserve much more than this. But…'

'But what?'

'Let me tell you something about the fire.'

'Only if you have the strength.'

There is silence again. Then Will speaks, and the rattle in his breathing fades and it seems almost as if he is talking to himself. 'It was a hot, bright day. Cruelly hot, so even the shadows sweated, and dogs lolled panting in open doorways. I was not at the Globe for the performance: I had business in the City. So the first I knew of the fire was black smoke, drifting over the house-tops as I hurried from St Paul's.' He pauses, and coughs again.

'As I reached Blackfriars Stairs, a cry went up. "The Globe is burning!" And I raised my head – for I was thinking of a verse that I was writing, and staring at the ground – and then I looked across the water and saw the flames, leaping into the summer sky. I paid the boatman half a crown to row quickly, and I ran from the south bank to the theatre door. What a sight it was! Like the Pit itself! The sun had crisped the thatch and dried out the walls, and the sound was terrible – the roaring of fire, and the crashing of timber. The heat smote me as I stood there, and I saw that the trees nearby were catching too.'

'Yet all were saved!'

'So Burbage told me. He came running up, with his shirt all soot-stained and his face as red as the flames. "We are all safe, praise God!" he shouted, tears pouring down his cheeks. "All safe, Will, every man!" But, as I looked at him, a thought came to me. I had been working on a play.'

'Was that so strange?'

He coughs again, and I can hear him struggling to find a clear way for his breath. 'That morning, I had brought it with me, to the tiring-room, because I wanted to get it done. Then I went off to see a printer at Paul's Churchyard, and I had left it behind, upon my table.'

He hesitates, and I wait. 'I have told no one of this but you, Aemilia. This play was to be the master-work that all my other writing led to – the play to end all plays. Such a piece that would always be remembered. Five hundred years – a thousand years

from now. The others might fade from memory, but this play…
this one would last.'

'And so you ran into the fire.'

'Ah, you are the only one who understands insanity. Yes, I ran,
shaking Dick off as I went. I hurtled through the entrance, into
the pit. The lintel was burning red – I could see that it would fall
at any moment. The pit itself was clear of fire, though the rushes
were black and shrivelled and glowed beneath my feet. I ran over
them, and up on to the stage. The canopy was flame; the Heavens
were Hell. I felt my clothes begin to char and burn my skin. But
still I went – into the tiring-room, where all the costumes burned
like Catholics – and there was my table. And – lo! – the pages
were still there. I praised God – then, as I ran forward, I looked
up and the flaming roof timbers were falling down. I snatched
the pages, and fled the room as it roared and crackled around
me. Ran back across the pit, and into the open air. My clothes,
my hair, my skin itself – all of this was flame. By some miracle, I
got outside, and it was Dick who saved me. He wrapped a cloak
around me and quenched the fire. I fell to the ground, clutching
my papers, my breath coming like sword-shafts.'

'Dear God! But you saved your pages?'

The chair creaks.

'What of your pages? What of your great play?'

'All dust,' he says. 'All charred to nothing.'

He is making a strange sound. He is laughing again, after a
wheezy fashion.

'Nothing left at all?'

'All that was left was one charred scrap of paper, with the
title wrote upon it.'

'And… what was the title?'

'It was *Dark Aemilia*. The story of a great lady, and her fall.'

'Oh!'

'It was a fable, concerning love, and poetry and fame. But
mostly love.'

I wipe my eyes. 'This was to be your great work?'

'I wanted to summon the spirit of our time together. Its passion and its madness and its joy.'

'Oh, my lord,' say I. 'My sweet, beloved Will.'

'My love,' he says, his voice weak and indistinct. 'We shall remember, shan't we? We have it still.'

After a moment, he says, 'Listen, I cannot speak for very much longer. I have three gifts for you. The first, most people might think was next to worthless, but I believe that you will see its value. As you are a poet.'

'I am overcome.'

I can hear him smile again. 'Wait till you hear what it is: you may think it a strange present. My foul pages. With all my crossings out and alterations.'

'Heminge said your pages are never blurred nor blotted.'

'That is because I keep my first draft to myself. Until now, that is. Now they are yours. You will be heartened by my short-comings, and perhaps you can learn from my mistakes.'

'Will... I... how can I thank you – ?'

'And also... also my bed.'

'Your *bed*?'

'Not the bed I sleep in now, which is of little value. No, the one where we last... went at it. Lord, what a night that was. It's still there – I could not bear to bring it back to Stratford, nor did I want to pay the fee the carrier wanted.'

I remember it well – the fug of love inside its curtains and its roof patterned with leaping porpoises.

'Aemilia?'

'Yes?'

'Still there – good.'

'Still here? I cannot bear to leave!'

'There is one final gift.'

'I don't need anything more. You have been kind enough.'

'I will put your name upon the play. Upon *Macbeth*. For, as sure as anything, the meat of that strange piece is yours.'

'Thank you. But – no. It would be wrong.'

He sighs. A long, rattling sigh.

'Aemilia, you are many things. You are a troublesome, noisy, cock-teasing, cock-tiring, wild-tongued termagant…' He stops, as if to gather his strength. 'But you are not evil.'

'I *am* evil. Tom died because of me.'

'How do you know?'

'You were there! You saw it! He fell down upon the stage. The spirit cursed him, and the crane fell.'

'Yes, the crane killed him. We don't know why it fell, but it was the crane that brought about his death. Burbage and I built it, and it was me who pushed to have it. But I haven't spent all these years believing that I am evil! It was an accident. All life brings risk.'

'Is that what you believe?'

'Of course. You are no more guilty of his death than I am. Nor are you the evil strumpet of those sonnets. You are Aemilia. And I loved you better than myself.'

'Loved?'

'Love. I still love you. Nothing has changed that.'

'No. Nothing has changed it.' The tears pour out of me.

'Shall we forgive each other?' he asks. His voice is weaker still.

'Oh, Will!' I sob. 'If we forgive each other, then we are all done.'

'My love, we *are* all done,' says Will. 'Open the shutters.'

His face is dark from the sun. His eyes are full of sky. His lips are swollen red from reckless kissing. 'Let's not quarrel,' he says. 'Let's make love, and I'll teach you poetry that way.'

I smooth the hair back from his forehead.

'Am I your mistress, then? Am I all the things you wanted?'

'You are indeed, and I am your obedient slave.'
I look at him, eye to eye, to see if I can peer inside his head.
'Do you want me?' he asks, very serious.
Oh, I do. I do.
Afterwards, we lie together, sticky and naked in the long grass. 'Be silent with me now, my love,' he whispers.

She sits me in the hall downstairs, beside a smouldering log fire, and hands me a cup of wine. Quite kindly, compared to what has gone before.

'I am sorry that you had to see him so,' she says.

'I didn't know.'

'No one is allowed to speak of it.'

'I understand.'

'He ran back into the Globe. When it was burning. They tried to stop him, but he struggled free.'

'A brave act.'

'Brave indeed. He wanted to be sure that no one had been left inside.'

'Did he tell you that?'

'Why else would he have entered an inferno, if not to save a human life? He is a good man.'

I cannot say that he is more than good, and less. I sip my tear-thinned wine in silence.

'Poor Will! What an ending!' I say at last.

'The doublet and the rapier are beside you,' she says, nodding to an iron-bound box. 'And his foul papers with them. Take care of those in particular. They are the workings of his mind.'

'I'll put them in safe-keeping.'

'Safe! Where in London's pit of malice and foul-doing do you call "safe"?'

'It is safe enough, madam, I can assure you. I have a little house at Aldgate, though I am soon to move to Pudding Lane.'

411

Mistress Shakespeare looks at me blankly. I realise that London names mean nothing to her. 'I make a habit of reading the Scriptures when I can,' she says. 'I put my trust in God and his angels now.' She picks up the Bible that is lying next to her on the oak settle.

'So must we all.'

Opening the book, she reads for a moment, but she is crying. 'I wanted him to come back so much. I prayed for it,' she says, without looking up. 'And now these prayers have been most cruelly answered.'

I shake my head sadly.

'It won't be long before Will is with God,' she says 'I try to see that. I try to bear it.'

The past is twisting in my mind, the greedy and illiterate country wife transformed into Patient Griselda. I try to think of words to comfort her – and me. But everything is muddled.

'I would like to ask one thing of you,' she says. 'Do not remember him as you just saw him. Remember him as he was.' She swallows and looks at me sharply. 'When you knew him. When he was young.'

'I shall.'

'He is a poet,' she says. 'And a magician. He is also my husband, but that is of less importance. I have learned to understand that, though I don't expect others to see it as I do.' Then, she closes her eyes. Is she about to pray? But no – she quotes these lines...

'I have bedimm'd
The noontide sun, call'd forth the mutinous winds,
And 'twixt the green sea and the azured vault
Set roaring war: to the dread rattling thunder
Have I given fire, and rifted Jove's stout oak
With his own bolt; the strong-bas'd promontory
Have I made shake and by the spurs pluck'd up

The pine and cedar: graves at my command
Have wak'd their sleepers, op'd, and let 'em forth
By my so potent Art. But this rough magic
I here abjure; and, when I have required
Some heavenly music, which even now I do,
To work mine end upon their senses that
This airy charm is for, I'll break my staff,
Bury it certain fathoms in the earth,
And deeper than did ever plummet sound
I'll drown my book.'

The words are so clear and bright that my neck pricks at their sound, and I sit there with my box of foul papers and stare at the sorcerer's wife in frank amazement.

I want to speak, of Prospero and love and endings. I want to say – our love was insubstantial, but magical. Like Ariel. But I can't. So I say, 'You had the best of him. A family, and a life here, and a home together.'

She stares at me. 'The best of him?'

'Yes.'

'What can you know of that? How can you presume to look into the minds or lives of others?'

'I don't presume to know anything, Mistress Shakespeare; you quite mistake me.'

'No, Mistress Lanyer, *you* mistake *me*. Of your own life you may be the witness, though no one knows when you are true and when you play false.'

'I am indeed the witness to it, mistress.'

'Of the rest of us, you can know next to nothing. Don't load us with your study, or your supposition. Do you *hear* me? Do you *understand?'*

We sit in silence. I watch a log glow red then crumble to a spume of fine grey ash. After a while, it falls to pieces in a rain of crackling stars.

Scene IV

The Globe, London, April 1616

Springtime, and the sky is streaked with fragile cloud. The meadows are white with lady smock and tender violets peer out from the hedgerow shade. Larks sing, cuckoos call, and a soft wind shakes the oaks which stand hard by the new-built Globe. The theatre is a splendid copy of its former self. But its roof is made from slate instead of thatch. God willing, this theatre will last longer than the old one.

'It's a fine thing,' says Henry, squeezing my arm. 'His work is born again.'

I cannot speak, but squeeze his arm in return. I have not set foot in the theatre since the day that Tom Flood died. Yesterday Ann Shakespeare sent me word that Will is dead too. He breathed his last while he was sleeping.

I am dressed in black. For Will would have his way, and this is his third present to me – a fine dress of ebony-coloured velvet. It was sent to me after I left Stratford, together with a caul of seed pearls. A single piece of paper was pinned to it, burned and charred so that at first the writing on it seemed illegible. Then I managed to make out two words: 'Dark Aemilia'. Now, I am wearing it on a bright spring day in a world in which he does not exist.

Henry persuaded me to come, full of pride for his dead father. He is wearing the Spanish doublet and the rapier is at his side. He is tall, and well-made, with thoughtful, shadowed eyes and a musician's ear for poetry. I could not bear a tragedy, or a

Roman rant, but the players are putting on *A Midsummer Night's Dream*, which I have never seen. A comedy for springtime, and for love, so Henry tells me, and the white flag that flutters over the theatre's cupola confirms that there will be no blood today.

We pass under the entrance, painted in myriad colours like the gateway to an ancient palace. Every detail of the old gate has been reproduced, even the likeness of Hercules with the world upon his shoulders. The world beyond the walls of the theatre is mutable and beyond our grasp. The world within is shaped and patterned for our understanding and diversion. We sit down in the gallery and Henry takes my hand. I look around at the pageant which surrounds me. The new pit is full to overflowing, and every seat on every tier of the gallery is taken. Those in the pit will find it hard to follow all the action, there is such a crowd of gallants seated upon the stage. The courtiers are rosetted and bombasted to the death, flaunting their warlike beards and girlish love-locks. The lesser folk are just as vivid in their cheaper finery, swarming together in a brawl of colour and vulgar show: yellow farthingales crushed by apple-women, stack-heels sinking in the mud. I wonder if the play-goers are wearing their finest clothing in Will's honour, just as I have put on my widow's gown.

The seething crowd is chatting, munching, singing, dicing, gaming, smoking, and swigging small beer. There are law students, strumpets, apprentices and oyster-sellers. Choirboys, pickpockets, servant girls and foists. I see a blur of movement; but also a multitude of London faces, looming and vanishing in the mob. A pretty Romeo and his pale Juliet, arms twined together. A handsome Moor and his whispering, rat-faced Iago. A stout and jocular Falstaff, drinking from an ale-pot, while a young blade laughs at his side. A student, in a black cloak, frowning deep as Hamlet as he reads his book. The sun shimmers on every button and scarlet pustule, every scar and cross-stitched codpiece, every tooth-stump and curling smile. So that the scene is as vibrant as a palace portrait, preserved in oils and distemper.

Here is Thomas Dekker, writing on his sleeve, head cocked to one side as if listening to the throng. Here is Moll Cutpurse, strumming her lute and singing out, full-throated. And see, there is my landlord Anthony Inchbald, propped high on one of the best seats, dressed in scarlet. Dogs run between the legs of the play-goers, snatching up the fallen chicken bones. The scent of tobacco smoke wafts into the balmy air. On the balcony above the stage, the musicians are playing. A nut-seller shouts for custom; a baby squeals; a drunk's song rages and stops.

And then I see them. A white-haired woman, overdressed in a tawny gown with a lace ruff. There is a younger woman next to her, with two little girls. They have black hair, wild and curly. The children are sitting side by side, so tight that they might be made of one flesh. I look closer. They *are* one flesh. It is Anne Flood, and Marie, and Anne's grandchildren, the joined twins. Anne leans close to Marie and whispers something to her, and Marie throws her head back and laughs.

I spring up, wanting to call to them, but Henry pulls me back into my seat. 'Mother! Sit down, sit down…'

Three trumpet calls blast out, to summon any latecomers. The musicians strike up a stately tune. Out comes Dick Burbage. He is head-to-toe in black: the only mortal here dressed as funereally as I am. His velvet cloak ripples behind him in the breeze. Behind him come two players. Oberon, in purple and cloth-of-gold, and his fair Titania in a gown of taffeta and *toile d'atour*. Their faces are painted white, their lips are scarlet, and the ostrich feathers in their jewelled crowns waft gently above their heads.

The audience is silent. Kites wheel to and fro in the blue sky, wing-beats rapid, then still as they soar upon the breeze. A bear screams from the pit next door, and the sound of cheering follows. Henry is smiling with tears upon his cheeks.

Burbage steps forward.

Historical Note

Dark Aemilia is a work of imagination, based on fact. I wanted to tell a story that was authentic and historically accurate. Equally importantly, I wanted to write about Shakespeare's London as if I was there. If a time machine had been available, I would have used it.

Historical fiction writers sometimes disagree about the extent to which people have changed over the centuries. It is certainly not accurate to suggest that a woman in the Elizabethan or Jacobean period would be 'feminist' in any sense that we recognise today. But the poetry that Aemilia Lanyer wrote shows her championing the cause of Eve, and drawing attention to the role of women in the Passion of Christ. Academics have referred to her poetry as 'proto-feminist'. So I felt I could work with that.

However, I believe that some aspects of human nature remain constant. Disease and death were part of everyday life in the past, but parents were still traumatised by the death of a child. There is certainly evidence for this, which ranges from the inscriptions and tombs in churchyards to the poem *Pearl*, a fourteenth-century allegory about bereavement and religious faith. And who can forget that most harrowing scene in all of Shakespeare – King Lear's lament over the body of Cordelia?

The starting point for this novel was the life of a real woman. Aemilia Bassano (later Lanyer) was born in Bishopsgate in 1569 and buried in Clerkenwell in 1645. She became the mistress of Henry Carey, Lord Hunsdon, in 1587. Six years later, she became pregnant and was married off to her cousin Alfonso, a recorder player in the Queen's consort. Her son Henry, born in 1593, is presumed to be Hunsdon's child.

There is no evidence that Lanyer was the lover of William Shakespeare, but she is one of the candidates for the shadowy role of the Dark Lady, the object of the later sonnets (127–154). However, there is no proof; only theory, opinion and the reinterpretation of existing facts. (The historian A.L. Rowse was one of the first scholars to suggest that Lanyer might be Shakespeare's muse.) In fact, there is no evidence that Shakespeare dedicated the sonnets to anyone at all, and many academics believe that the Fair Youth and the Dark Lady are symbolic figures.

We do know that Lanyer was one of the first women in England to be a published poet, and the first to be published in a professional way, as men were. *Salve Deus Rex Judaeorum* (Hail, God, King of the Jews) was printed by Valentine Simmes in 1611 and sold in Paul's Churchyard (the bookselling quarter of London) by Richard Bonian. Lanyer dedicated her collection, in a rather flamboyant manner, to a host of distinguished and wealthy women, starting with Queen Anne, the wife of James I.

Most of the surviving facts about Lanyer have been preserved in the notebooks of the physician and astrologer Simon Forman, who kept detailed accounts of his dealings with his clients. Forman was clearly fascinated by her, and hoped to seduce her. His notes indicate that, although he spent a night with her, she did not have sex with him. (Or 'halek', the word that Forman coined for sexual intercourse.)

Surviving church and court records provide the other information: her birth, marriage, death, the births and deaths of family members and her setting-up of a school at St Giles-in-the-Fields (1617–19). There is also a record of a legal dispute about her rights to Alfonso Lanyer's income after his death in 1613. We do not know if Lanyer's father, Baptiste Bassano, was murdered, but court records show that there was an attempt on his life a few years before he died.

There is no evidence that Lanyer wrote *Macbeth*, or any part of it. Forman does, however, mention that, on one of her visits to him, she asked for advice about conjuring demons. The current consensus is that Shakespeare sometimes worked with collaborators, including Thomas Middleton and Thomas Dekker.

The dating of Shakespeare's plays is an inexact science, and one of the themes of the novel is lost stories and knowledge and the frailty of the paper trail to the past. There are websites that give 'exact' dates for his plays, but academics are more circumspect. *The Taming of the Shrew* was probably written in 1590. *Othello*'s dates are very uncertain; the play could have been written and performed as early as 1600, or as late as 1604. The key issue with *Macbeth* is that academics now believe it was written after the Gunpowder Plot of November 1605, because it is agreed that there are references to the plot in the play. The date I have given in the novel is May 1606. There is no record of a performance of *A Midsummer Night's Dream* at the Globe after the death of Shakespeare in April 1616. But it is plausible that such a production might have taken place.

One of the 'lost works' is the book of sonnets that Will has published in 1605 while he and Aemilia are estranged. The sonnets which have survived were not published until 1609, and they do not refer to the 'Dark Lady'. The title of the publication was simply *Shakespeare's Sonnets*, the publisher was G. Eld for T.T. and the seller was William Aipley. It is thought that the sonnets could have been written as early as the 1590s, and that they would have been circulated in handwritten form, as suggested in the novel. Although the 1609 collection bears the promise 'Never before imprinted', as was customary at the time, it is plausible that some of the sonnets had been published before, and this was the first imprint of the whole collection.

At the end of the novel, Aemilia tells Ann Shakespeare that Will's papers will be safe with her in Pudding Lane. As readers will know, fifty years after this conversation takes place, the City of London was devastated by the Great Fire of 1666. I liked the idea of suggesting that Will's spoiled pages were somewhere in that huge conflagration. Just as an afterword, it is interesting to note that the Great Fire took several days to take hold, and the booksellers and printers of Paul's Churchyard and Paternoster Square stored their books, chap-books and pamphlets in St Paul's Cathedral for safekeeping. The building was stacked to the roof with paper. Three days later, it went up in smoke.

Historical Characters

William Shakespeare (1564–1616)

William Shakespeare was born and brought up in Stratford-upon-Avon. At eighteen, he married Ann Hathaway and they had three children: Susanna, and twins Hamnet and Judith. Few records of Shakespeare's life have survived. There is evidence, however, that Shakespeare worked in London as an actor and playwright in the late 1580s and early 1590s. (The first reference to him in London was made in the pamphlet *Greene's Groats-worth of Wit* published posthumously by his rival Robert Greene.)

Shakespeare became an actor, writer, and part-owner of the theatrical company the Lord Chamberlain's Men, which became known as the King's Men after James I came to the throne. Most of his surviving plays were written between 1589 and 1613. He is believed to have retired to Stratford around 1613 at the age of forty-nine, and he died there three years later. There is no evidence that Shakespeare was seriously injured in the Globe fire of 1613, but the theory has been put forward by Graham Philips and Martin Keatman in *The Shakespeare Conspiracy*.

Elizabeth I (1533–1603)

Elizabeth I was the last monarch of the Tudor dynasty, becoming Queen in 1558. The challenge with Elizabeth is that so much is known about her, and there have been so many fictional portrayals, that it is hard to find a new way of presenting her. I focus on her fragility and desperation at the end of her life.

The daughter of Henry VIII, she was born a princess, but was declared illegitimate after the execution of her mother Anne Boleyn. She had survived intense competition for the throne, and was imprisoned in the Tower for almost a year during her sister Mary's reign, on suspicion of supporting Protestant rebels.

One of her first acts as monarch was the establishment of an English Protestant Church, of which she became the Supreme Governor. This Elizabethan Religious Settlement later evolved into today's Church of England. It was a compromise between Catholicism and Protestantism.

Elizabeth I never married and became famous for the shrewd deployment of her virginity. In the novel, I make her the mother of Robert Devereux, Earl of Essex. The idea that Essex is not her lover but her secret, illegimate son links the themes of the novel together. It is a possible explanation for Essex's arrogance, his unreasonable behaviour and Elizabeth's inconsolable grief after his execution. There is of course no evidence for this, though there has been speculation that she may have had illegitimate children.

Alfonso Lanyer (1570s?–1613)

Most of what we know about Alfonso is taken from the notebooks of Simon Forman, and is based on his consultations with Aemilia. These state that Alfonso was her cousin and that he was a Queen's musician. Church records also show Alfonso and Aemilia were married in St Botolph's Church, Aldgate, on 18 October 1592.

It is known that the Lanyers were a French family, and that Alfonso was a profligate character. Aemilia told Simon Forman that he spent her dowry within a year. Even so, he does appear to have helped her in her quest for publication: the frontispiece of *Salve Deus Rex Judaeorum* includes a reference to 'Captain Alfonso Lanyer Servant to the King's Majestie'. We don't know if Alfonso actively assisted his wife, but his status helped her assert her respectability.

Alfonso Lanyer died in 1613. The cause is unknown.

Henry Lanyer (1593–1633)

Henry was the son of Aemilia Lanyer. His father is assumed to be Lord Hunsdon. Henry became a recorder player at the court, and died in 1633. Aemilia then bought up his two children.

There is no historical evidence that his father was William Shakespeare.

Baptiste Bassano (1520?–76)

Aemilia's father Baptiste is another obscure historical figure, and he only appears in the novel in Aemilia's memories of her childhood. As he is pivotal to the plot I think it is important to include a historical note which separates fact from fiction.

Baptiste came to England from Venice in the 1530s, and was certainly at Henry VIII's court in 1540, playing the sackbut (a kind of trombone) in the service of Edward Seymour, Earl of Hertford. He was the youngest of six brothers, who were originally from the town of Bassano del Grappa in the Veneto region. All of the brothers came to England, and only the eldest, Jacamo, returned to Venice. Henry VIII gave the brothers the right to live in apartments in the Charterhouse, a Carthusian monastery he had dissolved in 1537.

In 1563, conspirators Henry Dingley, Mark Anthony and a number of others were prosecuted for Bassano's attempted murder, and were sentenced to have their ears cut off and to be whipped, pilloried and banished for plotting to kill him. Nothing further is known about the incident. The murder that Aemilia witnesses is a fictional event, however; we do not know how Baptiste really died. In the novel, Margaret keeps it a secret, fearing for the rest of her family.

Baptiste was not formally married to Aemilia's mother Margaret Johnson, referring to her as his 'reputed wife' in his will.

In the novel, I make a reference to one of Margaret Johnson's cousins, Robert Johnson, who composed 'The Witch's Dance' (the tune that Alfonso is humming in Act II, Scene V). I liked the fact that he shares his name with the African-American blues guitarist Robert Johnson (1911–38) who is alleged to have sold his soul to the Devil at the crossroads. Popular myth has it that this is how Robert Johnson gained his phenomenal musical skill. He died in mysterious circumstances at the age of twenty-seven. In my story, Baptiste makes a similar pact with the witches at the crossroads at Tyburn, and then reneges on the deal, repenting and giving up his music.

Simon Forman (1552–1611)

Simon Forman studied at Oxford University, and later set up a medical practice in London, providing astrologically based treatments and predictions. Demand for his services increased after he (apparently) cured himself of plague. He was in dispute with the College of Physicians for many years, and the College banned him from practising as a doctor. He was eventually awarded this title.

Forman is one of the few people to have accurately predicted the date of his own death. His papers are now in the Bodleian Library in Oxford.

The distinction between 'high magic' and 'women's magic' was not made explicitly at the time, but it is accurate to suggest that men developed the intellectual side of magic via experimentation, while women used old lore to cure common ailments for small sums of money. If you want to know more about the importance of 'magic' and its connection to belief systems during this period, I recommend *Religion and the Decline of Magic* by Keith Thomas, a truly magisterial tome.

Henry Wriothesley, 3rd Earl of Southampton (1573–1624)

Wriothesley (pronounced 'Rizley') is often identified as the Fair Youth of Shakespeare's sonnets, though this is not a matter of historical fact. In addition, there is no evidence that Shakespeare and Henry Wriothesley were romantically or sexually involved, though many novelists have suggested this.

In the novel, I suggest that Wriothesley is bisexual, though not that he and Will are lovers. We have no information about Wriothesley's sexuality, though we do know that he was apparently happy with his wife, Elizabeth Vernon, and that they had several children. Surviving portraits of the handsome and highly elegant young man have been seen as evidence of his 'effeminacy' by some scholars, but his appearance could equally have been an expression of his interest in fashion, a widespread obsession at the Elizabethan court. Attitudes to sexuality were very different from today. Fulsome and seemingly romantic dedications, such as those made by Shakespeare to Wriothesley, were common. Young men were often physically affectionate towards each other. But male homosexuality was seen as a terrible sin, diverging from the natural order, and was a capital offence.

In the novel, I present Wriothesley as a young man intoxicated by his own power, who uses this to step beyond social norms. This is plausible, and fits in with the theme of over-reaching in the novel.

We do know that Wriothesley was involved in the rebellion led by the Earl of Essex in 1601, for which he was sentenced to death. Essex was beheaded – which Elizabeth apparently regretted – but after her death Wriothesley's sentence was commuted to life imprisonment in the Tower of London. He was released on the accession of James I.

Henry Carey, 1st Baron Hunsdon (1526–96)

Hunsdon was the son of Mary Boleyn, Anne Boleyn's sister. He was a blunt, outspoken man, a professional soldier rather than a courtier. As Lord Chamberlain, he was the patron of William Shakespeare's company from 1594.

Simon Forman's case-books record that Aemilia Bassano was his mistress for around six years (1586–92).

426

Hunsdon died in 1596 and was buried in Westminster Abbey. His tomb is indeed bizarre and ornate.

Ann Shakespeare, née Hathaway (1555/6–1623)

Very little is known about Ann Hathaway beyond a few references in legal documents, but her personality and marriage to Shakespeare have been the subject of a great deal of speculation.

Pregnant when she married William Shakespeare in 1582, Ann was seven years older than he was. Much has been made of this, and it has been suggested that Shakespeare was coerced into marrying her. We have no proof of this. Although Shakespeare worked in London, there is also no evidence that he disliked his wife.

Shakespeare famously bequeathed his 'second-best bed' to Ann. In my novel, he leaves his best bed to Aemilia. I feel that Ann has been poorly treated both by popular myth and (most) other fiction writers. Germaine Greer robustly challenges the idea that Ann was unintelligent or illiterate in *Shakespeare's Wife*; my version of Ann is inspired by Greer's book. Ann is as formidable as Aemilia in her own way. If you are interested in a ribald and witty fictional account of her life, read *Mrs Shakespeare: the Complete Works* by Robert Nye.

Thomas Dekker (1570?–1632)

Throughout his life, dramatist and pamphleteer Thomas Dekker had severe financial problems, and was imprisoned for debt several times. He is thought to have written about sixty plays, but only twenty have survived. Dekker wrote the city comedy *The Roaring Girle* (1610) in collaboration with Middleton. The heroine of this play, Moll Cutpurse, was based on the notorious London thief Mary Frith, who dressed as a man. His pamphlet *The Wonderful Year* (1603) describes London ravaged by the effects of the plague.

Moll Cutpurse (Mary Frith) (1584–1659)

Mary Frith (also known as Moll Cutpurse) was a cross-dressing fence and thief. She was mythologised even in her lifetime, and at least two plays were written about her. She smoked a pipe, played her lute on the stage, and swore. She lived into the time of Oliver Cromwell's Protectorate and is alleged to have fired a musket at one of his men. Her remarkable life story does indeed indicate that she enjoyed a level of personal freedom that was almost unknown among women at that time.

Richard Burbage (1567–1619)

Although Richard Burbage was a member of an acting family, his early career is poorly documented. Later he became one of London's best-known actors.

He was the lead actor with the Lord Chamberlain's Men, and a sharer in the company. Burbage played the title role in the first performances of many of Shakespeare's plays, including *Hamlet*, *Othello*, *Richard III*, and *King Lear*.

Background Events

1526	Birth of Henry Carey, Lord Hunsdon.
1533	Birth of Elizabeth I.
1569	Birth of Aemilia Bassano.
1576	Death of Baptiste Bassano, Aemilia's father, cause unknown.
1587	Death of Margaret Johnson, Aemilia's mother. The probable date of beginning of Aemilia's affair with Lord Hunsdon.
1591–92	Plague kills 15,000 people in London.
1592	Christopher Marlowe writes *Dr Faustus* (probable date).
1592	Aemilia falls pregnant and is married off to court musician (and cousin by marriage) Alfonso Lanyer.
1595	Robert Southwell, English Jesuit poet, hanged at Tyburn.
1596	Lord Hunsdon dies at Somerset House while still in office.
1597	Shakespeare's son Hamnet dies in Stratford.
1597	Aemilia visits Simon Forman for news about how her husband's 'business' will fare. This is the Islands Voyage trip to the Azores, 1597, led by Robert Devereux, 2nd Earl of Essex, the Queen's favourite.
1599	Globe Theatre built.
1600	Moll Cutpurse indicted in Middlesex for stealing 2s 11d. Two plays written about her in next ten years – *The Madde Pranckes of Mery Mall of the Bankside* by John Day, and *The Roaring Girle* by Thomas Dekker

and Thomas Middleton. Both dwell on the 'scandalous' issue of her dressing like a man.

1603	Queen Elizabeth dies.
1603	Alfonso is one of 59 musicians who played at Elizabeth's funeral. He is then employed by James I.
1603	King James 1 crowned.
1605	Gunpowder plot (known as the Treason Plot), November 5th.
1605–07	Probable date of first performance of *Macbeth*. Many scholars say that the play was probably written between 1603 and 1606. As it seems to celebrate the Stuart accession to the English throne, they argue that the play is unlikely to have been composed earlier than 1603, when James I was crowned. Others suggest a more specific date of 1605–06 because the play appears to refer to the Gunpowder Plot. *Macbeth* was first printed in the First Folio of 1623 and the Folio is the only source for the text.
1611	Aemilia Lanyer publishes *Salve Deus Rex Judaeorum*. She is one of the first women to be published as a poet in England, and the first to claim professional status for her work.
1611	Simon Forman writes first known review of *Macbeth* in his notebook.
1613	Alfonso Lanyer dies.
1613	Globe Theatre burns down during a performance of *Henry VIII*.
1614	Globe Theatre rebuilt (using brick rather than wood).
1616	William Shakespeare dies.
1645	Aemilia Lanyer dies, aged 76, a 'pensioner' therefore someone who has an income – not rich, but not a pauper.

Suggested Reading

If this story has made you want to find out more about the period, here are some suggestions for further reading:

Peter Ackroyd, *Shakespeare, The Biography* (Chatto & Windus, 2005)

Bill Bryson, *Shakespeare, The World as a Stage* (Harper Perennial, 2007)

Judith Cook, *Dr Simon Forman, a Most Notorious Physician* (Chatto & Windus, 2001)

Andrew Dickson, *The Rough Guide to Shakespeare* (Rough Guides, 2009)

Germaine Greer, *Shakespeare's Wife* (Bloomsbury, 2007)

Christopher Lee, *1603: The Death of Elizabeth I and the Birth of the Stuart Era* (Review, 2003)

Robert Nye, *Mrs Shakespeare: the Complete Works* (Sinclair-Stevenson, 1993)

Graham Philips and Martin Keatman, *The Shakespeare Conspiracy* (Arrow, 1995)

Lisa Picard, *Elizabeth's London: Everyday Life in Elizabethan London* (Phoenix, 2004)

Stephen Porter, *The Plagues of London* (Tempus, 2008)

Alison Sim, *The Tudor Housewife* (Sutton, 1996)

Keith Thomas, *Religion and the Decline of Magic* (Weidenfeld & Nicolson, 1971)

Susanne Woods, *The Poems of Aemilia Lanyer: Salve Deus Rex Judaeorum* (Oxford University Press, 1993)

Susanne Woods, *Lanyer: A Renaissance Woman Poet* (Oxford University Press, 1999)

Glossary

ale-pottle (noun) – beer bottle or tankard

bawdy (noun) – lewd or obscene talk or writing

bowelled – (adj) disembowelled

ceruse (noun) – a white lead pigment, used in cosmetics

chap-book (noun) – a small book or pamphlet containing poems, ballads, stories or religious tracts

cheat-bread (noun) – poor quality bread

coney (noun) – a tame rabbit raised for the table

coney catcher (noun) – a thief or trickster

the Corporation (noun) – the Corporation of London, the municipal governing body of the City of London

cozener (noun) – cheat or trickster (from verb, to cozen)

doxy (noun) – mistress or prostitute

dread-belly (noun) – Aemilia's own word, meaning stomach upset brought on by unwholesome food and/or anxiety about the Early Modern world

farthingale (noun) – a support, such as a hoop, worn beneath a skirt to extend it horizontally from the waist, used by European women in the sixteenth and seventeenth centuries

foolscap – (noun) paper cut to the size of 8.5 x 13.5 inches (216 x 343 mm) – traditional size used in Europe before A4 paper became the international standard

fribbling (adj) – time-wasting

grabble (verb) – Aemilia's own word: to catch at thin air in a desperate manner

gull (noun) – a gullible person, easily fooled or the victim of a trick (from verb, to gull)

halek (verb) – Simon Forman's own word, meaning to have sexual intercourse

hell-waines (noun) – creatures from hell ('waine' is an Old English name for boy)

jakes (noun) – an outside toilet

kennel (noun) – a gutter along a street

kersey (noun) – coarse woollen fabric

kinchin-mort (noun) – a child used by professional beggars to gain sympathy

the Liberties (noun) – an area on what is now the South Bank of London which was outside the jurisdiction of the Corporation of London

Marranos (noun) – Jews living in the Iberian peninsula who converted to Christianity, many of whom practised Judaism in secret

mouldiwarp (noun) – a mole

pattens (noun) – outdoor shoes with wooden soles worn over indoor shoes

pavane (noun) – a slow processional dance common in Europe during the sixteenth century

pigwidgeon (noun) – an insignificant or unimportant person; something petty or small that is worthy of contempt

plague-mort (noun) – Aemilia's own word, meaning someone afflicted with the plague

pottage (noun) – a thick soup or stew

prentice-boy (noun) – apprentice boy

scragged (adj) – Aemilia's own word, meaning scraggy, skinny, lined

scrimmage (noun) – Aemilia's own word, meaning a mess and tangle of mucky things

shave-grasse (noun) – a plant with a brush-like appearance

shippon (noun) – cowshed

shittle-cock (noun) – shuttlecock, used in *Volpone* and *The Fox*, by Ben Jonson

simples (noun) – medicinal plants or the medicine obtained from them

slip-shake (adj) – Parson John's own word, meaning slippery and unwholesome

small beer (noun) – a beer or ale that contains little alcohol

solar (noun) – upper sitting room, common in most houses of the period

squibbling (to squibble) (verb) – Aemilia's own word, meaning the male habit of quibbling and double-dealing, being deceitful and emotionally dishonest

truckle-bed (noun) – a low bed on casters, often pushed under another bed when not in use. Also called a trundle bed.

virginals (noun) – keyboard instrument of the harpsichord family widespread in Europe during the sixteenth and seventeenth centuries

vizard (noun) – mask for disguise or protection, alteration of Middle English *viser* mask

wherry (noun) – a river ferry-boat

Acknowledgements

This book has been a joy to write, and many people have helped it along the way.

First of all, my heartfelt thanks to everyone at Myriad Editions, especially Candida Lacey, Linda McQueen, Holly Ainley and Vicky Blunden. It is inspiring and exciting to work with people who love books and writing so much, and are so meticulous about the publishing process.

I'm also indebted to the writers and historians who gave me the benefit of their considerable wisdom while I drafted and re-drafted the novel. Fay Weldon, Celia Brayfield, Elizabeth Evenden, Sarah Penny, Matt Thorne and Linda Anderson – thank you so much. Sincere thanks also to Ronald Hutton, Professor of History at the University of Bristol. The ideas, themes and characters in the novel came together after many fascinating meetings and discussions. Any mistakes or inaccuracies are mine alone.

There were times when my energy and determination flagged – the friendship and support of Martin Cox, Susanna Jones, Alison Macleod, Lisa Seabourne and Kate Wade have kept me going.

A special mention too, for Julie Burchill. After a long and boozy lunch party during a rather gloomy hiatus in my career, Julie gave me three books by Patrick Hamilton and said, 'I don't know why you don't write something darker and more historical.' I think this book fulfils the brief.

I am also grateful to Brunel University. The university's Isambard Scholarship gave me the means to study for a PhD in English and Creative Writing, and this novel is the main component of that research.

(Nearly there now.) I couldn't function without my children and (extremely patient) husband. Georgia and Declan, you are probably the funniest teenagers on the planet, and definitely the messiest. I don't know what I have taught you, but you have taught me what motherhood feels like. Noel, you are the best reader I could hope for, and please carry on telling me when my writing isn't good enough – even when you would rather have a quiet life. And thank you, Mum, the only person I know who is as forceful and unstoppable as Aemilia Bassano Lanyer.

Last of all – thank you, Aemilia. This book was meant to be about Lady Macbeth. Then I found you, threw away 30,000 words – and never looked back.